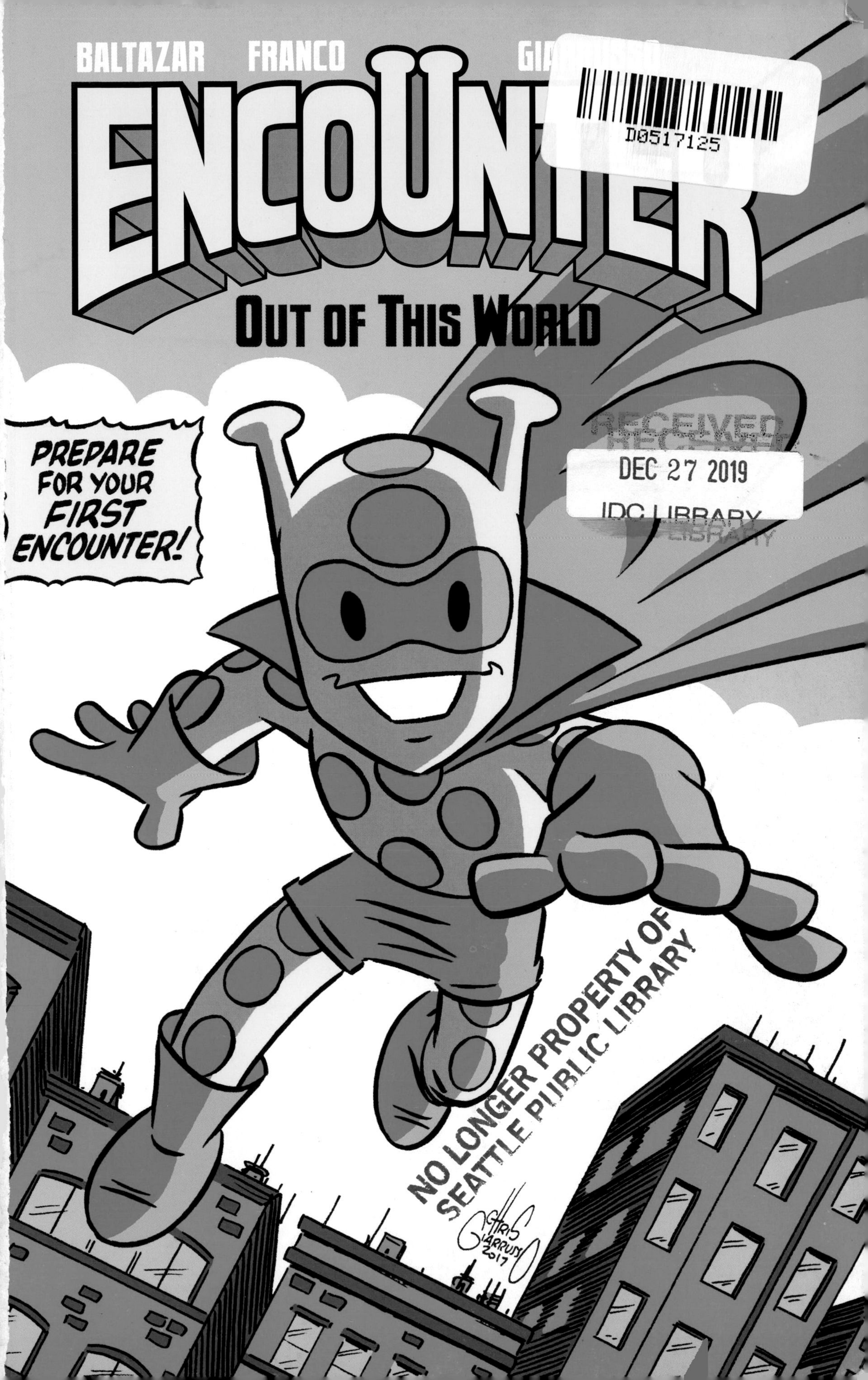
BALTAZAR
FRANCO
ENCOUNTER
OUT OF THIS WORLD
PREPARE FOR YOUR FIRST ENCOUNTER!

CARACAL™

Encounter Volume 1: Out of This World, published 2018 by The Lion Forge, LLC. © 2018 The Lion Forge, LLC. Portions of this book were previously published in Encounter, Vol. 1, Issues 1-5 © 2018 The Lion Forge, LLC. All rights reserved. ENCOUNTER™, LION FORGE™ and CARACAL™ and all associated distinctive designs as well as the characters featured in this book and the distinctive names and likenesses thereof, and all related indicia are trademarks of The Lion Forge, LLC. No similarity between any of the names, characters, persons, or institutions in this issue with those of any living or dead person or institution is intended, and any such similarity which may exist is purely coincidental. Printed in China.

ISBN: 978-1-5493-0270-1
Library of Congress Control Number: 2018932769
10 9 8 7 6 5 4 3 2 1

ENCOÜNTER™

OUT OF THIS WORLD

STORY BY
ART BALTAZAR, FRANCO & CHRIS GIARRUSSO

ART, LETTERING & COVER BY
CHRIS GIARRUSSO

ISSUE 1 COLORS BY
CHRIS GIARRUSSO

ISSUES 2–5 COLORS BY
STEPHEN MAYER

BACKUP STORY BY
ART BALTAZAR & FRANCO

BACKUP ART, COLORS & LETTERING BY
ART BALTAZAR

EDITOR
HAZEL NEWLEVANT

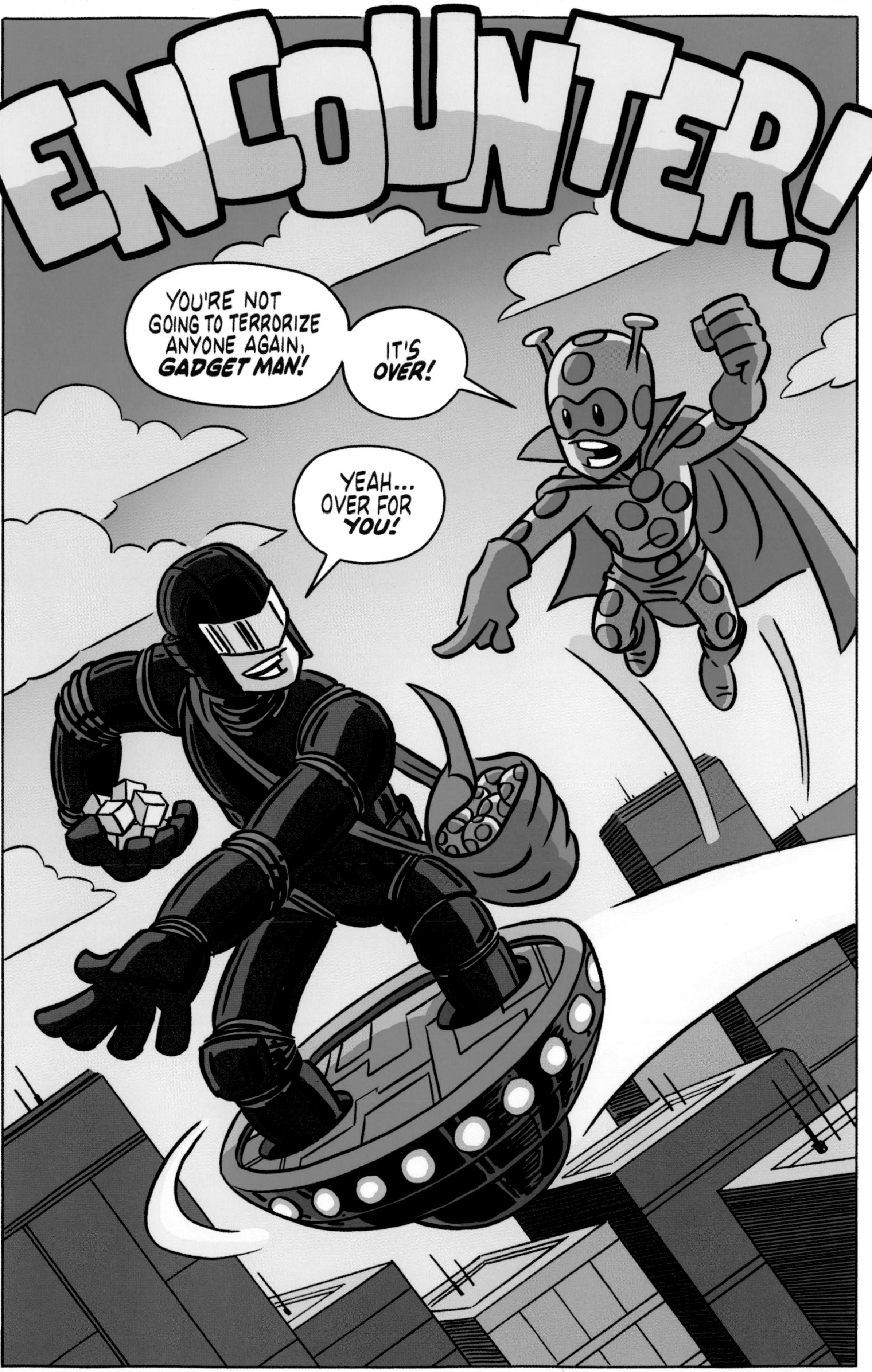
ENCOUNTER!
YOU'RE NOT GOING TO TERRORIZE ANYONE AGAIN, GADGET MAN!
IT'S OVER!
YEAH... OVER FOR YOU!

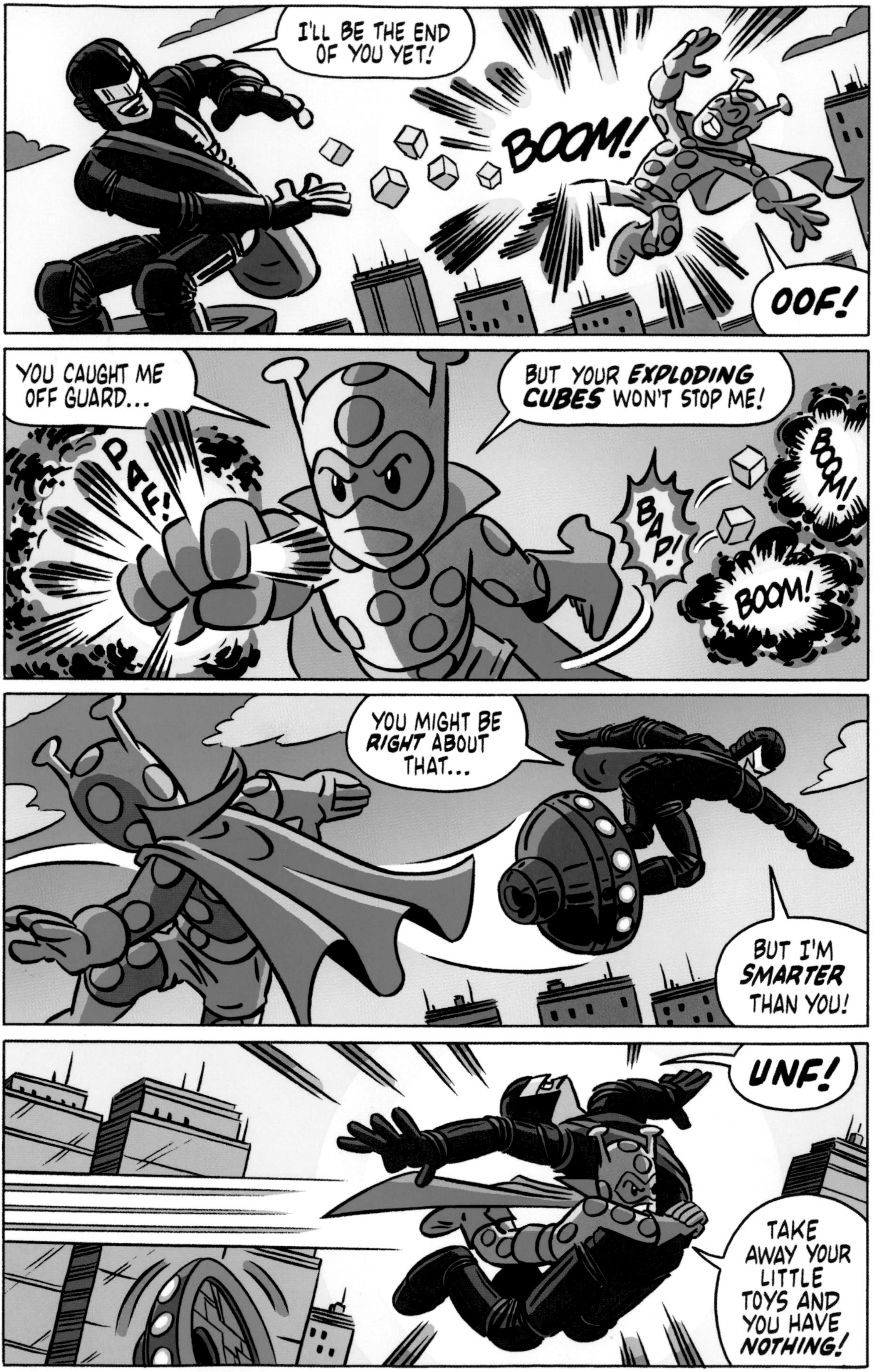
I'LL BE THE END OF YOU YET!
BOOM!
OOF!
YOU CAUGHT ME OFF GUARD...
BUT YOUR EXPLODING CUBES WON'T STOP ME!
PAF!
BAP!
BOOM!
BOOM!
YOU MIGHT BE RIGHT ABOUT THAT...
BUT I'M SMARTER THAN YOU!
UNF!
TAKE AWAY YOUR LITTLE TOYS AND YOU HAVE NOTHING!

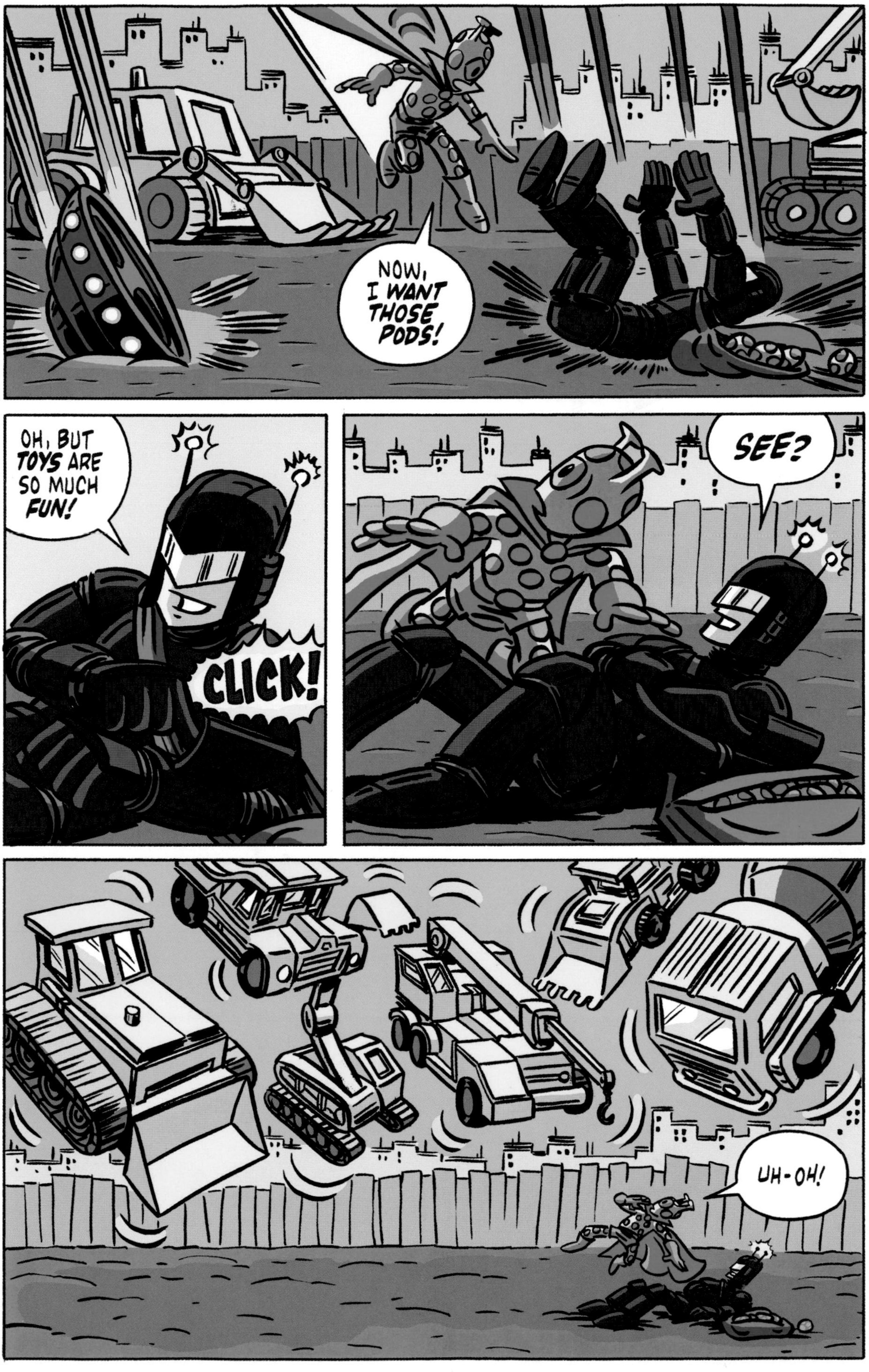
NOW, I WANT THOSE PODS!
OH, BUT TOYS ARE SO MUCH FUN!
CLICK!
SEE?
UH-OH!

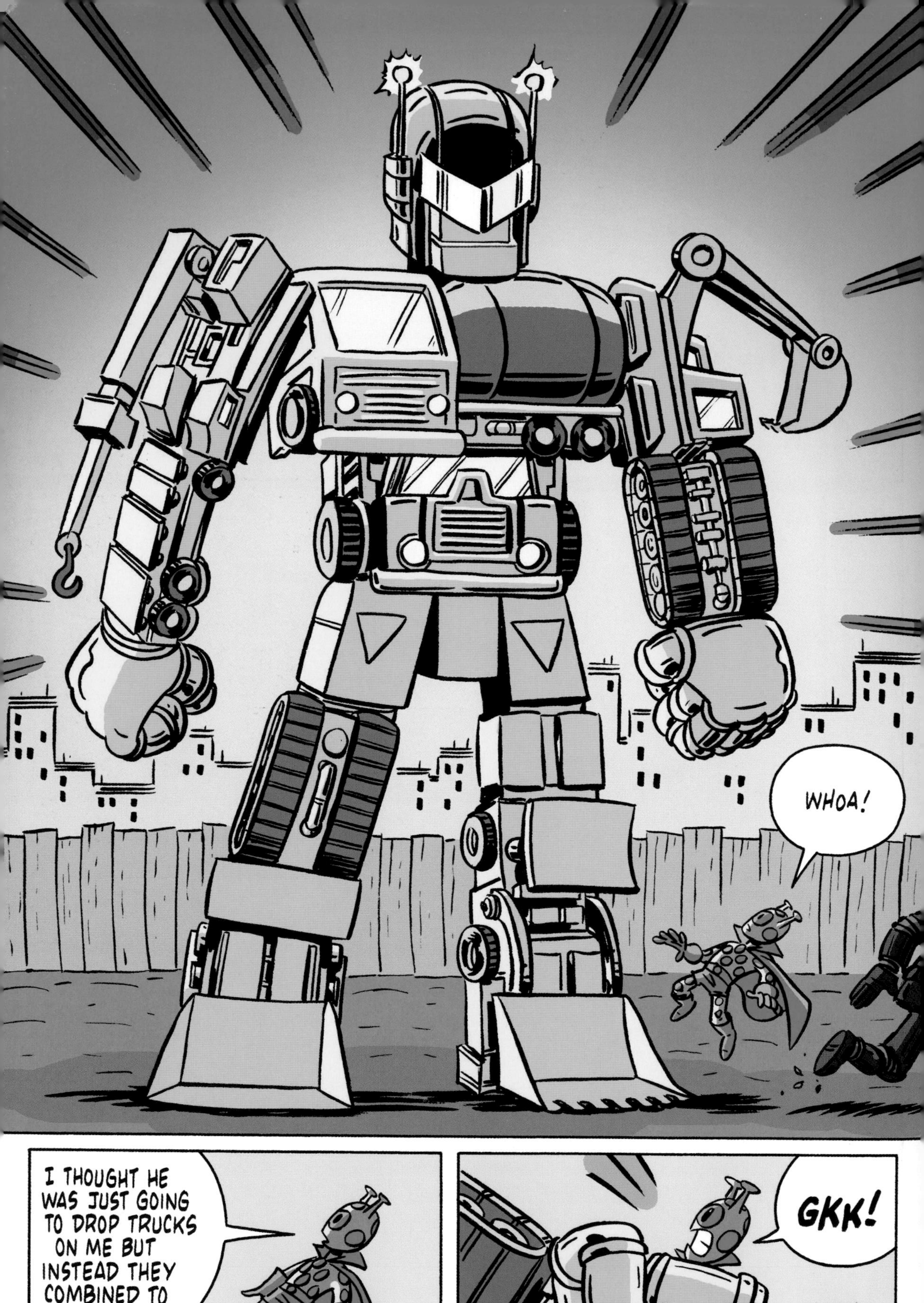
WHOA!

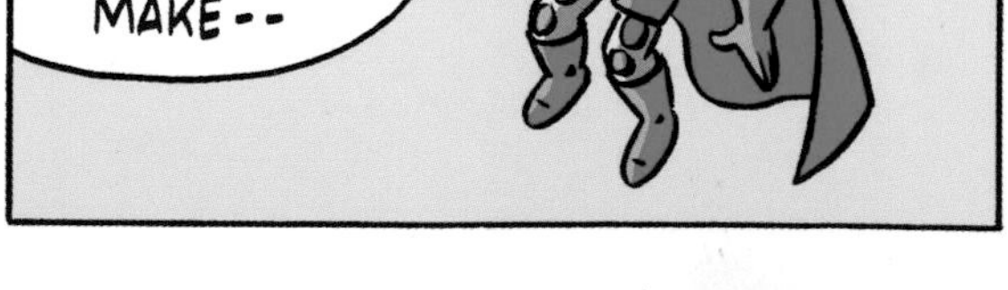
I THOUGHT HE WAS JUST GOING TO DROP TRUCKS ON ME BUT INSTEAD THEY COMBINED TO MAKE--

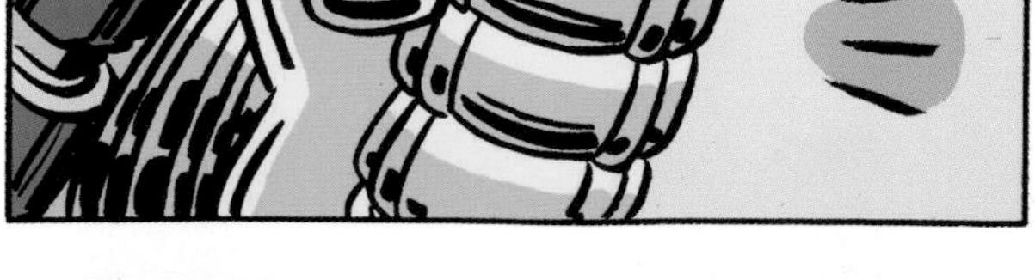
GKK!

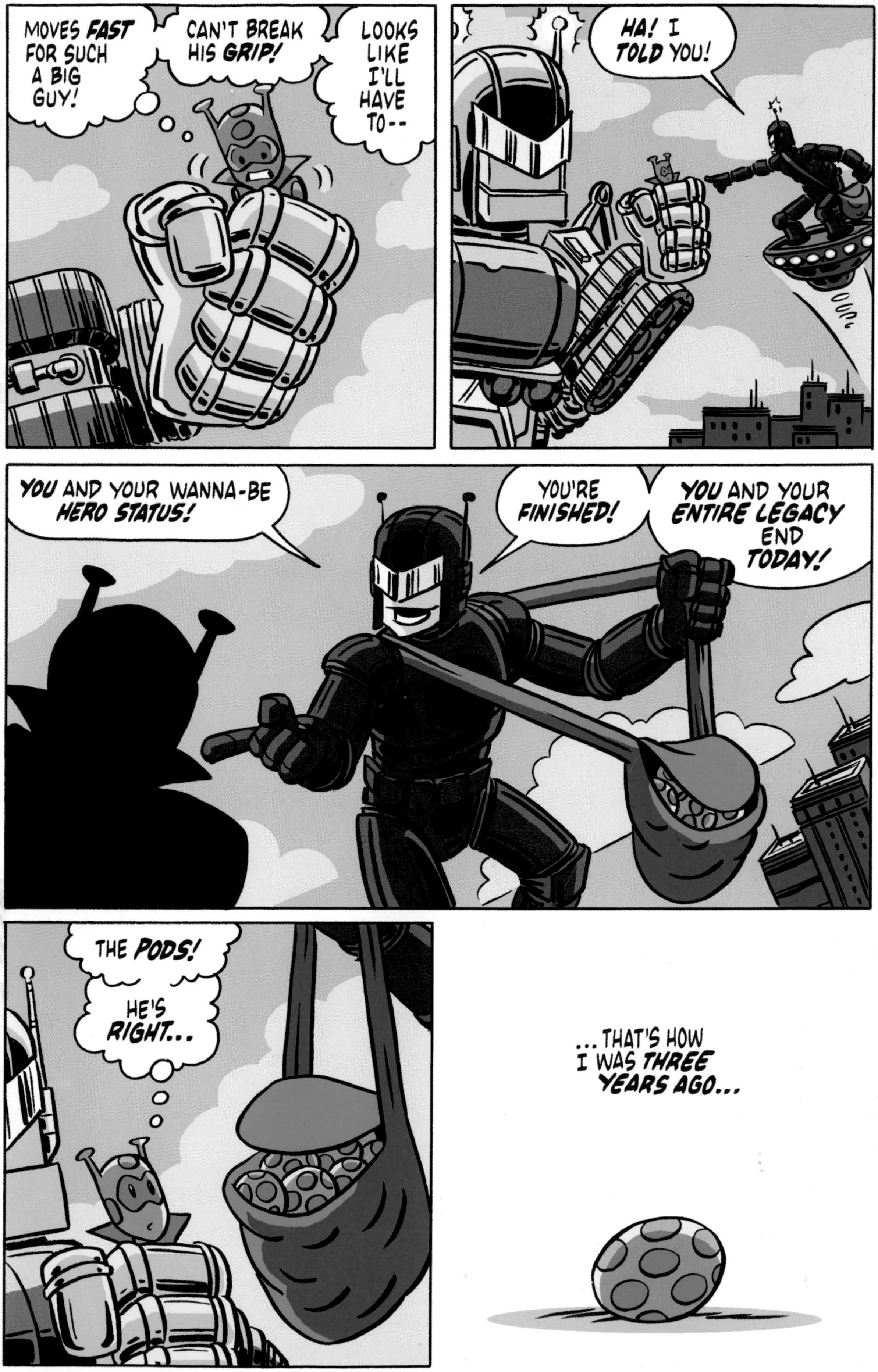
MOVES FAST FOR SUCH A BIG GUY!
CAN'T BREAK HIS GRIP!
LOOKS LIKE I'LL HAVE TO--
HA! I TOLD YOU!
YOU AND YOUR WANNA-BE HERO STATUS!
YOU'RE FINISHED!
YOU AND YOUR ENTIRE LEGACY END TODAY!
THE PODS!
HE'S RIGHT...
...THAT'S HOW I WAS THREE YEARS AGO...

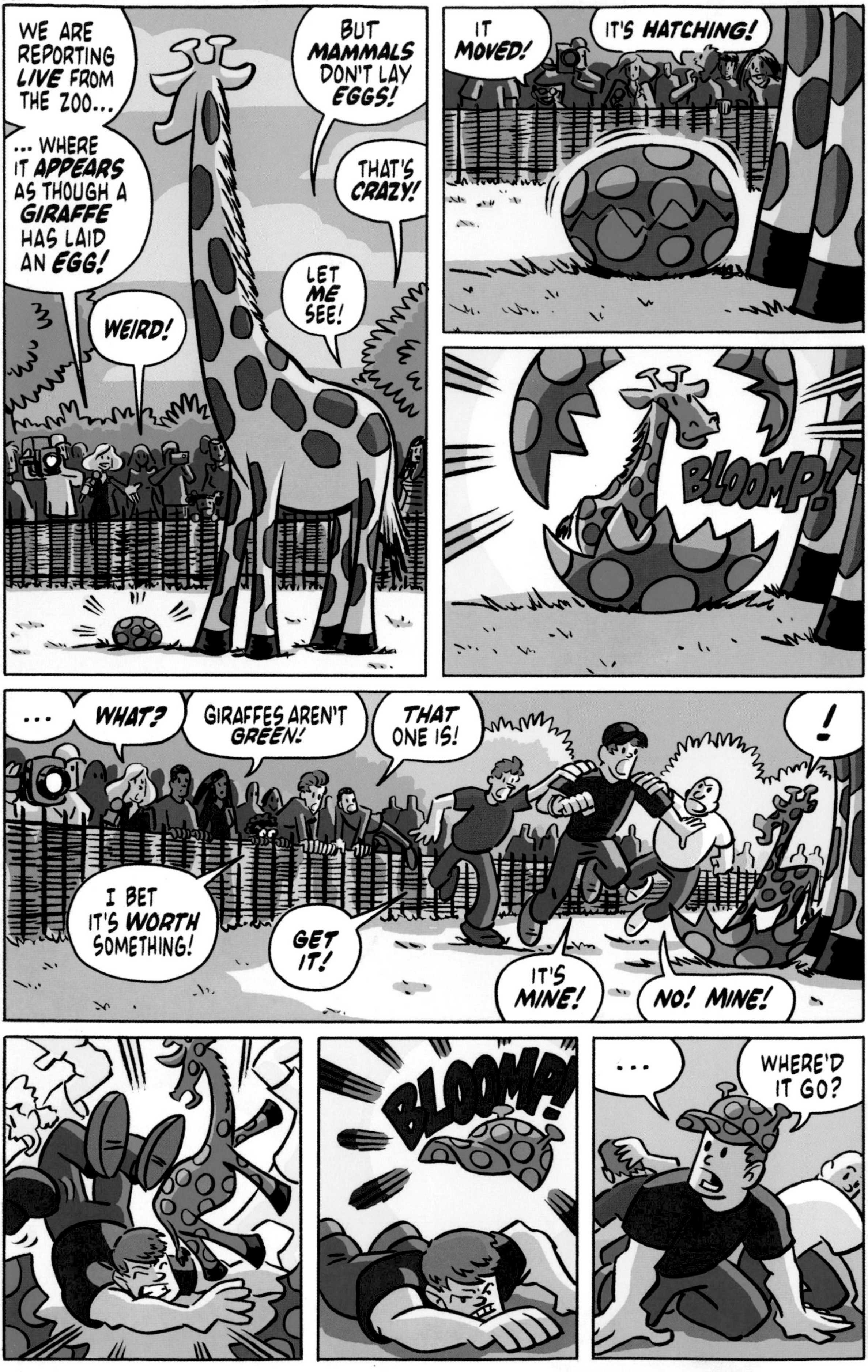
WE ARE REPORTING LIVE FROM THE ZOO...
... WHERE IT APPEARS AS THOUGH A GIRAFFE HAS LAID AN EGG!
BUT MAMMALS DON'T LAY EGGS!
THAT'S CRAZY!
WEIRD!
LET ME SEE!
IT MOVED!
IT'S HATCHING!
BLOOMP!
...
WHAT?
GIRAFFES AREN'T GREEN!
THAT ONE IS!
!
I BET IT'S WORTH SOMETHING!
GET IT!
IT'S MINE!
NO! MINE!
BLOOMP!
...
WHERE'D IT GO?

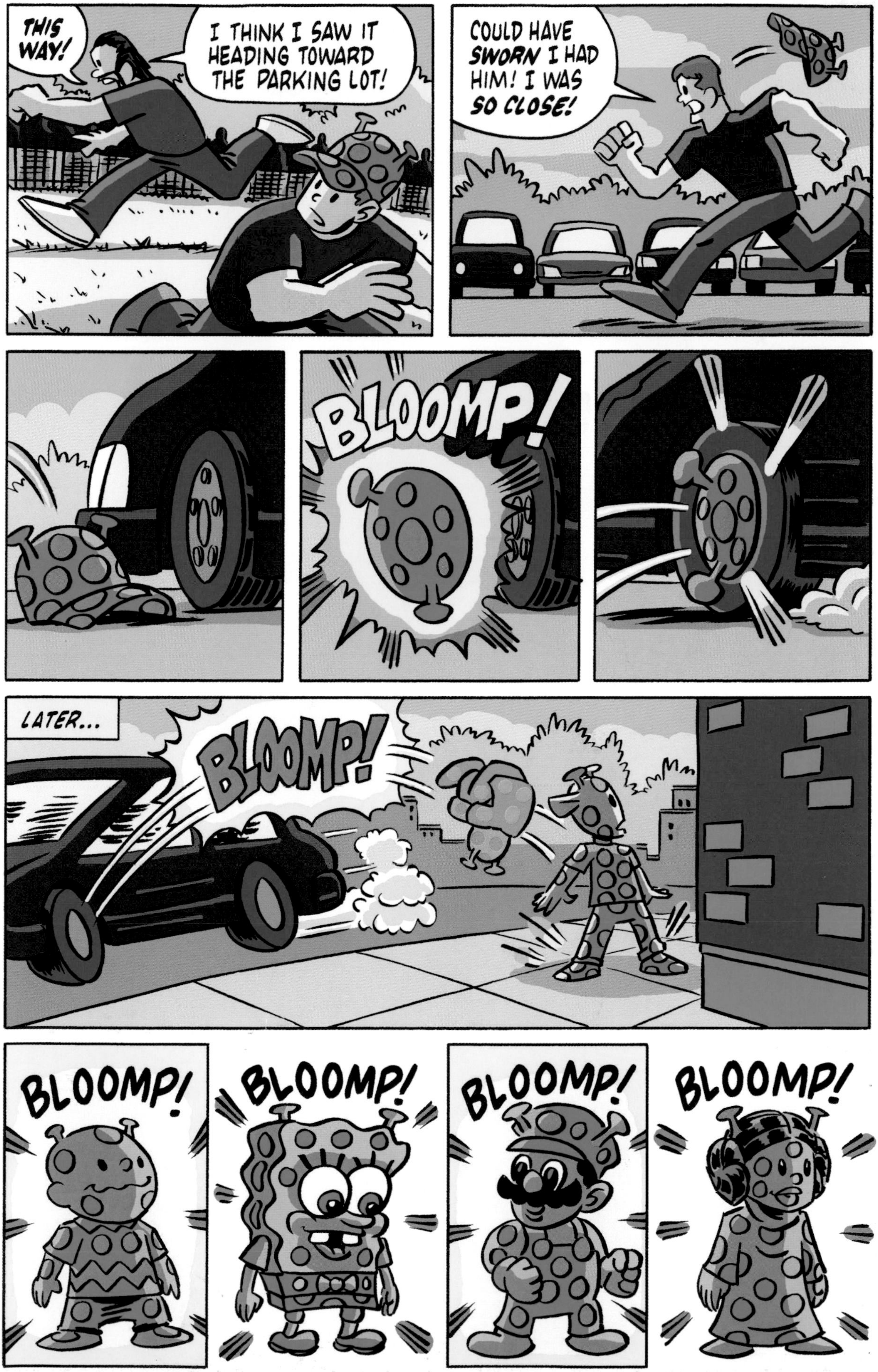

THIS WAY!
I THINK I SAW IT HEADING TOWARD THE PARKING LOT!
COULD HAVE SWORN I HAD HIM! I WAS SO CLOSE!
BLOOMP!
LATER...
BLOOMP!
BLOOMP!
BLOOMP!
BLOOMP!
BLOOMP!

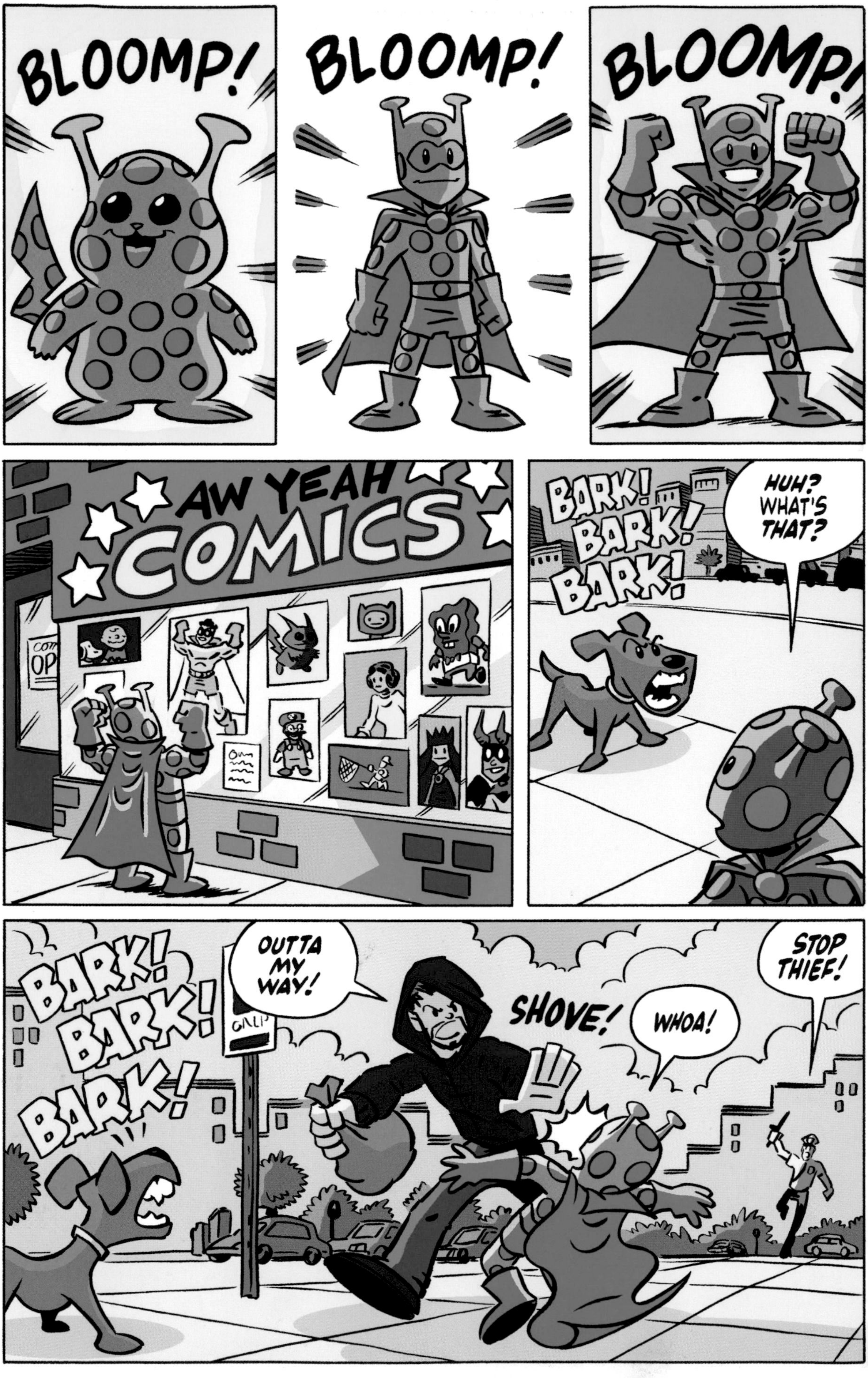
BLOOMP!
BLOOMP!
BLOOMP!
AW YEAH COMICS
BARK! BARK! BARK!
HUH? WHAT'S THAT?
BARK! BARK! BARK!
OUTTA MY WAY!
SHOVE!
WHOA!
STOP THIEF!

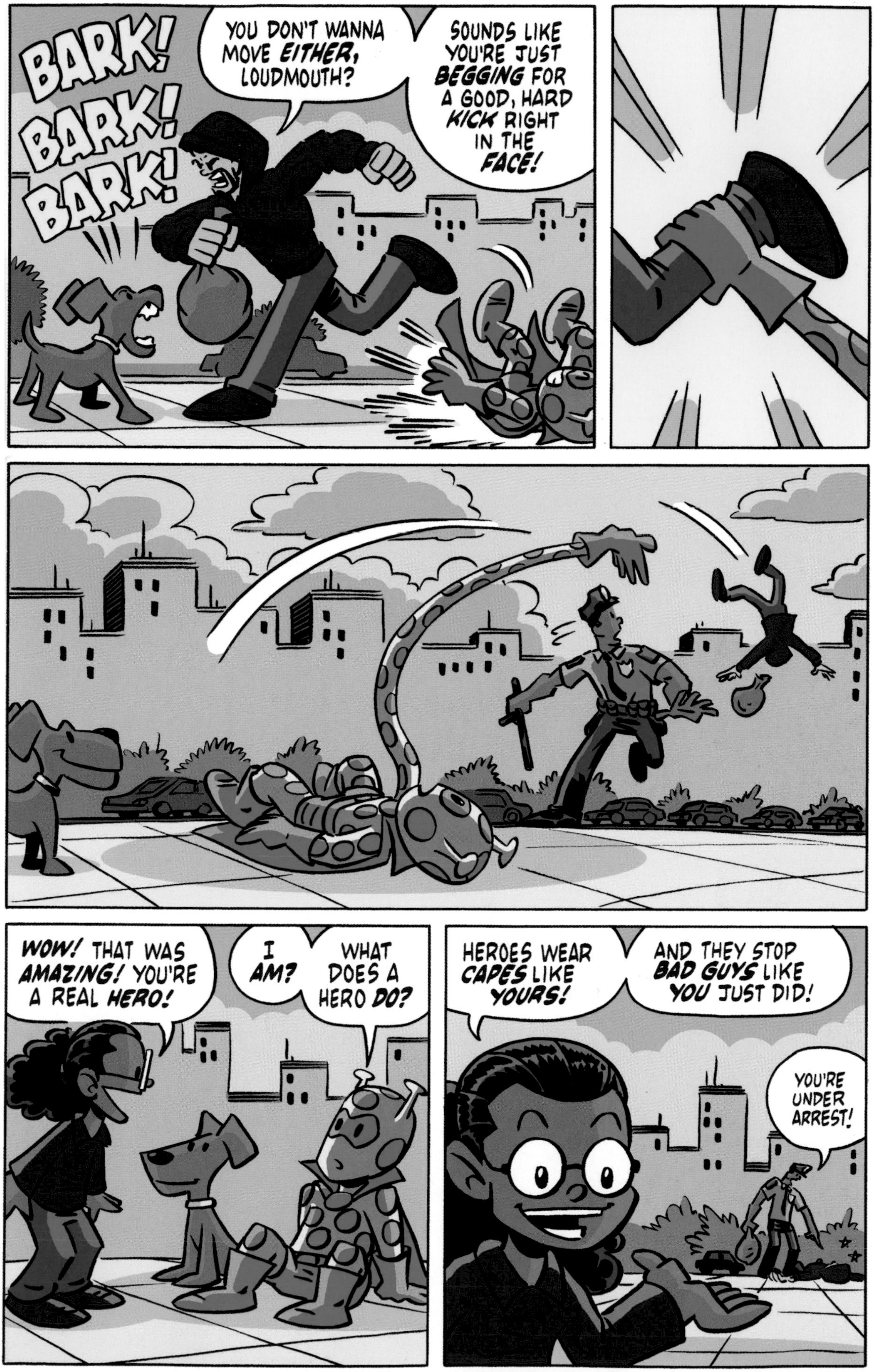
BARK! BARK! BARK!
YOU DON'T WANNA MOVE EITHER, LOUDMOUTH?
SOUNDS LIKE YOU'RE JUST BEGGING FOR A GOOD, HARD KICK RIGHT IN THE FACE!
WOW! THAT WAS AMAZING! YOU'RE A REAL HERO!
I AM?
WHAT DOES A HERO DO?
HEROES WEAR CAPES LIKE YOURS!
AND THEY STOP BAD GUYS LIKE YOU JUST DID!
YOU'RE UNDER ARREST!

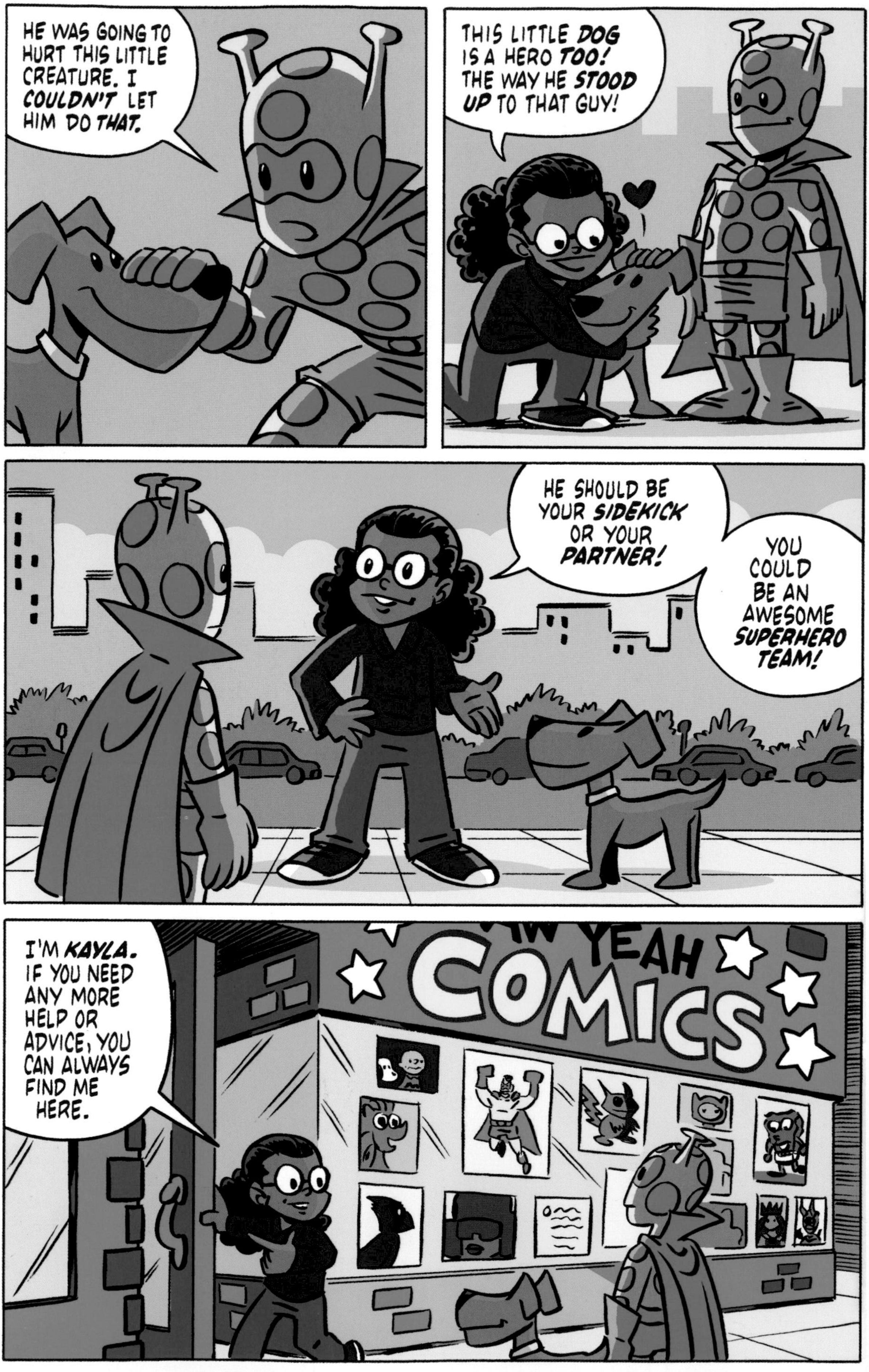
HE WAS GOING TO HURT THIS LITTLE CREATURE. I *COULDN'T* LET HIM *DO THAT.*
THIS LITTLE *DOG* IS A HERO *TOO!* THE WAY HE *STOOD UP* TO THAT GUY!
HE SHOULD BE YOUR *SIDEKICK* OR YOUR *PARTNER!*
YOU COULD BE AN AWESOME *SUPERHERO TEAM!*
YEAH COMICS
I'M *KAYLA.* IF YOU NEED ANY MORE HELP OR ADVICE, YOU CAN ALWAYS FIND ME HERE.

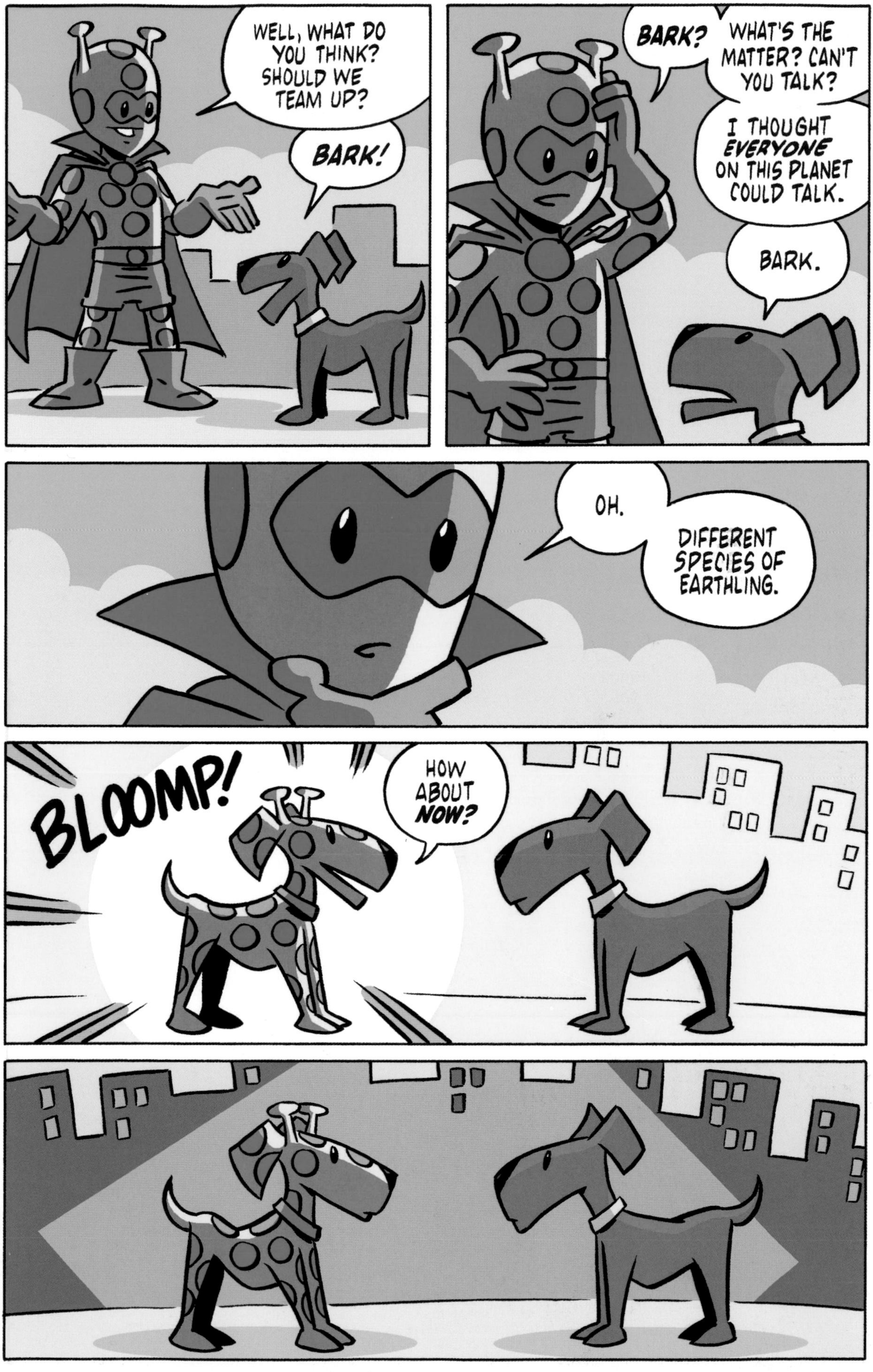
WELL, WHAT DO YOU THINK? SHOULD WE TEAM UP?
BARK!
BARK?
WHAT'S THE MATTER? CAN'T YOU TALK?
I THOUGHT EVERYONE ON THIS PLANET COULD TALK.
BARK.
OH.
DIFFERENT SPECIES OF EARTHLING.
BLOOMP!
HOW ABOUT NOW?

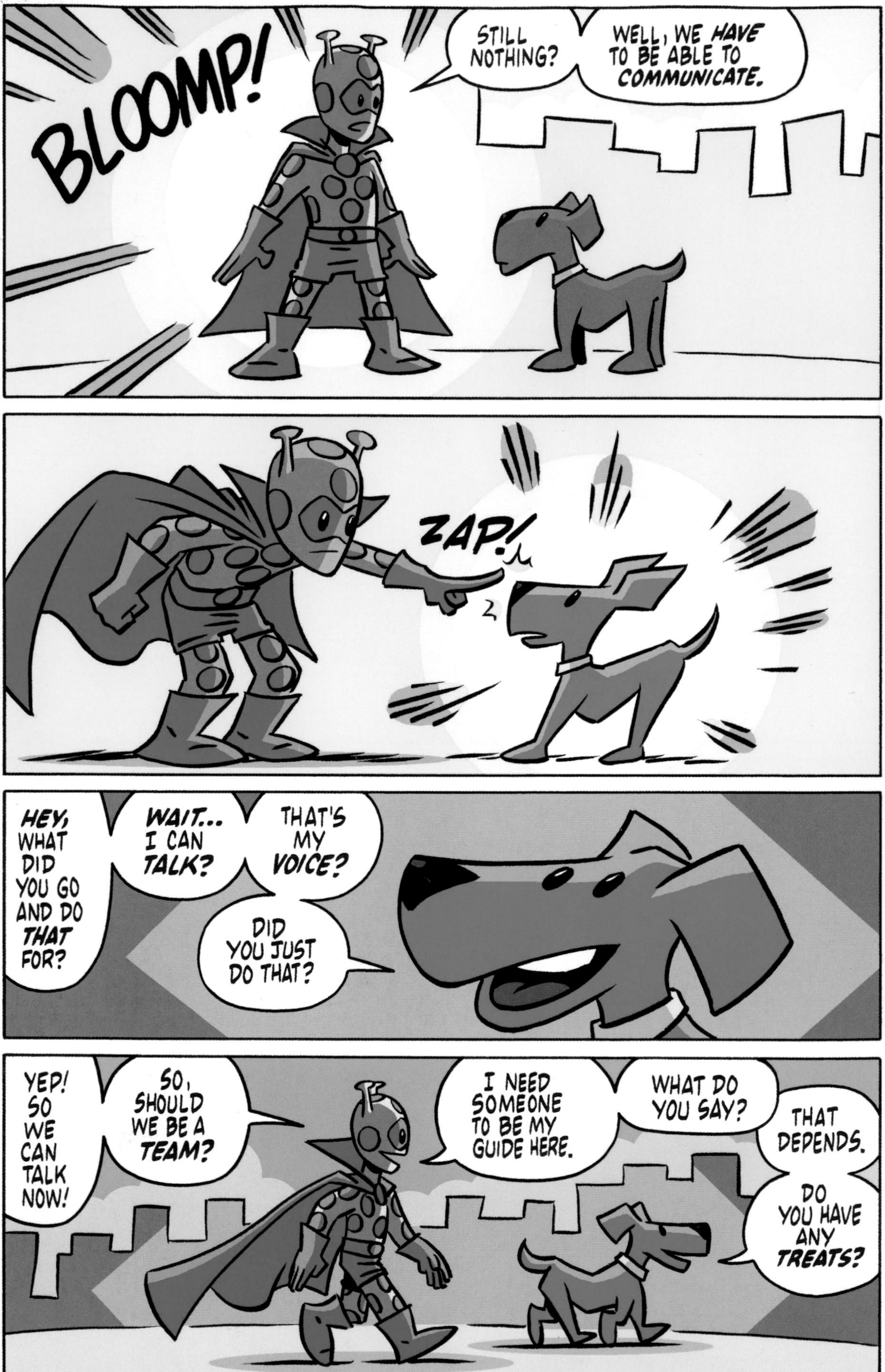
BLOOMP!
STILL NOTHING?
WELL, WE HAVE TO BE ABLE TO COMMUNICATE.
ZAP!
HEY, WHAT DID YOU GO AND DO THAT FOR?
WAIT... I CAN TALK?
THAT'S MY VOICE?
DID YOU JUST DO THAT?
YEP! SO WE CAN TALK NOW!
SO, SHOULD WE BE A TEAM?
I NEED SOMEONE TO BE MY GUIDE HERE.
WHAT DO YOU SAY?
THAT DEPENDS.
DO YOU HAVE ANY TREATS?

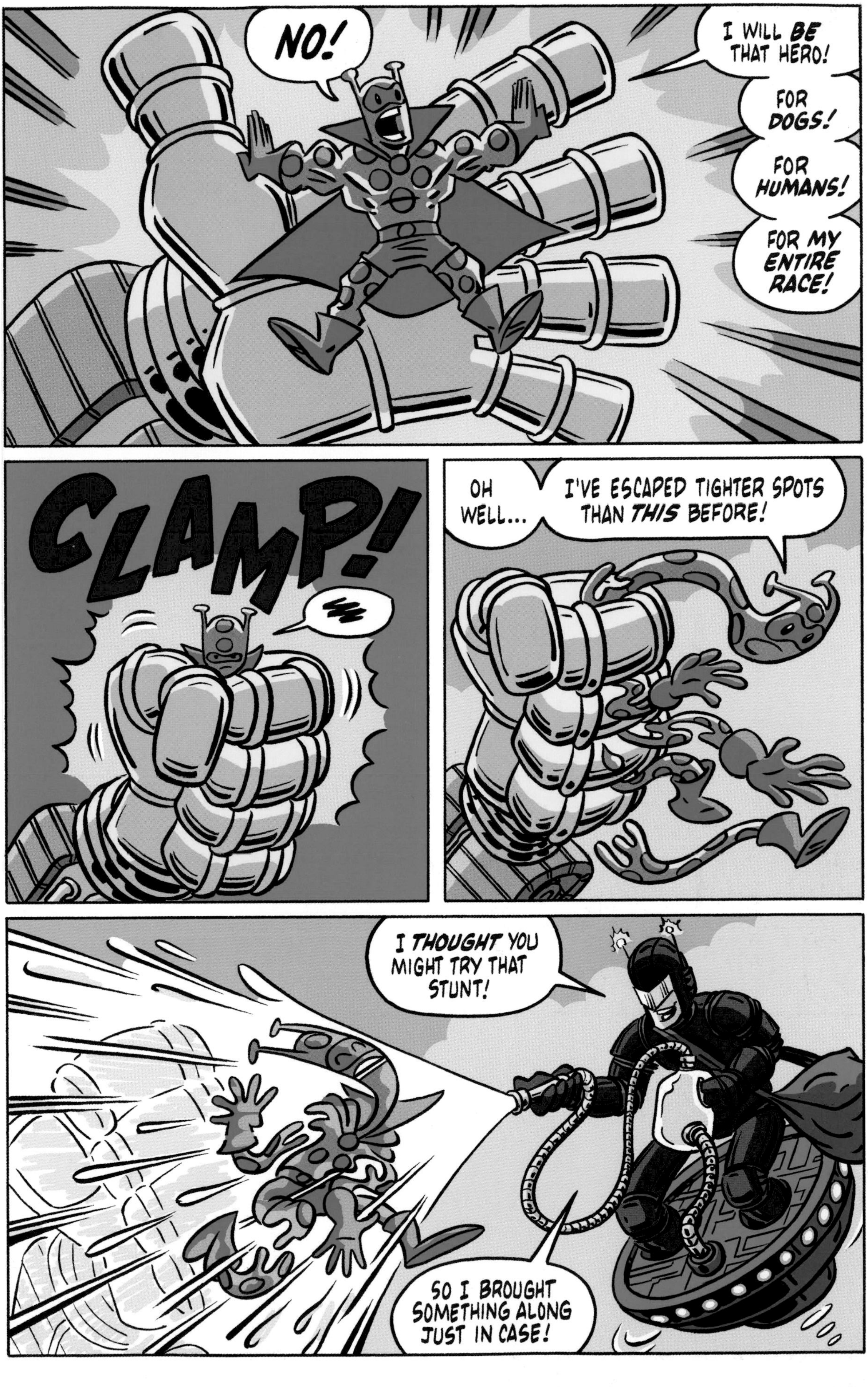
NO!
I WILL BE THAT HERO!
FOR DOGS!
FOR HUMANS!
FOR MY ENTIRE RACE!
CLAMP!
OH WELL...
I'VE ESCAPED TIGHTER SPOTS THAN THIS BEFORE!
I THOUGHT YOU MIGHT TRY THAT STUNT!
SO I BROUGHT SOMETHING ALONG JUST IN CASE!

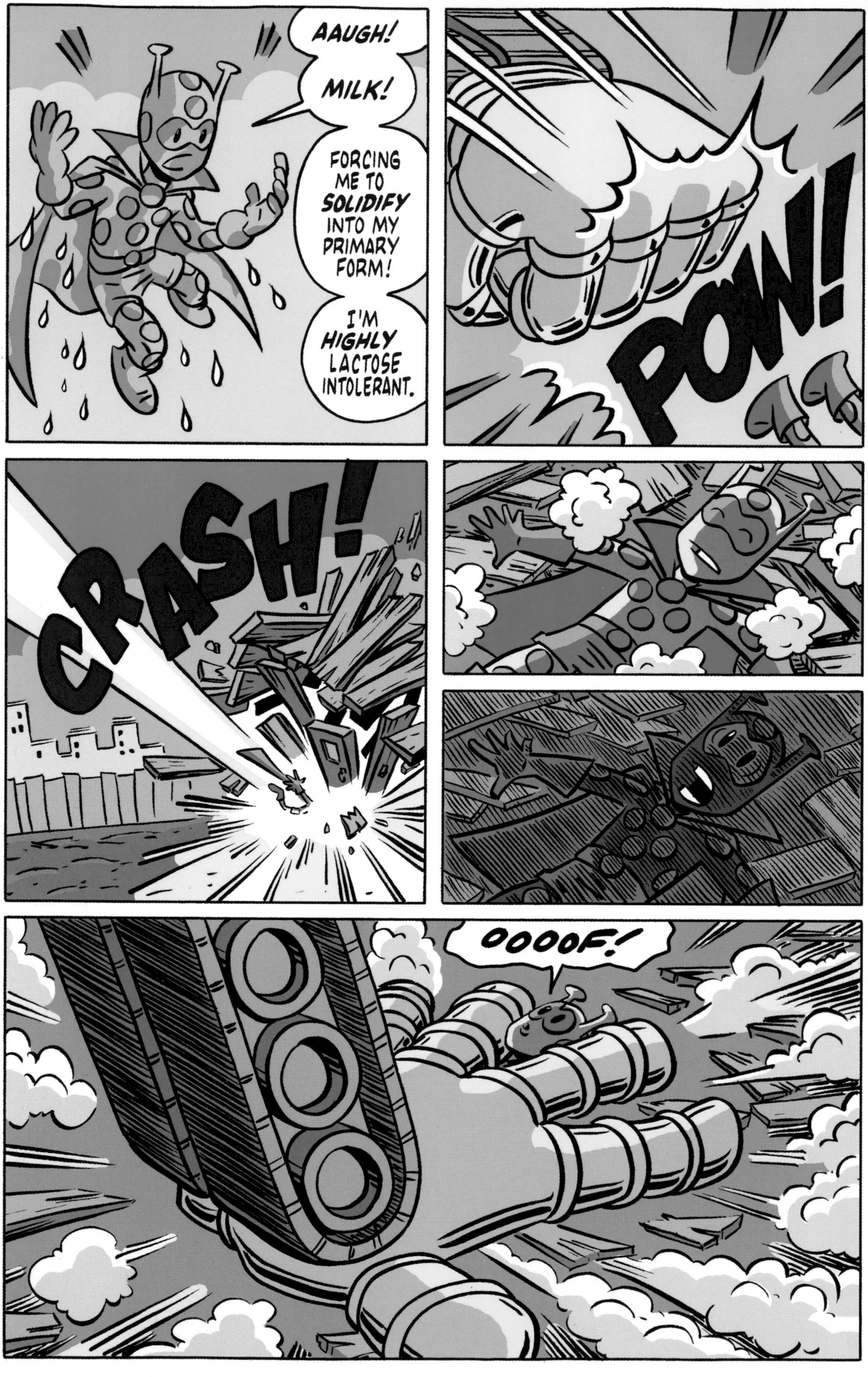
AAUGH!
MILK!
FORCING ME TO SOLIDIFY INTO MY PRIMARY FORM!
I'M HIGHLY LACTOSE INTOLERANT.
POW!!
CRASH!
OOOOF!

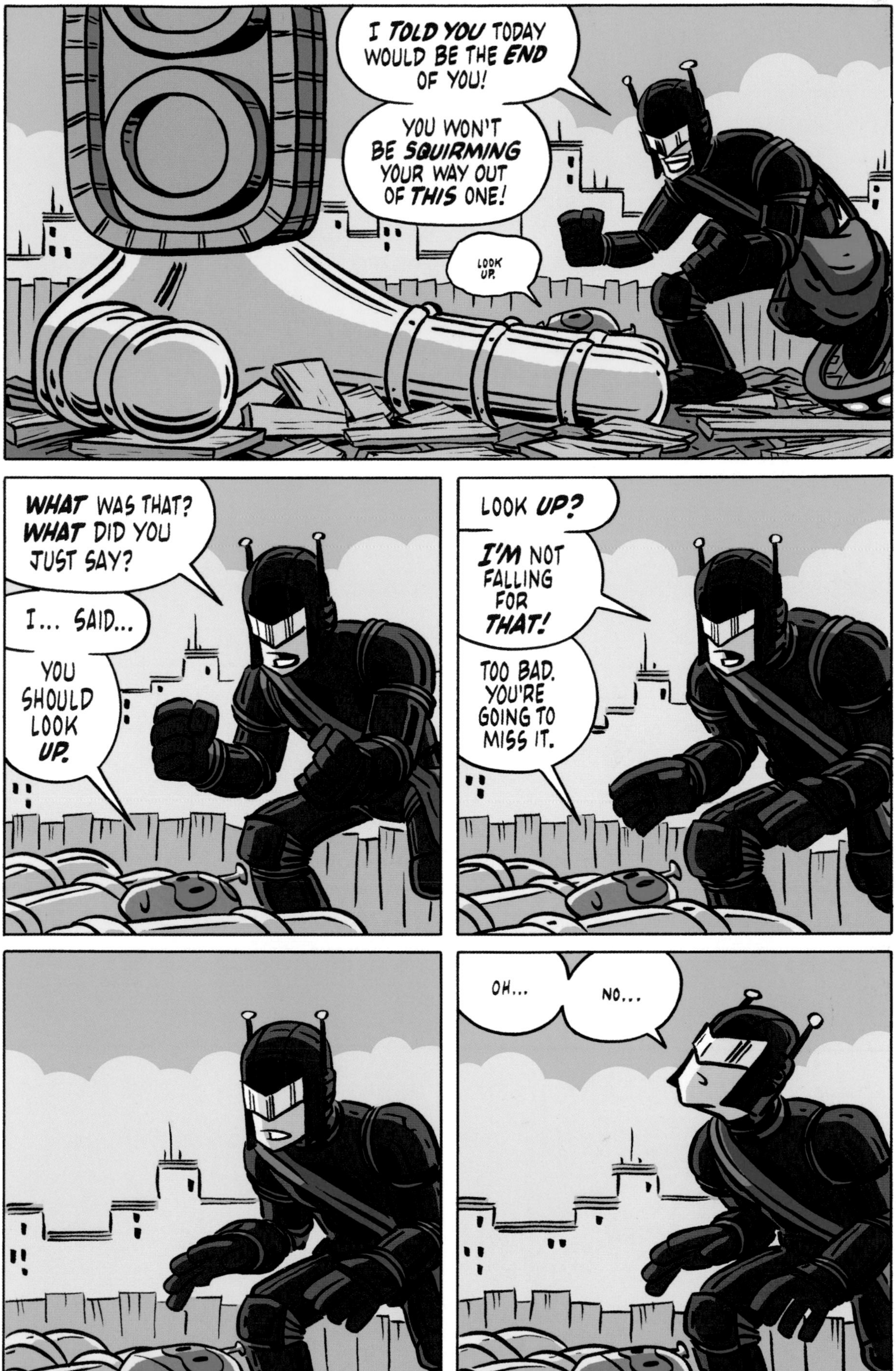
I TOLD YOU TODAY WOULD BE THE END OF YOU!
YOU WON'T BE SQUIRMING YOUR WAY OUT OF THIS ONE!
LOOK UP.
WHAT WAS THAT? WHAT DID YOU JUST SAY?
I... SAID...
YOU SHOULD LOOK UP.
LOOK UP?
I'M NOT FALLING FOR THAT!
TOO BAD. YOU'RE GOING TO MISS IT.
OH...
NO...

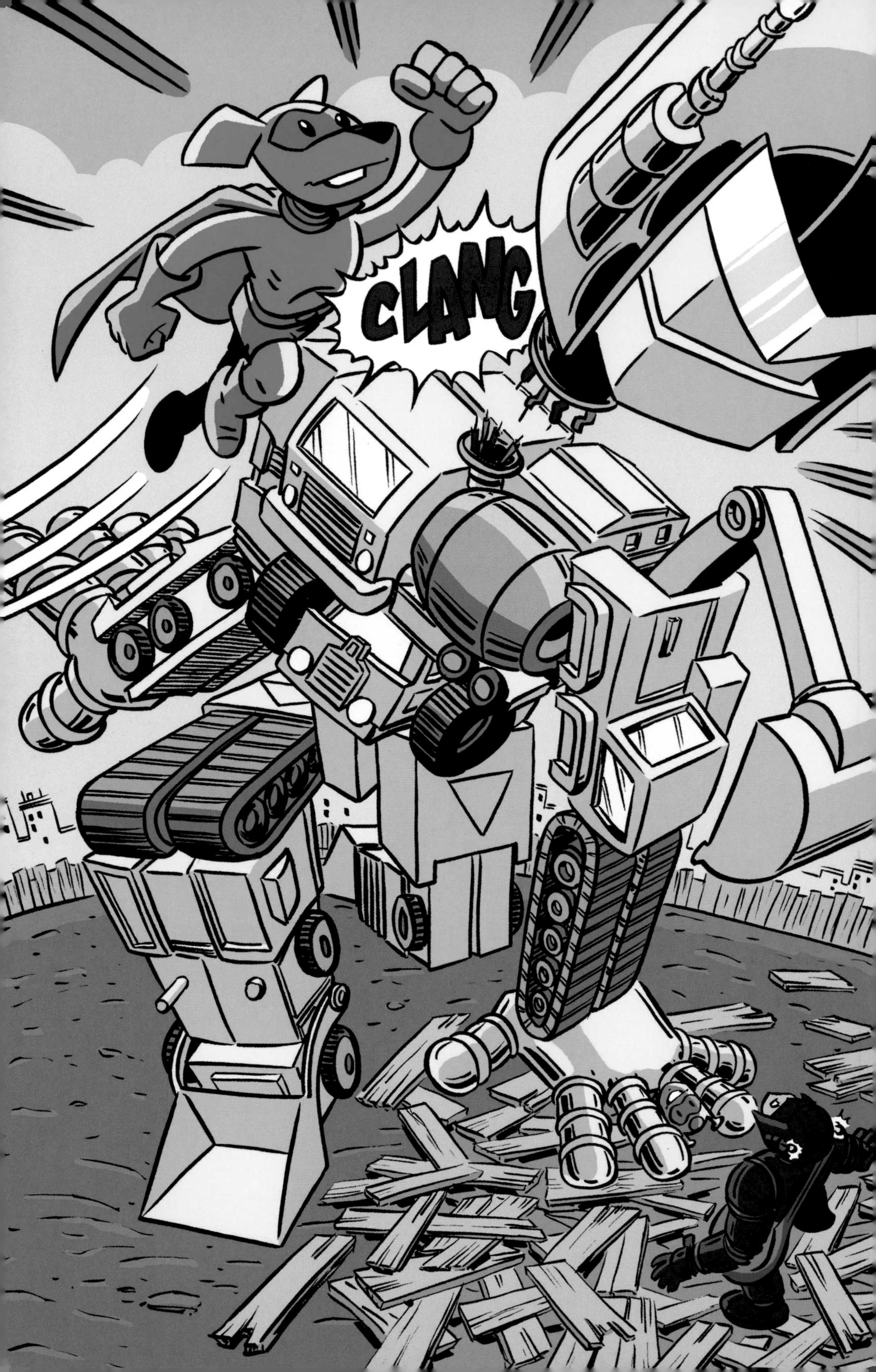
CLANG

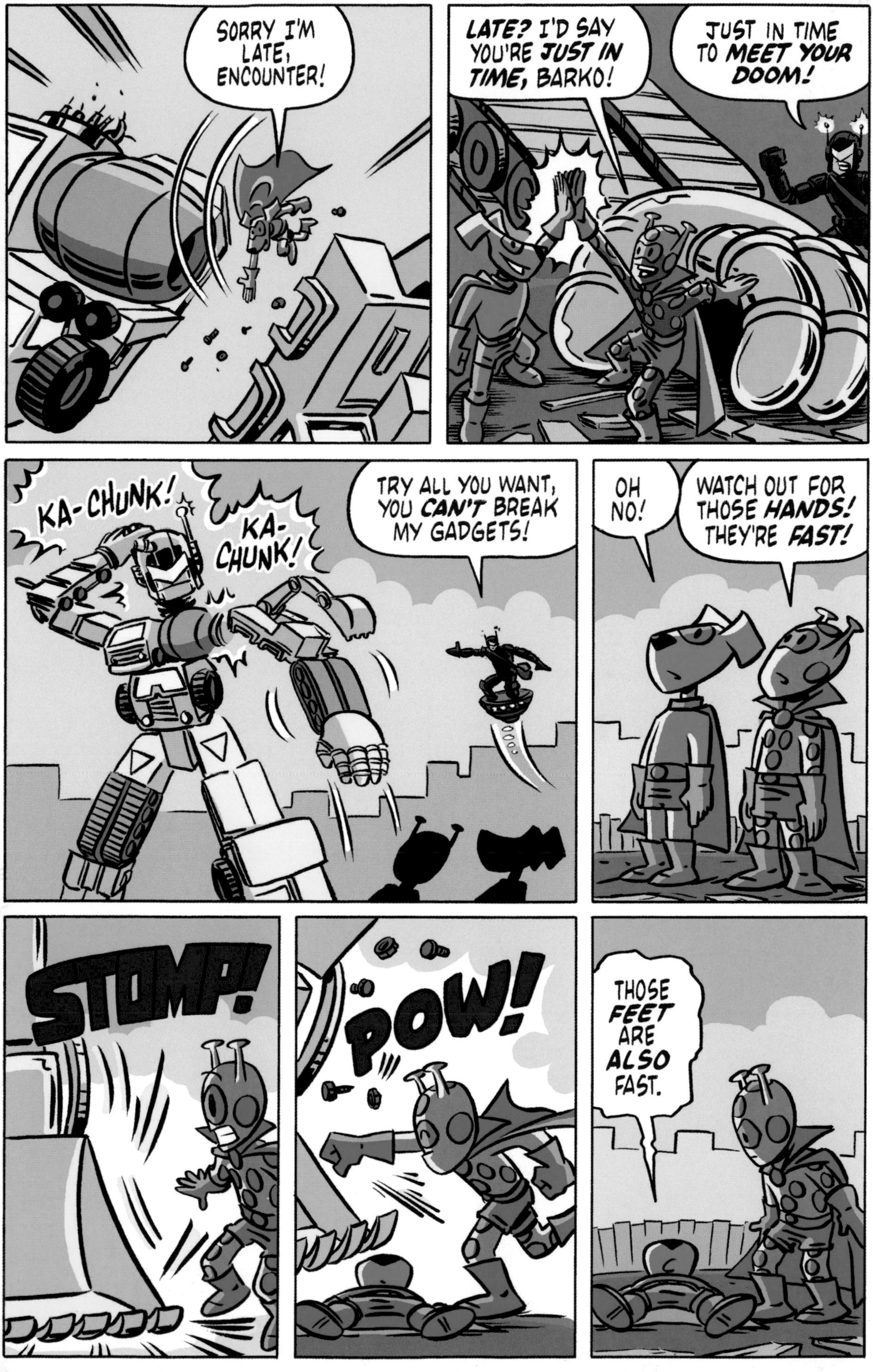
SORRY I'M LATE, ENCOUNTER!
LATE? I'D SAY YOU'RE JUST IN TIME, BARKO!
JUST IN TIME TO MEET YOUR DOOM!
KA-CHUNK!
KA-CHUNK!
TRY ALL YOU WANT, YOU CAN'T BREAK MY GADGETS!
OH NO!
WATCH OUT FOR THOSE HANDS! THEY'RE FAST!
STOMP!
POW!
THOSE FEET ARE ALSO FAST.

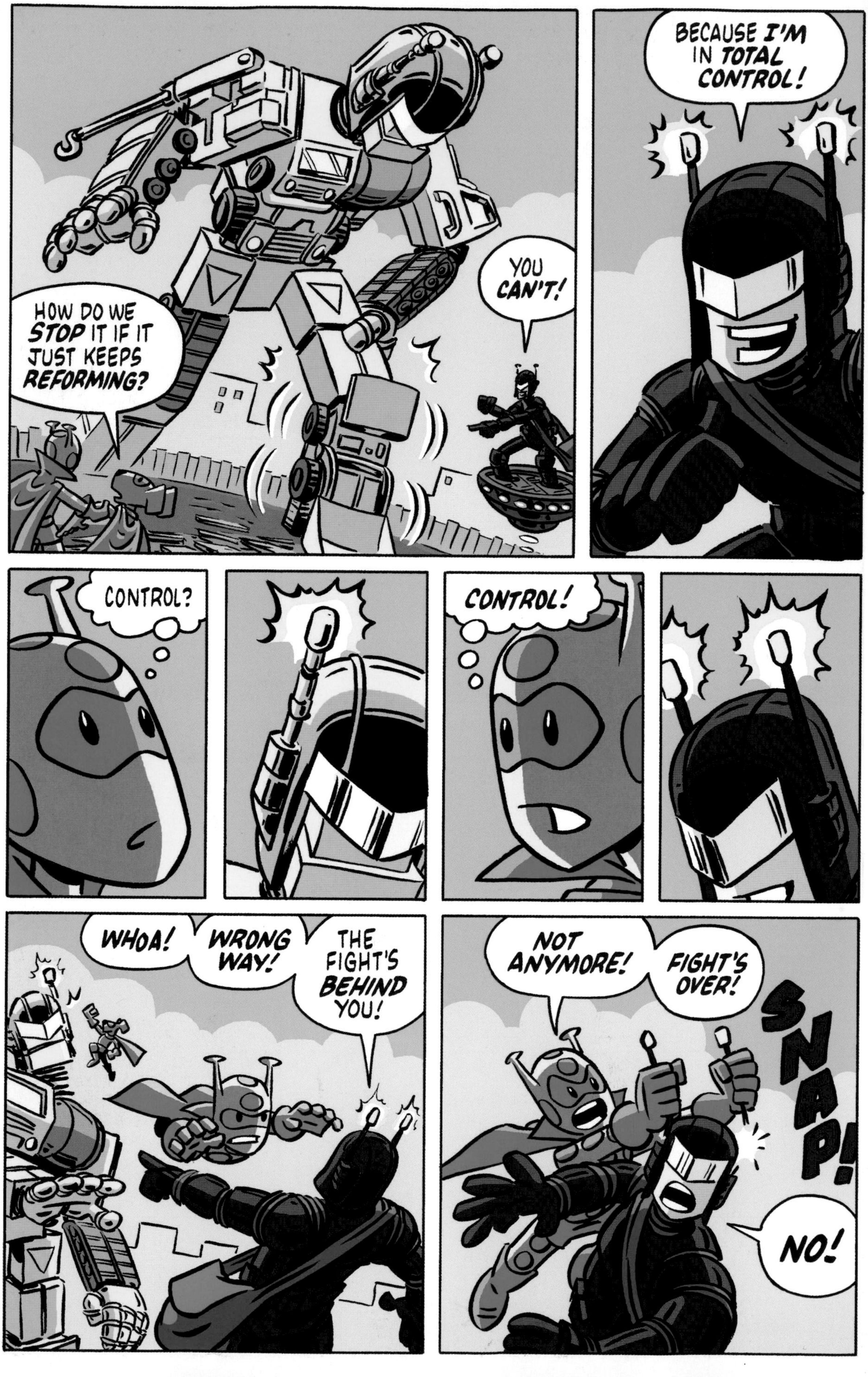
HOW DO WE STOP IT IF IT JUST KEEPS REFORMING?
YOU CAN'T!
BECAUSE I'M IN TOTAL CONTROL!
CONTROL?
CONTROL!
WHOA!
WRONG WAY!
THE FIGHT'S BEHIND YOU!
NOT ANYMORE!
FIGHT'S OVER!
SNAP!
NO!

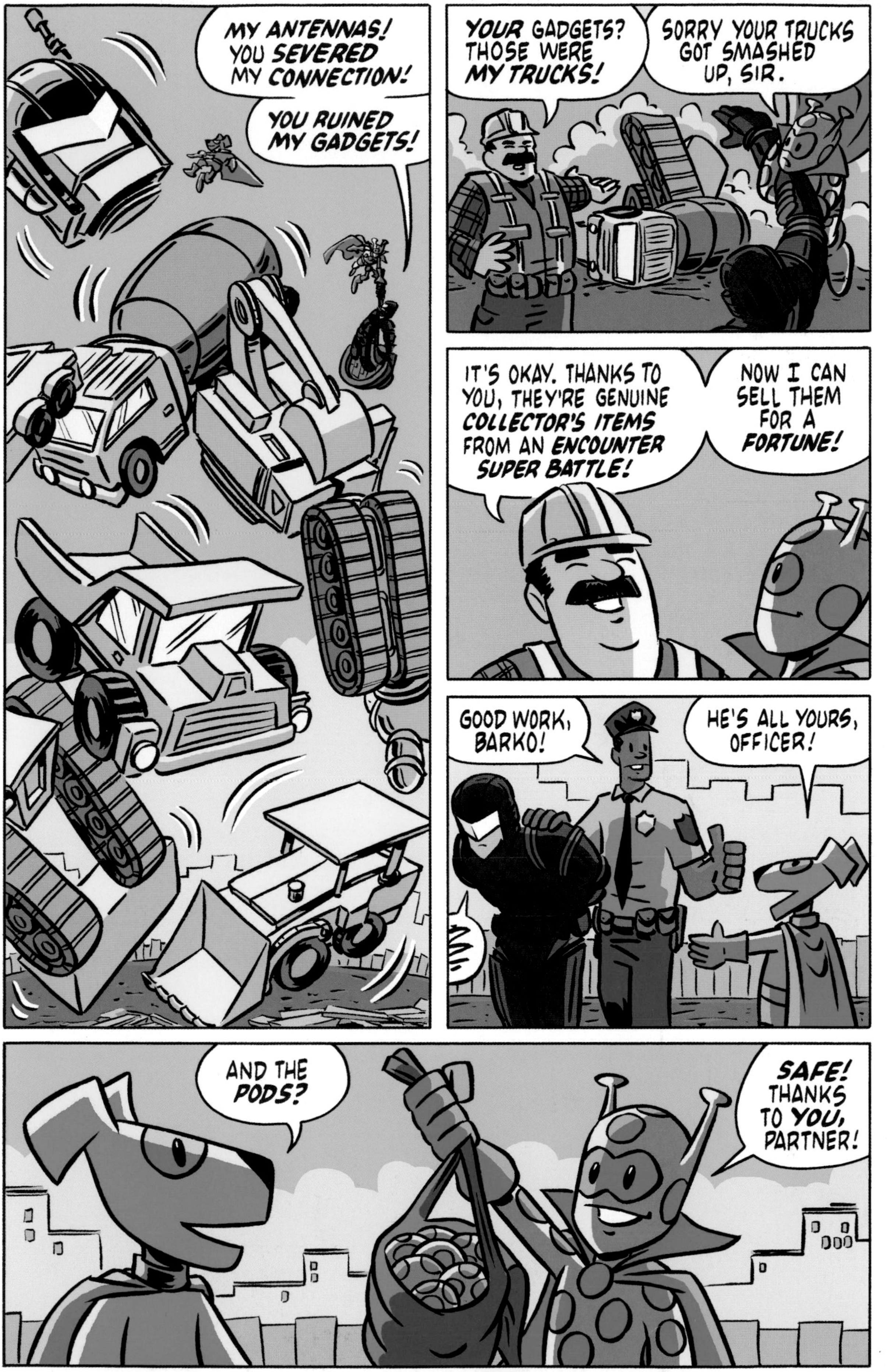
MY ANTENNAS! YOU SEVERED MY CONNECTION!
YOU RUINED MY GADGETS!
YOUR GADGETS? THOSE WERE MY TRUCKS!
SORRY YOUR TRUCKS GOT SMASHED UP, SIR.
IT'S OKAY. THANKS TO YOU, THEY'RE GENUINE COLLECTOR'S ITEMS FROM AN ENCOUNTER SUPER BATTLE!
NOW I CAN SELL THEM FOR A FORTUNE!
GOOD WORK, BARKO!
HE'S ALL YOURS, OFFICER!
AND THE PODS?
SAFE! THANKS TO YOU, PARTNER!

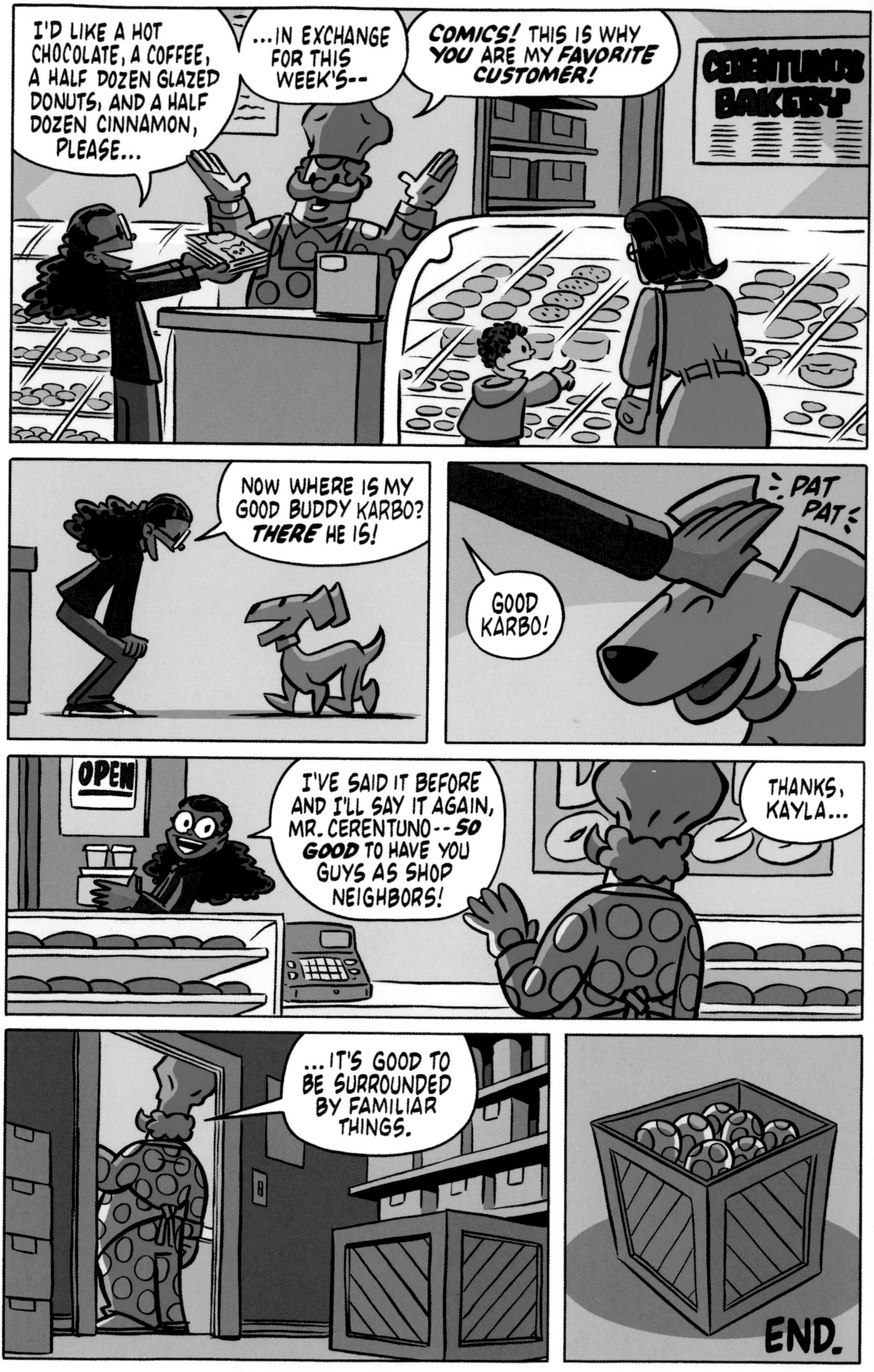
I'D LIKE A HOT CHOCOLATE, A COFFEE, A HALF DOZEN GLAZED DONUTS, AND A HALF DOZEN CINNAMON, PLEASE...
...IN EXCHANGE FOR THIS WEEK'S--
COMICS! THIS IS WHY YOU ARE MY FAVORITE CUSTOMER!
CERENTUNO'S BAKERY
NOW WHERE IS MY GOOD BUDDY KARBO? THERE HE IS!
PAT PAT
GOOD KARBO!
OPEN
I'VE SAID IT BEFORE AND I'LL SAY IT AGAIN, MR. CERENTUNO--SO GOOD TO HAVE YOU GUYS AS SHOP NEIGHBORS!
THANKS, KAYLA...
...IT'S GOOD TO BE SURROUNDED BY FAMILIAR THINGS.
END.

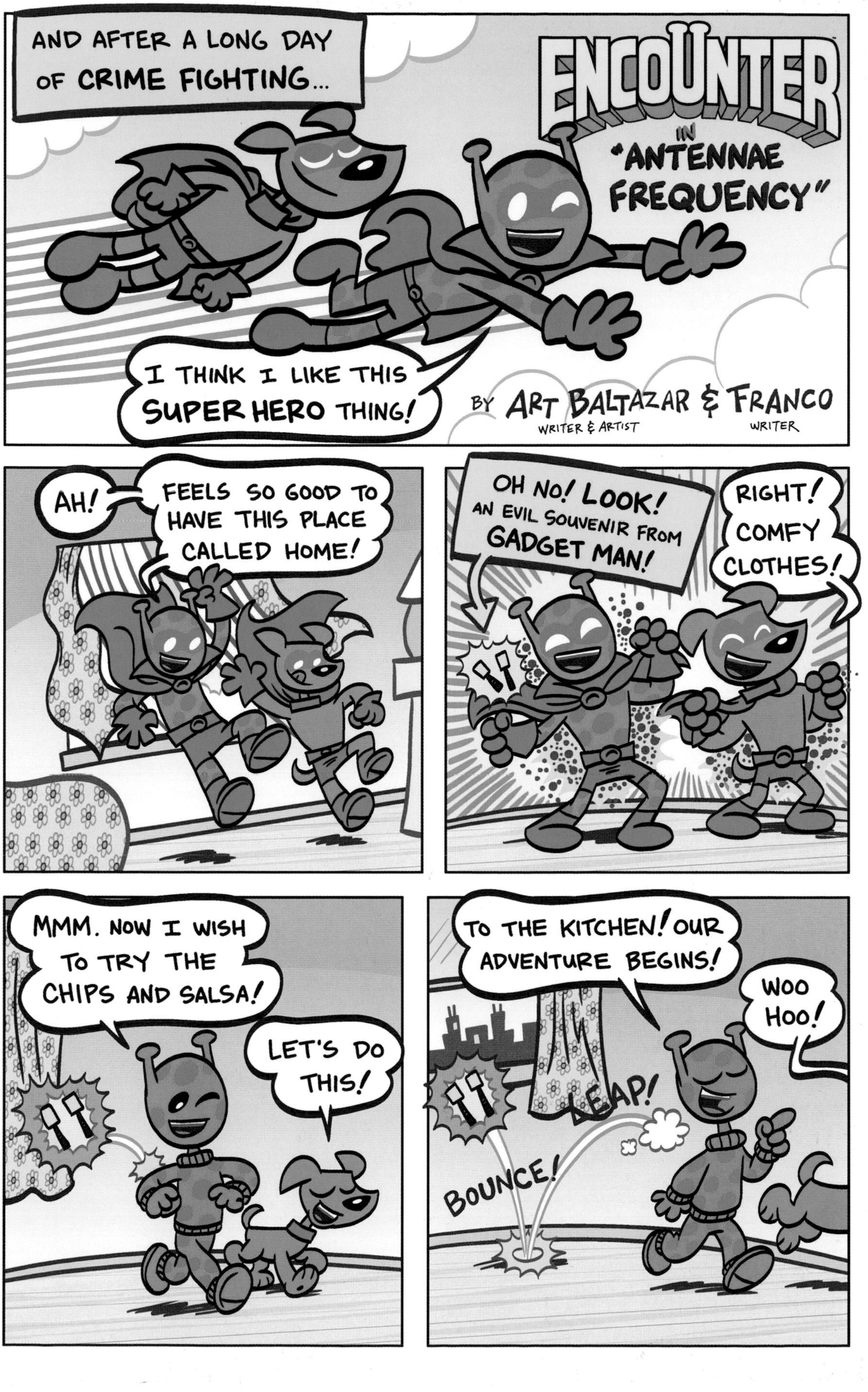
AND AFTER A LONG DAY OF CRIME FIGHTING...
ENCOUNTER
IN "ANTENNAE FREQUENCY"
I THINK I LIKE THIS SUPER HERO THING!
BY ART BALTAZAR & FRANCO
WRITER & ARTIST
WRITER
AH!
FEELS SO GOOD TO HAVE THIS PLACE CALLED HOME!
OH NO! LOOK! AN EVIL SOUVENIR FROM GADGET MAN!
RIGHT! COMFY CLOTHES!
MMM. NOW I WISH TO TRY THE CHIPS AND SALSA!
LET'S DO THIS!
TO THE KITCHEN! OUR ADVENTURE BEGINS!
WOO HOO!
LEAP!
BOUNCE!

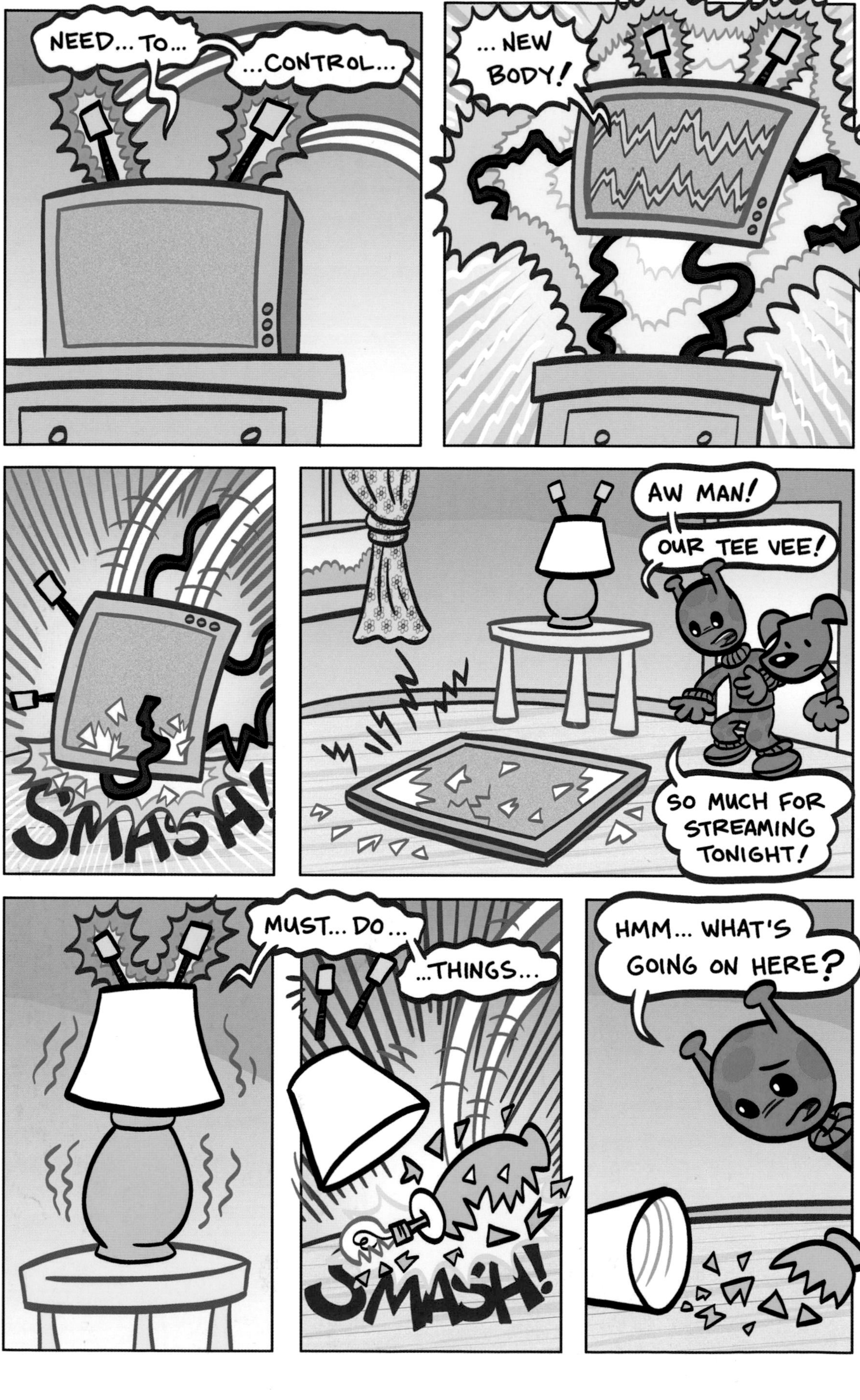
NEED... TO...
...CONTROL...
... NEW BODY!
SMASH!
AW MAN!
OUR TEE VEE!
SO MUCH FOR STREAMING TONIGHT!
MUST... DO...
...THINGS...
SMASH!
HMM... WHAT'S GOING ON HERE?

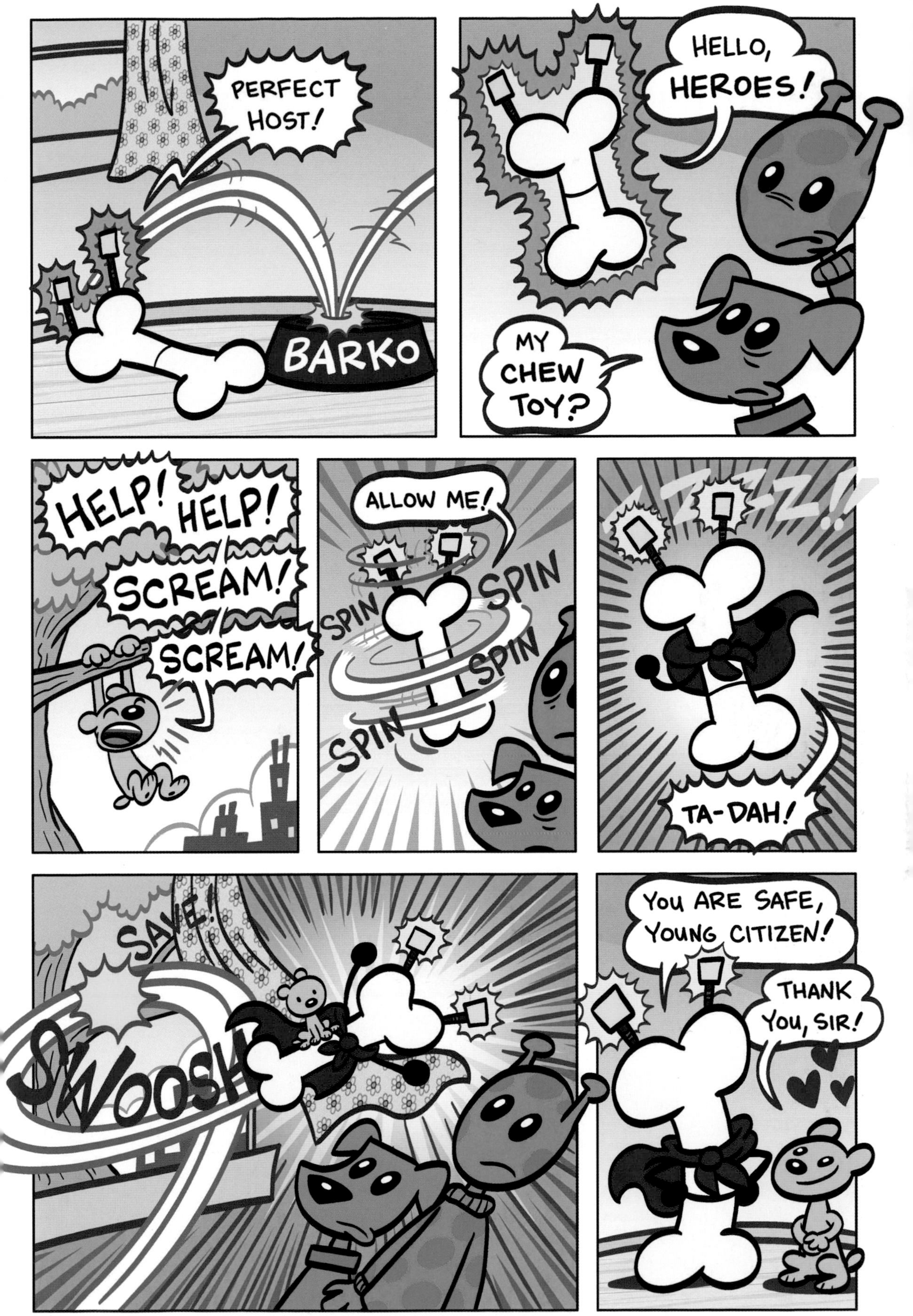
PERFECT HOST!
BARKO
HELLO, HEROES!
MY CHEW TOY?
HELP! HELP!
SCREAM!
SCREAM!
ALLOW ME!
SPIN SPIN SPIN SPIN
TA-DAH!
SAVE!
SWOOSH
YOU ARE SAFE, YOUNG CITIZEN!
THANK YOU, SIR!

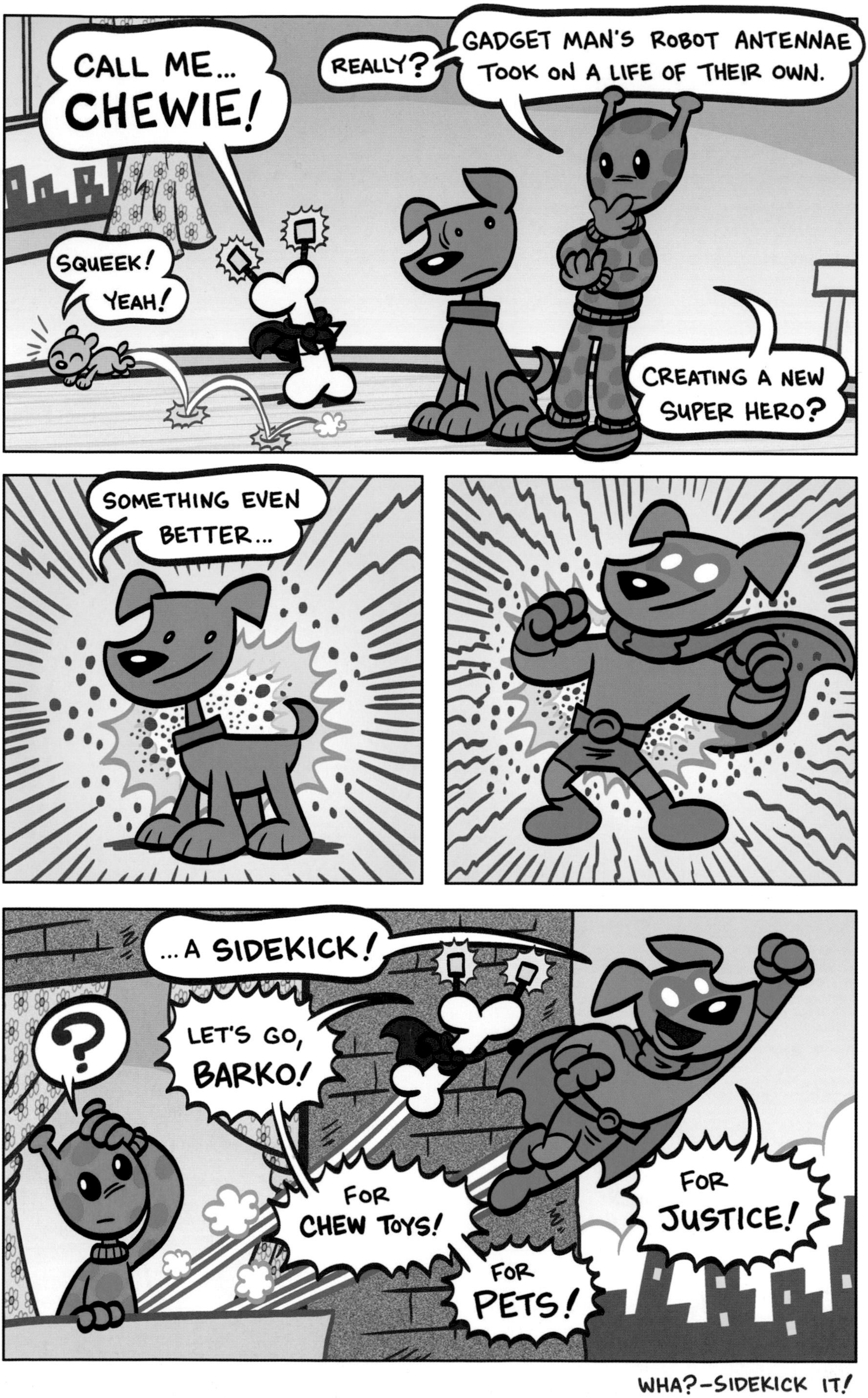
CALL ME... CHEWIE!
REALLY?
GADGET MAN'S ROBOT ANTENNAE TOOK ON A LIFE OF THEIR OWN.
SQUEEK! YEAH!
CREATING A NEW SUPER HERO?
SOMETHING EVEN BETTER...
...A SIDEKICK!
?
LET'S GO, BARKO!
FOR CHEW TOYS!
FOR PETS!
FOR JUSTICE!

WHA?-SIDEKICK IT!

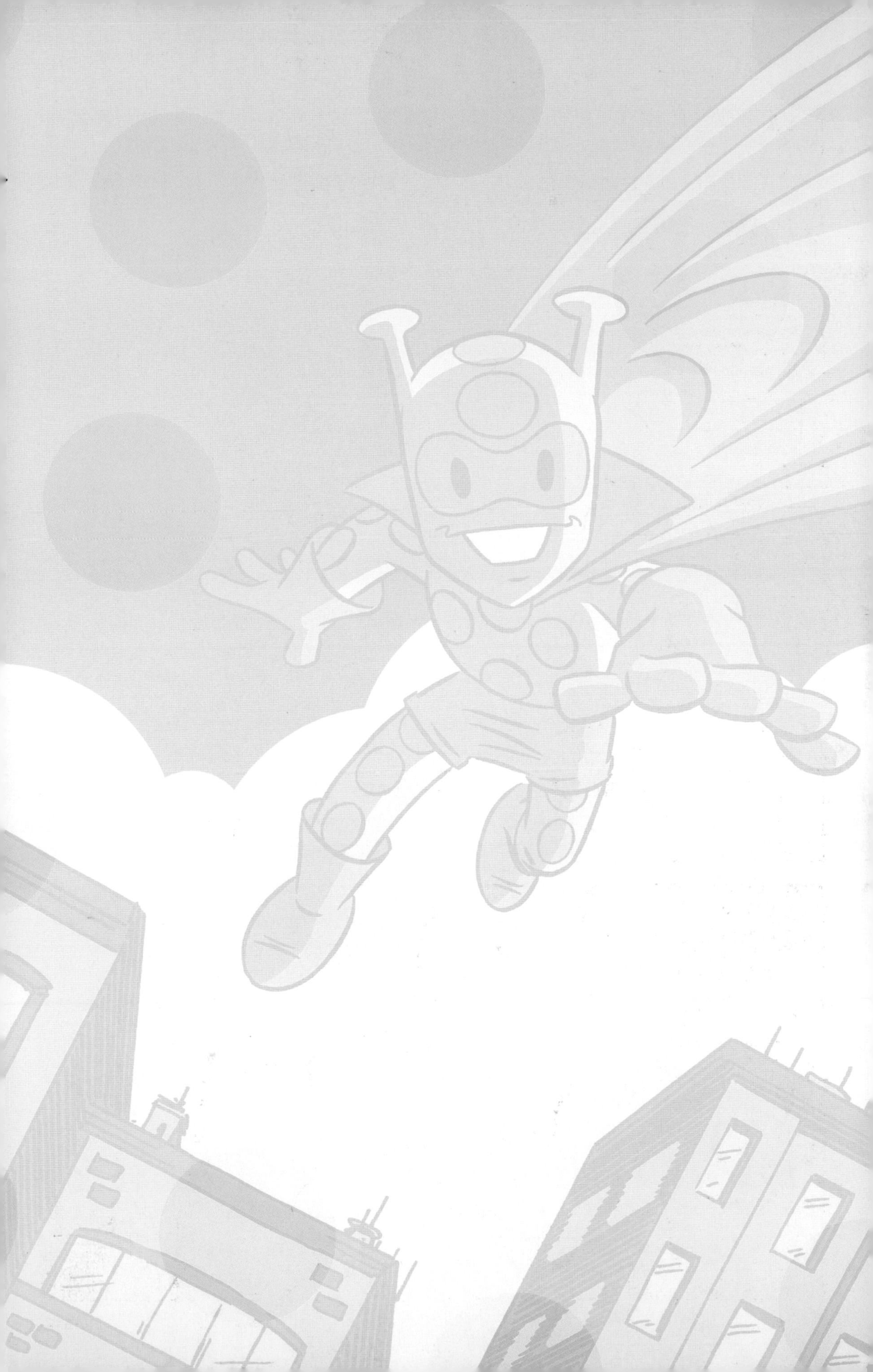

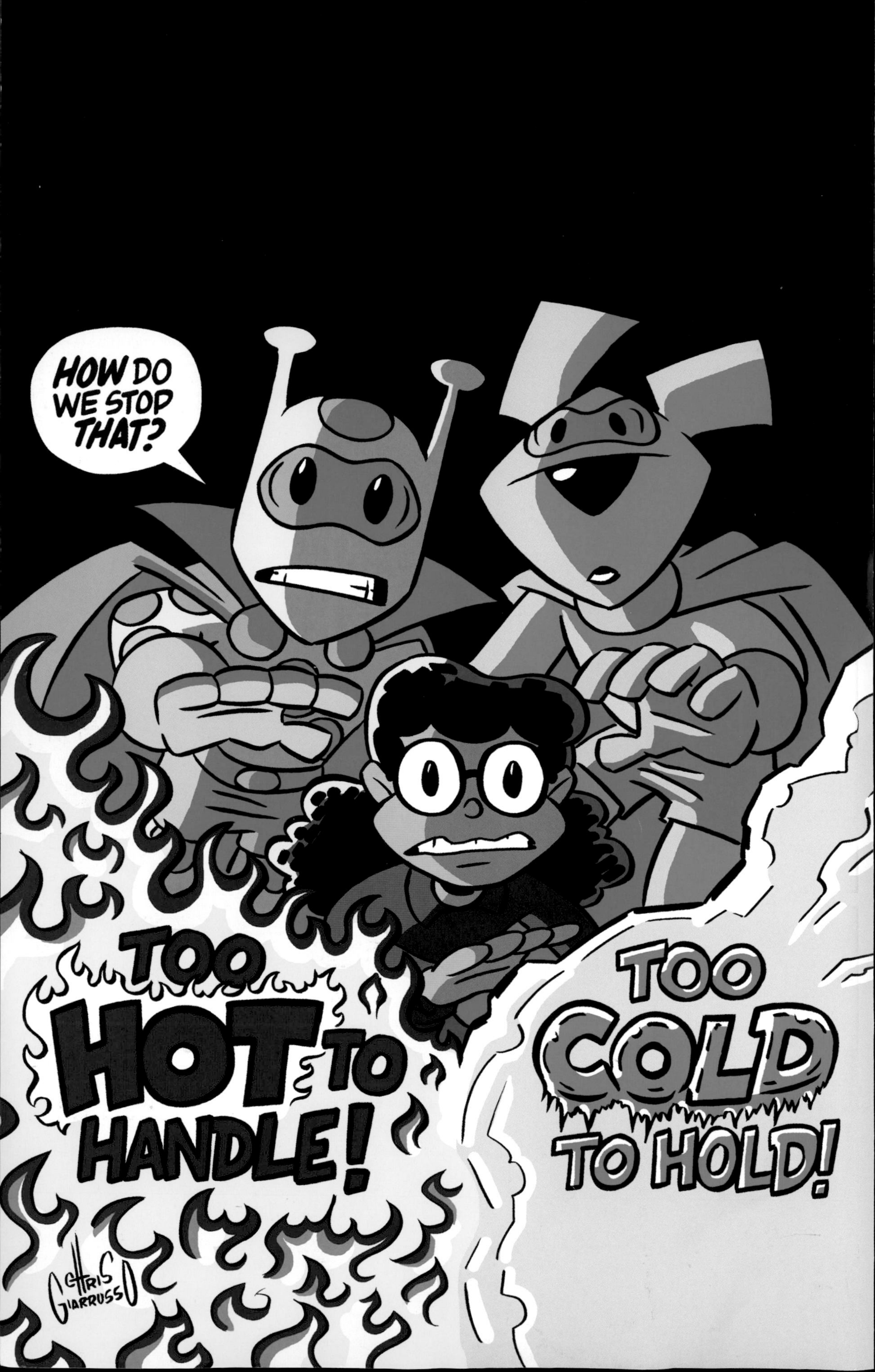
HOW DO WE STOP THAT?
TOO HOT TO HANDLE!
TOO COLD TO HOLD!
CHRIS GIARRUSSO

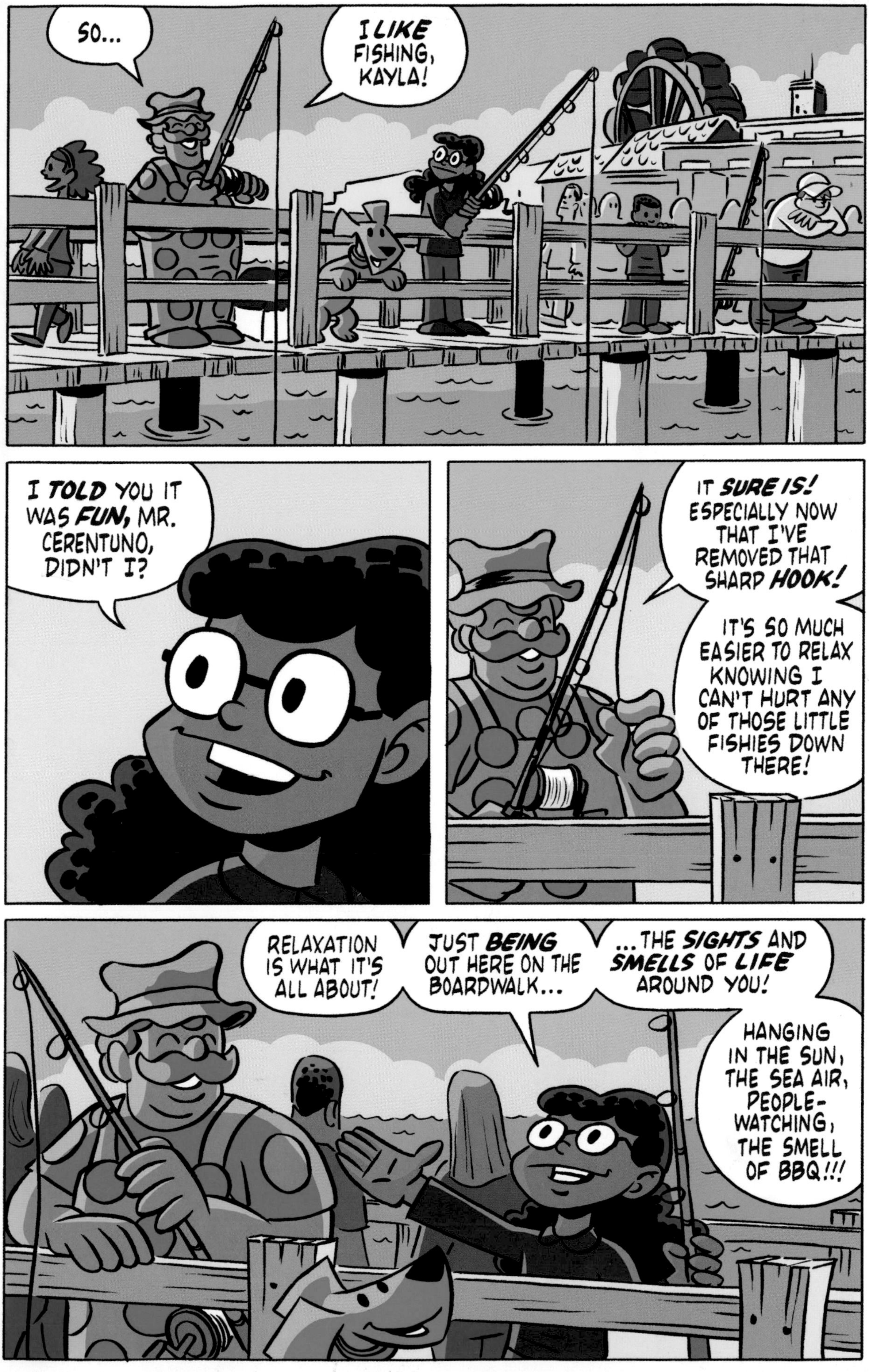
SO...
I LIKE FISHING, KAYLA!
I TOLD YOU IT WAS FUN, MR. CERENTUNO, DIDN'T I?
IT SURE IS! ESPECIALLY NOW THAT I'VE REMOVED THAT SHARP HOOK!
IT'S SO MUCH EASIER TO RELAX KNOWING I CAN'T HURT ANY OF THOSE LITTLE FISHIES DOWN THERE!
RELAXATION IS WHAT IT'S ALL ABOUT!
JUST BEING OUT HERE ON THE BOARDWALK...
...THE SIGHTS AND SMELLS OF LIFE AROUND YOU!
HANGING IN THE SUN, THE SEA AIR, PEOPLE-WATCHING, THE SMELL OF BBQ!!!

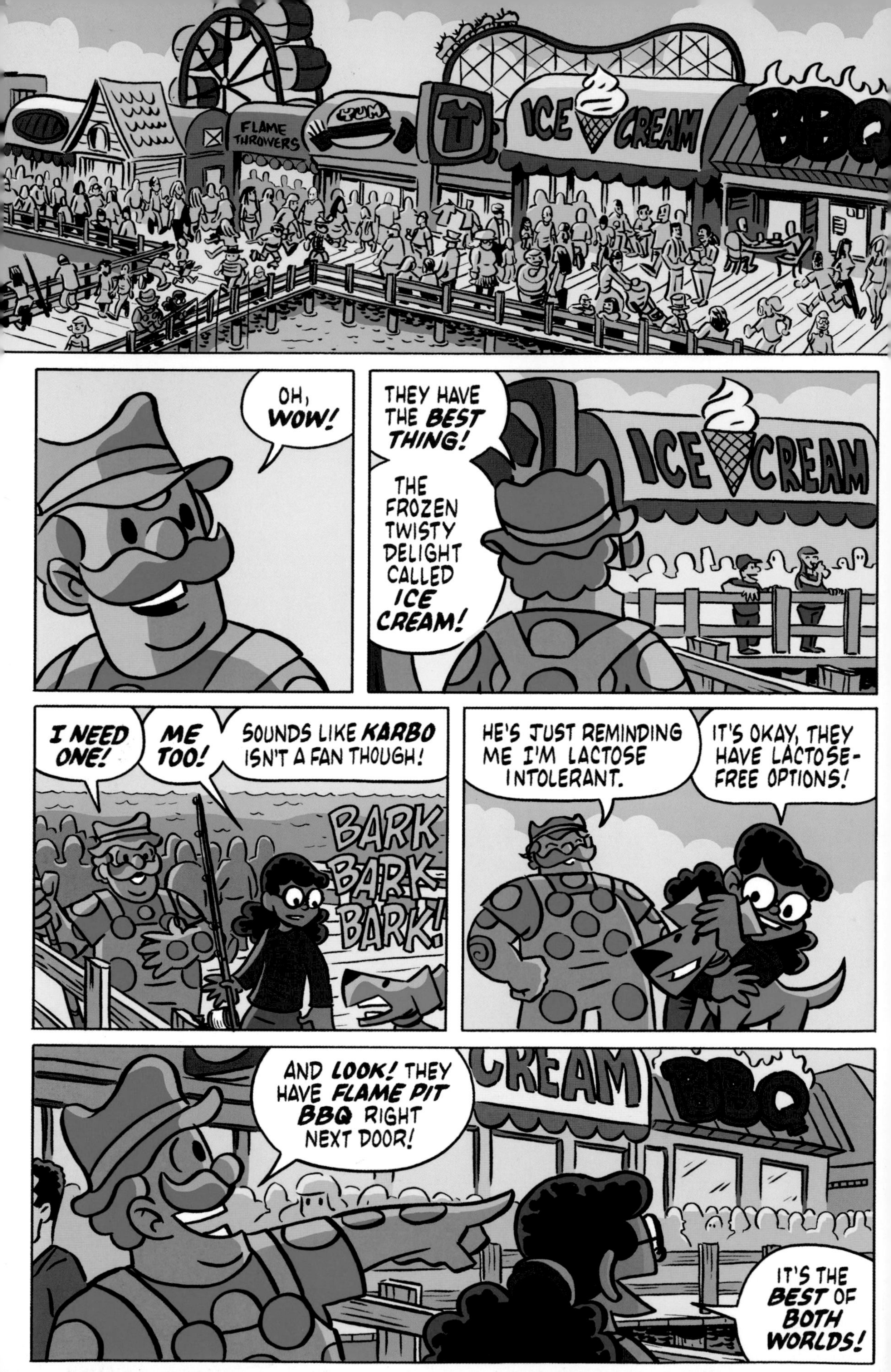

FLAME THROWERS
YUM
ICE CREAM
BBQ
OH, WOW!
THEY HAVE THE BEST THING!
THE FROZEN TWISTY DELIGHT CALLED ICE CREAM!
ICE CREAM
I NEED ONE!
ME TOO!
SOUNDS LIKE KARBO ISN'T A FAN THOUGH!
BARK BARK BARK!
HE'S JUST REMINDING ME I'M LACTOSE INTOLERANT.
IT'S OKAY, THEY HAVE LACTOSE-FREE OPTIONS!
AND LOOK! THEY HAVE FLAME PIT BBQ RIGHT NEXT DOOR!
CREAM
BBQ
IT'S THE BEST OF BOTH WORLDS!

WE SHALL BE RIGHT BACK WITH DELICIOUS MEATS AND FROZEN TREATS!

HA HA, DON'T MIX THEM UP! *HOT* SIDE *HOT*, *COOL* SIDE *COOL!*

CHOMP!

WHAT WAS *THAT?*

CH OMP!

ANOTHER ONE!

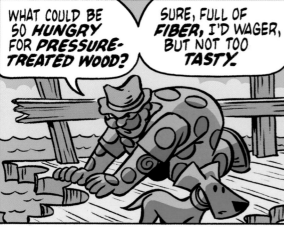

WHAT COULD BE SO *HUNGRY* FOR *PRESSURE-TREATED WOOD?*

SURE, FULL OF *FIBER*, I'D WAGER, BUT NOT TOO *TASTY.*

SHARK!

BUT IT'S... ON FIRE?

THAT SEEMS *WRONG.*

I HAVE READ ABOUT SHARKS.

THEY ARE NOT SUPPOSED TO BE ON FIRE.

IT'S COMING BACK!

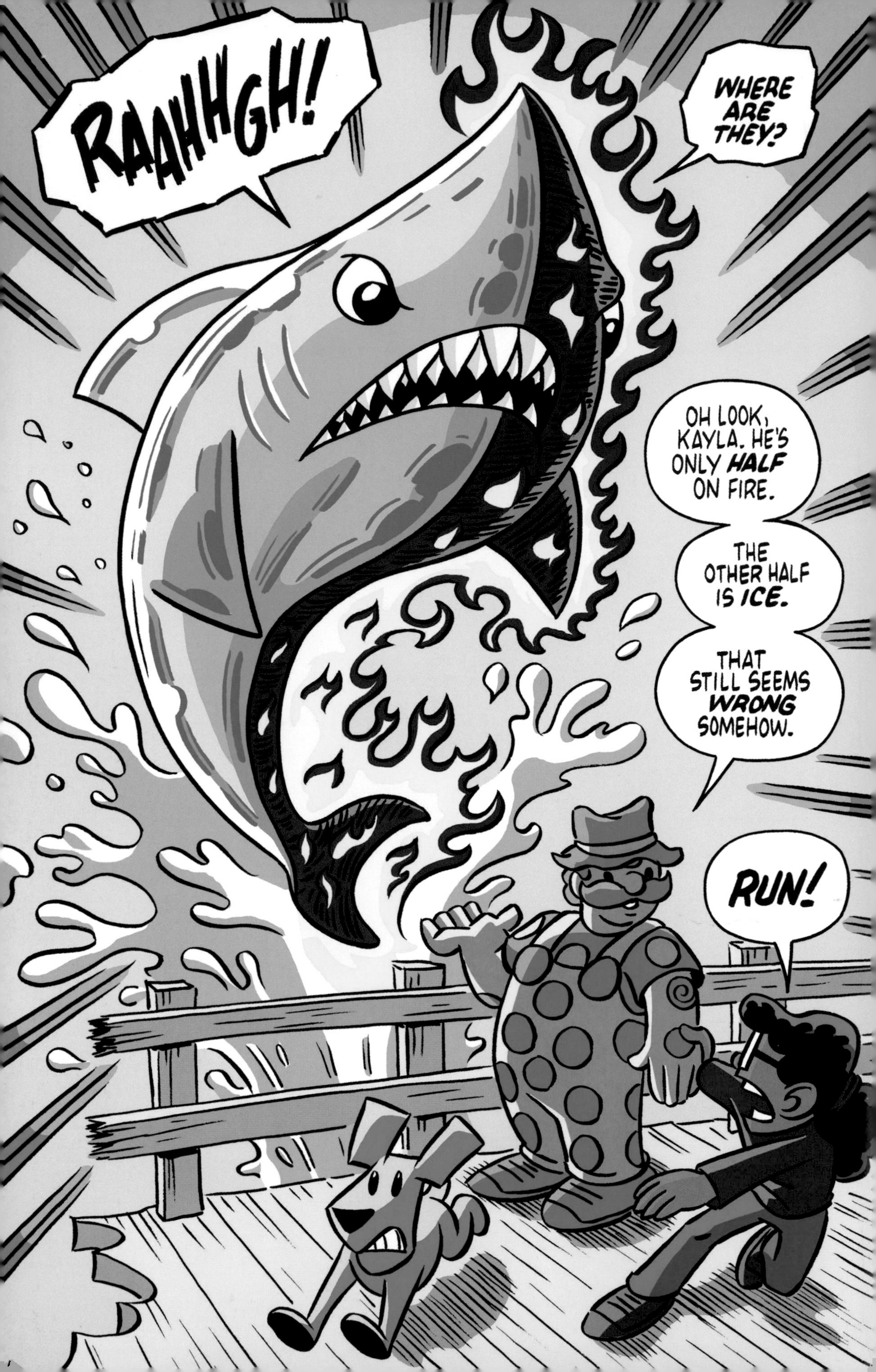
RAAHHGH!
WHERE ARE THEY?
OH LOOK, KAYLA. HE'S ONLY HALF ON FIRE.
THE OTHER HALF IS ICE.
THAT STILL SEEMS WRONG SOMEHOW.
RUN!

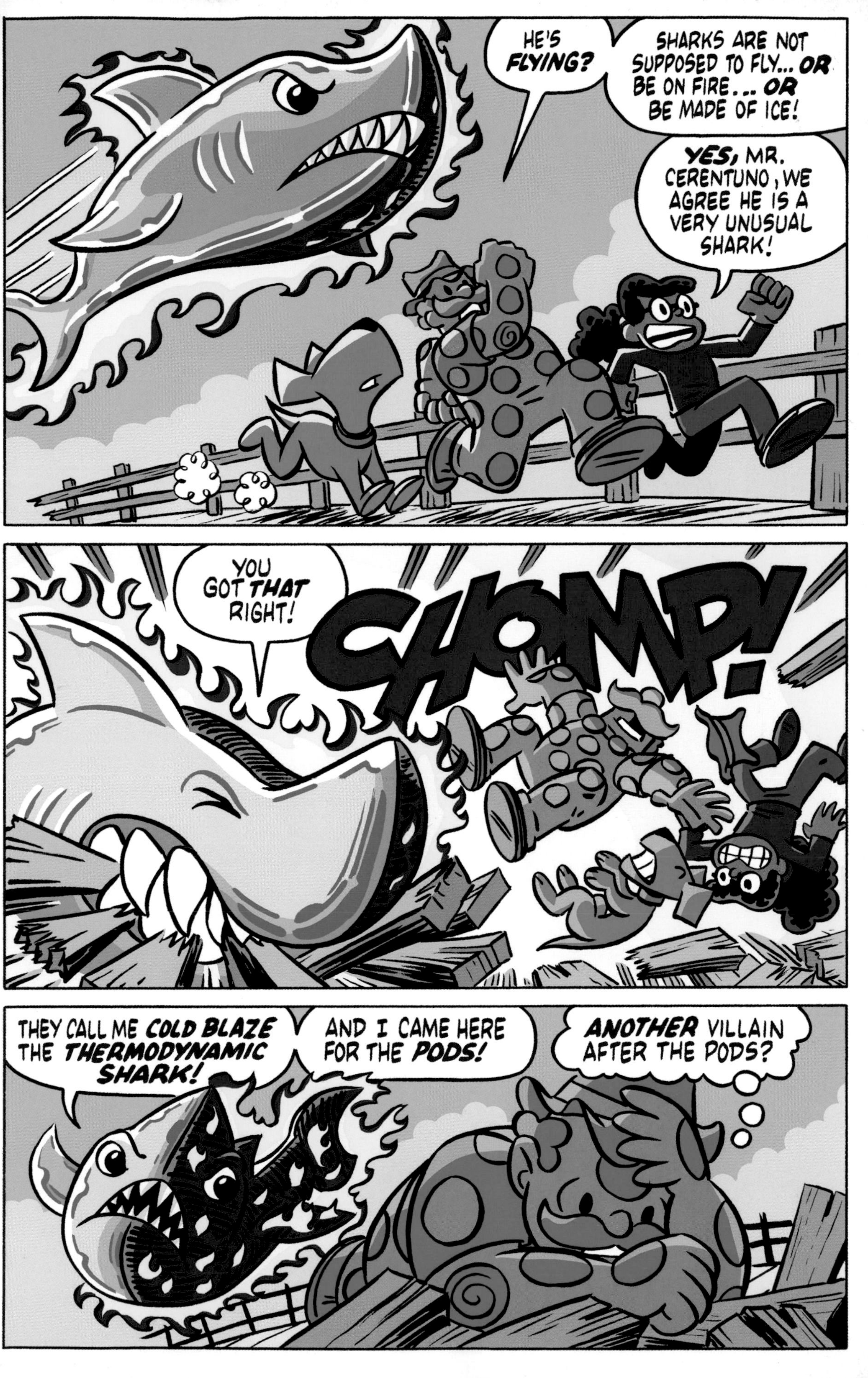
HE'S *FLYING?*
SHARKS ARE NOT SUPPOSED TO FLY... *OR* BE ON FIRE... *OR* BE MADE OF ICE!
YES, MR. CERENTUNO, WE AGREE HE IS A VERY UNUSUAL SHARK!
YOU GOT *THAT* RIGHT!
CHOMP!
THEY CALL ME *COLD BLAZE* THE *THERMODYNAMIC SHARK!*
AND I CAME HERE FOR THE *PODS!*
ANOTHER VILLAIN AFTER THE PODS?

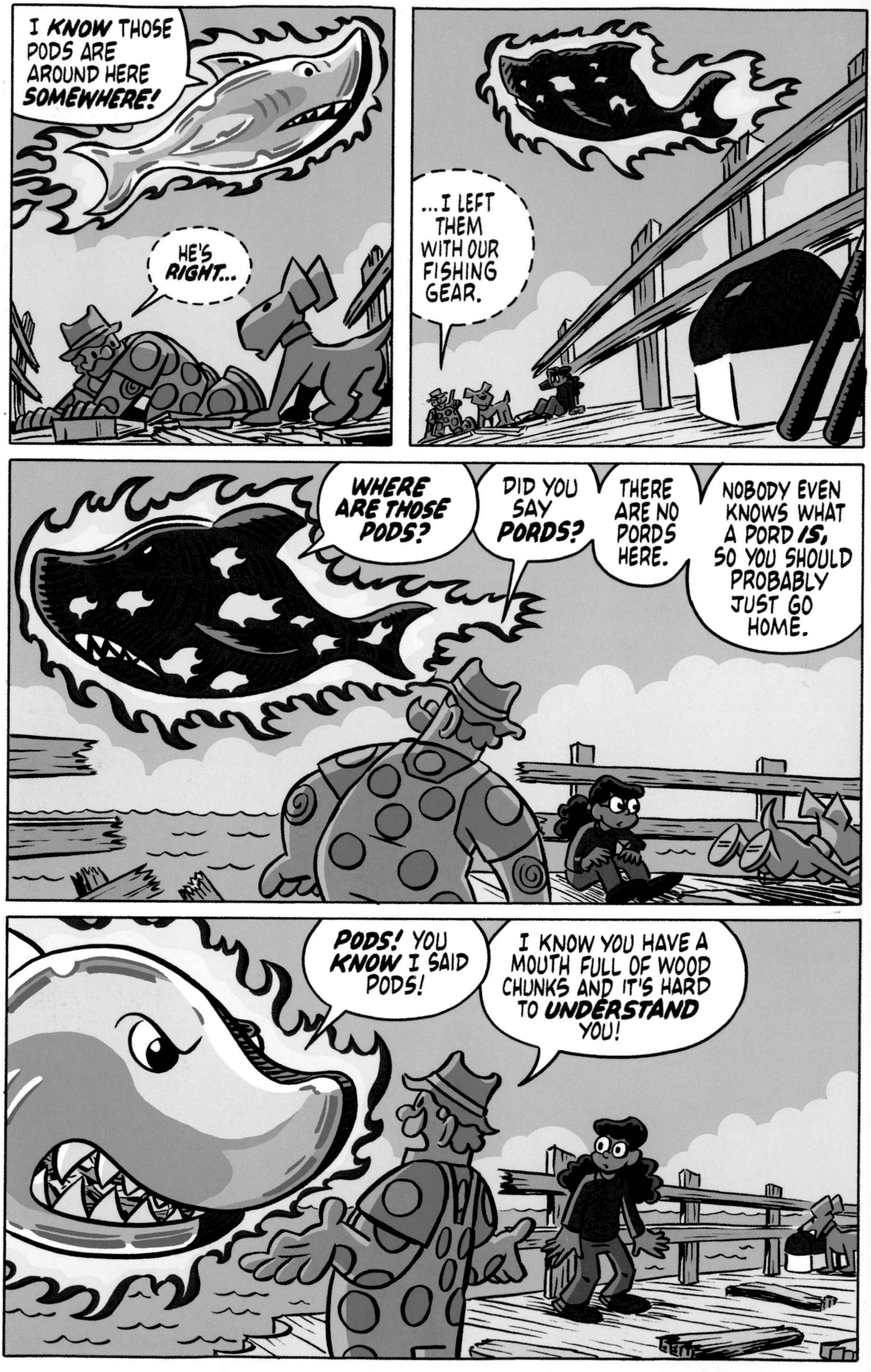
I KNOW THOSE PODS ARE AROUND HERE SOMEWHERE!
HE'S RIGHT...
...I LEFT THEM WITH OUR FISHING GEAR.
WHERE ARE THOSE PODS?
DID YOU SAY PORDS?
THERE ARE NO PORDS HERE.
NOBODY EVEN KNOWS WHAT A PORD IS, SO YOU SHOULD PROBABLY JUST GO HOME.
PODS! YOU KNOW I SAID PODS!
I KNOW YOU HAVE A MOUTH FULL OF WOOD CHUNKS AND IT'S HARD TO UNDERSTAND YOU!

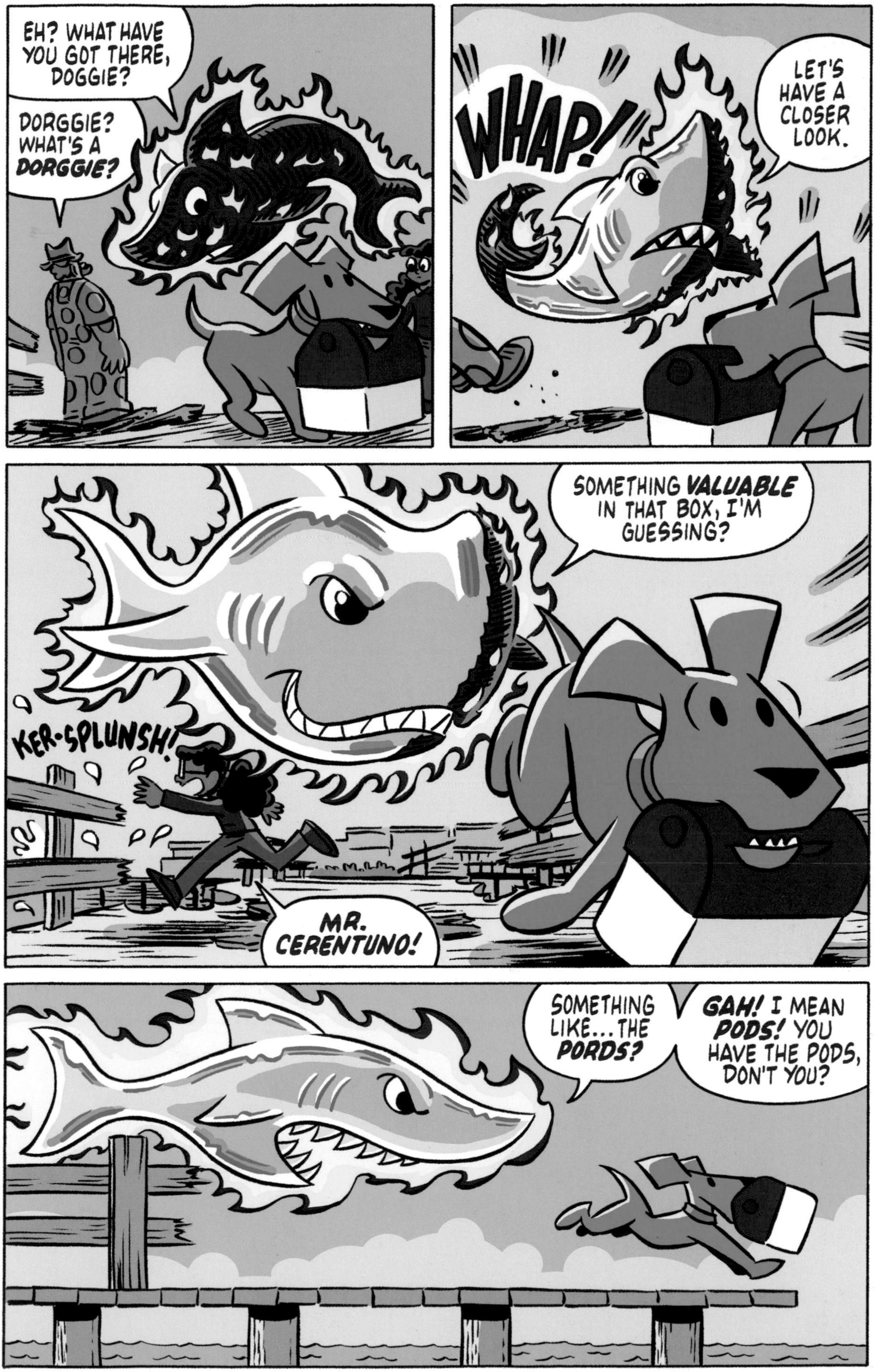
EH? WHAT HAVE YOU GOT THERE, DOGGIE?
DORGGIE? WHAT'S A DORGGIE?
WHAP!
LET'S HAVE A CLOSER LOOK.
SOMETHING VALUABLE IN THAT BOX, I'M GUESSING?
KER-SPLUNSH!
MR. CERENTUNO!
SOMETHING LIKE...THE PORDS?
GAH! I MEAN PODS! YOU HAVE THE PODS, DON'T YOU?

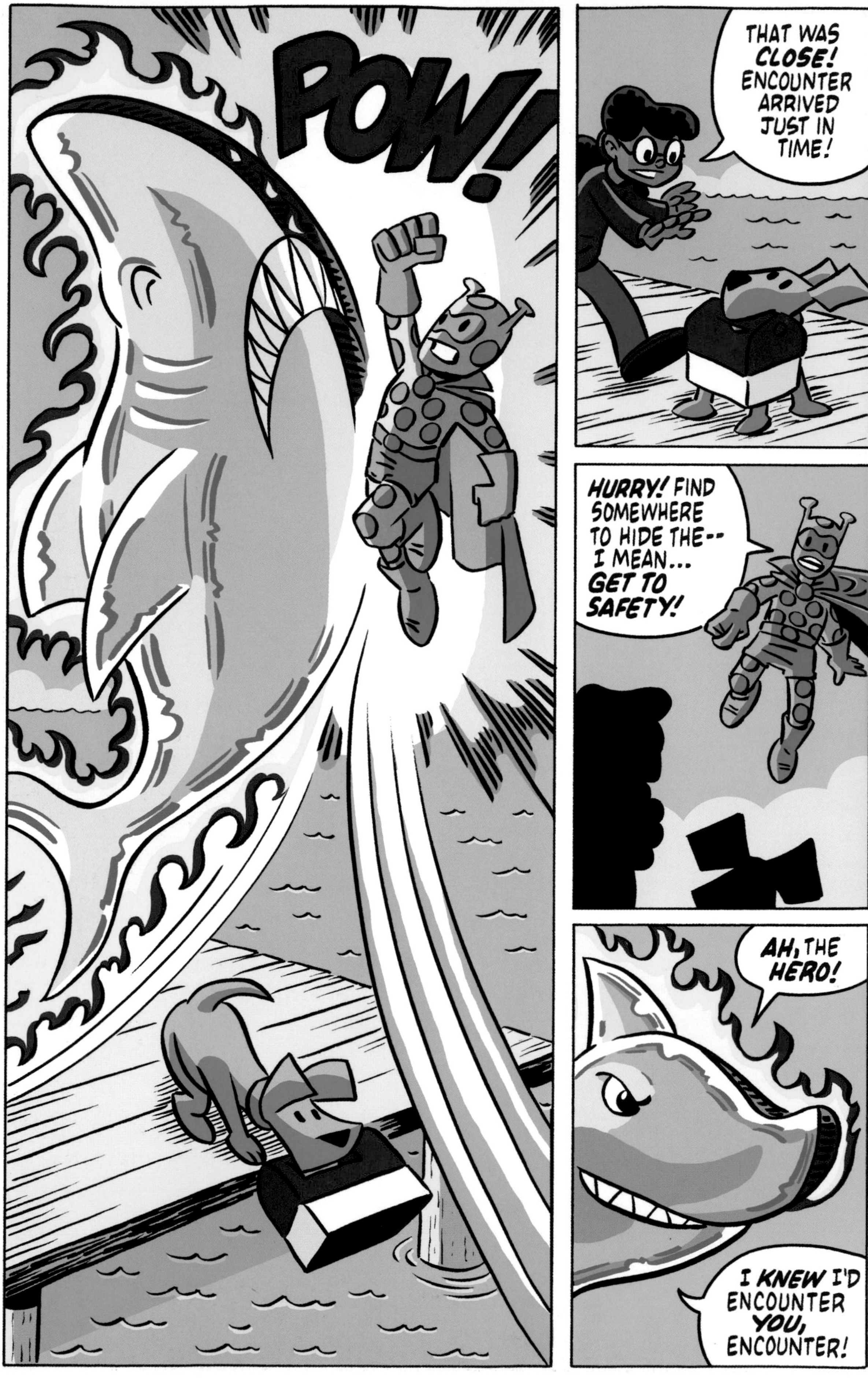
POW!
THAT WAS CLOSE! ENCOUNTER ARRIVED JUST IN TIME!
HURRY! FIND SOMEWHERE TO HIDE THE-- I MEAN... GET TO SAFETY!
AH, THE HERO!
I KNEW I'D ENCOUNTER YOU, ENCOUNTER!

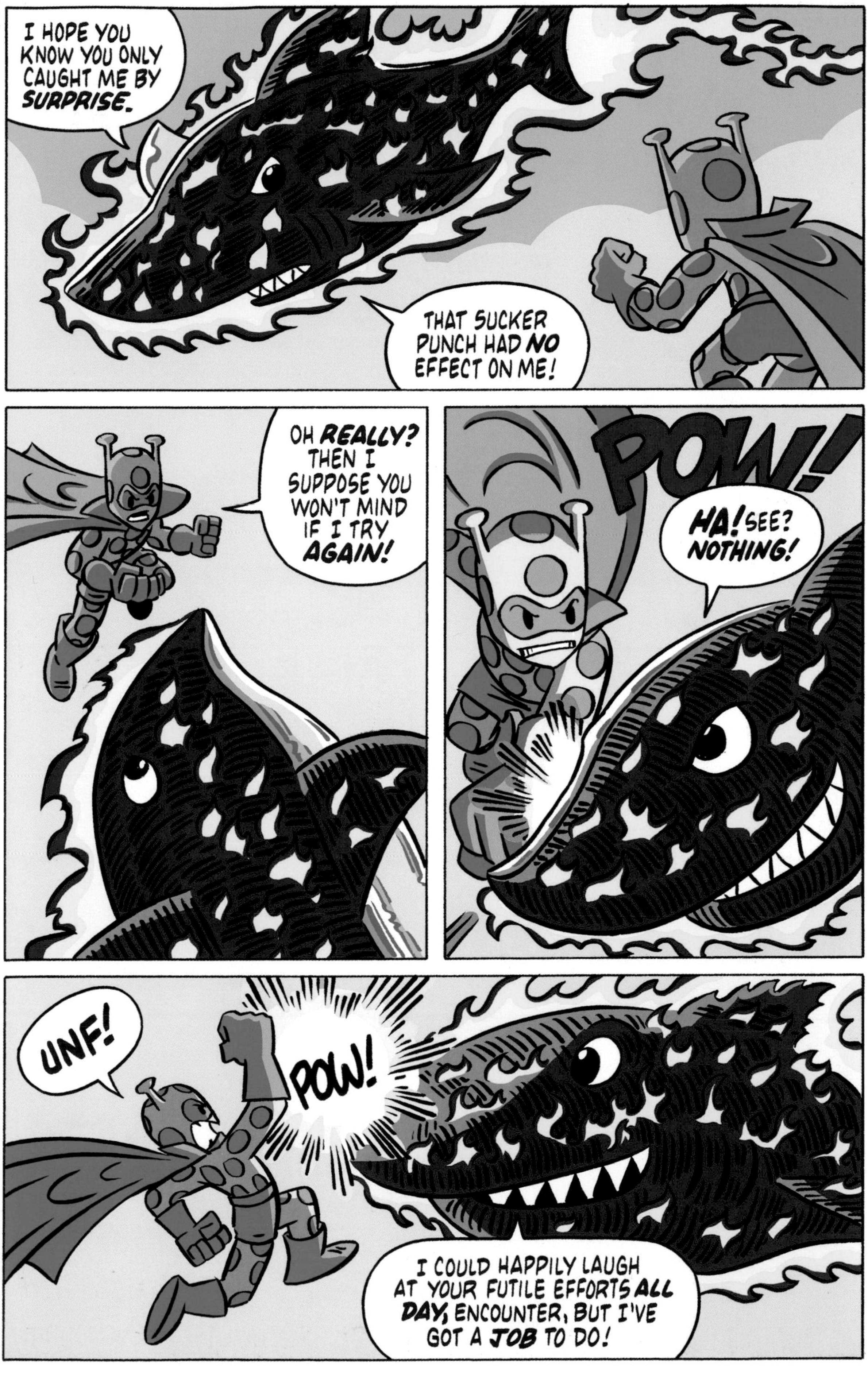
I HOPE YOU KNOW YOU ONLY CAUGHT ME BY **SURPRISE.**
THAT SUCKER PUNCH HAD **NO** EFFECT ON ME!
OH **REALLY?** THEN I SUPPOSE YOU WON'T MIND IF I TRY **AGAIN!**
POW!
HA! SEE? **NOTHING!**
UNF!
POW!
I COULD HAPPILY LAUGH AT YOUR FUTILE EFFORTS **ALL DAY,** ENCOUNTER, BUT I'VE GOT A **JOB** TO DO!

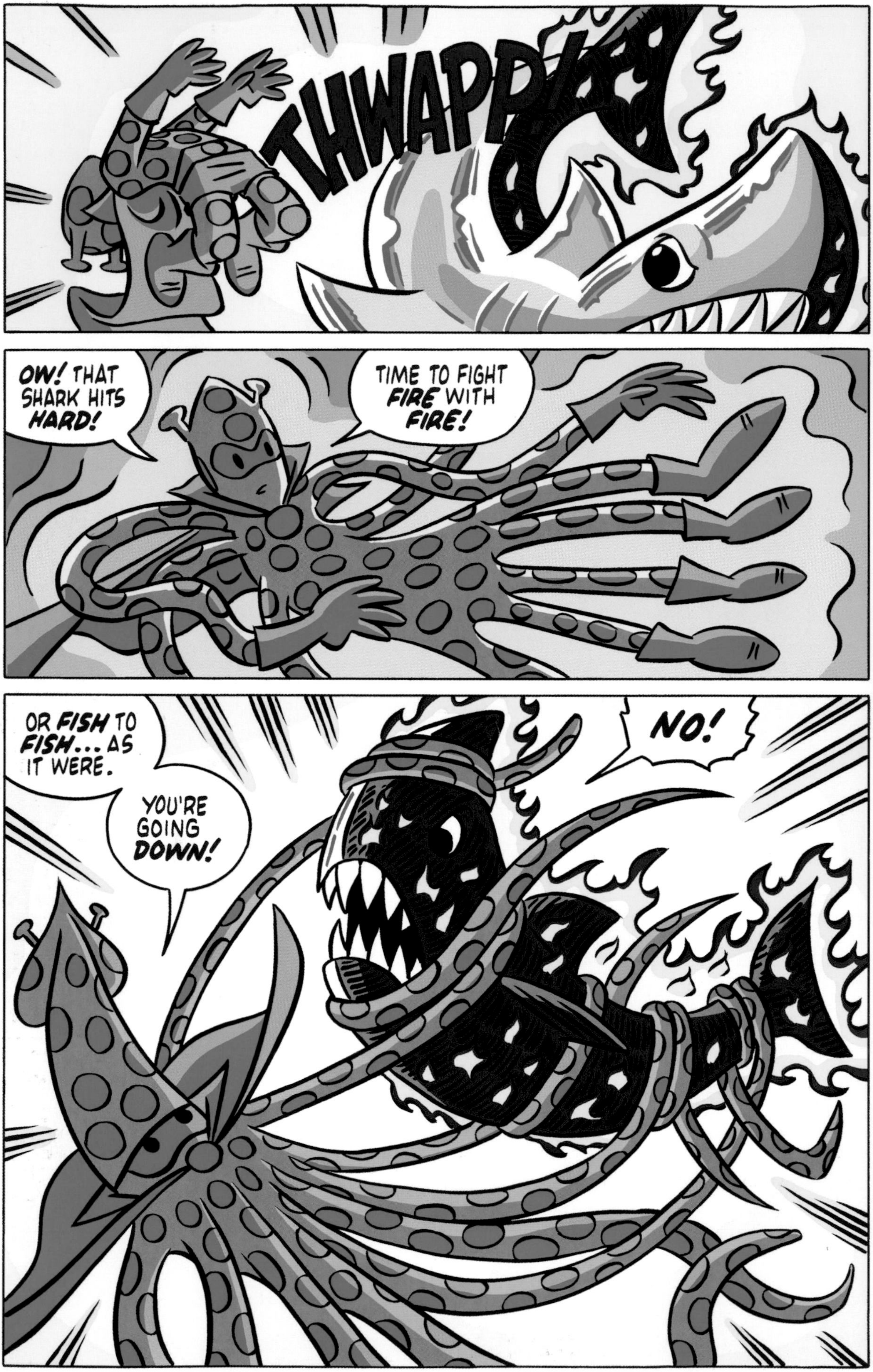
THWAPP!
OW! THAT SHARK HITS HARD!
TIME TO FIGHT FIRE WITH FIRE!
OR FISH TO FISH... AS IT WERE.
YOU'RE GOING DOWN!
NO!

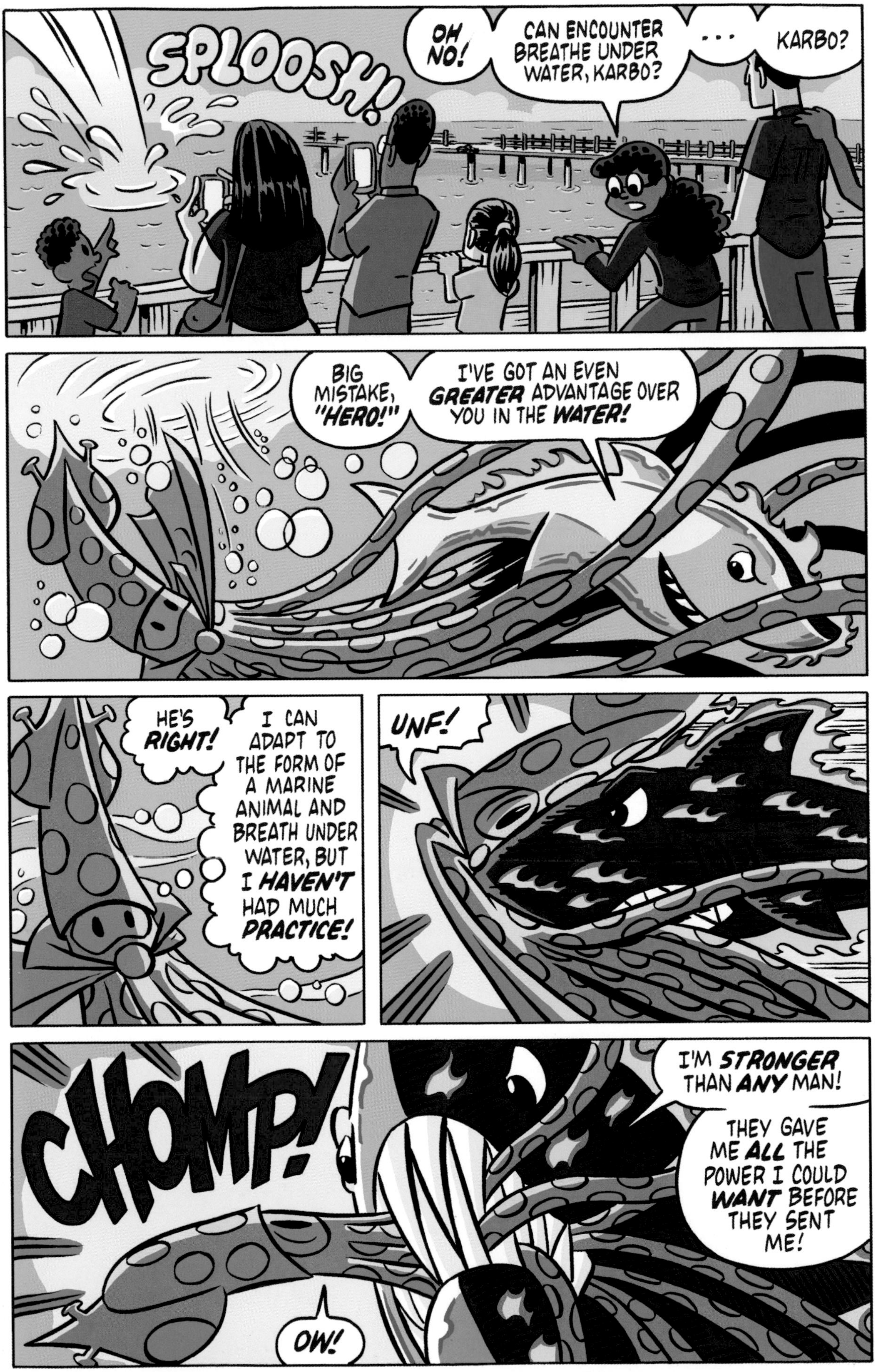
SPLOOSH!
OH NO!
CAN ENCOUNTER BREATHE UNDER WATER, KARBO?
...
KARBO?
BIG MISTAKE, "HERO!"
I'VE GOT AN EVEN GREATER ADVANTAGE OVER YOU IN THE WATER!
HE'S RIGHT!
I CAN ADAPT TO THE FORM OF A MARINE ANIMAL AND BREATH UNDER WATER, BUT I HAVEN'T HAD MUCH PRACTICE!
UNF!
CHOMP!
I'M STRONGER THAN ANY MAN!
THEY GAVE ME ALL THE POWER I COULD WANT BEFORE THEY SENT ME!
OW!

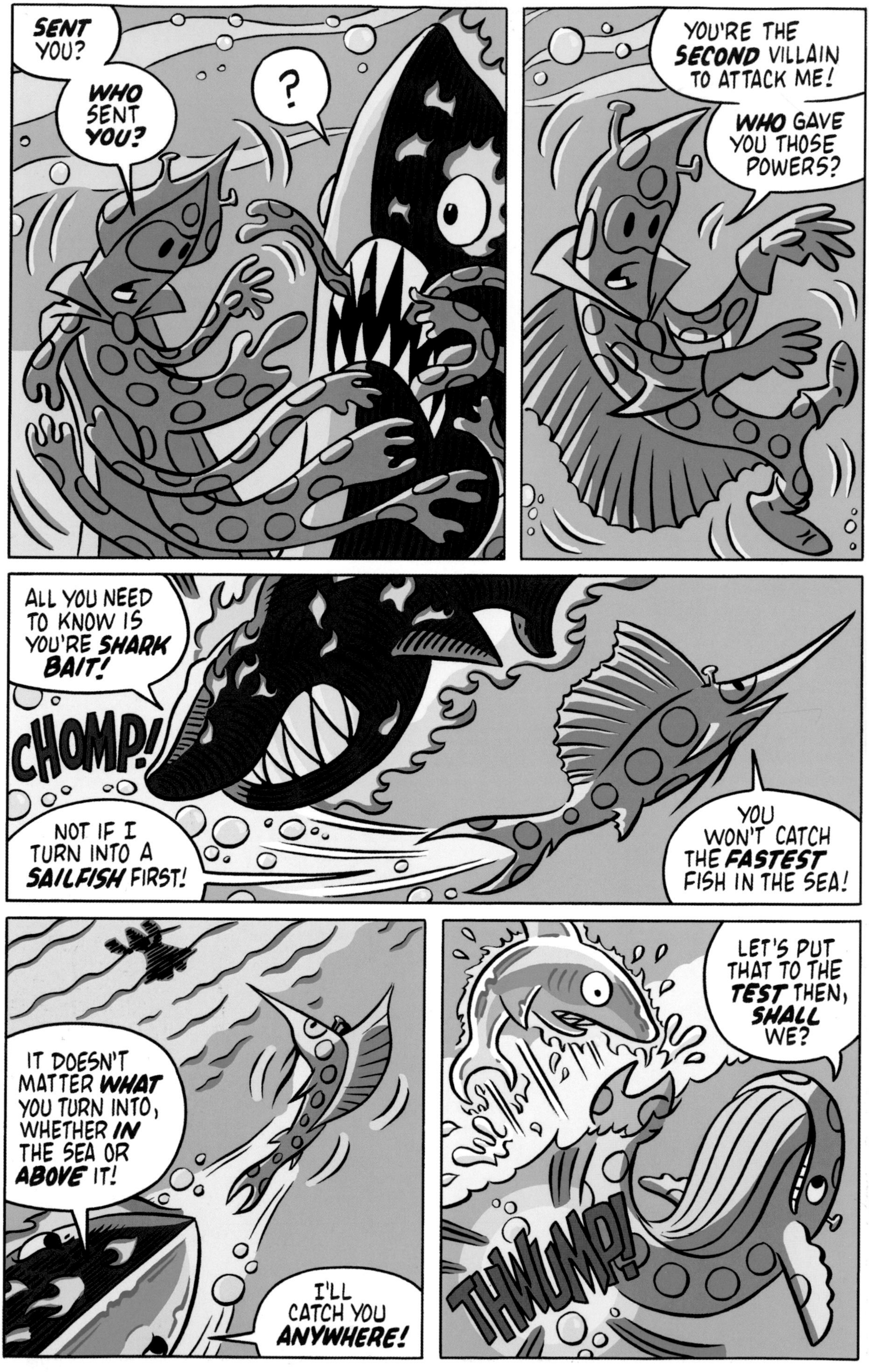
SENT YOU?
WHO SENT YOU?
?
YOU'RE THE SECOND VILLAIN TO ATTACK ME!
WHO GAVE YOU THOSE POWERS?
ALL YOU NEED TO KNOW IS YOU'RE SHARK BAIT!
CHOMP!
NOT IF I TURN INTO A SAILFISH FIRST!
YOU WON'T CATCH THE FASTEST FISH IN THE SEA!
IT DOESN'T MATTER WHAT YOU TURN INTO, WHETHER IN THE SEA OR ABOVE IT!
I'LL CATCH YOU ANYWHERE!
LET'S PUT THAT TO THE TEST THEN, SHALL WE?
THWUMP!

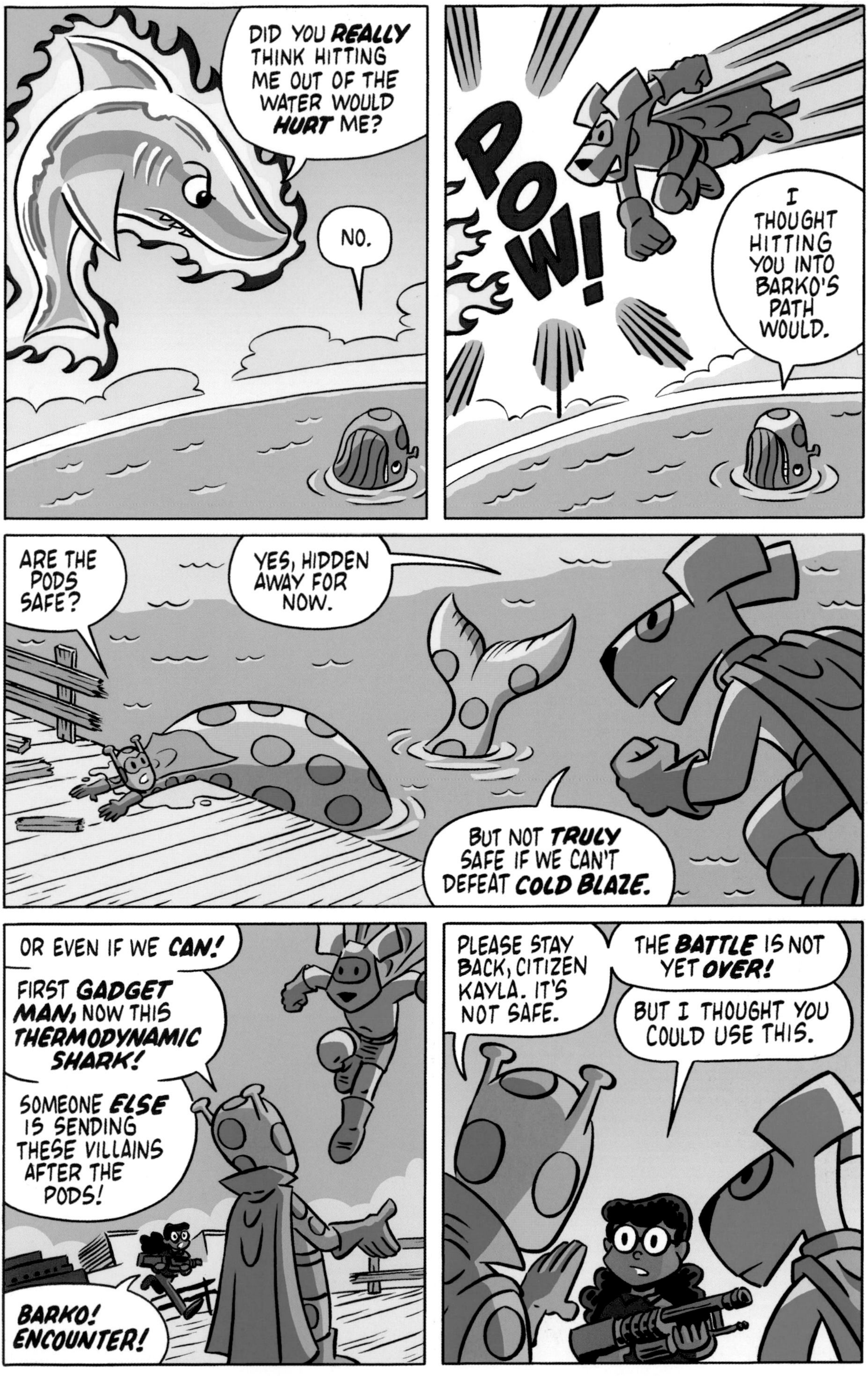
DID YOU REALLY THINK HITTING ME OUT OF THE WATER WOULD HURT ME?
NO.
POW!
I THOUGHT HITTING YOU INTO BARKO'S PATH WOULD.
ARE THE PODS SAFE?
YES, HIDDEN AWAY FOR NOW.
BUT NOT TRULY SAFE IF WE CAN'T DEFEAT COLD BLAZE.
OR EVEN IF WE CAN!
FIRST GADGET MAN, NOW THIS THERMODYNAMIC SHARK!
SOMEONE ELSE IS SENDING THESE VILLAINS AFTER THE PODS!
BARKO! ENCOUNTER!
PLEASE STAY BACK, CITIZEN KAYLA. IT'S NOT SAFE.
THE BATTLE IS NOT YET OVER!
BUT I THOUGHT YOU COULD USE THIS.

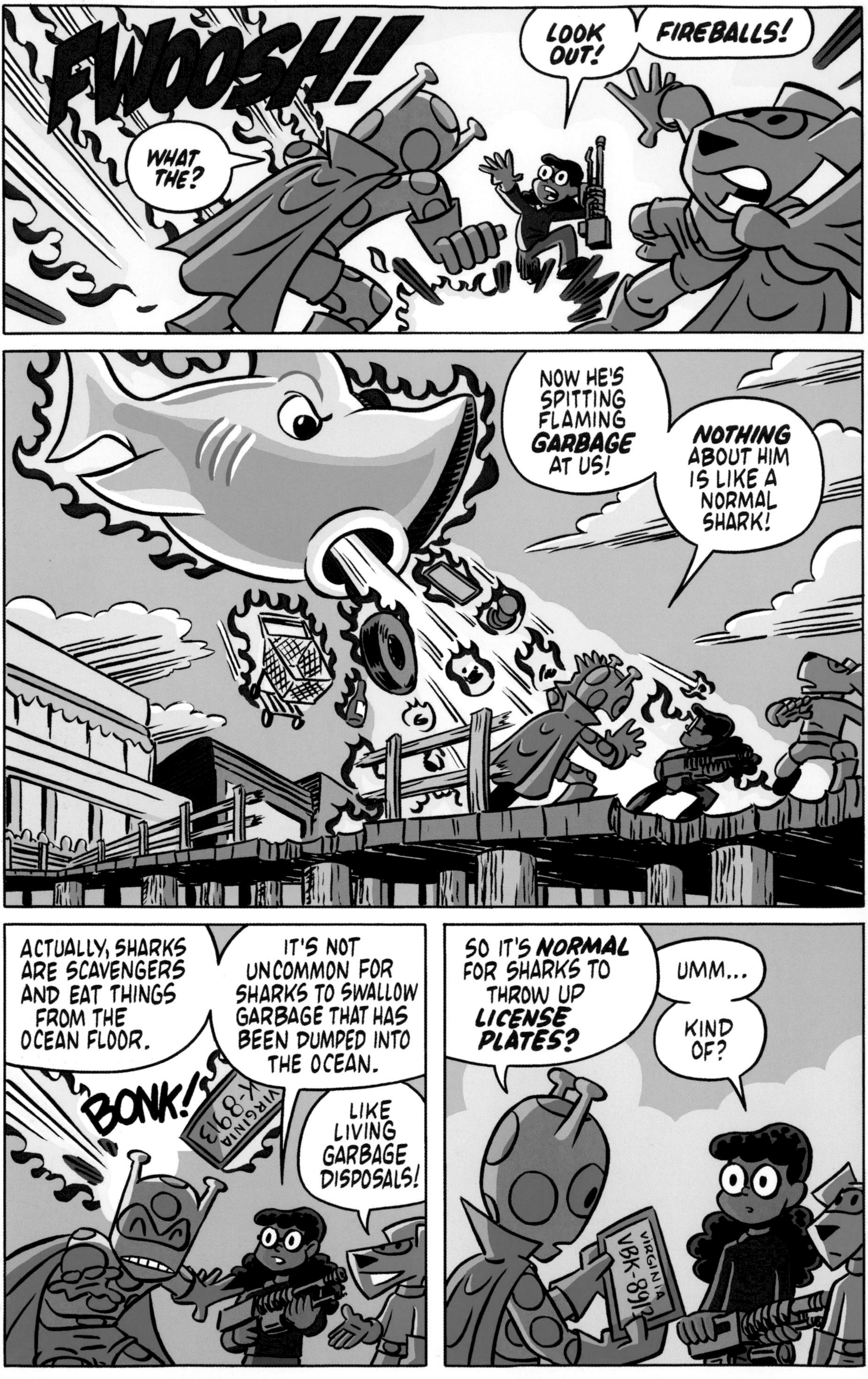
FWOOSH!!
WHAT THE?
LOOK OUT!
FIREBALLS!
NOW HE'S SPITTING FLAMING **GARBAGE** AT US!
NOTHING ABOUT HIM IS LIKE A NORMAL SHARK!
ACTUALLY, SHARKS ARE SCAVENGERS AND EAT THINGS FROM THE OCEAN FLOOR.
IT'S NOT UNCOMMON FOR SHARKS TO SWALLOW GARBAGE THAT HAS BEEN DUMPED INTO THE OCEAN.
BONK!
VIRGINIA
K-8913
LIKE LIVING GARBAGE DISPOSALS!
SO IT'S **NORMAL** FOR SHARKS TO THROW UP **LICENSE PLATES?**
UMM...
KIND OF?
VIRGINIA
VBK-8912

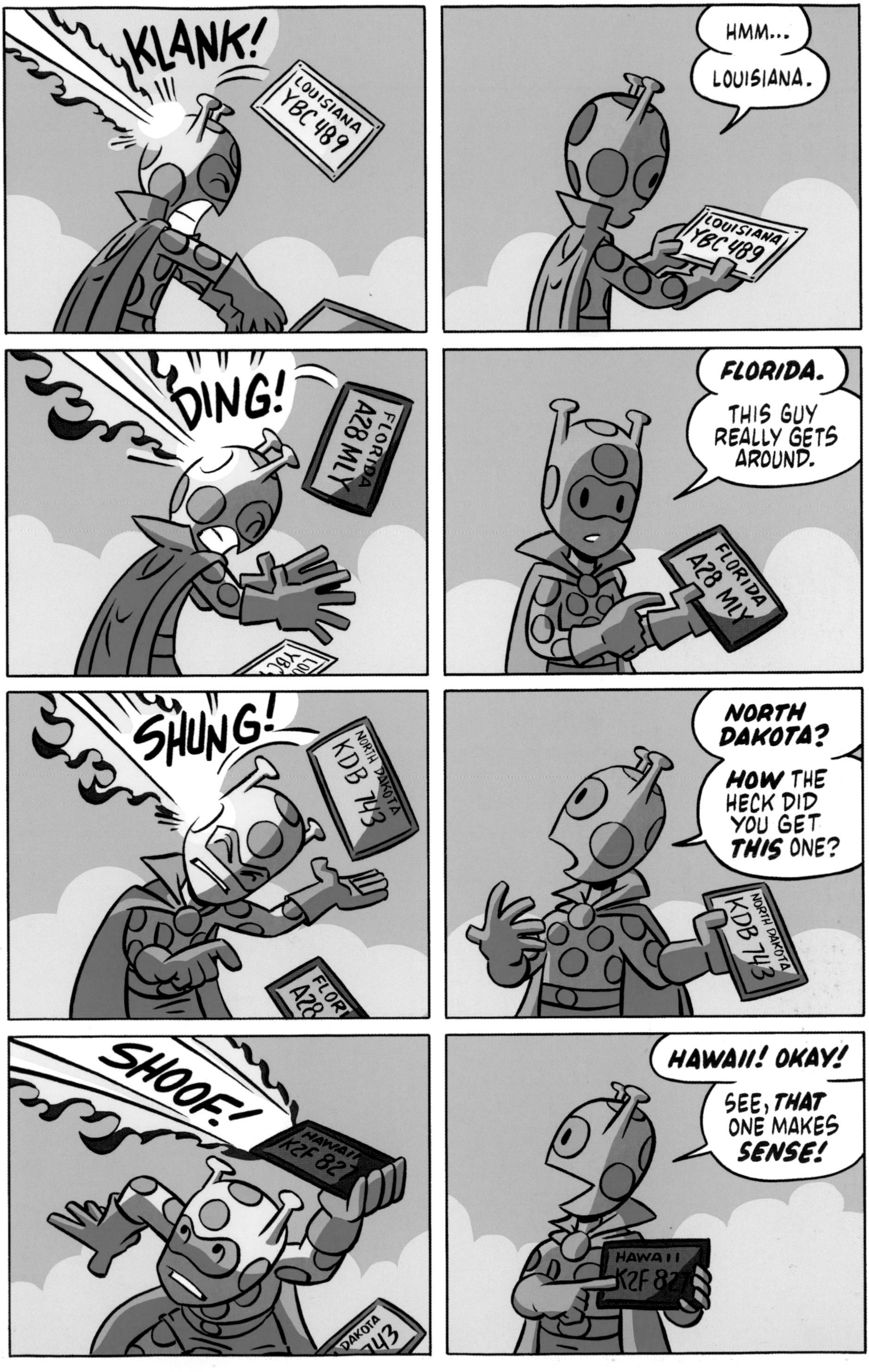
KLANK!
LOUISIANA
YBC 489
HMM...
LOUISIANA.
LOUISIANA
YBC 489
DING!
FLORIDA
A28 MLY
FLORIDA.
THIS GUY REALLY GETS AROUND.
FLORIDA
A28 MLY
SHUNG!
NORTH DAKOTA
KDB 743
NORTH DAKOTA?
HOW THE HECK DID YOU GET THIS ONE?
NORTH DAKOTA
KDB 743
SHOOF!
HAWAII
K2F 827
HAWAII! OKAY!
SEE, THAT ONE MAKES SENSE!

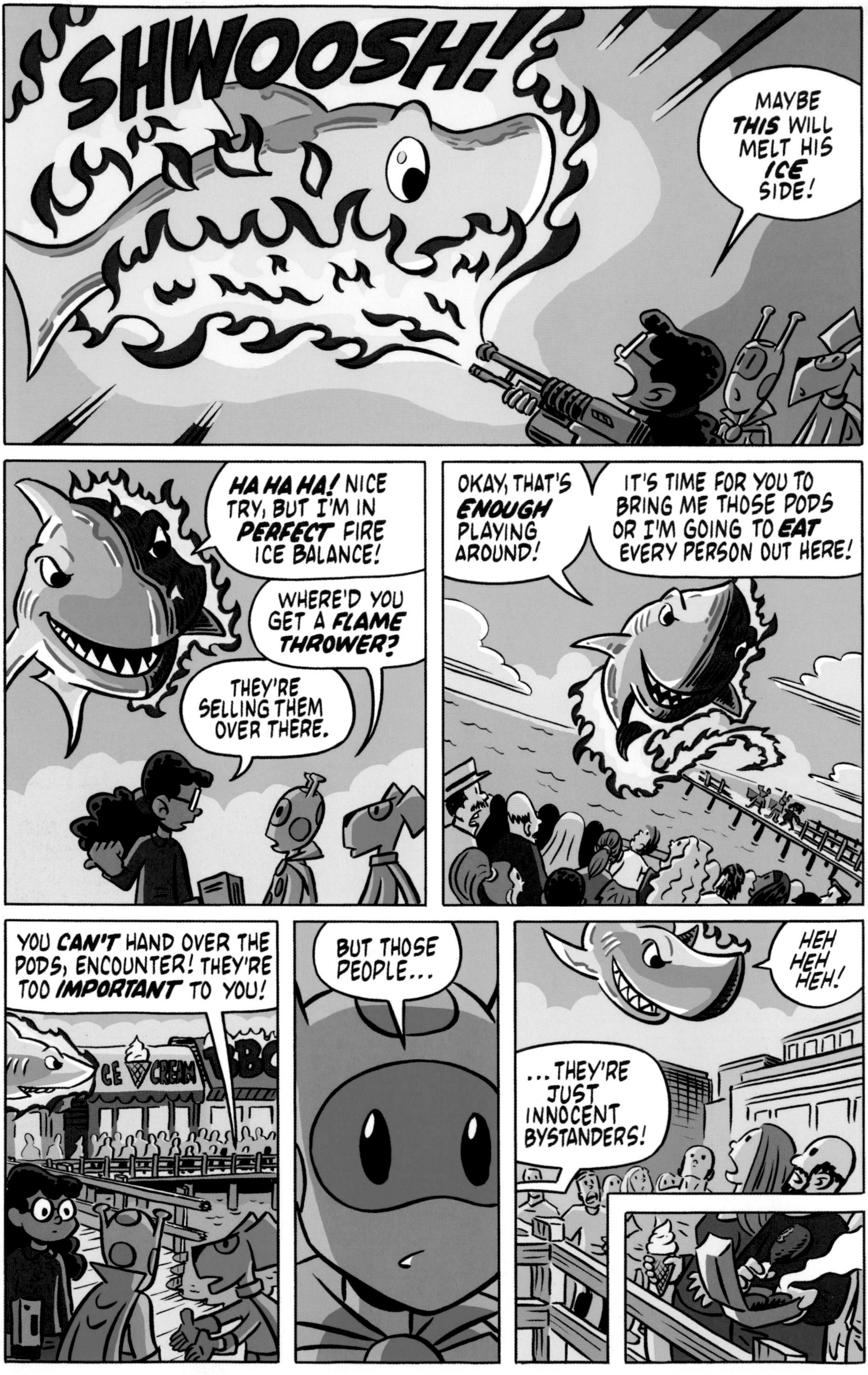
SHWOOSH!
MAYBE THIS WILL MELT HIS ICE SIDE!
HA HA HA! NICE TRY, BUT I'M IN PERFECT FIRE ICE BALANCE!
WHERE'D YOU GET A FLAME THROWER?
THEY'RE SELLING THEM OVER THERE.
OKAY, THAT'S ENOUGH PLAYING AROUND!
IT'S TIME FOR YOU TO BRING ME THOSE PODS OR I'M GOING TO EAT EVERY PERSON OUT HERE!
YOU CAN'T HAND OVER THE PODS, ENCOUNTER! THEY'RE TOO IMPORTANT TO YOU!
ICE CREAM
BUT THOSE PEOPLE...
HEH HEH HEH!
...THEY'RE JUST INNOCENT BYSTANDERS!

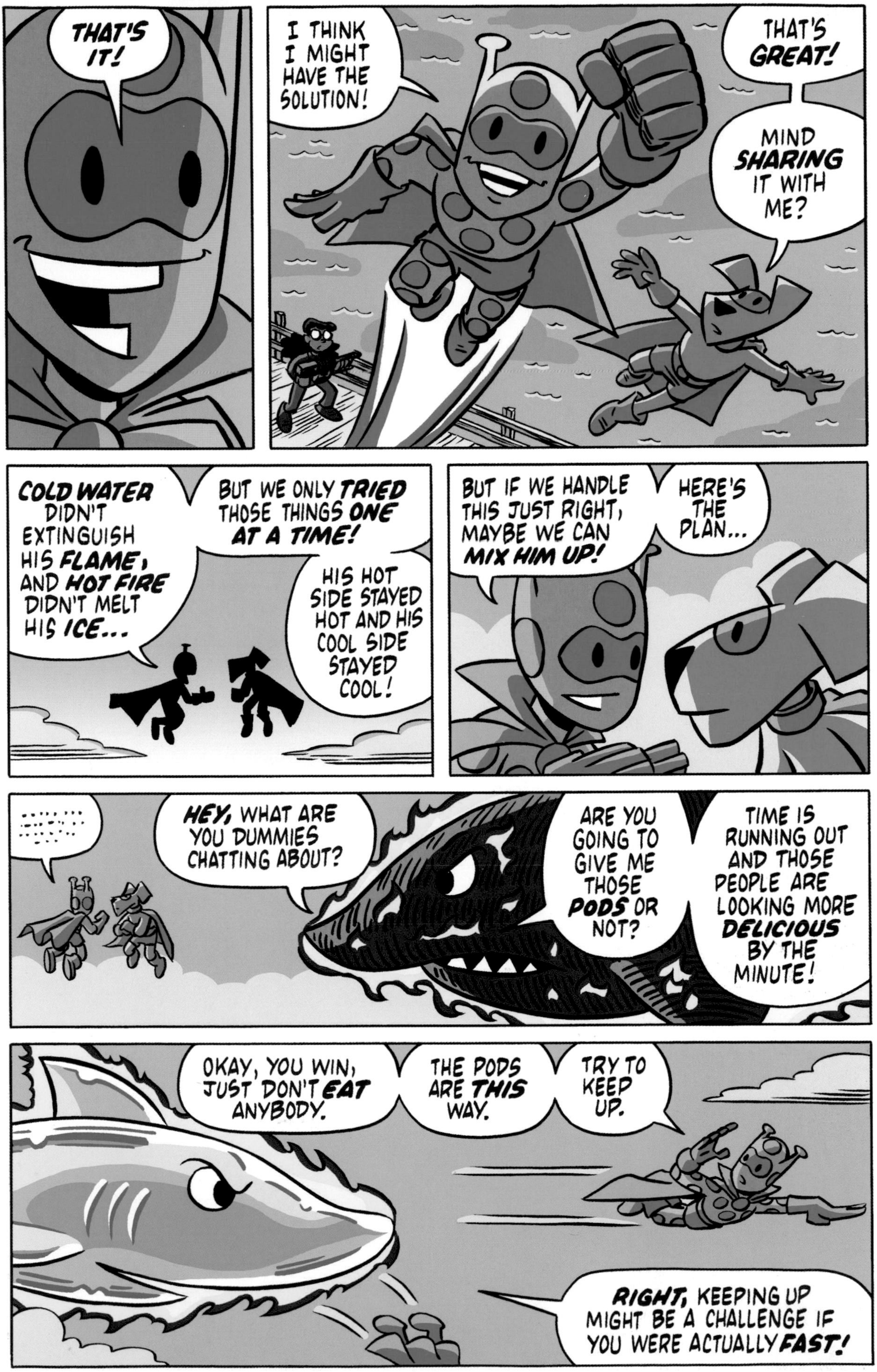
THAT'S IT!
I THINK I MIGHT HAVE THE SOLUTION!
THAT'S GREAT!
MIND SHARING IT WITH ME?
COLD WATER DIDN'T EXTINGUISH HIS FLAME, AND HOT FIRE DIDN'T MELT HIS ICE...
BUT WE ONLY TRIED THOSE THINGS ONE AT A TIME!
HIS HOT SIDE STAYED HOT AND HIS COOL SIDE STAYED COOL!
BUT IF WE HANDLE THIS JUST RIGHT, MAYBE WE CAN MIX HIM UP!
HERE'S THE PLAN...
HEY, WHAT ARE YOU DUMMIES CHATTING ABOUT?
ARE YOU GOING TO GIVE ME THOSE PODS OR NOT?
TIME IS RUNNING OUT AND THOSE PEOPLE ARE LOOKING MORE DELICIOUS BY THE MINUTE!
OKAY, YOU WIN, JUST DON'T EAT ANYBODY.
THE PODS ARE THIS WAY.
TRY TO KEEP UP.
RIGHT, KEEPING UP MIGHT BE A CHALLENGE IF YOU WERE ACTUALLY FAST!

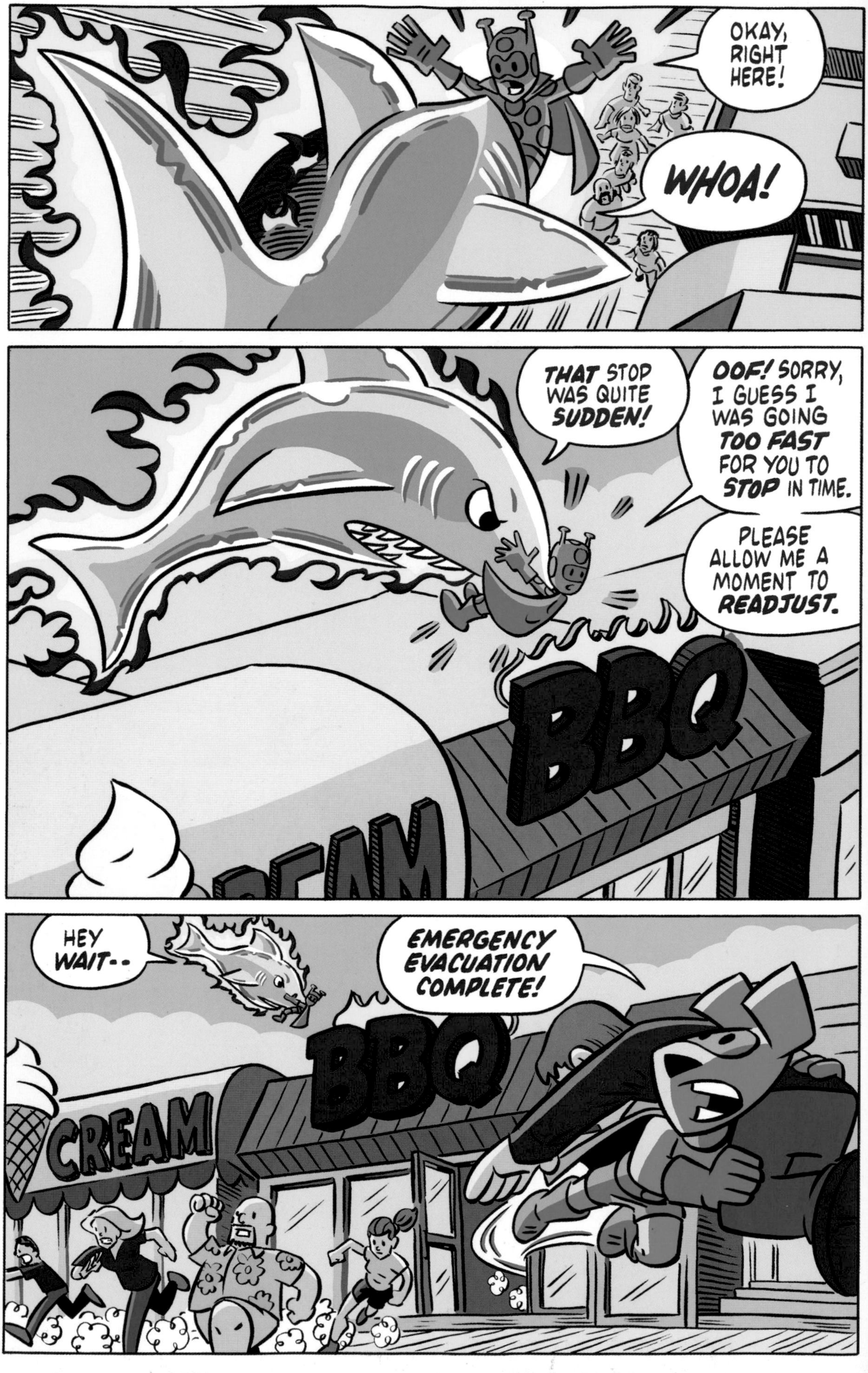
OKAY, RIGHT HERE!
WHOA!
THAT STOP WAS QUITE SUDDEN!
OOF! SORRY, I GUESS I WAS GOING TOO FAST FOR YOU TO STOP IN TIME.
PLEASE ALLOW ME A MOMENT TO READJUST.
BBQ
HEY WAIT--
EMERGENCY EVACUATION COMPLETE!
BBQ
CREAM

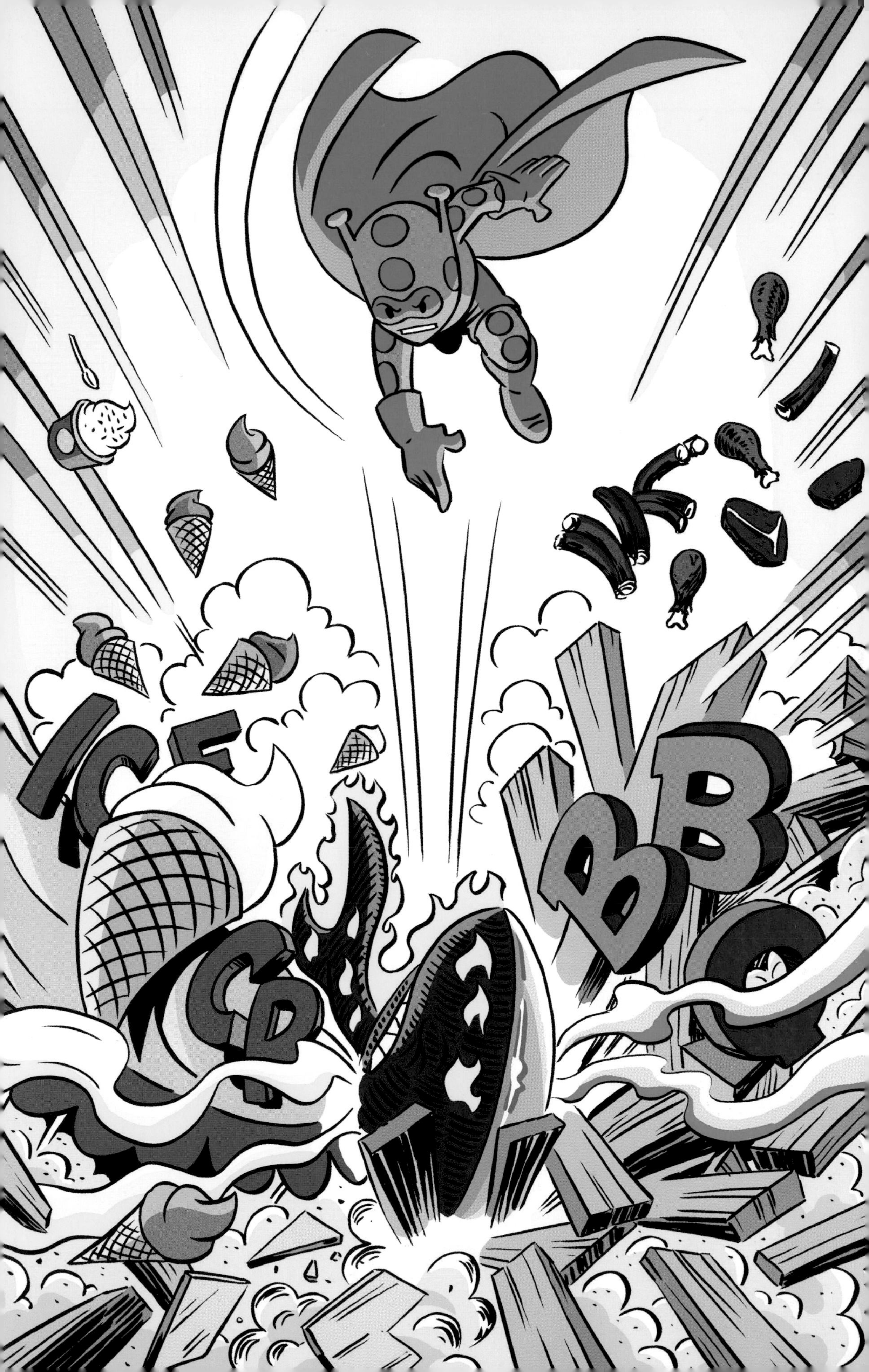
ICE
BBQ

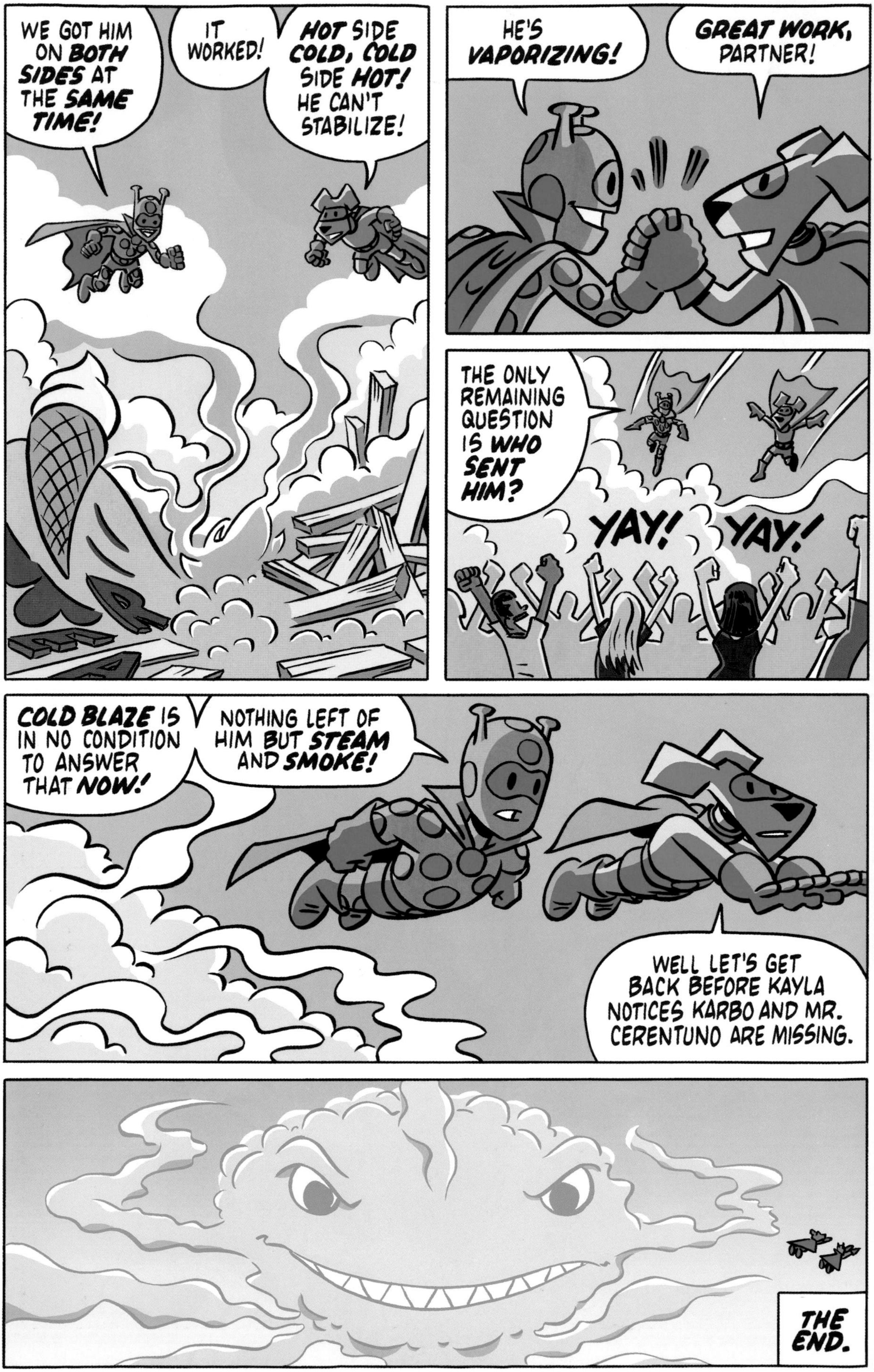
WE GOT HIM ON BOTH SIDES AT THE SAME TIME!
IT WORKED!
HOT SIDE COLD, COLD SIDE HOT! HE CAN'T STABILIZE!
HE'S VAPORIZING!
GREAT WORK, PARTNER!
THE ONLY REMAINING QUESTION IS WHO SENT HIM?
YAY! YAY!
COLD BLAZE IS IN NO CONDITION TO ANSWER THAT NOW!
NOTHING LEFT OF HIM BUT STEAM AND SMOKE!
WELL LET'S GET BACK BEFORE KAYLA NOTICES KARBO AND MR. CERENTUNO ARE MISSING.
THE END.

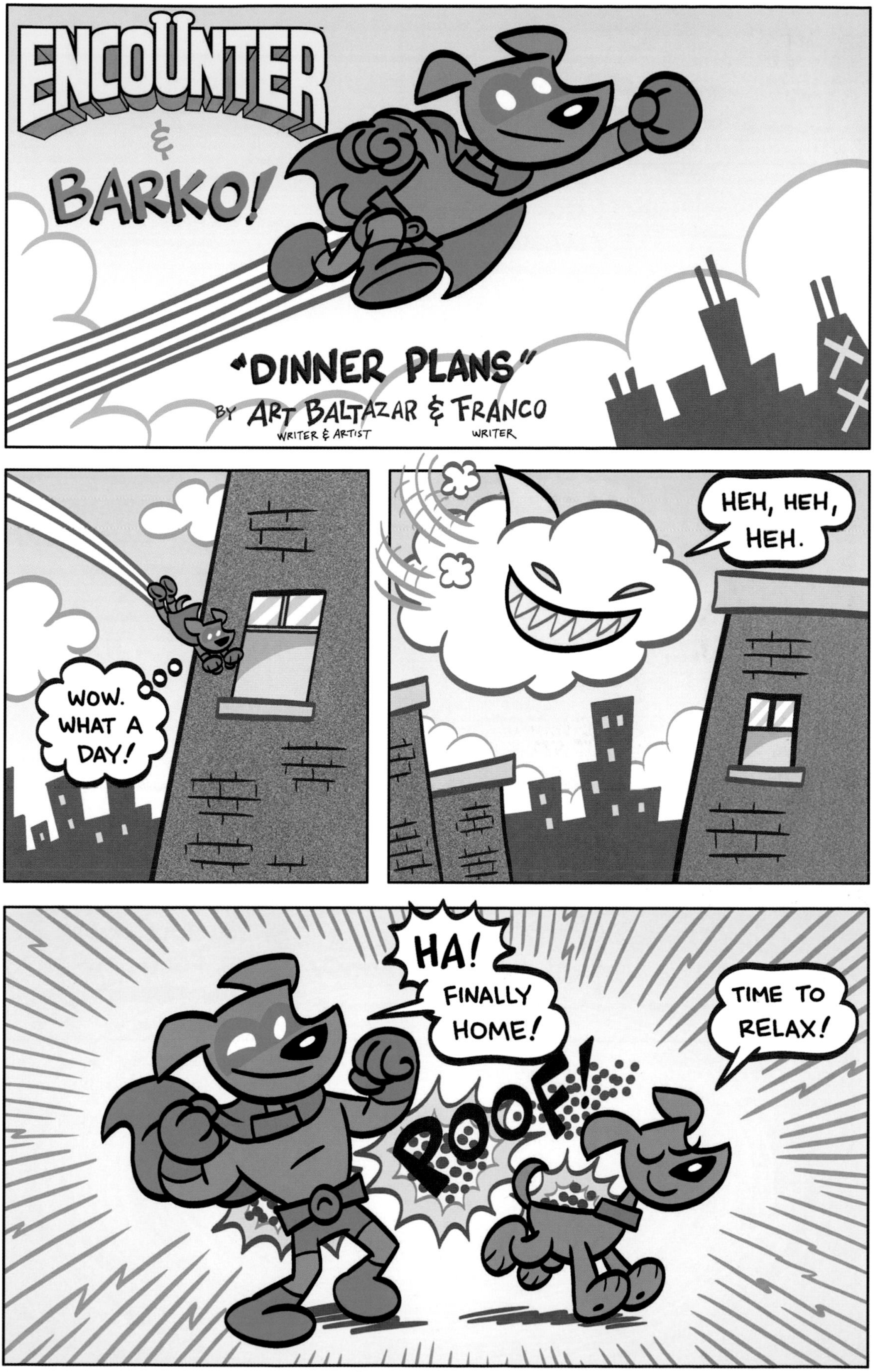
ENCOUNTER
&
BARKO!
"DINNER PLANS"
BY ART BALTAZAR & FRANCO
WRITER & ARTIST
WRITER
WOW. WHAT A DAY!
HEH, HEH, HEH.
HA! FINALLY HOME!
POOF!
TIME TO RELAX!

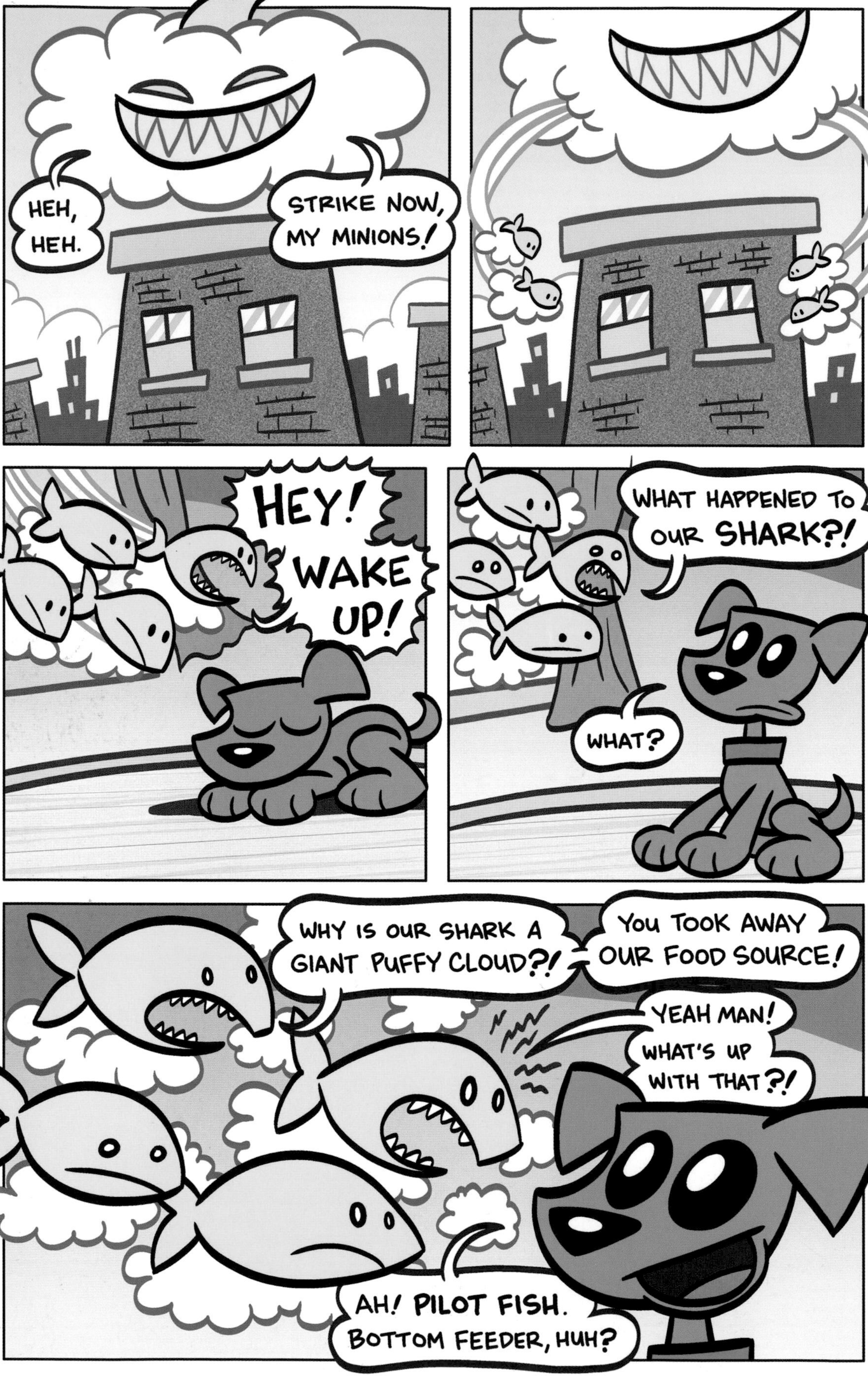
HEH, HEH.
STRIKE NOW, MY MINIONS!
HEY! WAKE UP!
WHAT HAPPENED TO OUR SHARK?!
WHAT?
WHY IS OUR SHARK A GIANT PUFFY CLOUD?!
YOU TOOK AWAY OUR FOOD SOURCE!
YEAH MAN! WHAT'S UP WITH THAT?!
AH! PILOT FISH. BOTTOM FEEDER, HUH?

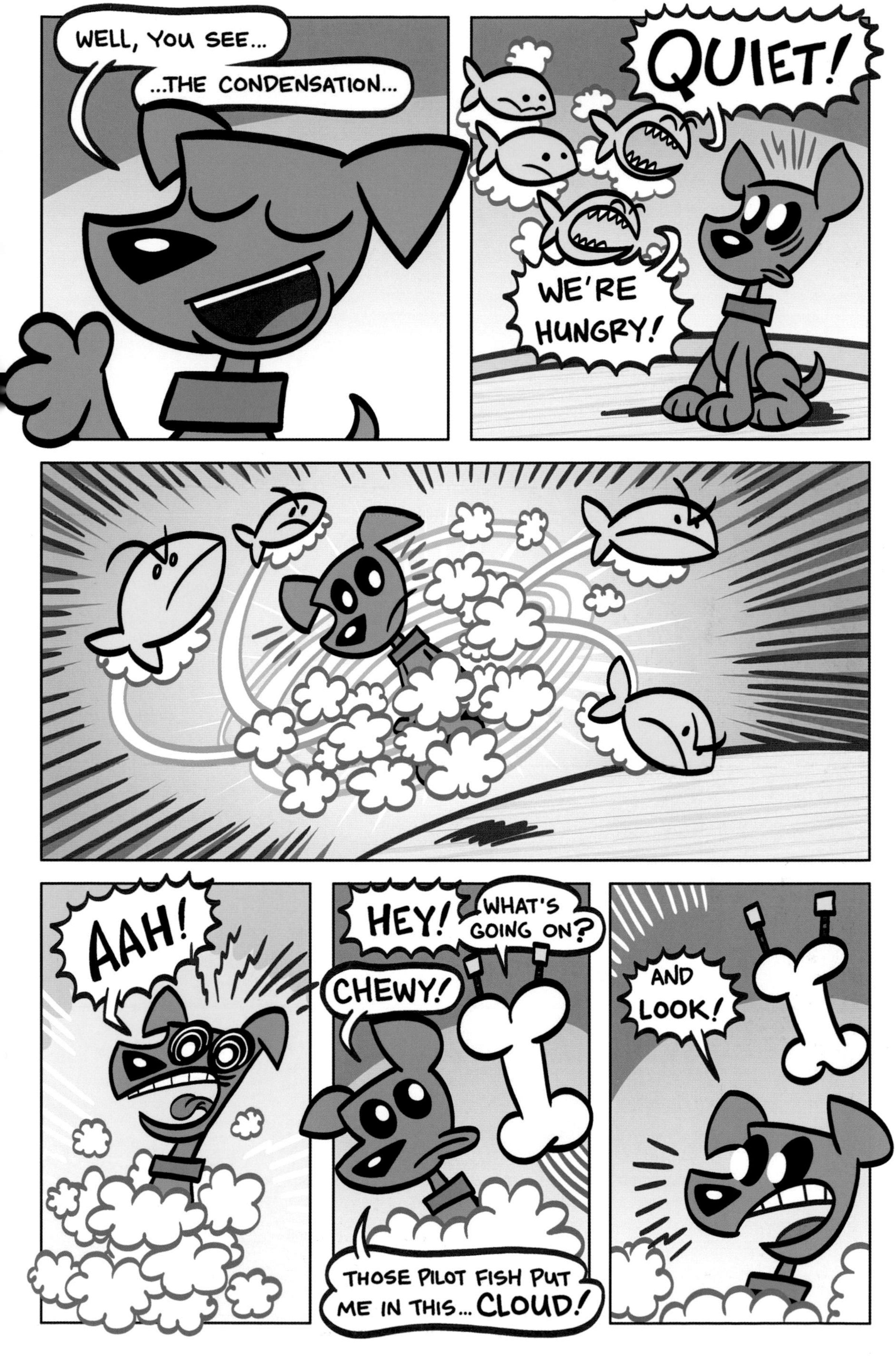

WELL, YOU SEE...
...THE CONDENSATION...
QUIET!
WE'RE HUNGRY!
AAH!
HEY!
WHAT'S GOING ON?
CHEWY!
THOSE PILOT FISH PUT ME IN THIS... CLOUD!
AND LOOK!

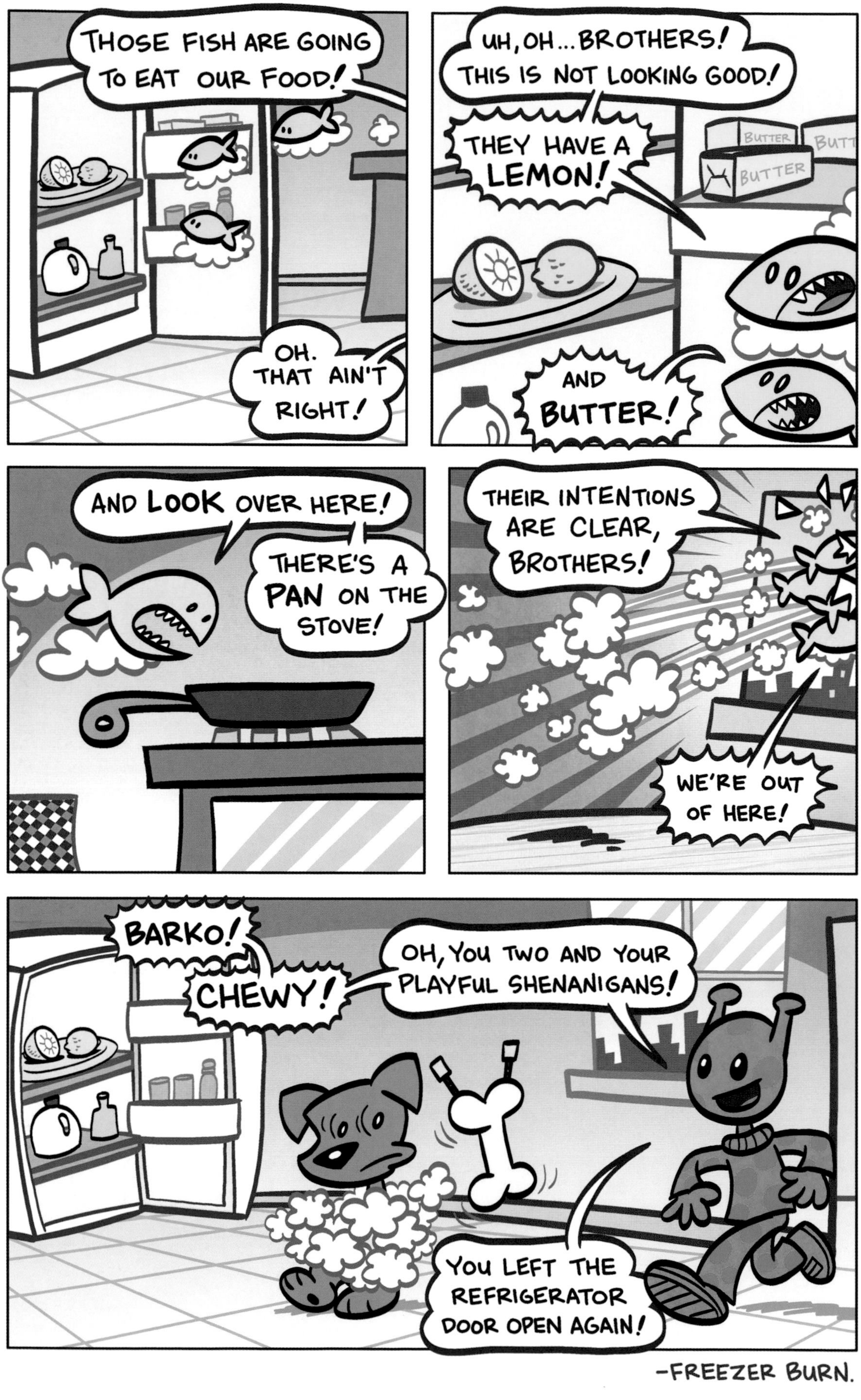
THOSE FISH ARE GOING TO EAT OUR FOOD!
OH. THAT AIN'T RIGHT!
UH, OH... BROTHERS! THIS IS NOT LOOKING GOOD!
THEY HAVE A LEMON!
AND BUTTER!
BUTTER
AND LOOK OVER HERE!
THERE'S A PAN ON THE STOVE!
THEIR INTENTIONS ARE CLEAR, BROTHERS!
WE'RE OUT OF HERE!
BARKO!
CHEWY!
OH, YOU TWO AND YOUR PLAYFUL SHENANIGANS!
YOU LEFT THE REFRIGERATOR DOOR OPEN AGAIN!

-FREEZER BURN.

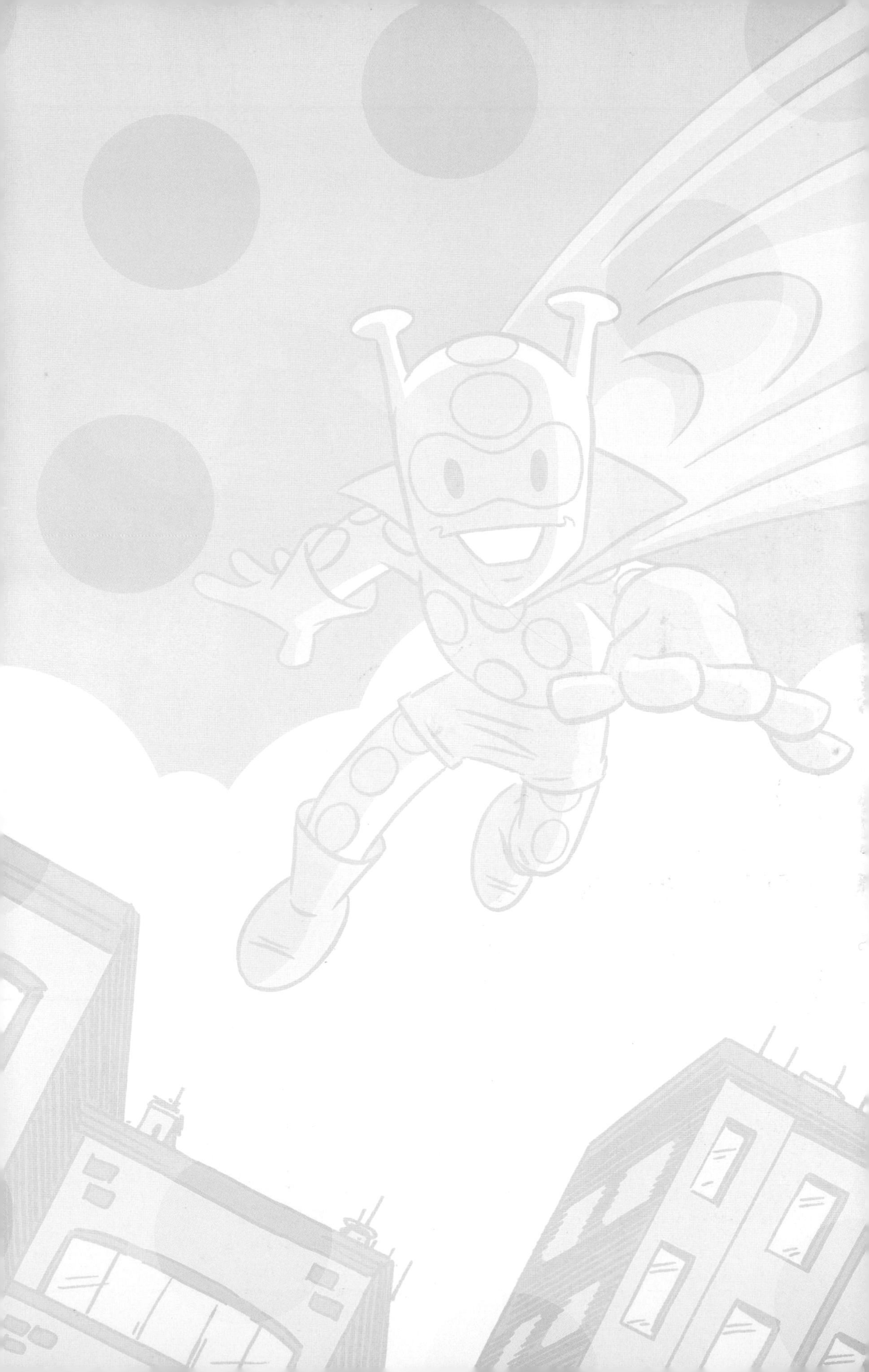

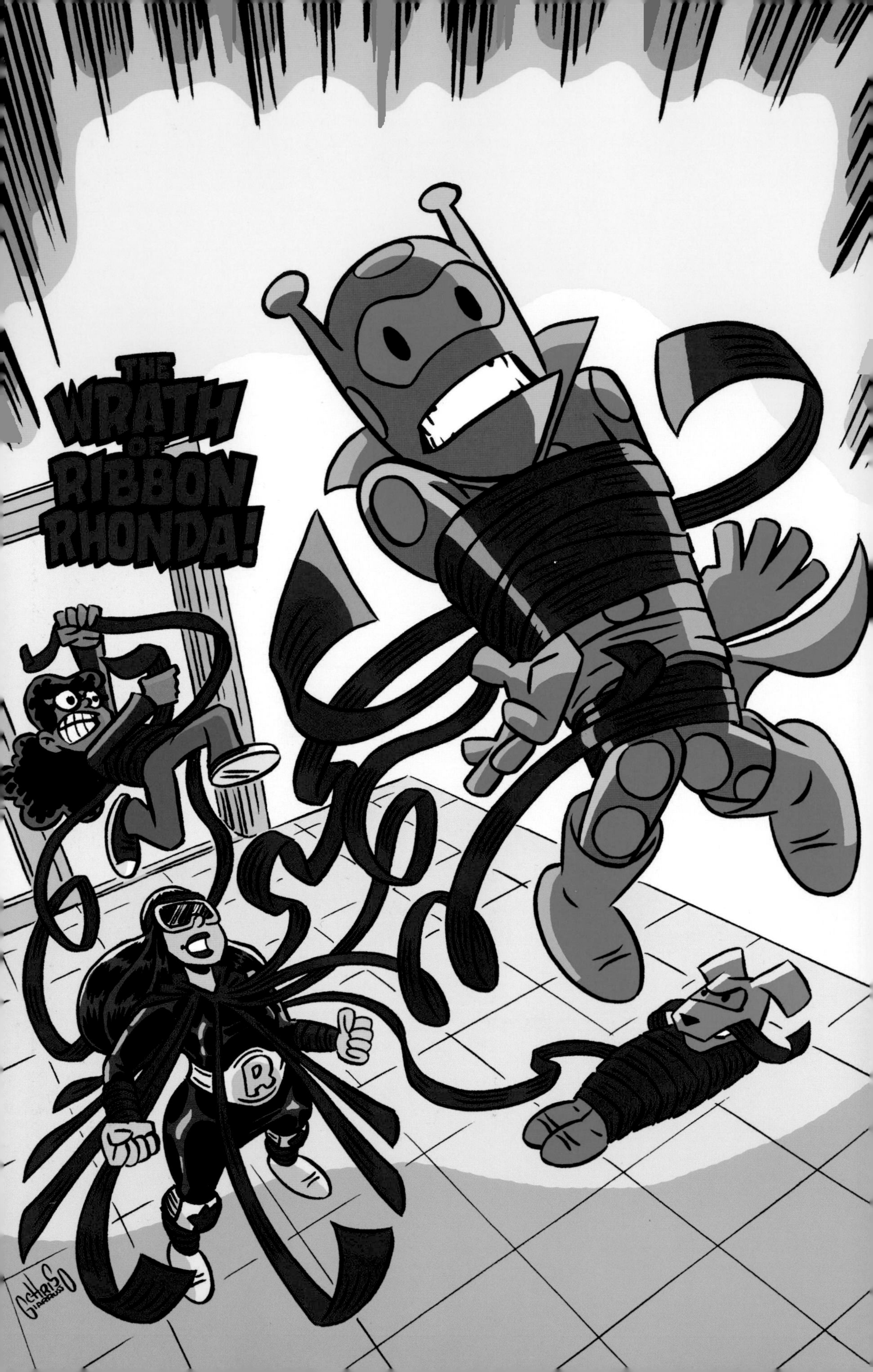
THE WRATH OF RIBBON RHONDA!

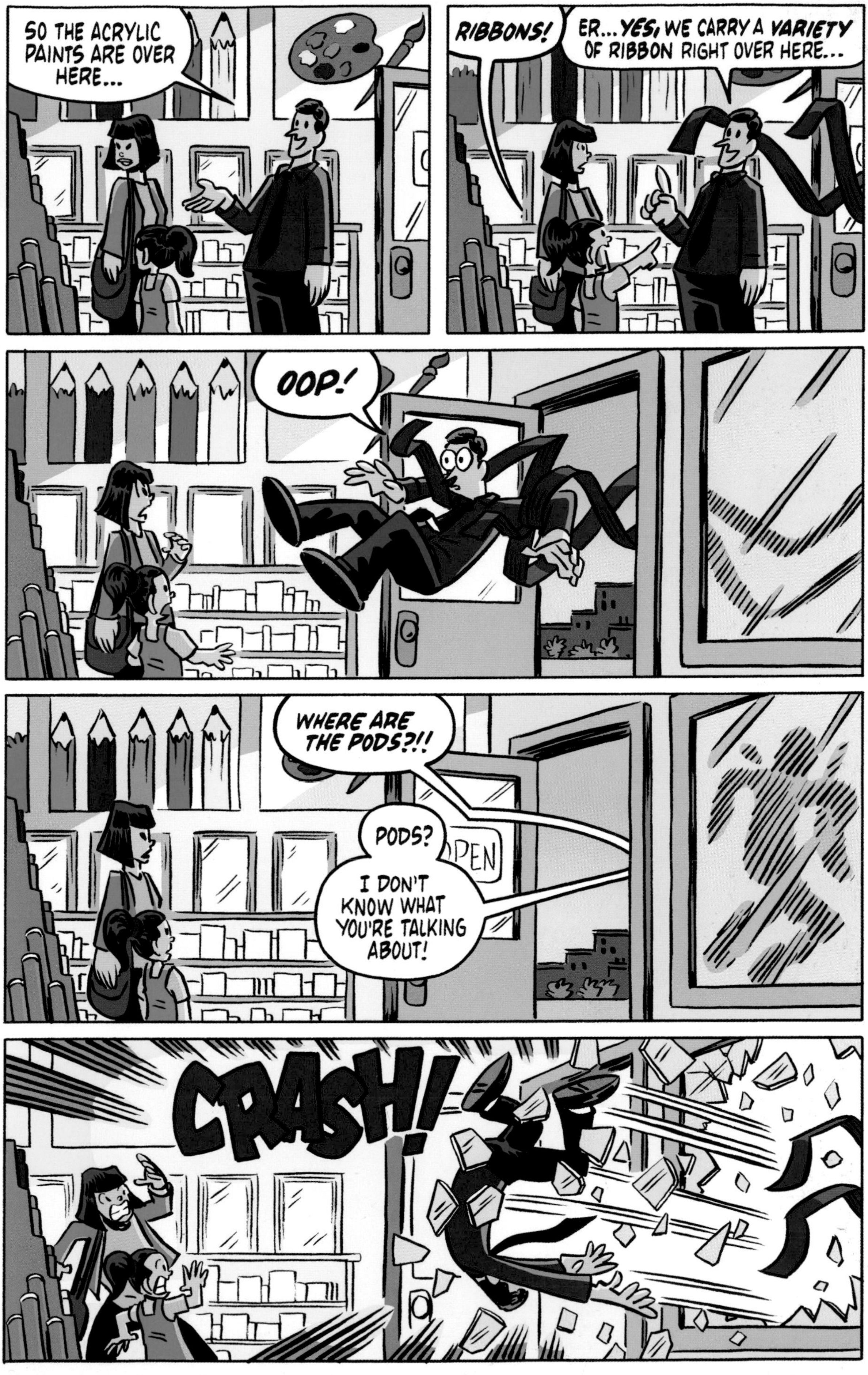
SO THE ACRYLIC PAINTS ARE OVER HERE...
RIBBONS!
ER...YES, WE CARRY A VARIETY OF RIBBON RIGHT OVER HERE...
OOP!
WHERE ARE THE PODS?!!
PODS?
OPEN
I DON'T KNOW WHAT YOU'RE TALKING ABOUT!
CRASH!

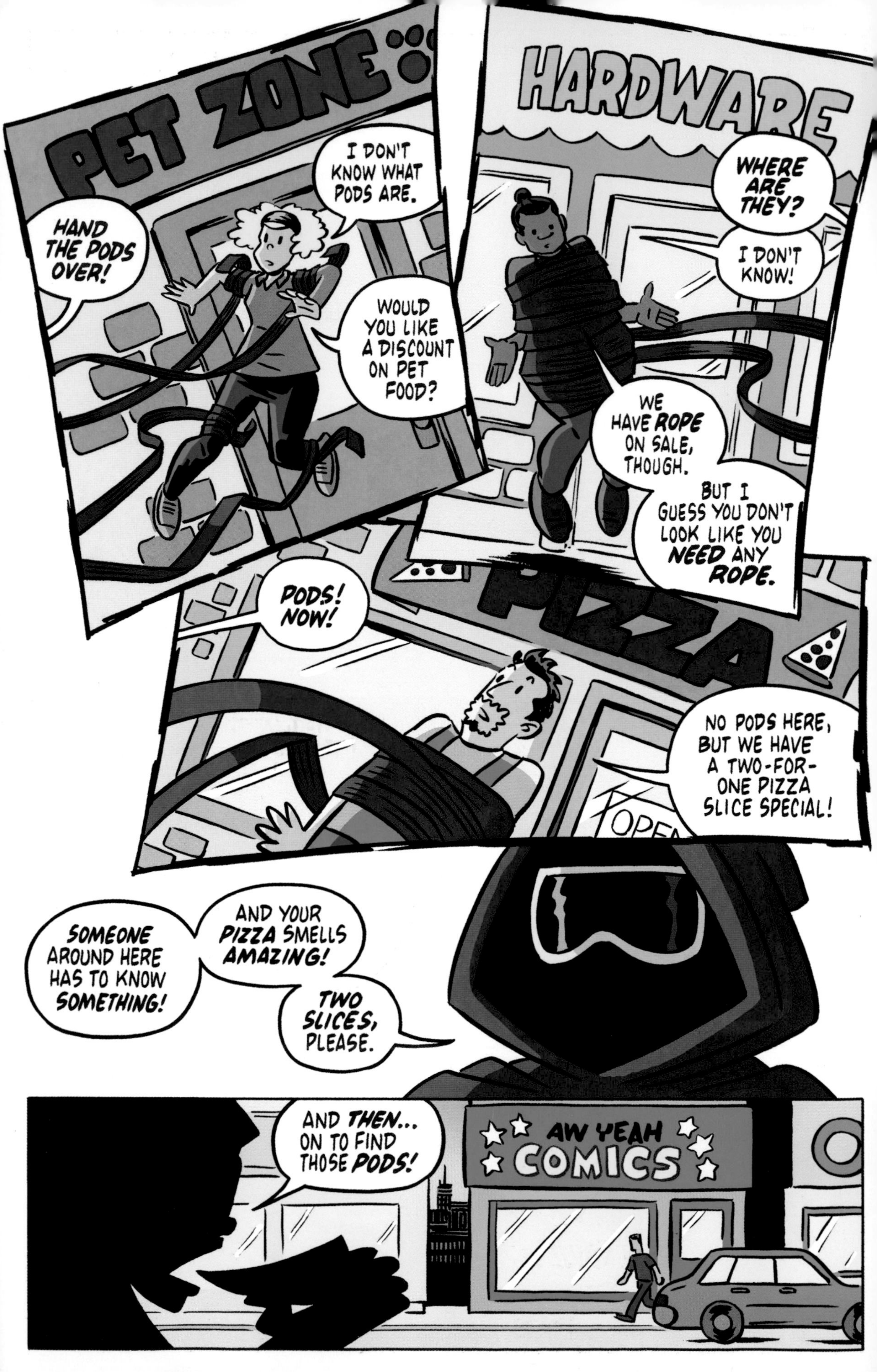

PET ZONE
HAND THE PODS OVER!
I DON'T KNOW WHAT PODS ARE.
WOULD YOU LIKE A DISCOUNT ON PET FOOD?
HARDWARE
WHERE ARE THEY?
I DON'T KNOW!
WE HAVE ROPE ON SALE, THOUGH.
BUT I GUESS YOU DON'T LOOK LIKE YOU NEED ANY ROPE.
PIZZA
PODS! NOW!
NO PODS HERE, BUT WE HAVE A TWO-FOR-ONE PIZZA SLICE SPECIAL!
SOMEONE AROUND HERE HAS TO KNOW SOMETHING!
AND YOUR PIZZA SMELLS AMAZING!
TWO SLICES, PLEASE.
AND THEN... ON TO FIND THOSE PODS!
AW YEAH COMICS

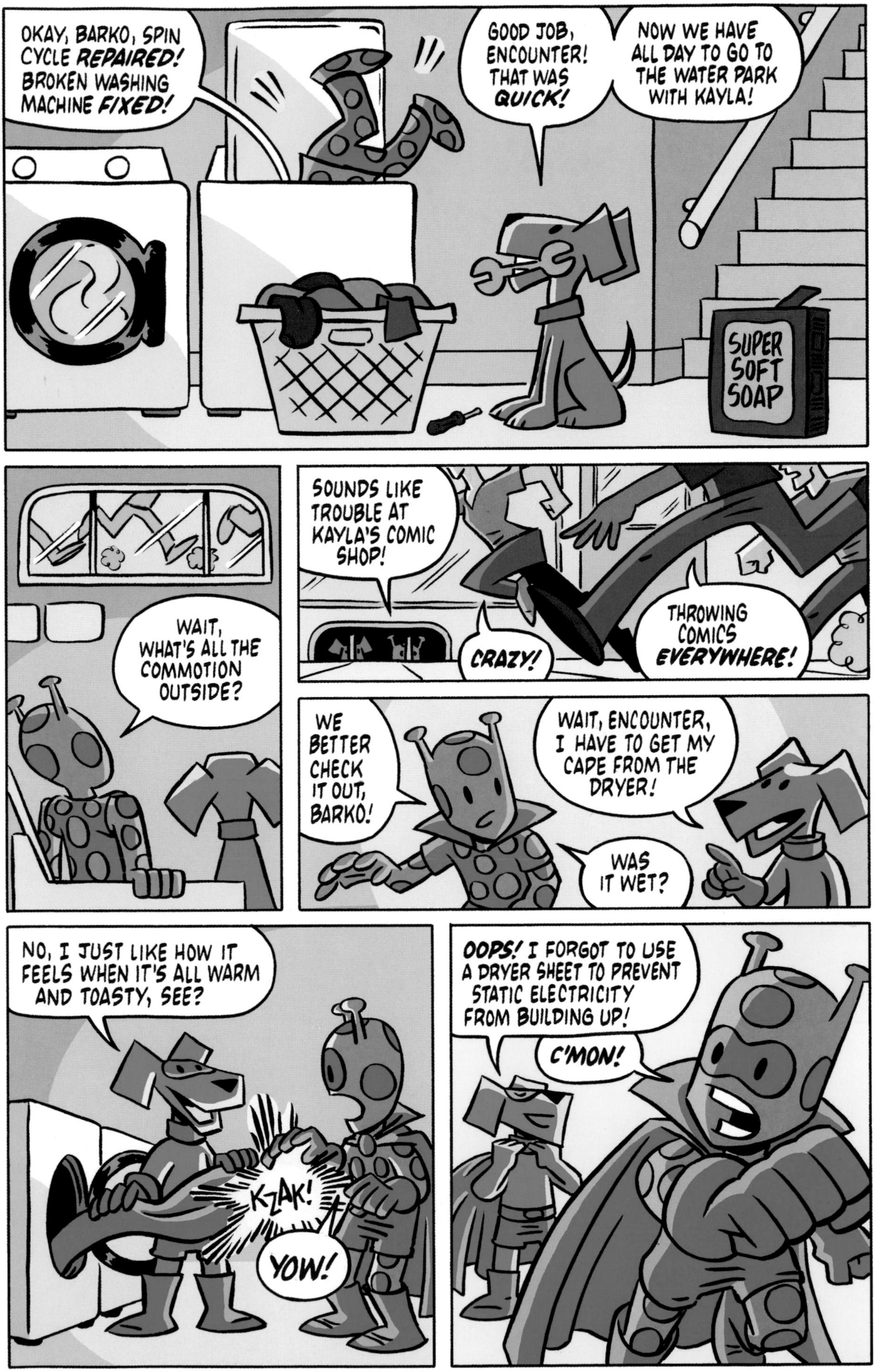
OKAY, BARKO, SPIN CYCLE REPAIRED! BROKEN WASHING MACHINE FIXED!
GOOD JOB, ENCOUNTER! THAT WAS QUICK!
NOW WE HAVE ALL DAY TO GO TO THE WATER PARK WITH KAYLA!
SUPER SOFT SOAP
WAIT, WHAT'S ALL THE COMMOTION OUTSIDE?
SOUNDS LIKE TROUBLE AT KAYLA'S COMIC SHOP!
CRAZY!
THROWING COMICS EVERYWHERE!
WE BETTER CHECK IT OUT, BARKO!
WAIT, ENCOUNTER, I HAVE TO GET MY CAPE FROM THE DRYER!
WAS IT WET?
NO, I JUST LIKE HOW IT FEELS WHEN IT'S ALL WARM AND TOASTY, SEE?
KZAK!
YOW!
OOPS! I FORGOT TO USE A DRYER SHEET TO PREVENT STATIC ELECTRICITY FROM BUILDING UP!
C'MON!

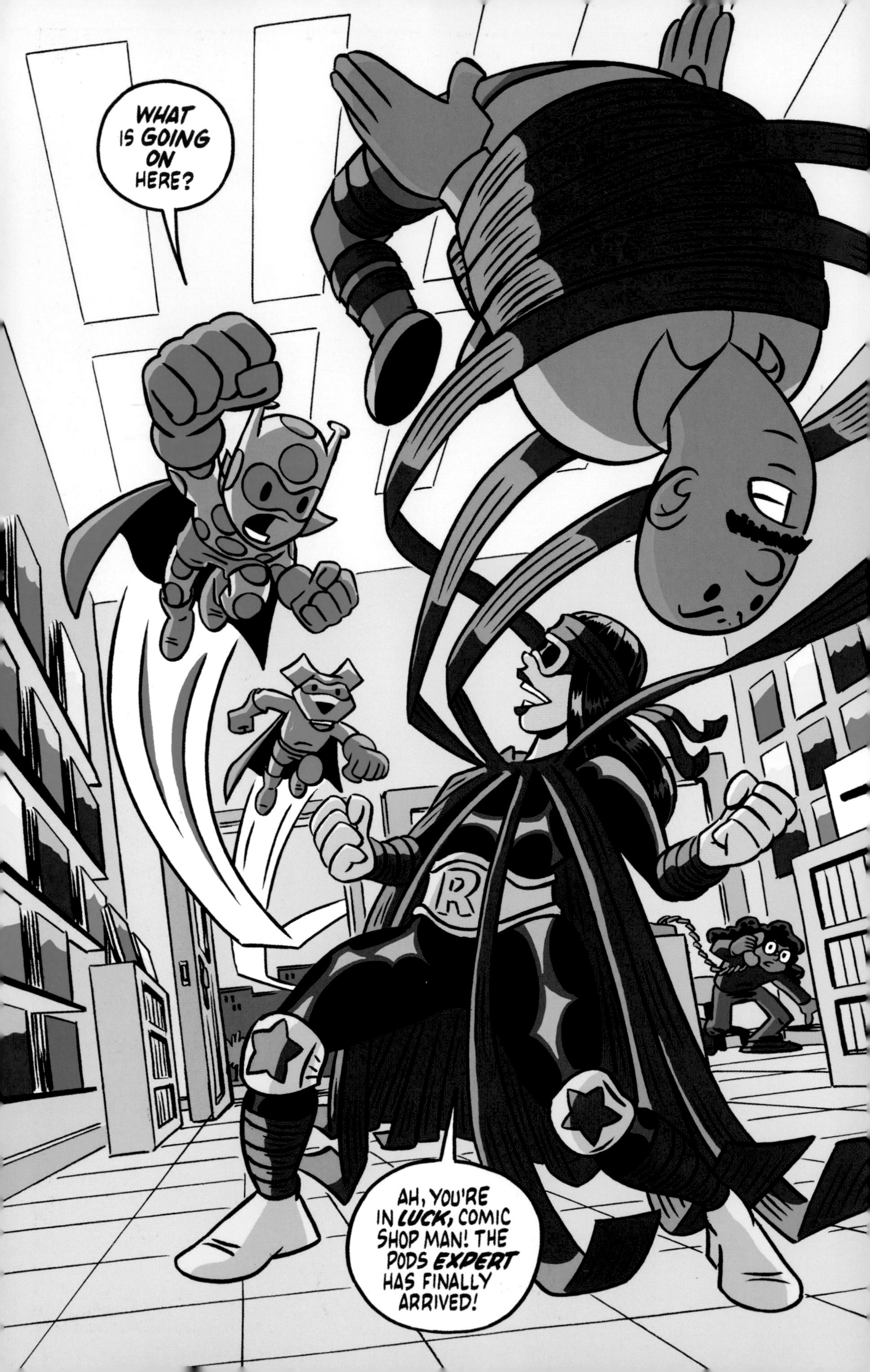
WHAT IS GOING ON HERE?
AH, YOU'RE IN LUCK, COMIC SHOP MAN! THE PODS EXPERT HAS FINALLY ARRIVED!

AND DON'T YOU EVEN *THINK* ABOUT CALLING THE POLICE!

SNAP

LET HIM *GO!*

AS YOU WISH.

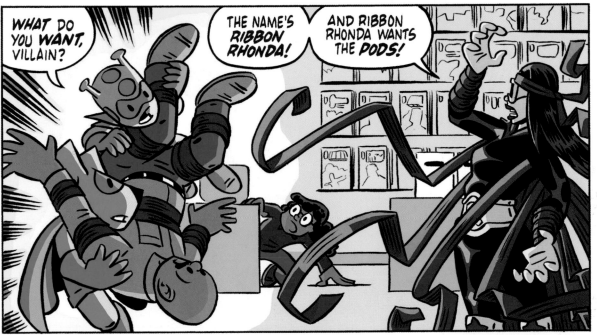

WHAT DO YOU *WANT,* VILLAIN?

THE NAME'S *RIBBON RHONDA!*

AND RIBBON RHONDA WANTS THE *PODS!*

THE PODS *AGAIN?*

YOU'RE THE *THIRD* CRIMINAL WHO'S COME AFTER THEM!

WHO'S BEEN SENDING ALL OF YOU?

HERE'S THE DEAL, ENCOUNTER...

RIBBON RHONDA WILL TELL YOU WHO SENT HER...

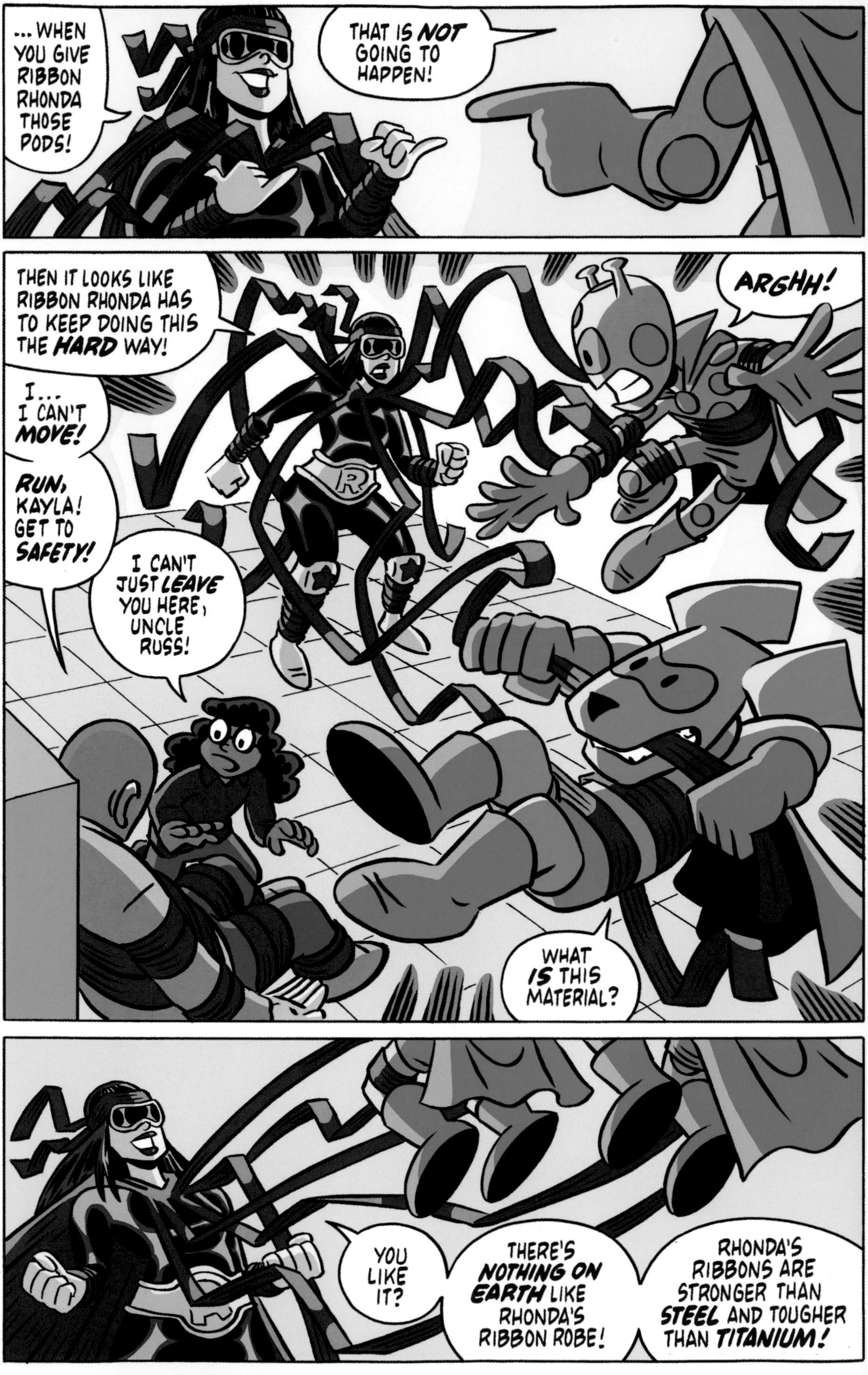
...WHEN YOU GIVE RIBBON RHONDA THOSE PODS!
THAT IS NOT GOING TO HAPPEN!
THEN IT LOOKS LIKE RIBBON RHONDA HAS TO KEEP DOING THIS THE HARD WAY!
ARGHH!
I... I CAN'T MOVE!
RUN, KAYLA! GET TO SAFETY!
I CAN'T JUST LEAVE YOU HERE, UNCLE RUSS!
WHAT IS THIS MATERIAL?
YOU LIKE IT?
THERE'S NOTHING ON EARTH LIKE RHONDA'S RIBBON ROBE!
RHONDA'S RIBBONS ARE STRONGER THAN STEEL AND TOUGHER THAN TITANIUM!

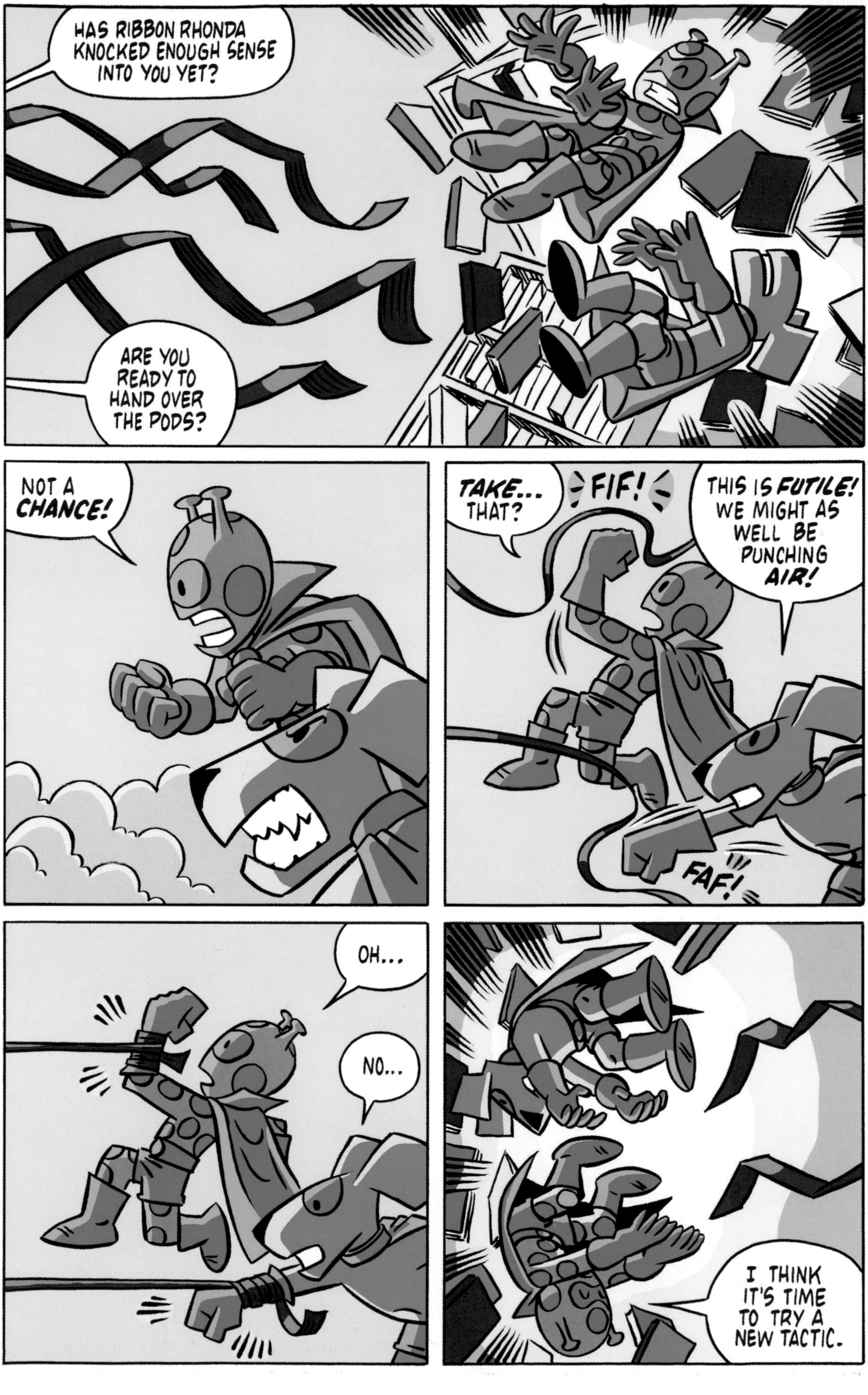
HAS RIBBON RHONDA KNOCKED ENOUGH SENSE INTO YOU YET?
ARE YOU READY TO HAND OVER THE PODS?
NOT A CHANCE!
TAKE... THAT?
FIF!
THIS IS FUTILE! WE MIGHT AS WELL BE PUNCHING AIR!
FAF!
OH...
NO...
I THINK IT'S TIME TO TRY A NEW TACTIC.

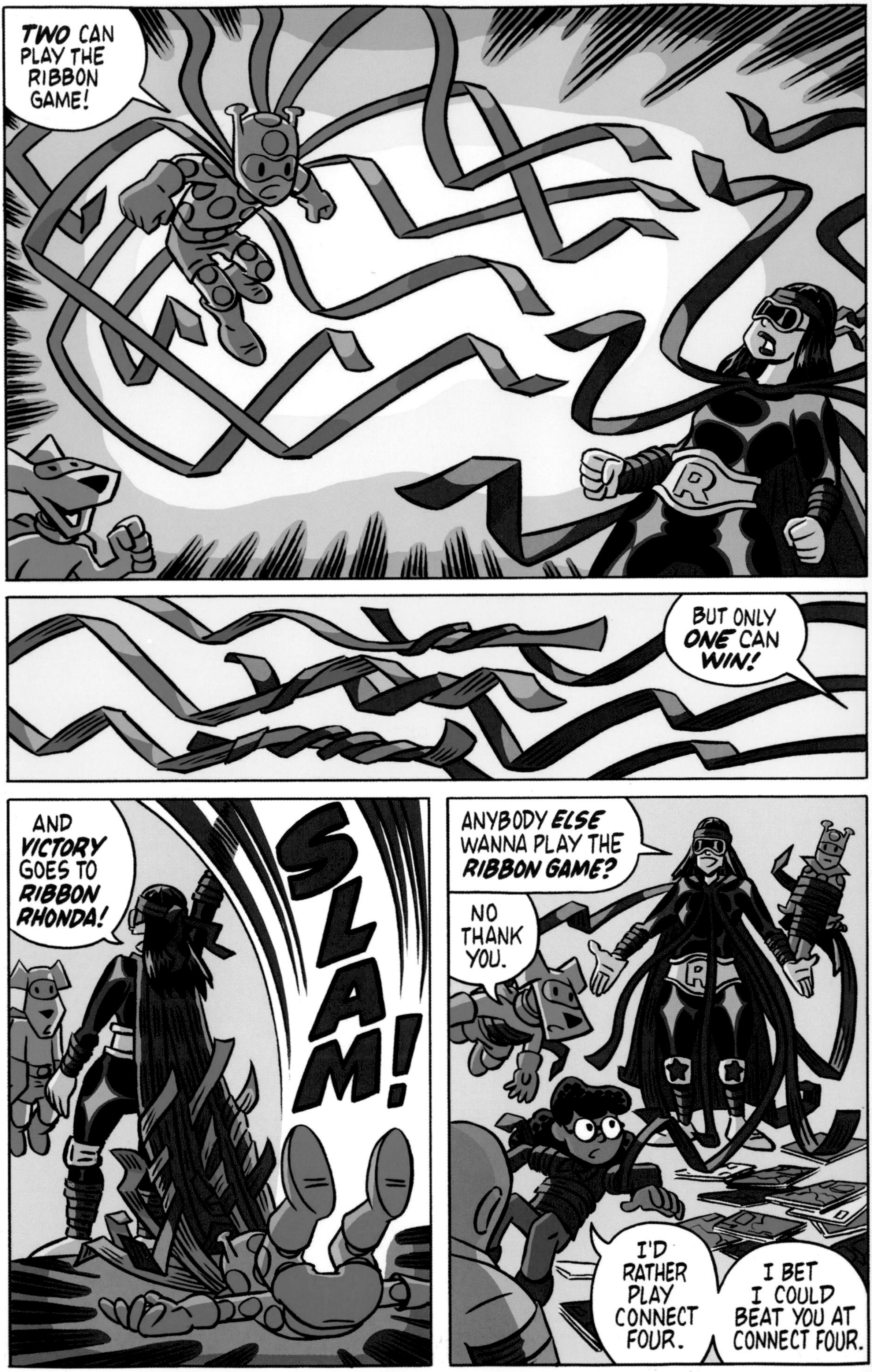
TWO CAN PLAY THE RIBBON GAME!
BUT ONLY ONE CAN WIN!
AND VICTORY GOES TO RIBBON RHONDA!
SLAM!
ANYBODY ELSE WANNA PLAY THE RIBBON GAME?
NO THANK YOU.
I'D RATHER PLAY CONNECT FOUR.
I BET I COULD BEAT YOU AT CONNECT FOUR.

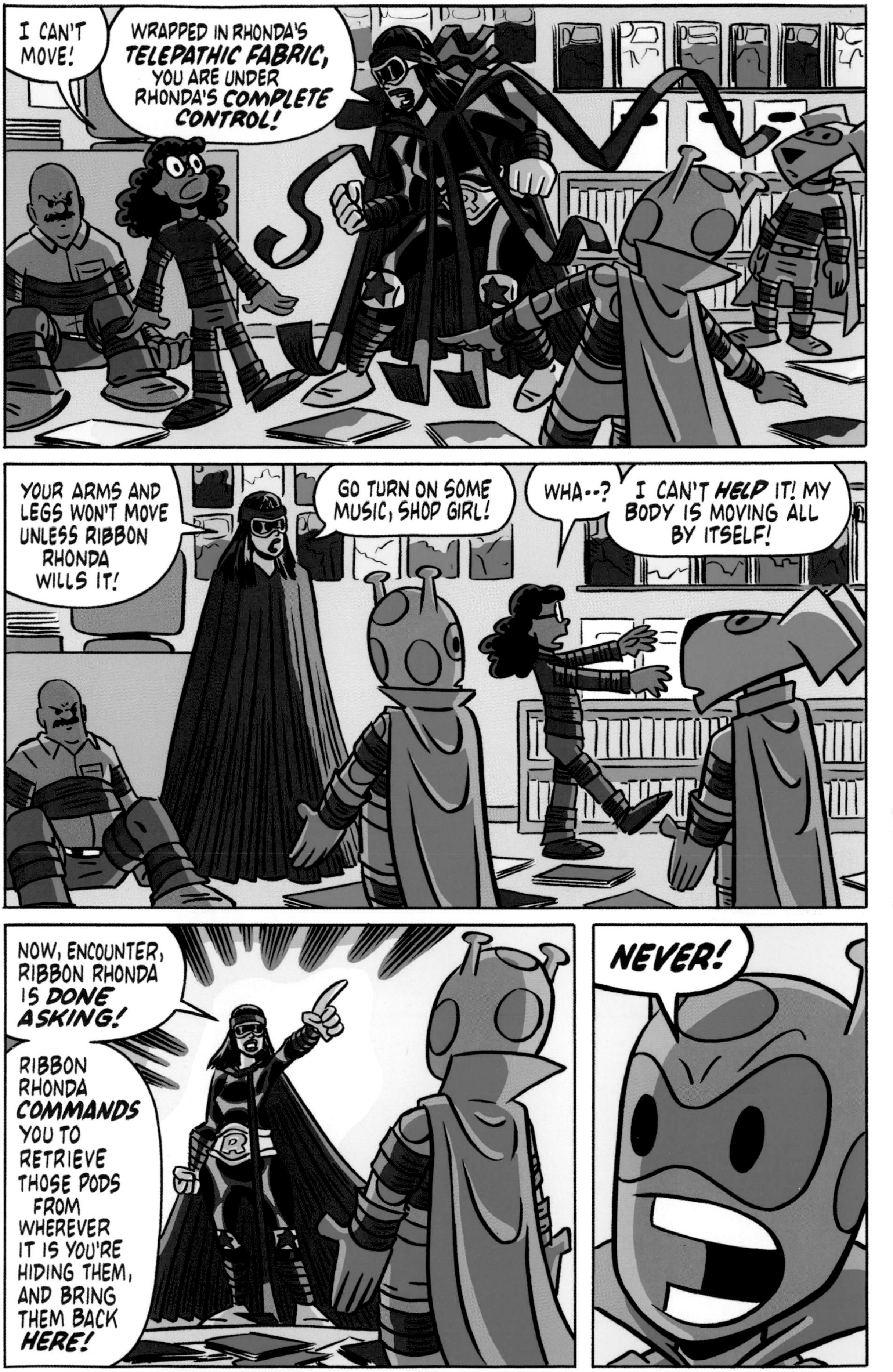

I CAN'T MOVE!
WRAPPED IN RHONDA'S TELEPATHIC FABRIC, YOU ARE UNDER RHONDA'S COMPLETE CONTROL!
YOUR ARMS AND LEGS WON'T MOVE UNLESS RIBBON RHONDA WILLS IT!
GO TURN ON SOME MUSIC, SHOP GIRL!
WHA--?
I CAN'T HELP IT! MY BODY IS MOVING ALL BY ITSELF!
NOW, ENCOUNTER, RIBBON RHONDA IS DONE ASKING!
RIBBON RHONDA COMMANDS YOU TO RETRIEVE THOSE PODS FROM WHEREVER IT IS YOU'RE HIDING THEM, AND BRING THEM BACK HERE!
NEVER!

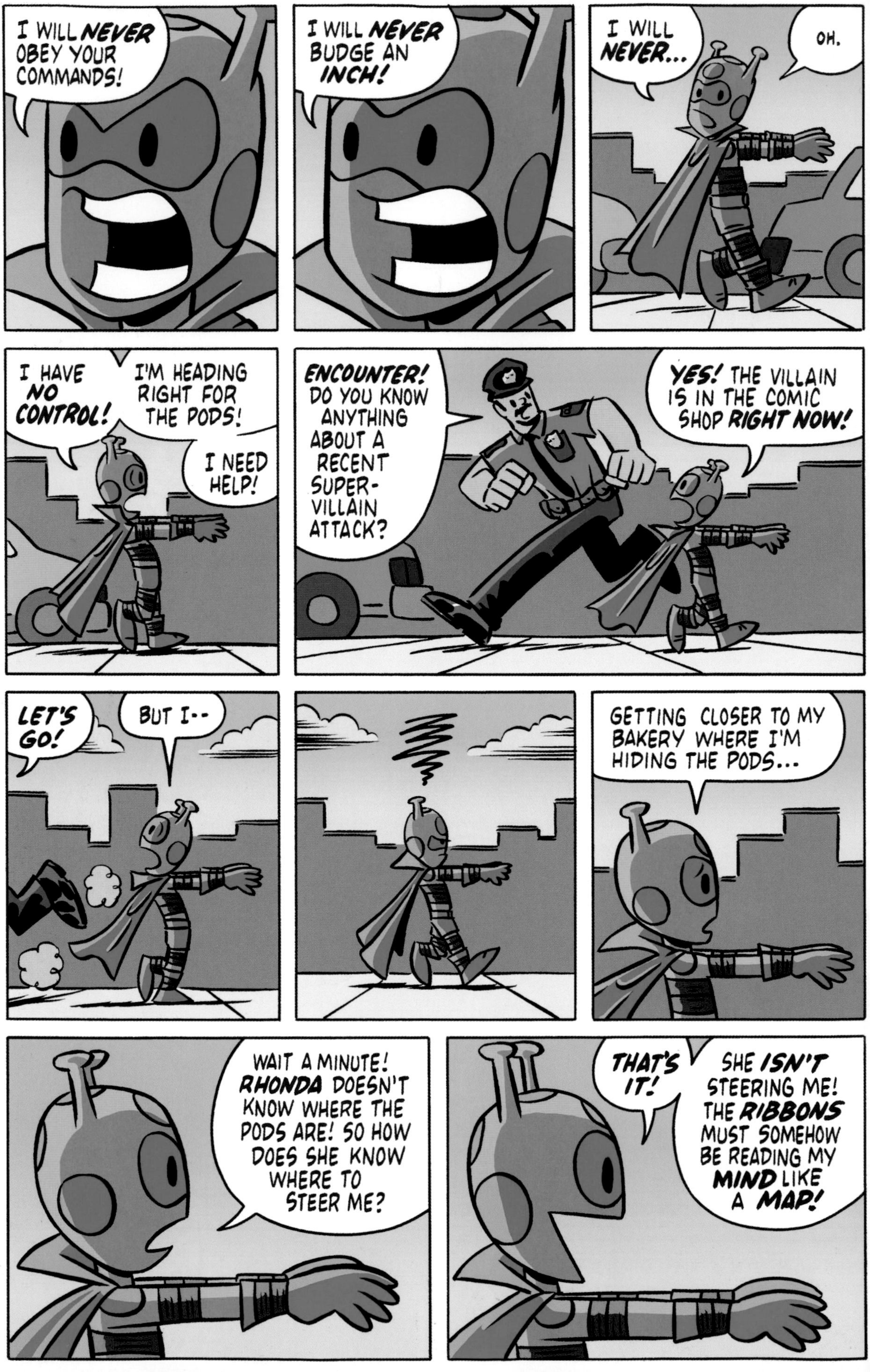
I WILL NEVER OBEY YOUR COMMANDS!
I WILL NEVER BUDGE AN INCH!
I WILL NEVER...
OH.
I HAVE NO CONTROL!
I'M HEADING RIGHT FOR THE PODS!
I NEED HELP!
ENCOUNTER! DO YOU KNOW ANYTHING ABOUT A RECENT SUPER-VILLAIN ATTACK?
YES! THE VILLAIN IS IN THE COMIC SHOP RIGHT NOW!
LET'S GO!
BUT I--
GETTING CLOSER TO MY BAKERY WHERE I'M HIDING THE PODS...
WAIT A MINUTE! RHONDA DOESN'T KNOW WHERE THE PODS ARE! SO HOW DOES SHE KNOW WHERE TO STEER ME?
THAT'S IT!
SHE ISN'T STEERING ME! THE RIBBONS MUST SOMEHOW BE READING MY MIND LIKE A MAP!

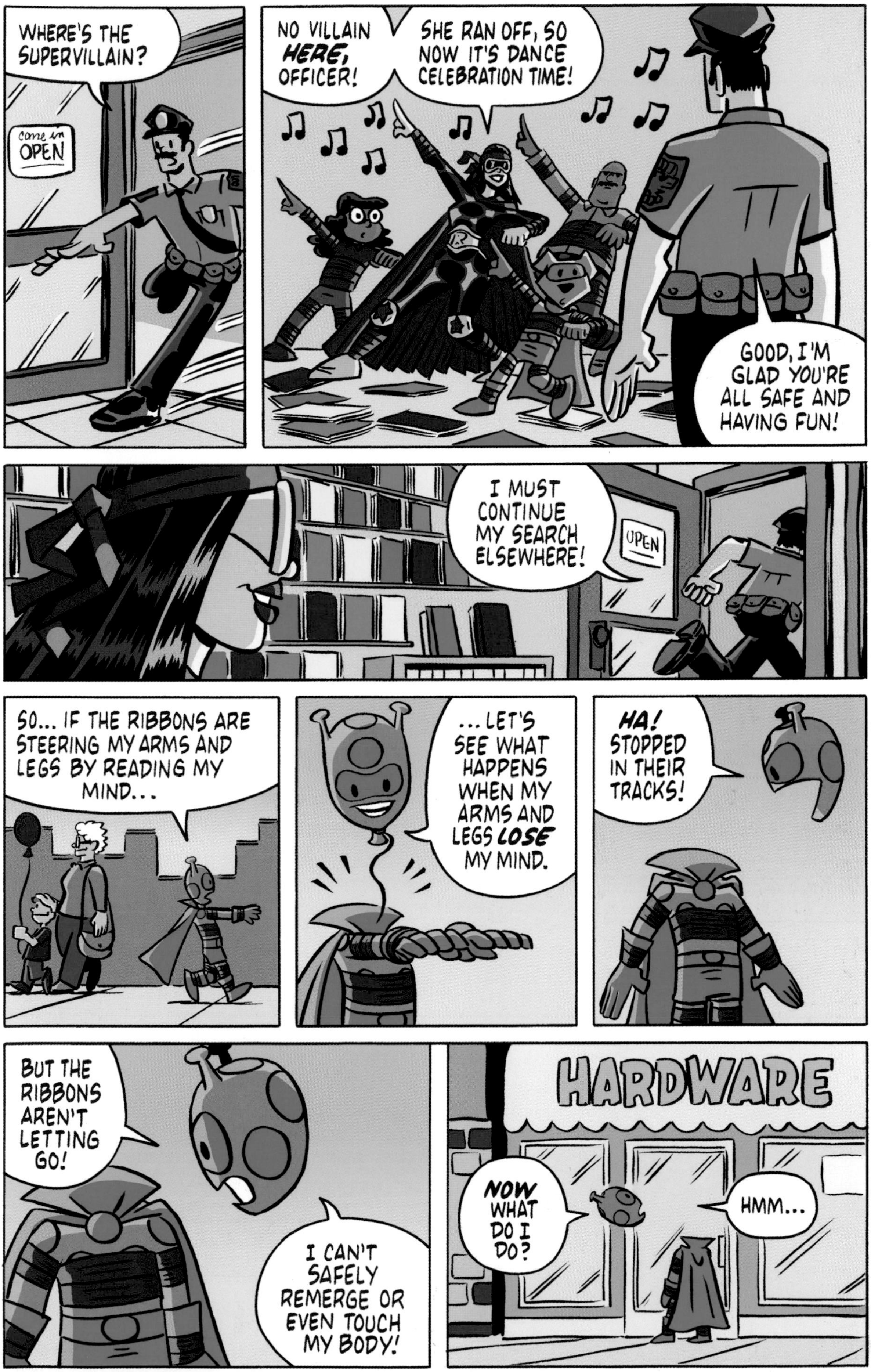
WHERE'S THE SUPERVILLAIN?
come in OPEN
NO VILLAIN *HERE,* OFFICER!
SHE RAN OFF, SO NOW IT'S DANCE CELEBRATION TIME!
GOOD, I'M GLAD YOU'RE ALL SAFE AND HAVING FUN!
I MUST CONTINUE MY SEARCH ELSEWHERE!
OPEN
SO... IF THE RIBBONS ARE STEERING MY ARMS AND LEGS BY READING MY MIND...
...LET'S SEE WHAT HAPPENS WHEN MY ARMS AND LEGS *LOSE* MY MIND.
HA! STOPPED IN THEIR TRACKS!
BUT THE RIBBONS AREN'T LETTING GO!
I CAN'T SAFELY REMERGE OR EVEN TOUCH MY BODY!
HARDWARE
NOW WHAT DO I DO?
HMM...

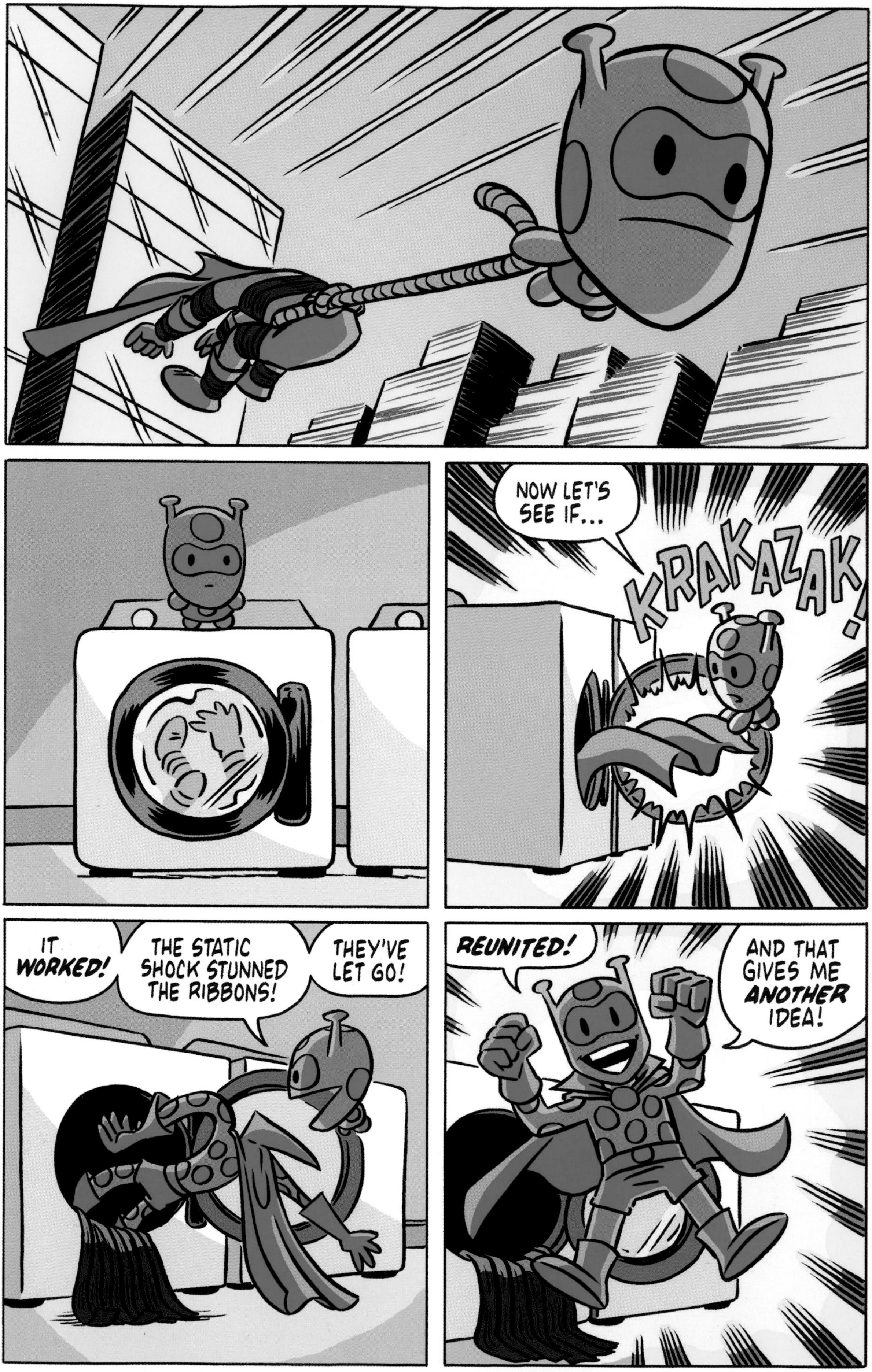
NOW LET'S SEE IF...
KRAKAZAK!
IT WORKED!
THE STATIC SHOCK STUNNED THE RIBBONS!
THEY'VE LET GO!
REUNITED!
AND THAT GIVES ME ANOTHER IDEA!

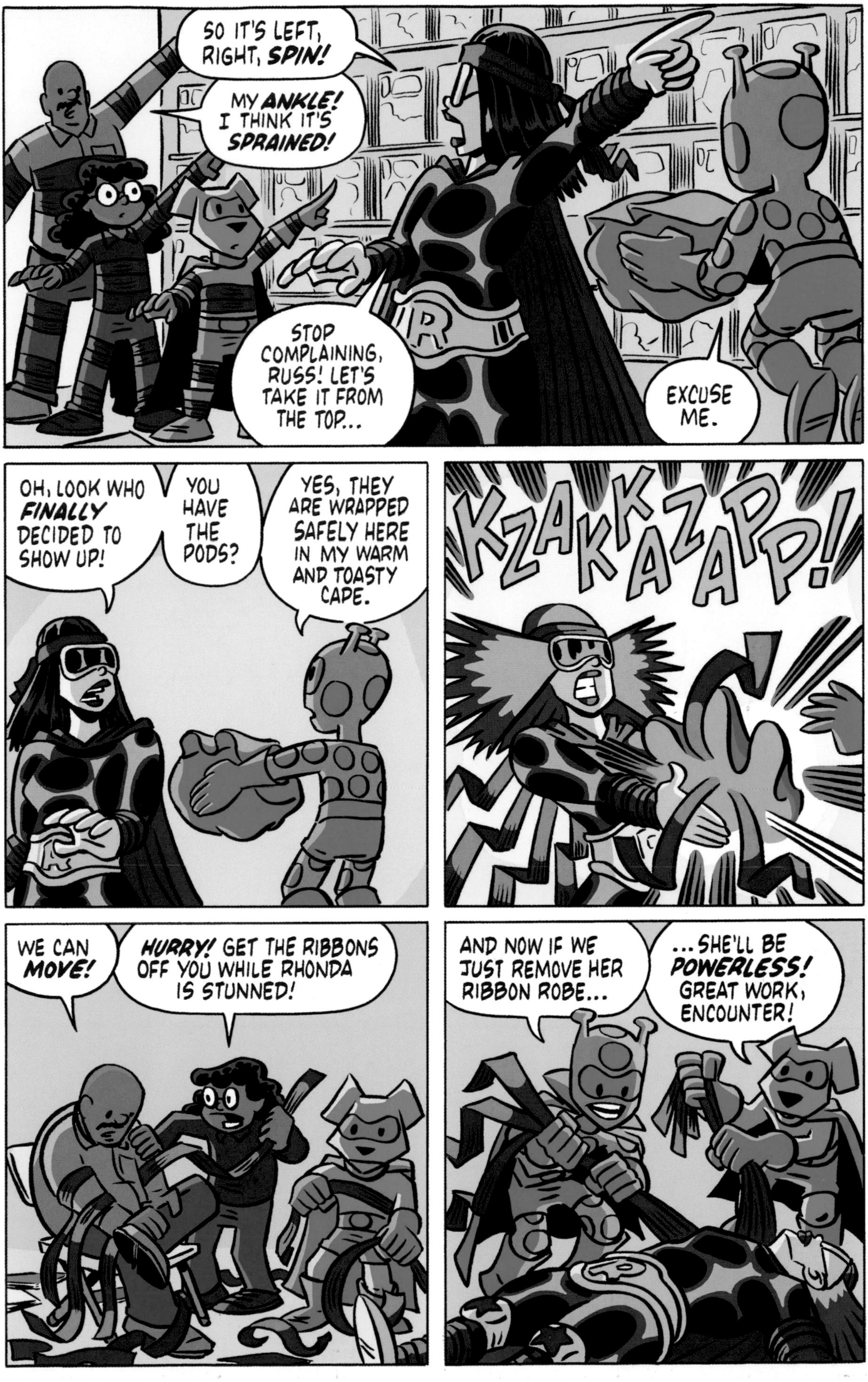
SO IT'S LEFT, RIGHT, SPIN!
MY ANKLE! I THINK IT'S SPRAINED!
STOP COMPLAINING, RUSS! LET'S TAKE IT FROM THE TOP...
EXCUSE ME.
OH, LOOK WHO FINALLY DECIDED TO SHOW UP!
YOU HAVE THE PODS?
YES, THEY ARE WRAPPED SAFELY HERE IN MY WARM AND TOASTY CAPE.
KZAKKZAPP!
KZAKKZAPP!
WE CAN MOVE!
HURRY! GET THE RIBBONS OFF YOU WHILE RHONDA IS STUNNED!
AND NOW IF WE JUST REMOVE HER RIBBON ROBE...
...SHE'LL BE POWERLESS! GREAT WORK, ENCOUNTER!

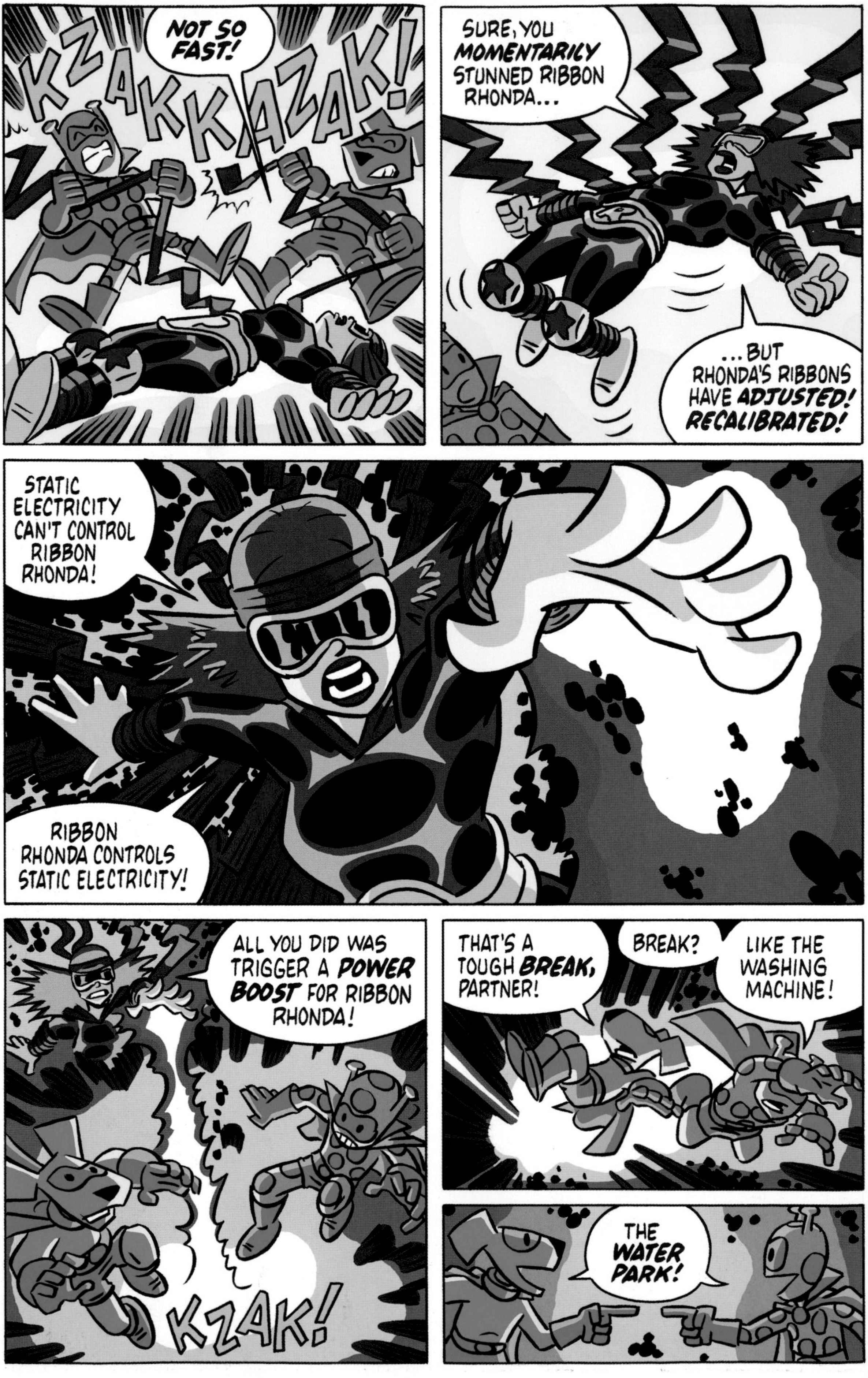
NOT SO FAST!
KZAKKAZAK!
SURE, YOU *MOMENTARILY* STUNNED RIBBON RHONDA...
...BUT RHONDA'S RIBBONS HAVE *ADJUSTED! RECALIBRATED!*
STATIC ELECTRICITY CAN'T CONTROL RIBBON RHONDA!
RIBBON RHONDA CONTROLS STATIC ELECTRICITY!
ALL YOU DID WAS TRIGGER A *POWER BOOST* FOR RIBBON RHONDA!
KZAK!
THAT'S A TOUGH *BREAK,* PARTNER!
BREAK?
LIKE THE WASHING MACHINE!
THE *WATER PARK!*

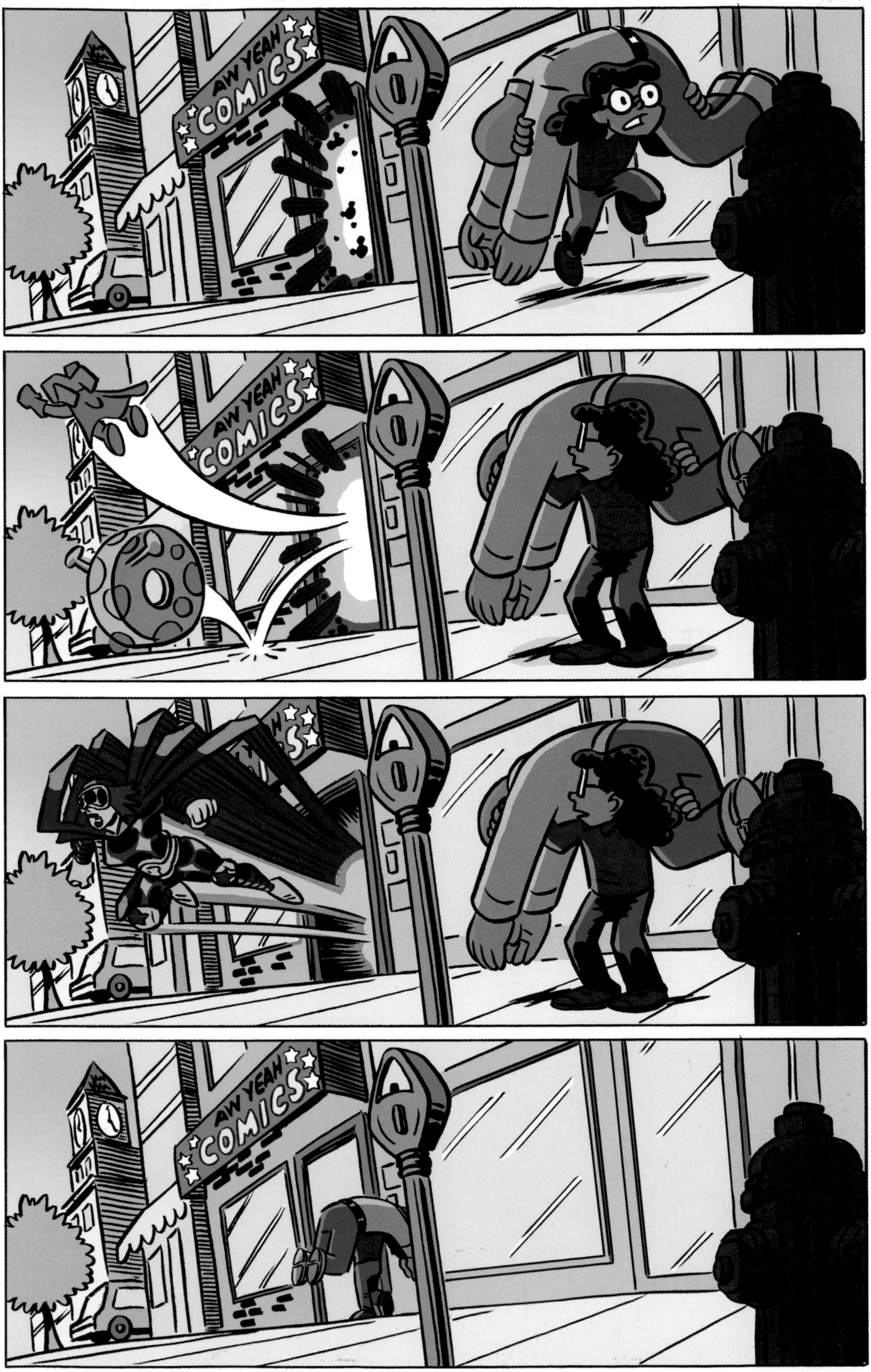
AW YEAH COMICS

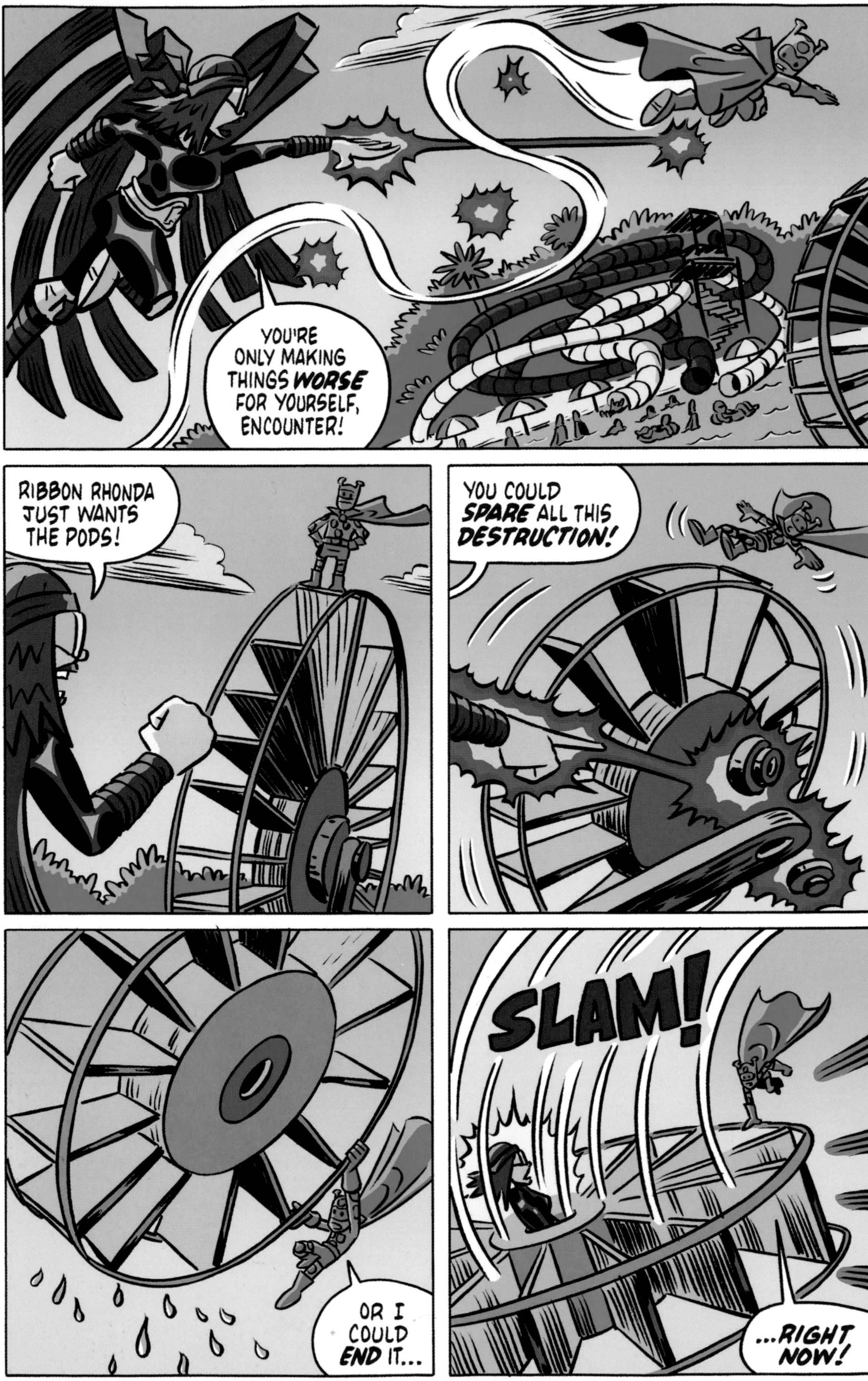
YOU'RE ONLY MAKING THINGS WORSE FOR YOURSELF, ENCOUNTER!
RIBBON RHONDA JUST WANTS THE PODS!
YOU COULD SPARE ALL THIS DESTRUCTION!
OR I COULD END IT...
SLAM!
...RIGHT NOW!

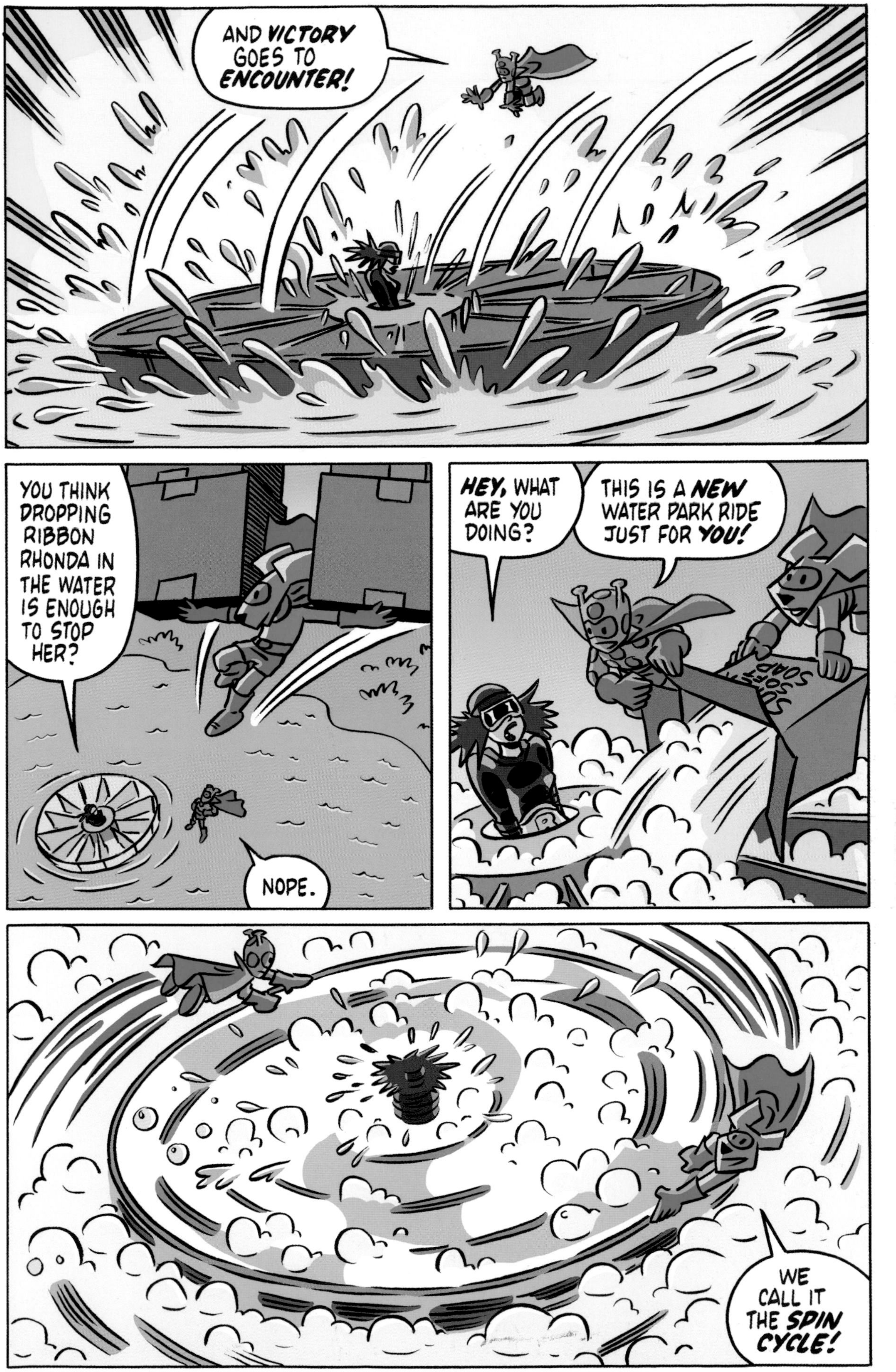
AND VICTORY GOES TO ENCOUNTER!
YOU THINK DROPPING RIBBON RHONDA IN THE WATER IS ENOUGH TO STOP HER?
NOPE.
HEY, WHAT ARE YOU DOING?
THIS IS A NEW WATER PARK RIDE JUST FOR YOU!
SUPER SOFT SOAP
WE CALL IT THE SPIN CYCLE!

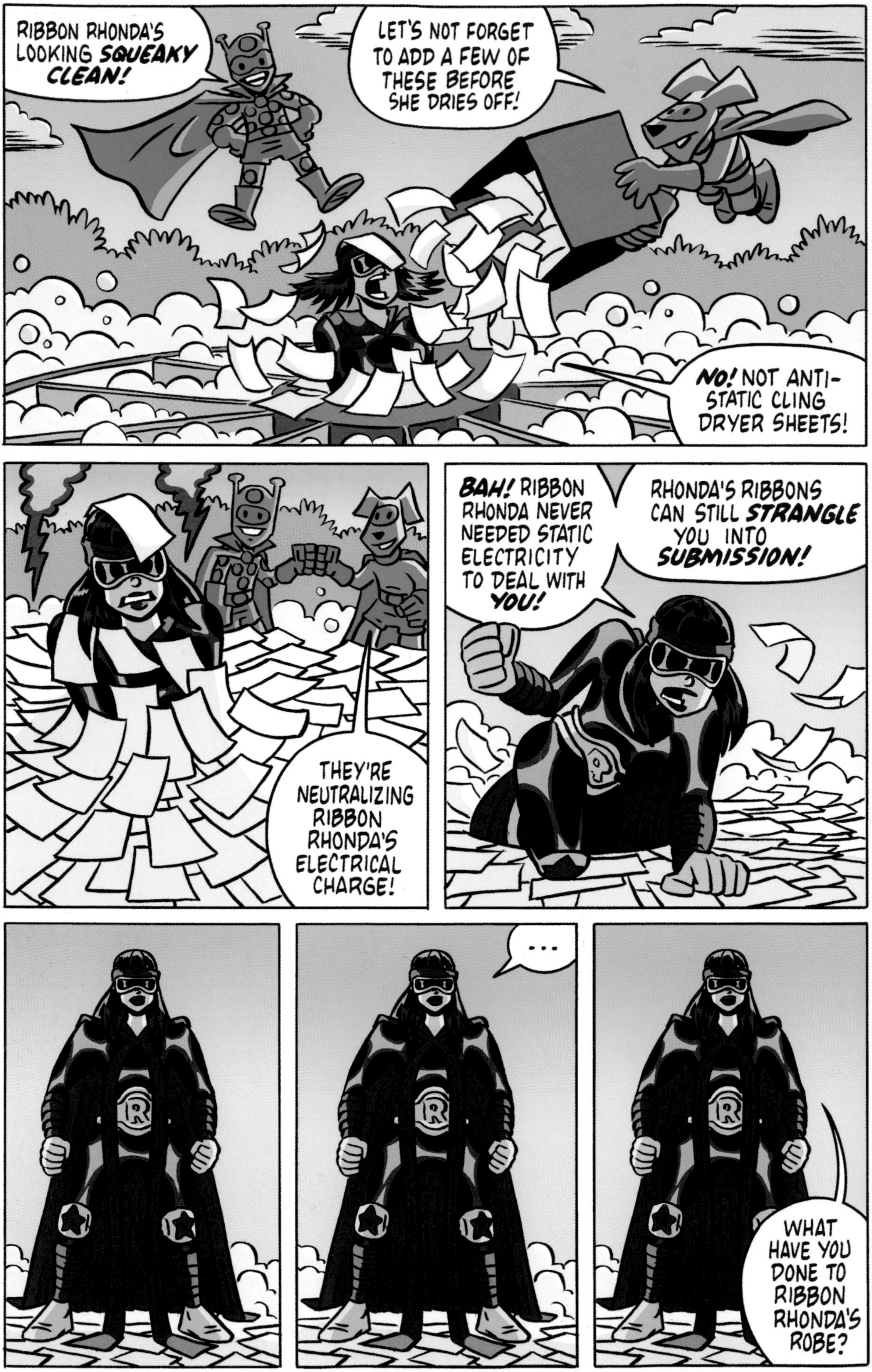
RIBBON RHONDA'S LOOKING SQUEAKY CLEAN!
LET'S NOT FORGET TO ADD A FEW OF THESE BEFORE SHE DRIES OFF!
NO! NOT ANTI-STATIC CLING DRYER SHEETS!
THEY'RE NEUTRALIZING RIBBON RHONDA'S ELECTRICAL CHARGE!
BAH! RIBBON RHONDA NEVER NEEDED STATIC ELECTRICITY TO DEAL WITH YOU!
RHONDA'S RIBBONS CAN STILL STRANGLE YOU INTO SUBMISSION!
...
WHAT HAVE YOU DONE TO RIBBON RHONDA'S ROBE?

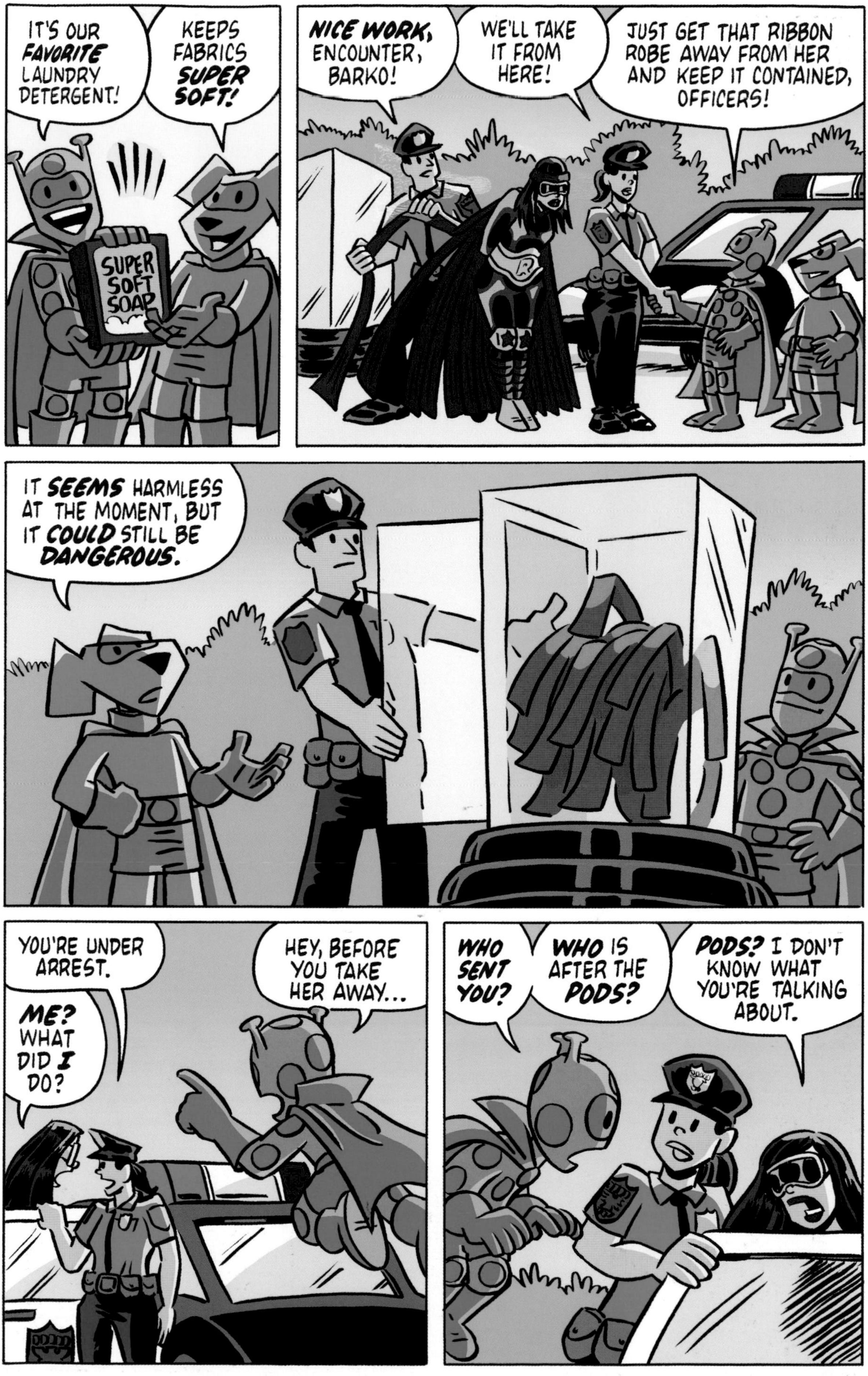
IT'S OUR FAVORITE LAUNDRY DETERGENT!
KEEPS FABRICS SUPER SOFT!
SUPER SOFT SOAP
NICE WORK, ENCOUNTER, BARKO!
WE'LL TAKE IT FROM HERE!
JUST GET THAT RIBBON ROBE AWAY FROM HER AND KEEP IT CONTAINED, OFFICERS!
IT SEEMS HARMLESS AT THE MOMENT, BUT IT COULD STILL BE DANGEROUS.
YOU'RE UNDER ARREST.
ME? WHAT DID I DO?
HEY, BEFORE YOU TAKE HER AWAY...
WHO SENT YOU?
WHO IS AFTER THE PODS?
PODS? I DON'T KNOW WHAT YOU'RE TALKING ABOUT.

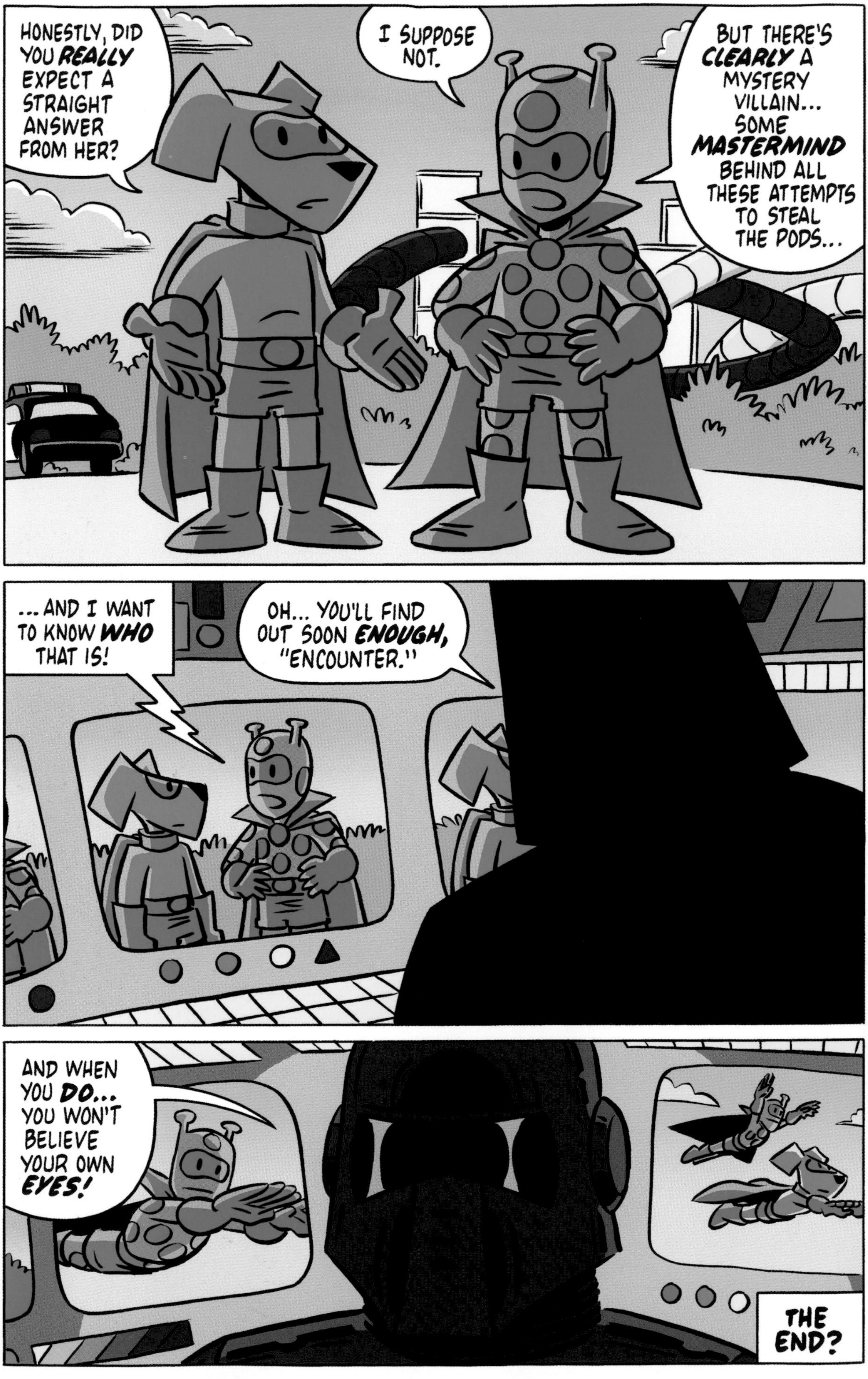
HONESTLY, DID YOU REALLY EXPECT A STRAIGHT ANSWER FROM HER?
I SUPPOSE NOT.
BUT THERE'S CLEARLY A MYSTERY VILLAIN... SOME MASTERMIND BEHIND ALL THESE ATTEMPTS TO STEAL THE PODS...
...AND I WANT TO KNOW WHO THAT IS!
OH... YOU'LL FIND OUT SOON ENOUGH, "ENCOUNTER."
AND WHEN YOU DO... YOU WON'T BELIEVE YOUR OWN EYES!
THE END?

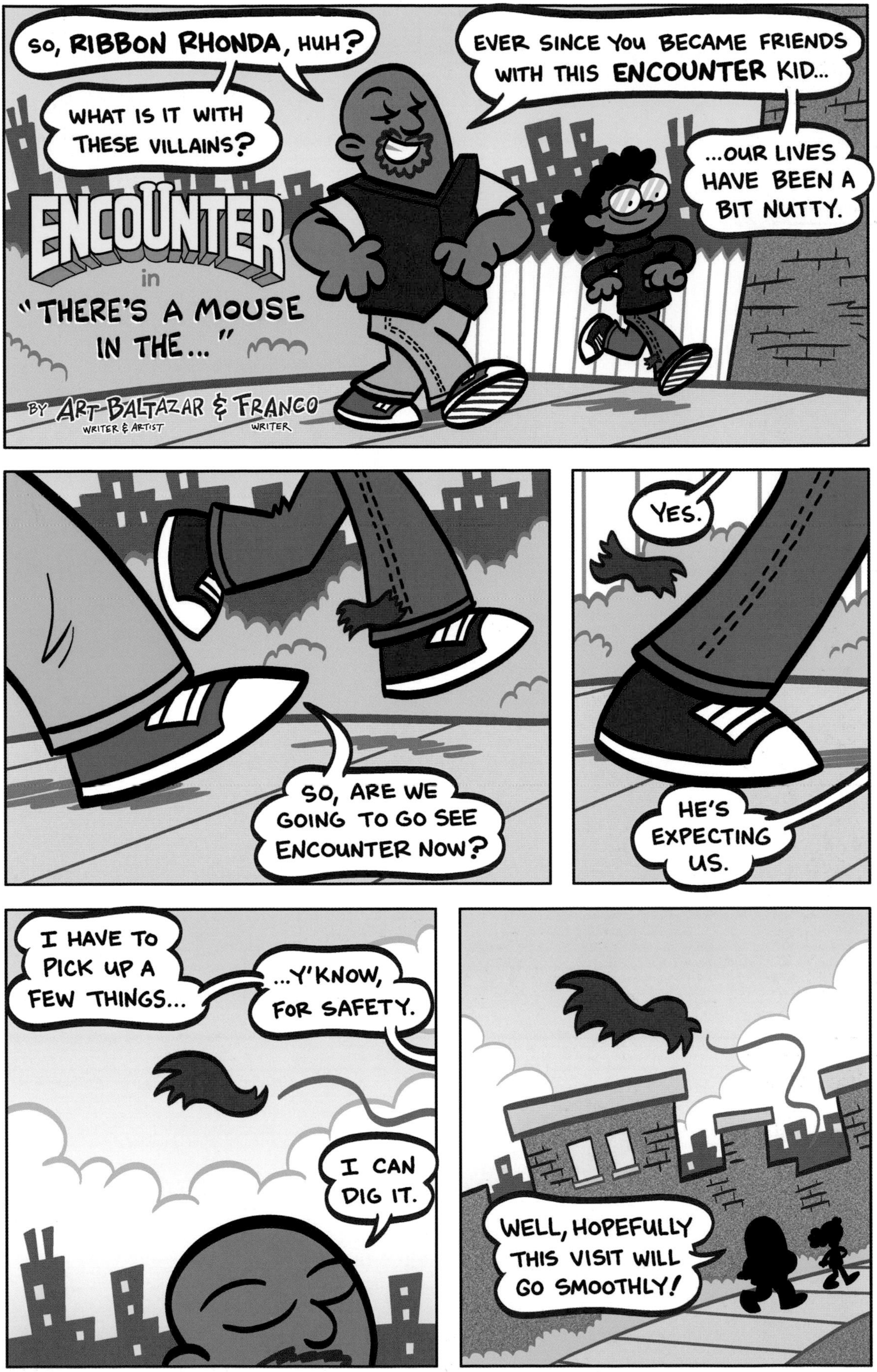
SO, RIBBON RHONDA, HUH?
WHAT IS IT WITH THESE VILLAINS?
EVER SINCE YOU BECAME FRIENDS WITH THIS ENCOUNTER KID...
...OUR LIVES HAVE BEEN A BIT NUTTY.
ENCOUNTER
in
"THERE'S A MOUSE IN THE..."
BY ART BALTAZAR & FRANCO
WRITER & ARTIST
WRITER
SO, ARE WE GOING TO GO SEE ENCOUNTER NOW?
YES.
HE'S EXPECTING US.
I HAVE TO PICK UP A FEW THINGS...
...Y'KNOW, FOR SAFETY.
I CAN DIG IT.
WELL, HOPEFULLY THIS VISIT WILL GO SMOOTHLY!

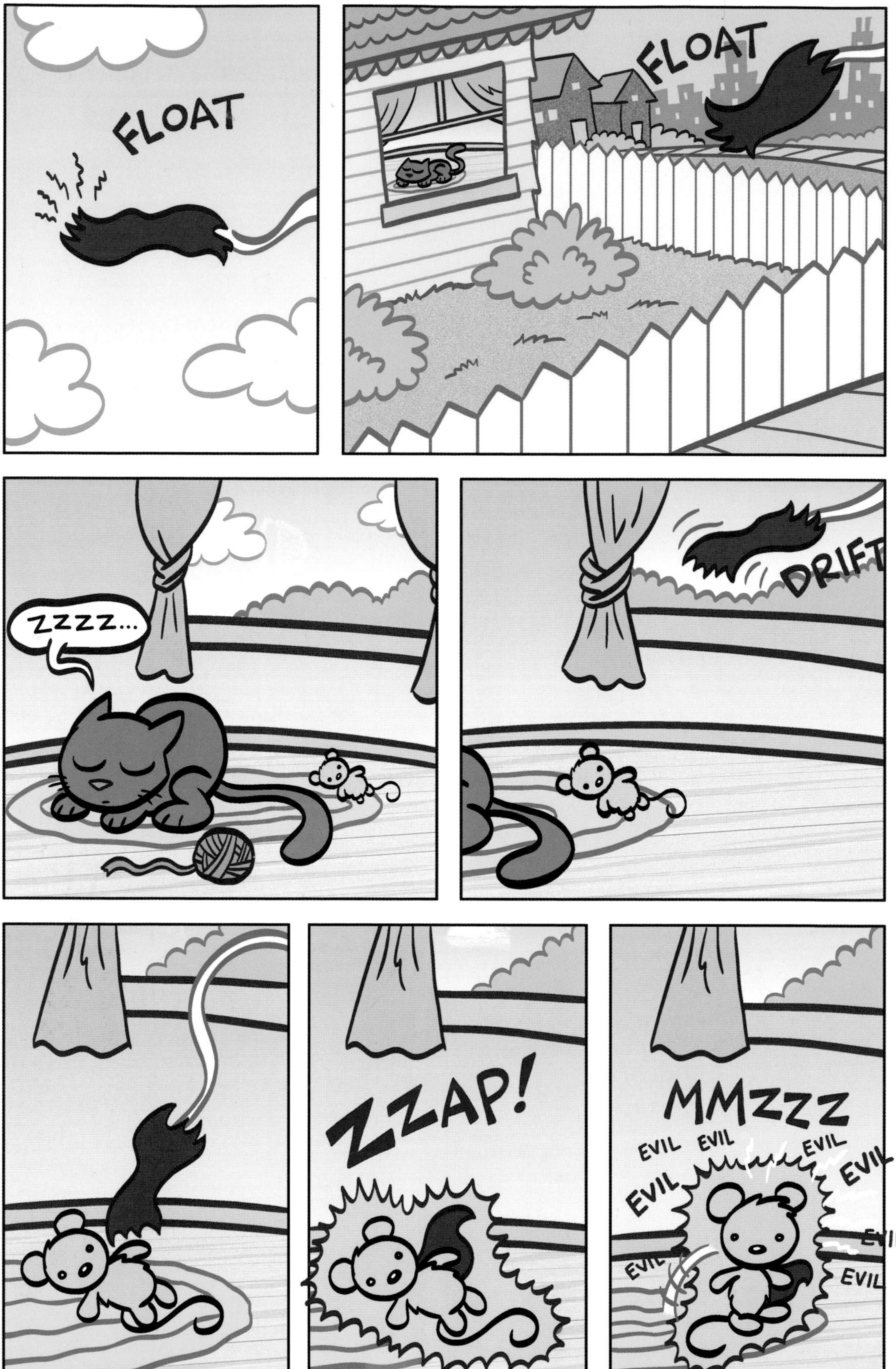
FLOAT
FLOAT
ZZZZ...
DRIFT
ZZAP!
MMZZZ
EVIL EVIL EVIL
EVIL EVIL
EVIL EVIL
EVIL

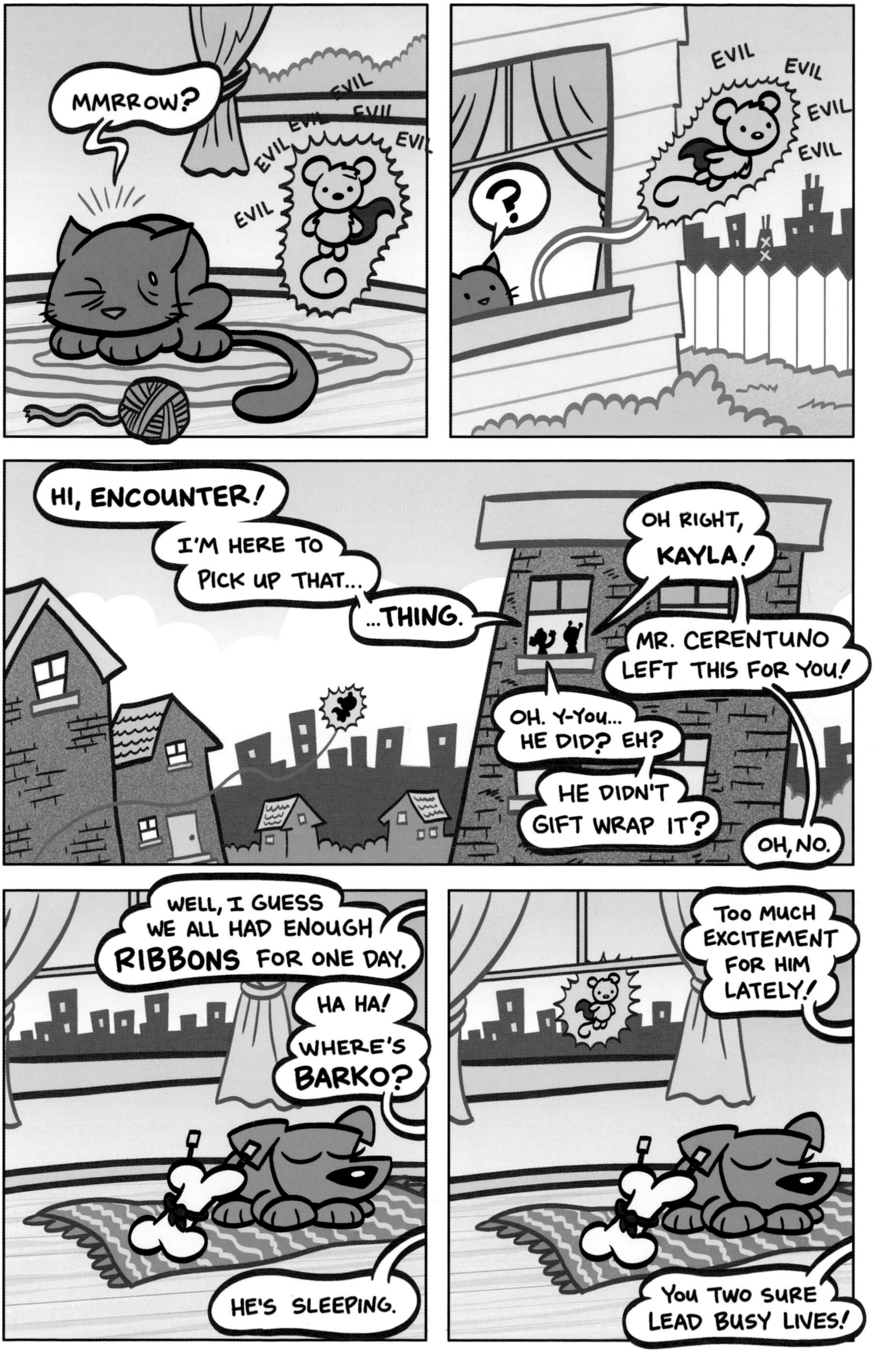
MMRROW?
EVIL
EVIL
EVIL
EVIL
EVIL
EVIL
?
EVIL
EVIL
EVIL
EVIL
HI, ENCOUNTER!
I'M HERE TO PICK UP THAT...
...THING.
OH RIGHT, KAYLA!
MR. CERENTUNO LEFT THIS FOR YOU!
OH. Y-YOU... HE DID? EH?
HE DIDN'T GIFT WRAP IT?
OH, NO.
WELL, I GUESS WE ALL HAD ENOUGH RIBBONS FOR ONE DAY.
HA HA!
WHERE'S BARKO?
HE'S SLEEPING.
TOO MUCH EXCITEMENT FOR HIM LATELY!
YOU TWO SURE LEAD BUSY LIVES!

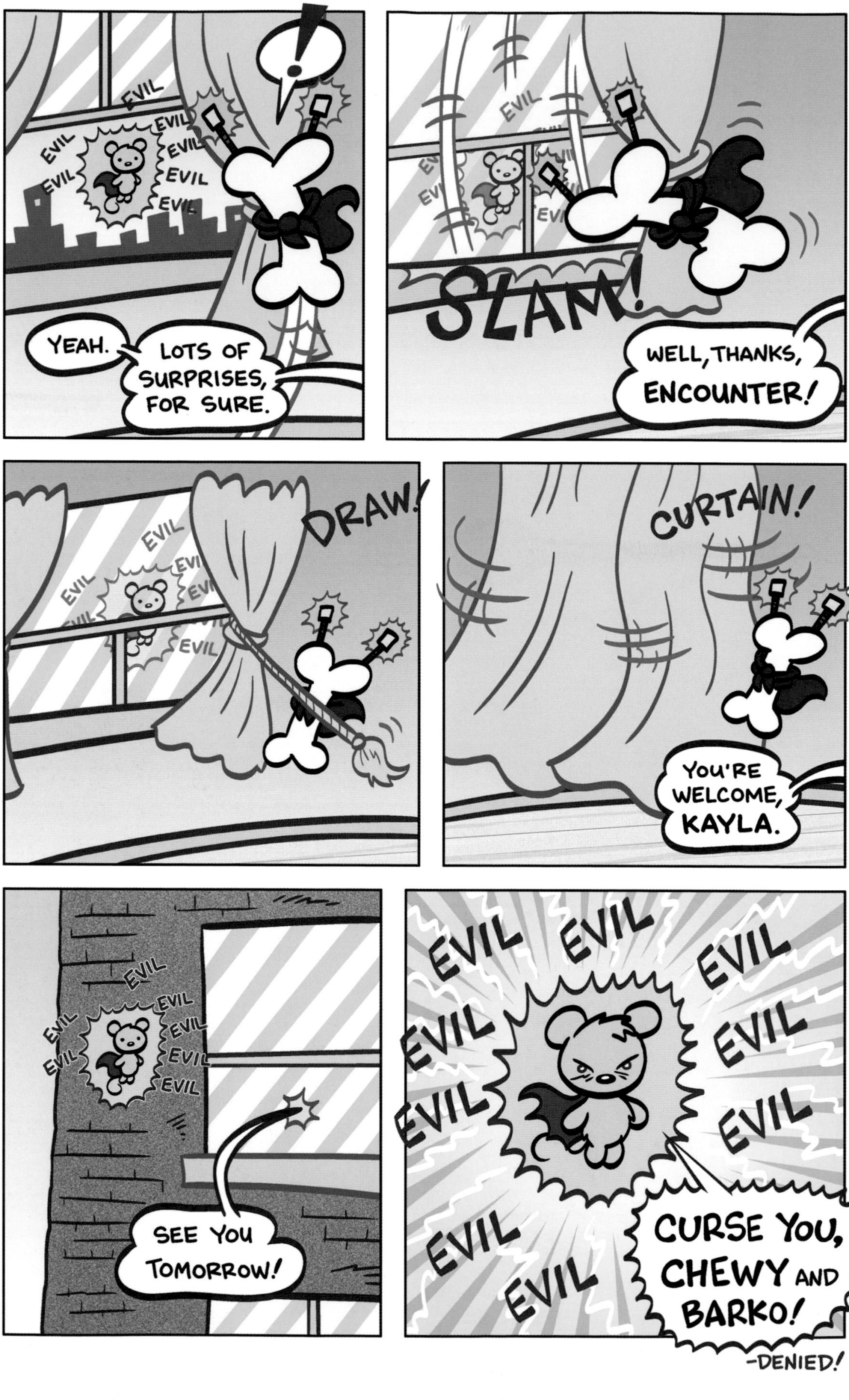
EVIL
EVIL
EVIL
EVIL
EVIL
EVIL
EVIL
!
YEAH.
LOTS OF SURPRISES, FOR SURE.
EVIL
SLAM!
WELL, THANKS, ENCOUNTER!
EVIL
DRAW!
CURTAIN!
YOU'RE WELCOME, KAYLA.
EVIL
EVIL
EVIL
EVIL
EVIL
EVIL
EVIL
SEE YOU TOMORROW!
EVIL
EVIL
EVIL
EVIL
EVIL
EVIL
EVIL
EVIL
EVIL
CURSE YOU, CHEWY AND BARKO!
-DENIED!

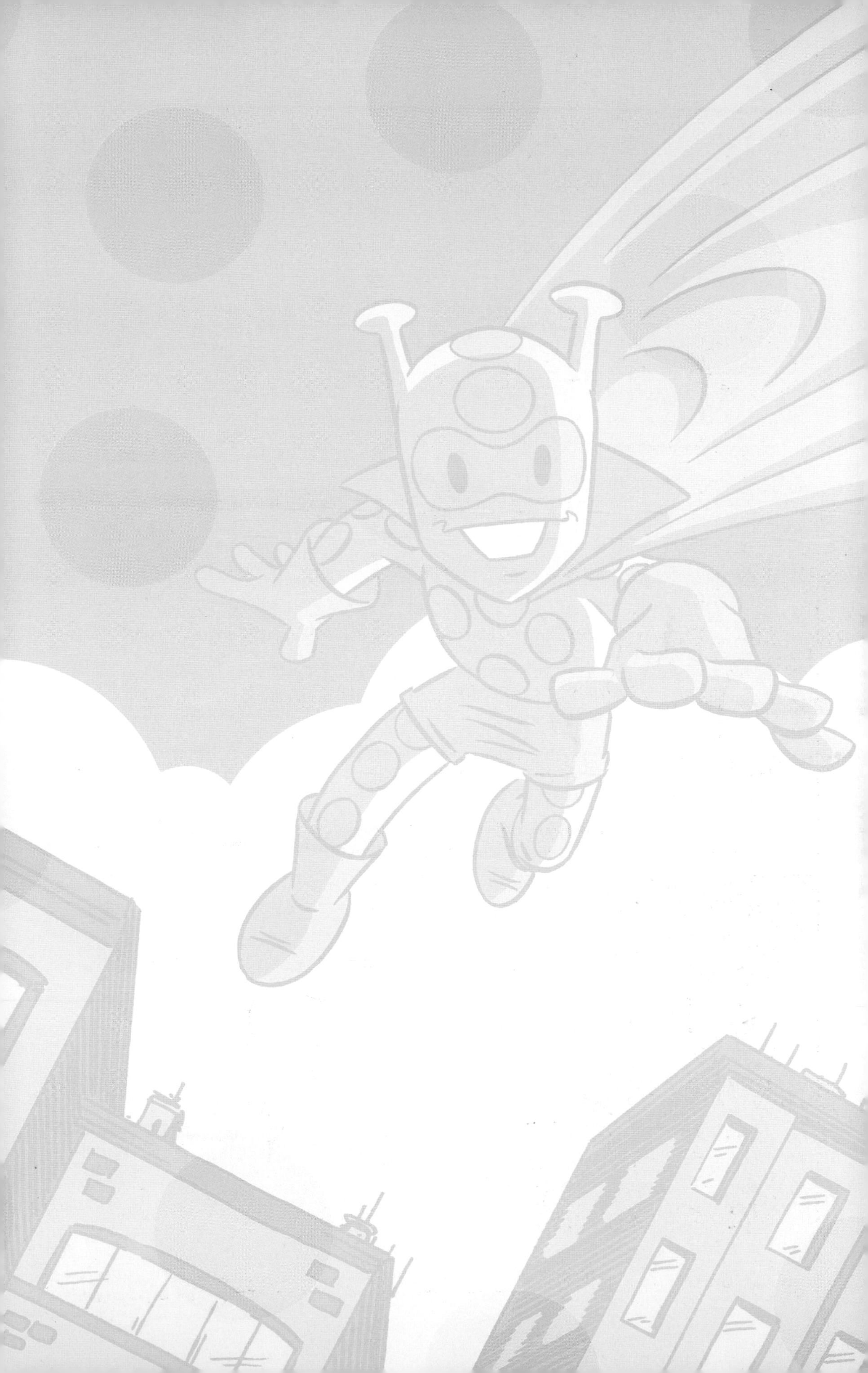

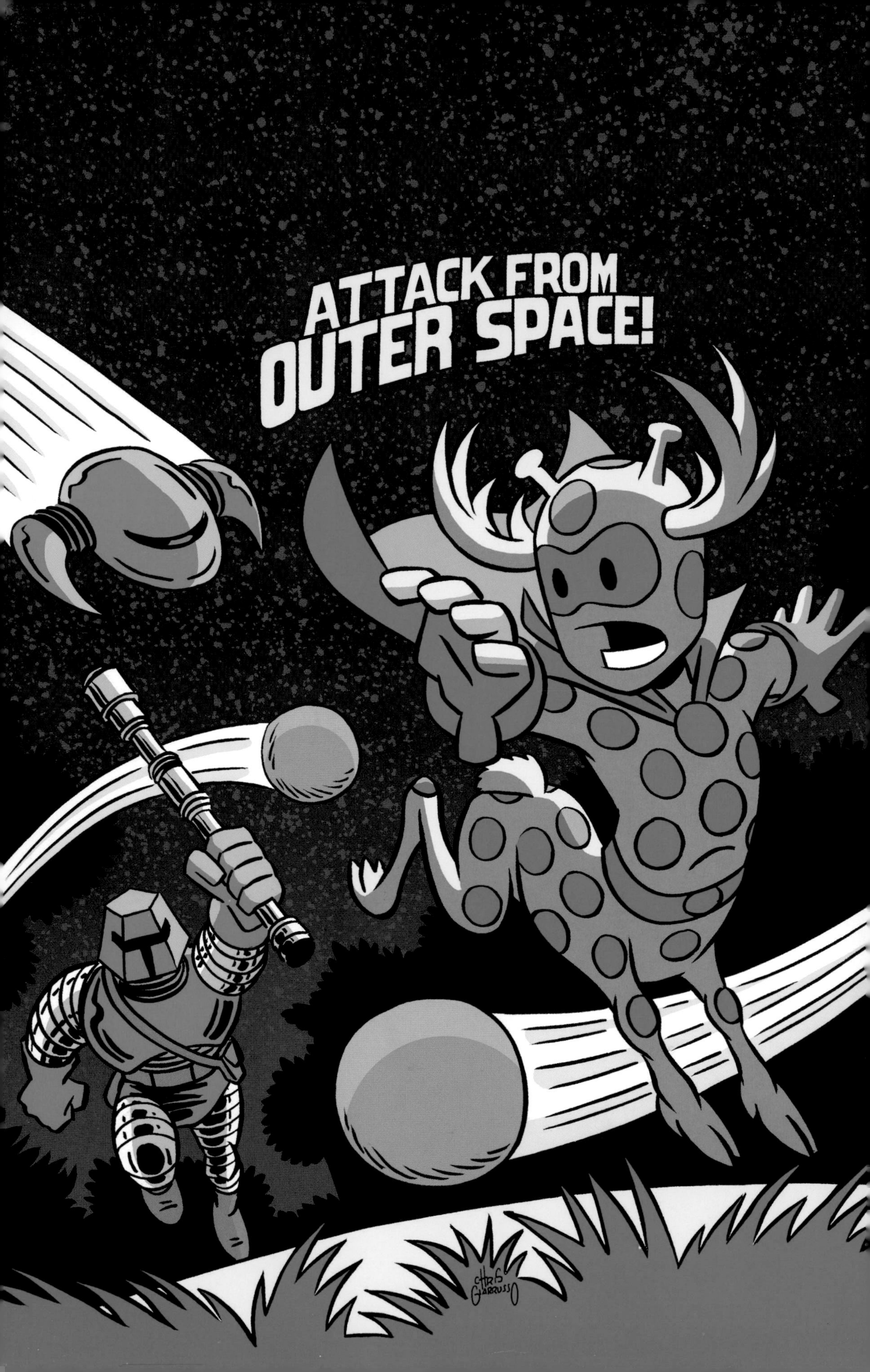
ATTACK FROM
OUTER SPACE!

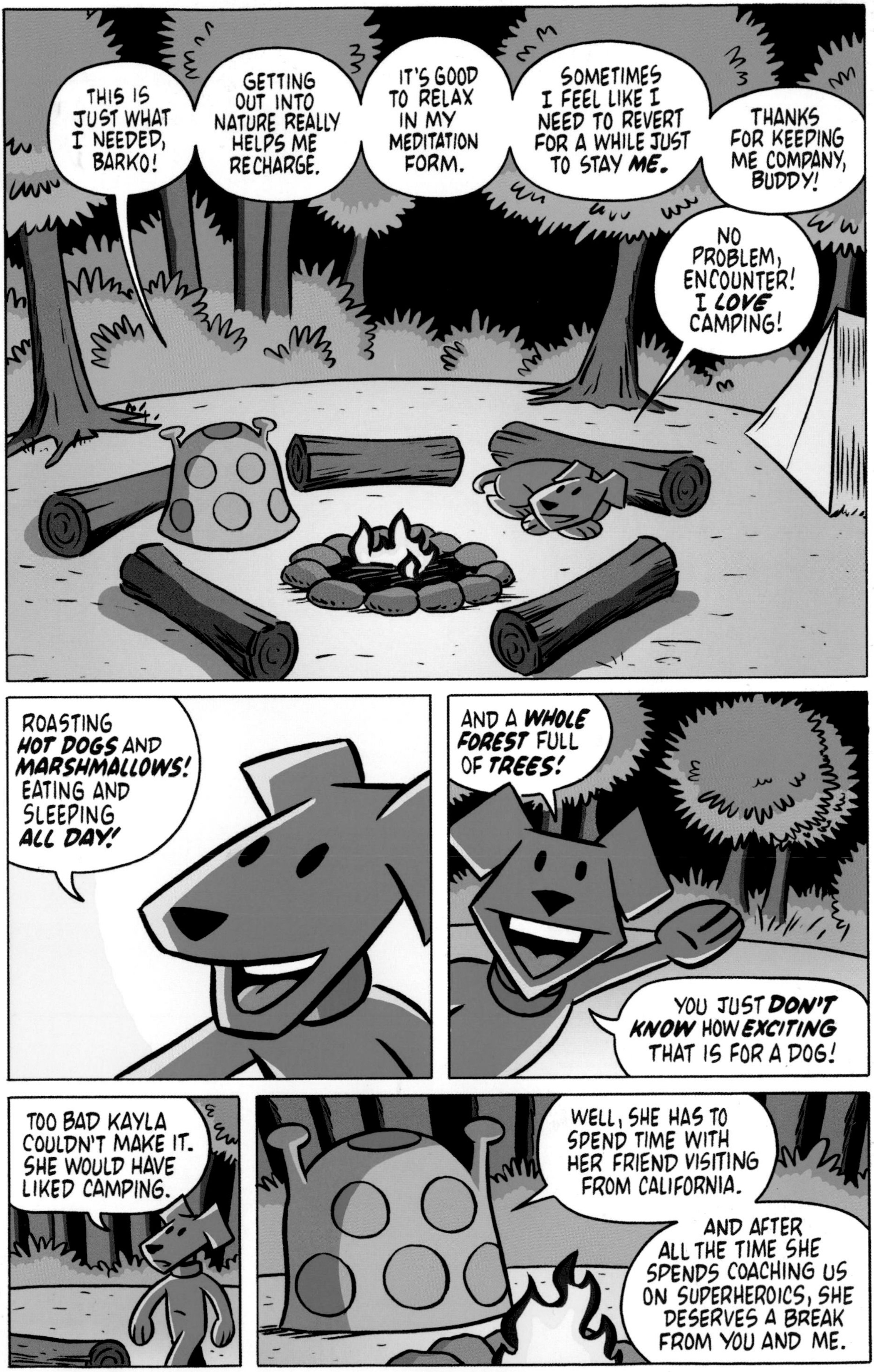
THIS IS JUST WHAT I NEEDED, BARKO!
GETTING OUT INTO NATURE REALLY HELPS ME RECHARGE.
IT'S GOOD TO RELAX IN MY MEDITATION FORM.
SOMETIMES I FEEL LIKE I NEED TO REVERT FOR A WHILE JUST TO STAY *ME.*
THANKS FOR KEEPING ME COMPANY, BUDDY!
NO PROBLEM, ENCOUNTER! I *LOVE* CAMPING!
ROASTING ***HOT DOGS*** AND ***MARSHMALLOWS!*** EATING AND SLEEPING ***ALL DAY!***
AND A ***WHOLE FOREST*** FULL OF ***TREES!***
YOU JUST ***DON'T KNOW*** HOW ***EXCITING*** THAT IS FOR A DOG!
TOO BAD KAYLA COULDN'T MAKE IT. SHE WOULD HAVE LIKED CAMPING.
WELL, SHE HAS TO SPEND TIME WITH HER FRIEND VISITING FROM CALIFORNIA.
AND AFTER ALL THE TIME SHE SPENDS COACHING US ON SUPERHEROICS, SHE DESERVES A BREAK FROM YOU AND ME.

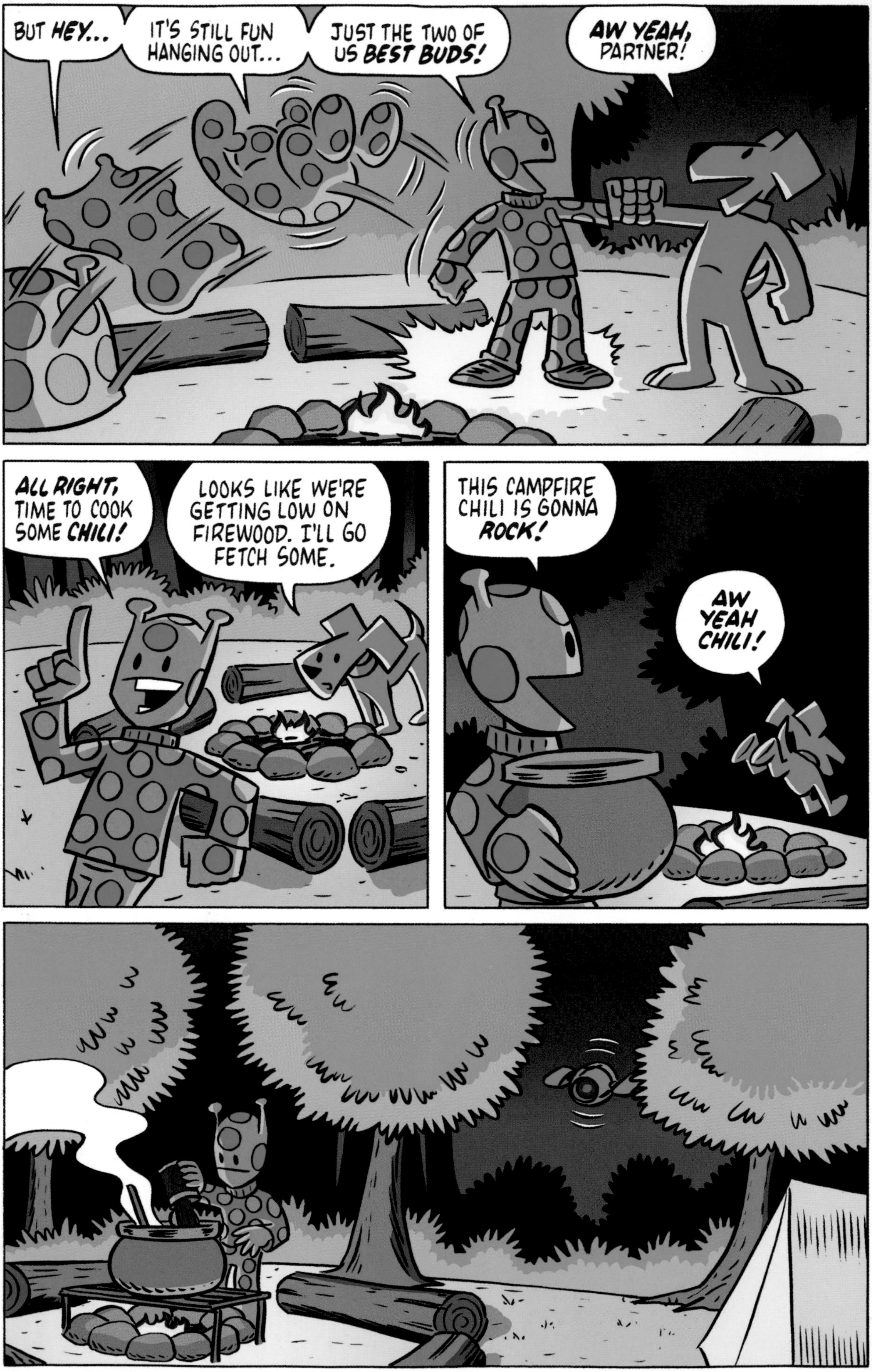
BUT HEY...
IT'S STILL FUN HANGING OUT...
JUST THE TWO OF US BEST BUDS!
AW YEAH, PARTNER!
ALL RIGHT, TIME TO COOK SOME CHILI!
LOOKS LIKE WE'RE GETTING LOW ON FIREWOOD. I'LL GO FETCH SOME.
THIS CAMPFIRE CHILI IS GONNA ROCK!
AW YEAH CHILI!

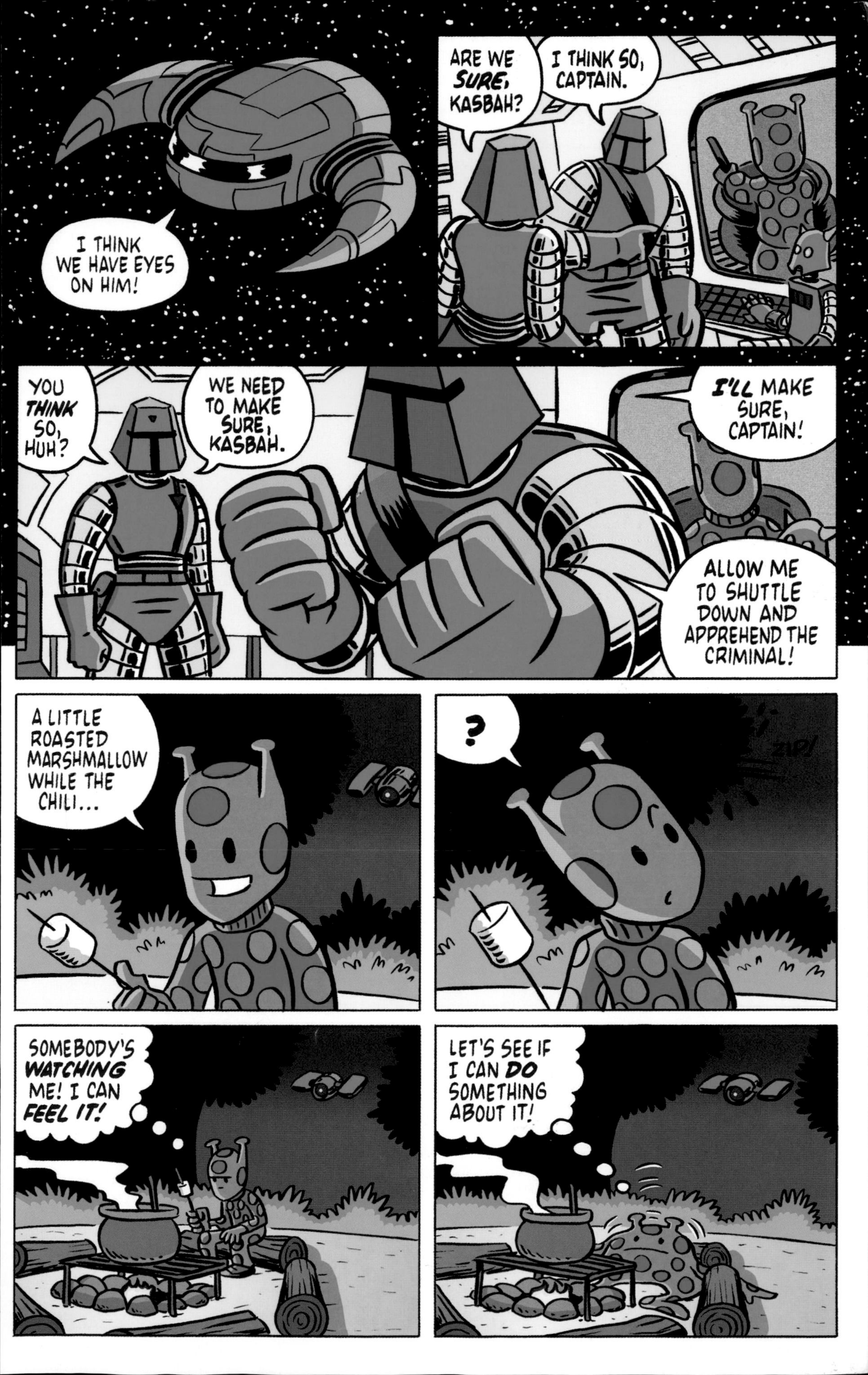
I THINK WE HAVE EYES ON HIM!
ARE WE SURE, KASBAH?
I THINK SO, CAPTAIN.
YOU THINK SO, HUH?
WE NEED TO MAKE SURE, KASBAH.
I'LL MAKE SURE, CAPTAIN!
ALLOW ME TO SHUTTLE DOWN AND APPREHEND THE CRIMINAL!
A LITTLE ROASTED MARSHMALLOW WHILE THE CHILI...
?
ZIP!
SOMEBODY'S WATCHING ME! I CAN FEEL IT!
LET'S SEE IF I CAN DO SOMETHING ABOUT IT!

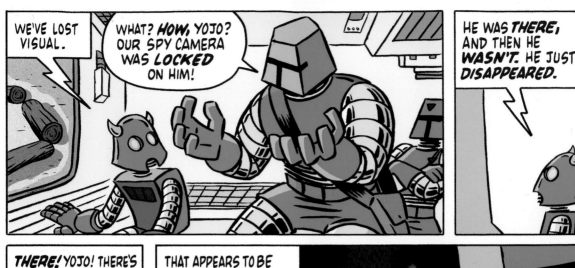

WE'VE LOST VISUAL.

WHAT? *HOW*, YOJO? OUR SPY CAMERA WAS *LOCKED* ON HIM!

HE WAS *THERE*, AND THEN HE *WASN'T*. HE JUST *DISAPPEARED*.

THERE! YOJO! THERE'S MOVEMENT TO THE RIGHT! *FOCUS!*

THAT APPEARS TO BE THE CRYPTOZOIC EARTH CREATURE CALLED *SASQUATCH.*

WHY'S IT SO *BLURRY?* I SAID *FOCUS!*

REFOCUSING. WE HAVE... SOMETHING.

THAT'S NOT HIM EITHER. THAT'S A *TREE SQUID.*

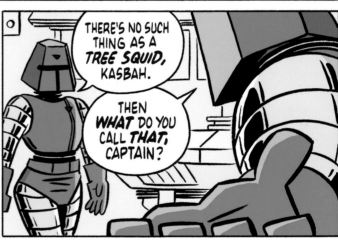

THERE'S NO SUCH THING AS A *TREE SQUID,* KASBAH.

THEN *WHAT* DO YOU CALL *THAT,* CAPTAIN?

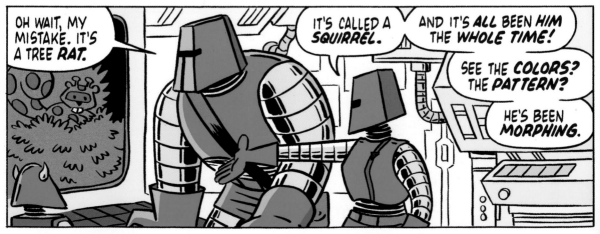

OH WAIT, MY MISTAKE. IT'S A TREE *RAT.*

IT'S CALLED A *SQUIRREL.*

AND IT'S *ALL BEEN HIM* THE *WHOLE TIME!*

SEE THE *COLORS?* THE *PATTERN?*

HE'S BEEN *MORPHING.*

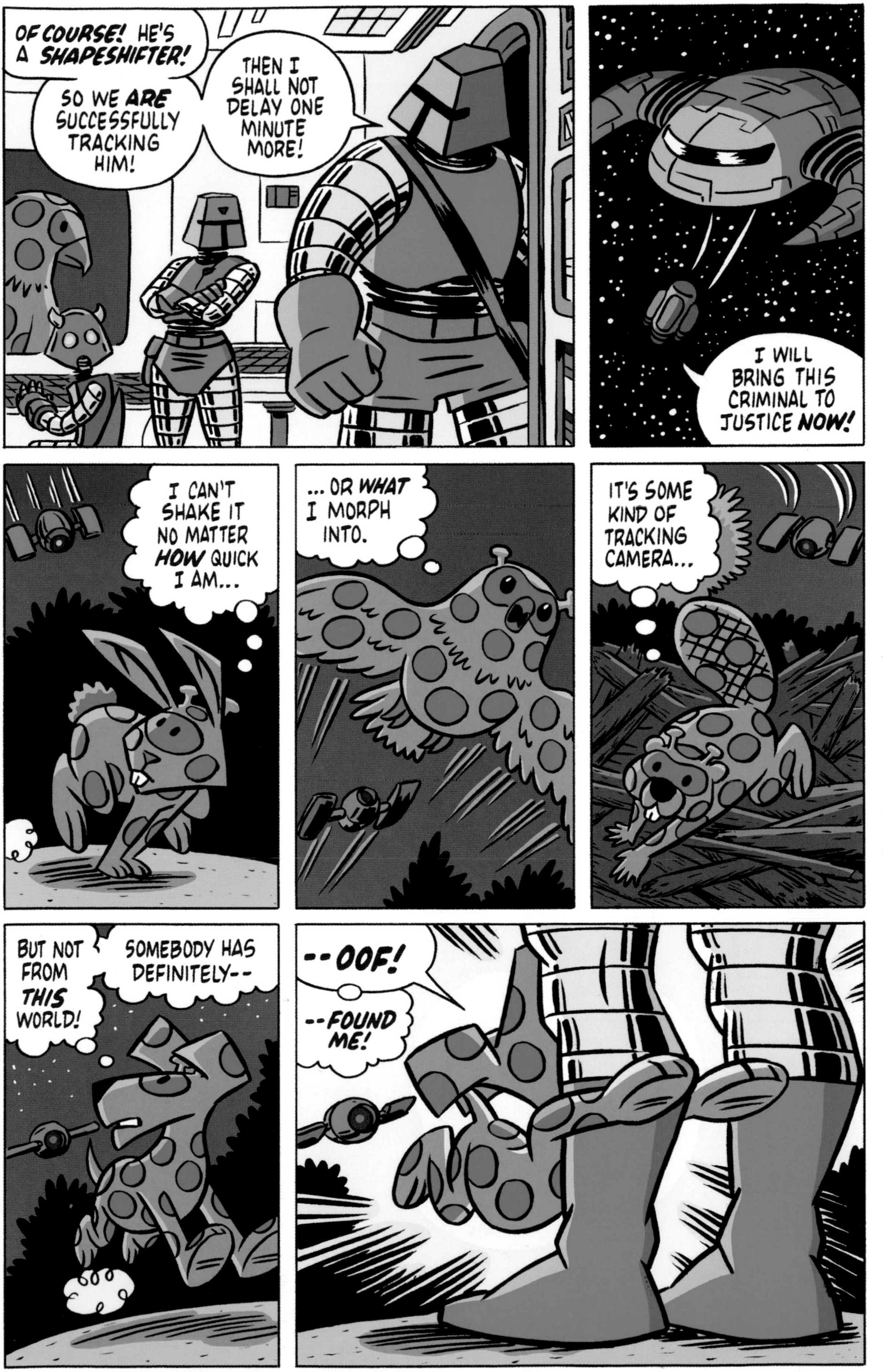
OF COURSE! HE'S A SHAPESHIFTER!
SO WE ARE SUCCESSFULLY TRACKING HIM!
THEN I SHALL NOT DELAY ONE MINUTE MORE!
I WILL BRING THIS CRIMINAL TO JUSTICE NOW!
I CAN'T SHAKE IT NO MATTER HOW QUICK I AM...
...OR WHAT I MORPH INTO.
IT'S SOME KIND OF TRACKING CAMERA...
SOMEBODY HAS DEFINITELY--
BUT NOT FROM THIS WORLD!
--OOF!
--FOUND ME!

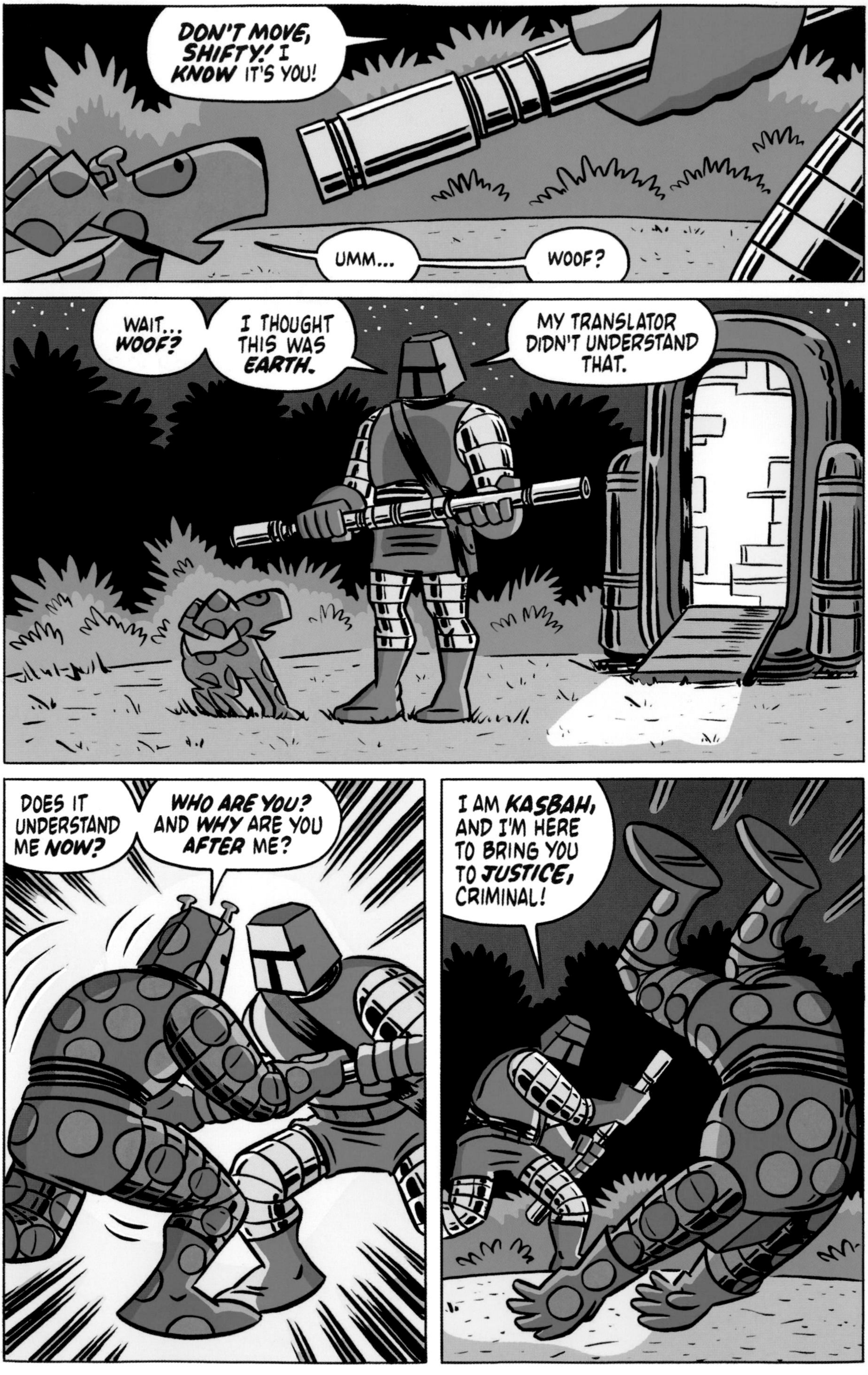
DON'T MOVE, SHIFTY! I KNOW IT'S YOU!
UMM...
WOOF?
WAIT... WOOF?
I THOUGHT THIS WAS EARTH.
MY TRANSLATOR DIDN'T UNDERSTAND THAT.
DOES IT UNDERSTAND ME NOW?
WHO ARE YOU? AND WHY ARE YOU AFTER ME?
I AM KASBAH, AND I'M HERE TO BRING YOU TO JUSTICE, CRIMINAL!

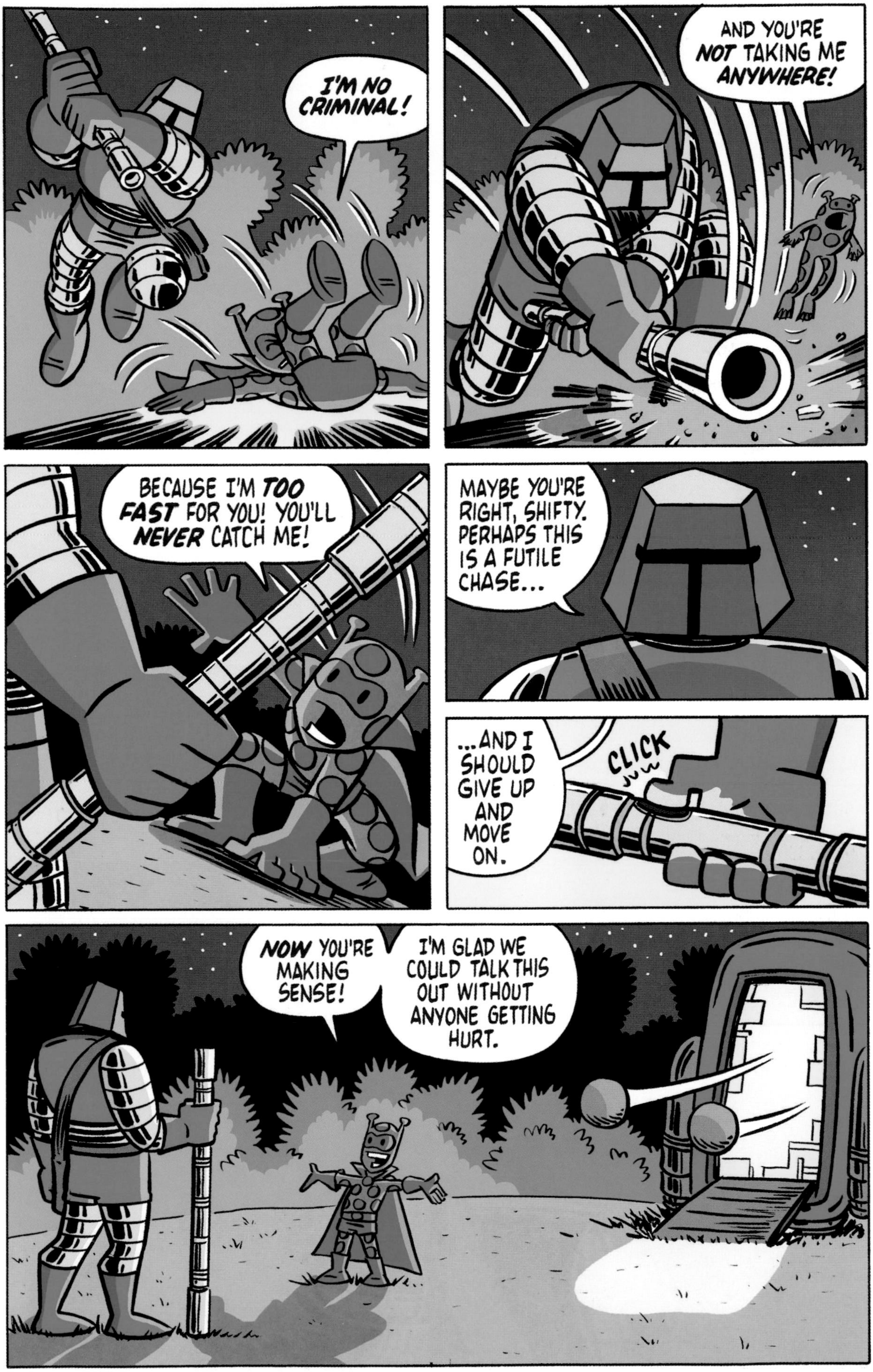
I'M NO CRIMINAL!
AND YOU'RE NOT TAKING ME ANYWHERE!
BECAUSE I'M TOO FAST FOR YOU! YOU'LL NEVER CATCH ME!
MAYBE YOU'RE RIGHT, SHIFTY. PERHAPS THIS IS A FUTILE CHASE...
...AND I SHOULD GIVE UP AND MOVE ON.
CLICK
NOW YOU'RE MAKING SENSE!
I'M GLAD WE COULD TALK THIS OUT WITHOUT ANYONE GETTING HURT.

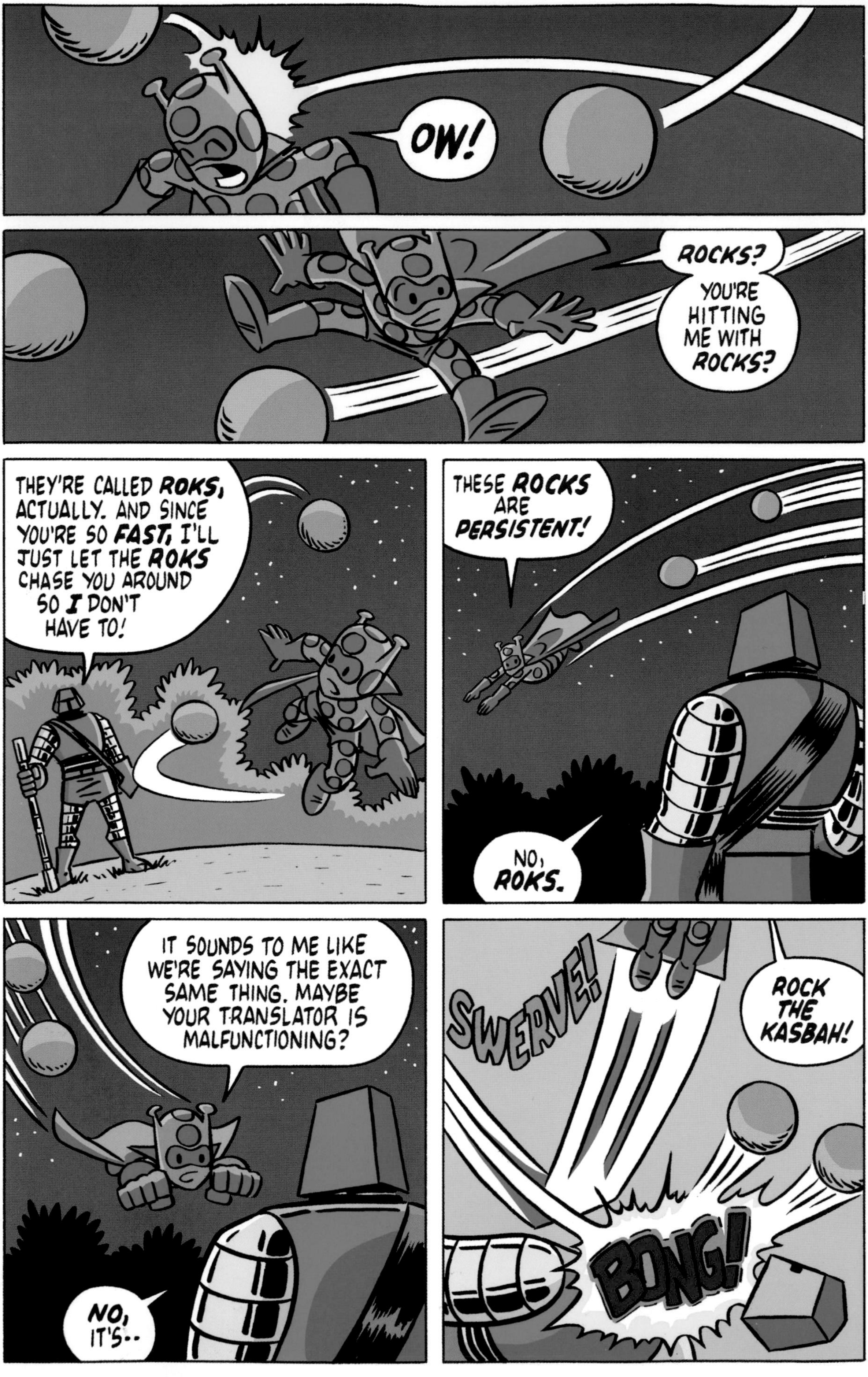
OW!
ROCKS?
YOU'RE HITTING ME WITH ROCKS?
THEY'RE CALLED ROKS, ACTUALLY. AND SINCE YOU'RE SO FAST, I'LL JUST LET THE ROKS CHASE YOU AROUND SO I DON'T HAVE TO!
THESE ROCKS ARE PERSISTENT!
NO, ROKS.
IT SOUNDS TO ME LIKE WE'RE SAYING THE EXACT SAME THING. MAYBE YOUR TRANSLATOR IS MALFUNCTIONING?
NO, IT'S..
SWERVE!
ROCK THE KASBAH!
BONG!

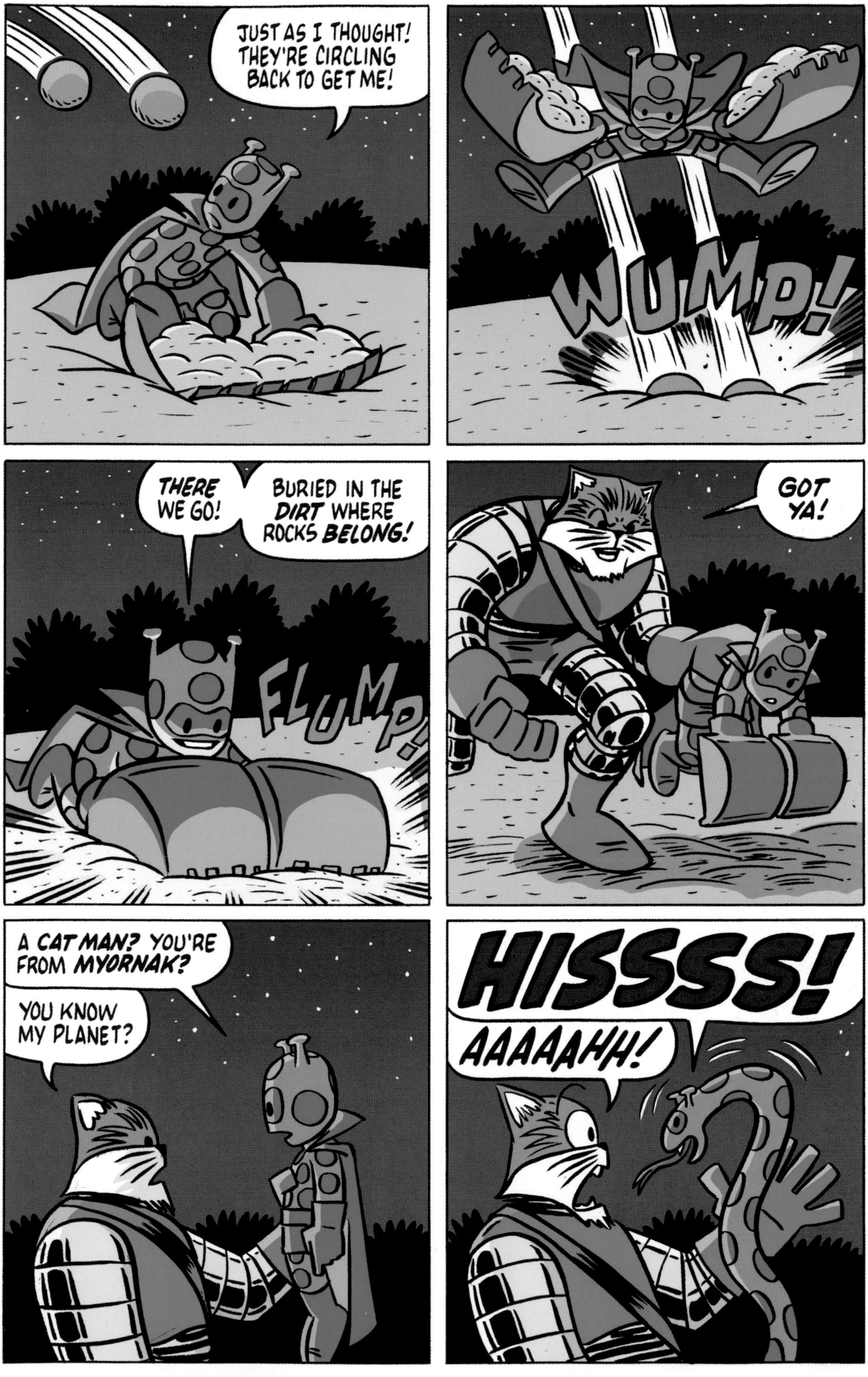
JUST AS I THOUGHT! THEY'RE CIRCLING BACK TO GET ME!
WUMP!
THERE WE GO!
BURIED IN THE DIRT WHERE ROCKS BELONG!
FLUMP!
GOT YA!
A CAT MAN? YOU'RE FROM MYORNAK?
YOU KNOW MY PLANET?
HISSSS!
AAAAAHH!

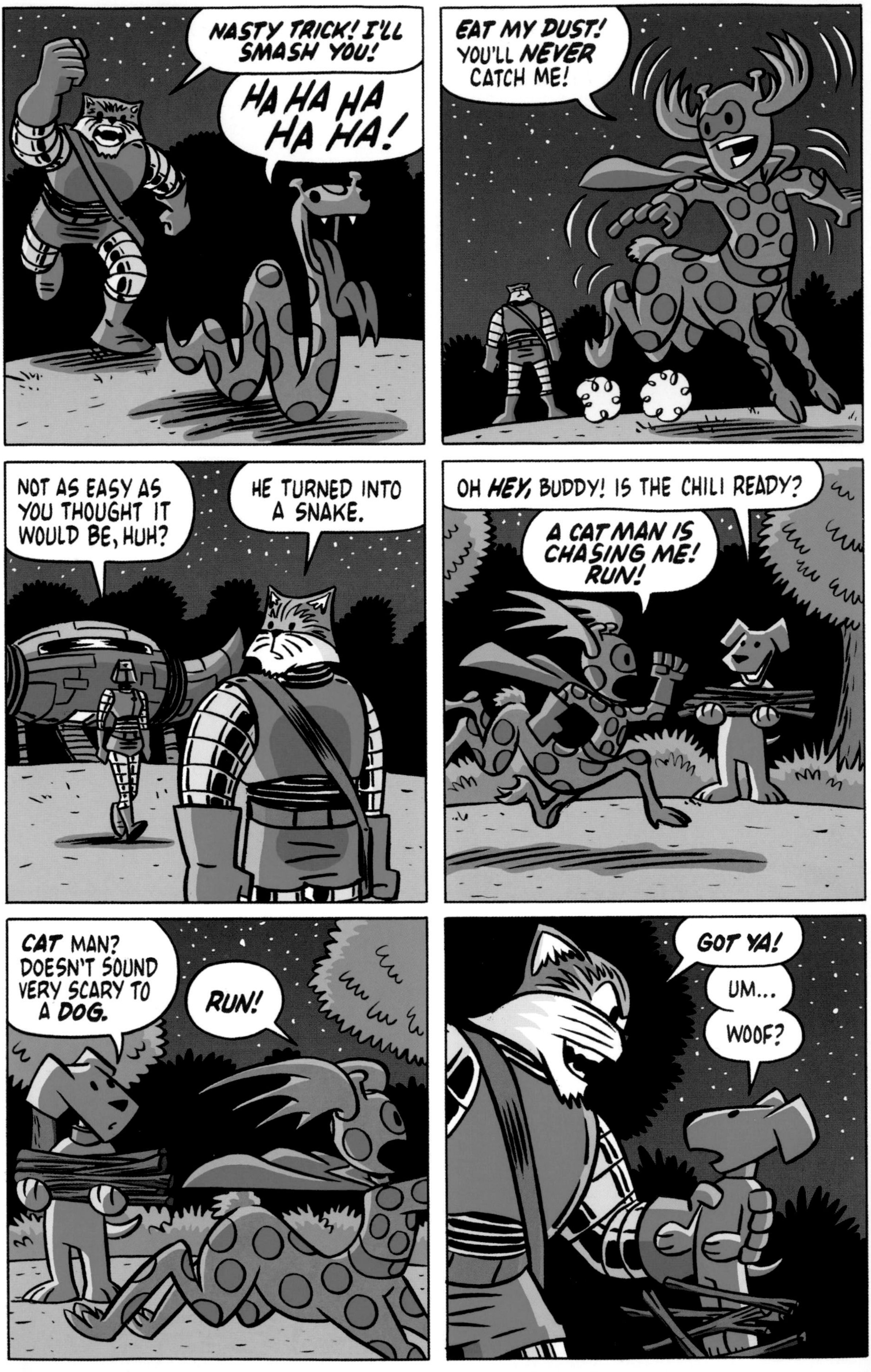
NASTY TRICK! I'LL SMASH YOU!
HA HA HA HA HA!
EAT MY DUST! YOU'LL NEVER CATCH ME!
NOT AS EASY AS YOU THOUGHT IT WOULD BE, HUH?
HE TURNED INTO A SNAKE.
OH HEY, BUDDY! IS THE CHILI READY?
A CAT MAN IS CHASING ME! RUN!
CAT MAN? DOESN'T SOUND VERY SCARY TO A DOG.
RUN!
GOT YA!
UM...
WOOF?

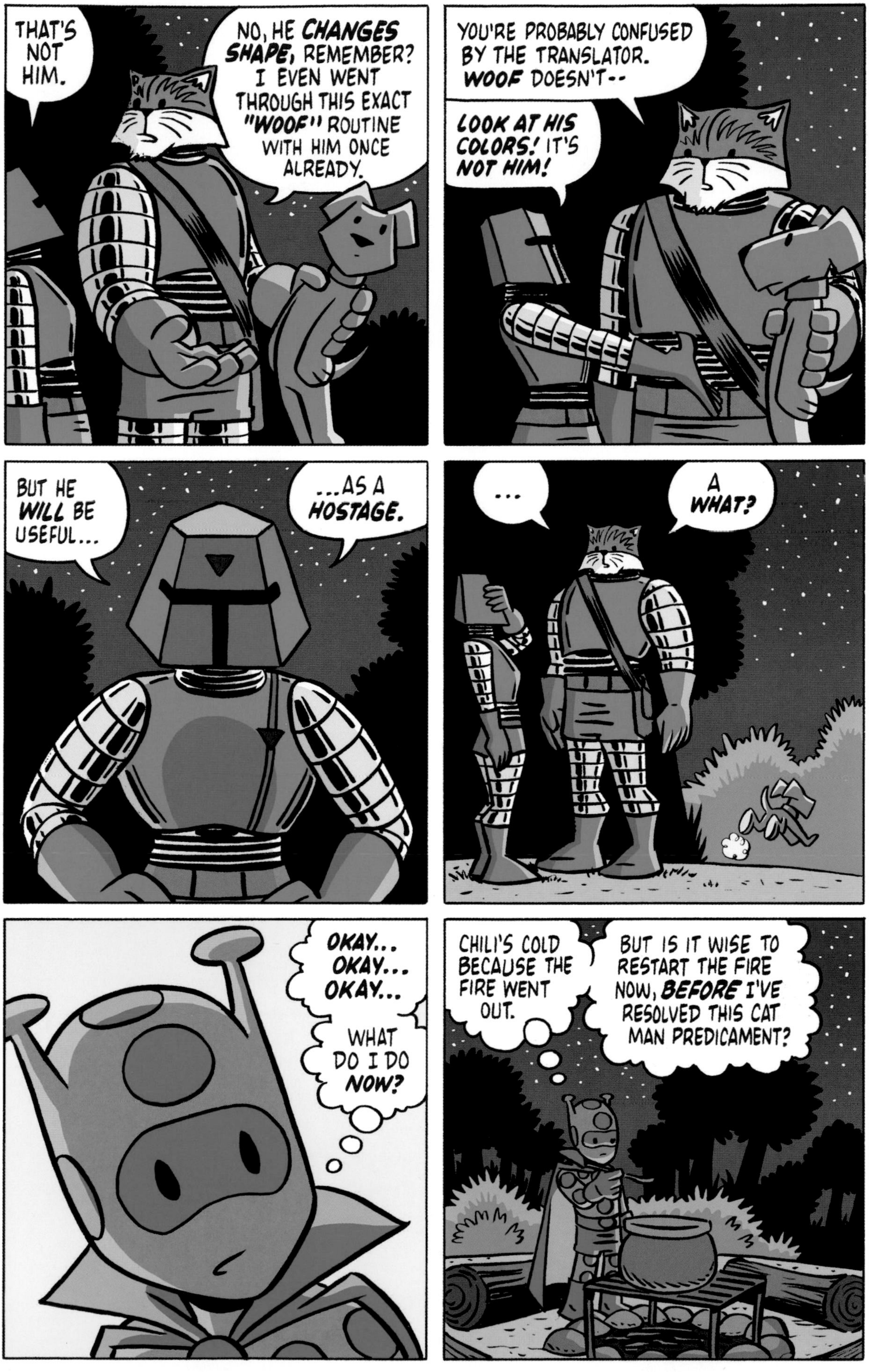
THAT'S NOT HIM.
NO, HE **CHANGES SHAPE**, REMEMBER? I EVEN WENT THROUGH THIS EXACT **"WOOF"** ROUTINE WITH HIM ONCE ALREADY.
YOU'RE PROBABLY CONFUSED BY THE TRANSLATOR. **WOOF** DOESN'T--
LOOK AT HIS COLORS! IT'S **NOT HIM!**
BUT HE **WILL** BE USEFUL...
...AS A **HOSTAGE.**
...
A **WHAT?**
OKAY... OKAY... OKAY...
WHAT DO I DO **NOW?**
CHILI'S COLD BECAUSE THE FIRE WENT OUT.
BUT IS IT WISE TO RESTART THE FIRE NOW, **BEFORE** I'VE RESOLVED THIS CAT MAN PREDICAMENT?

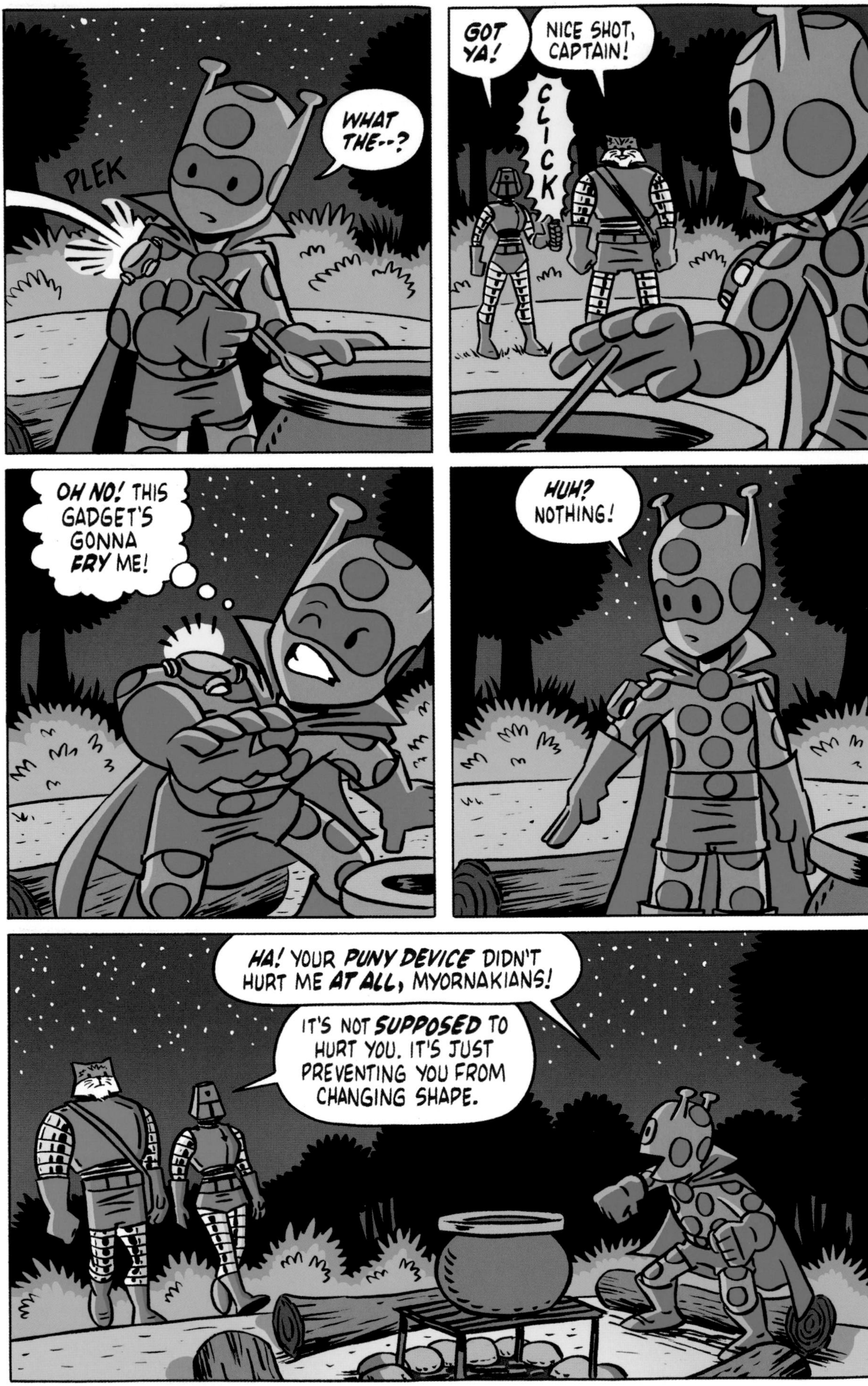
PLEK
WHAT THE--?
GOT YA!
NICE SHOT, CAPTAIN!
CLICK
OH NO! THIS GADGET'S GONNA FRY ME!
HUH? NOTHING!
HA! YOUR PUNY DEVICE DIDN'T HURT ME AT ALL, MYORNAKIANS!
IT'S NOT SUPPOSED TO HURT YOU. IT'S JUST PREVENTING YOU FROM CHANGING SHAPE.

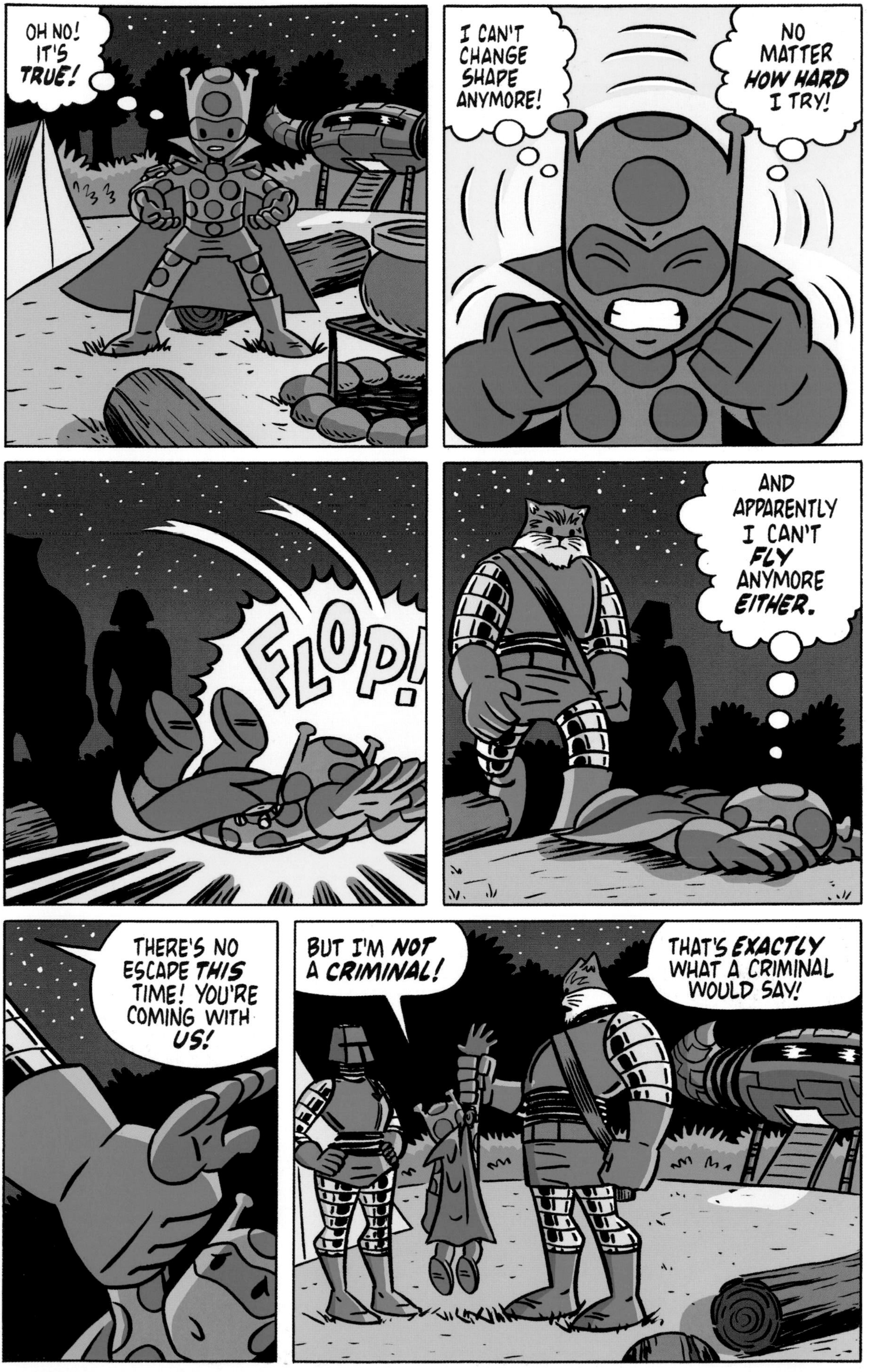
OH NO! IT'S TRUE!
I CAN'T CHANGE SHAPE ANYMORE!
NO MATTER HOW HARD I TRY!
FLOP!
AND APPARENTLY I CAN'T FLY ANYMORE EITHER.
THERE'S NO ESCAPE THIS TIME! YOU'RE COMING WITH US!
BUT I'M NOT A CRIMINAL!
THAT'S EXACTLY WHAT A CRIMINAL WOULD SAY!

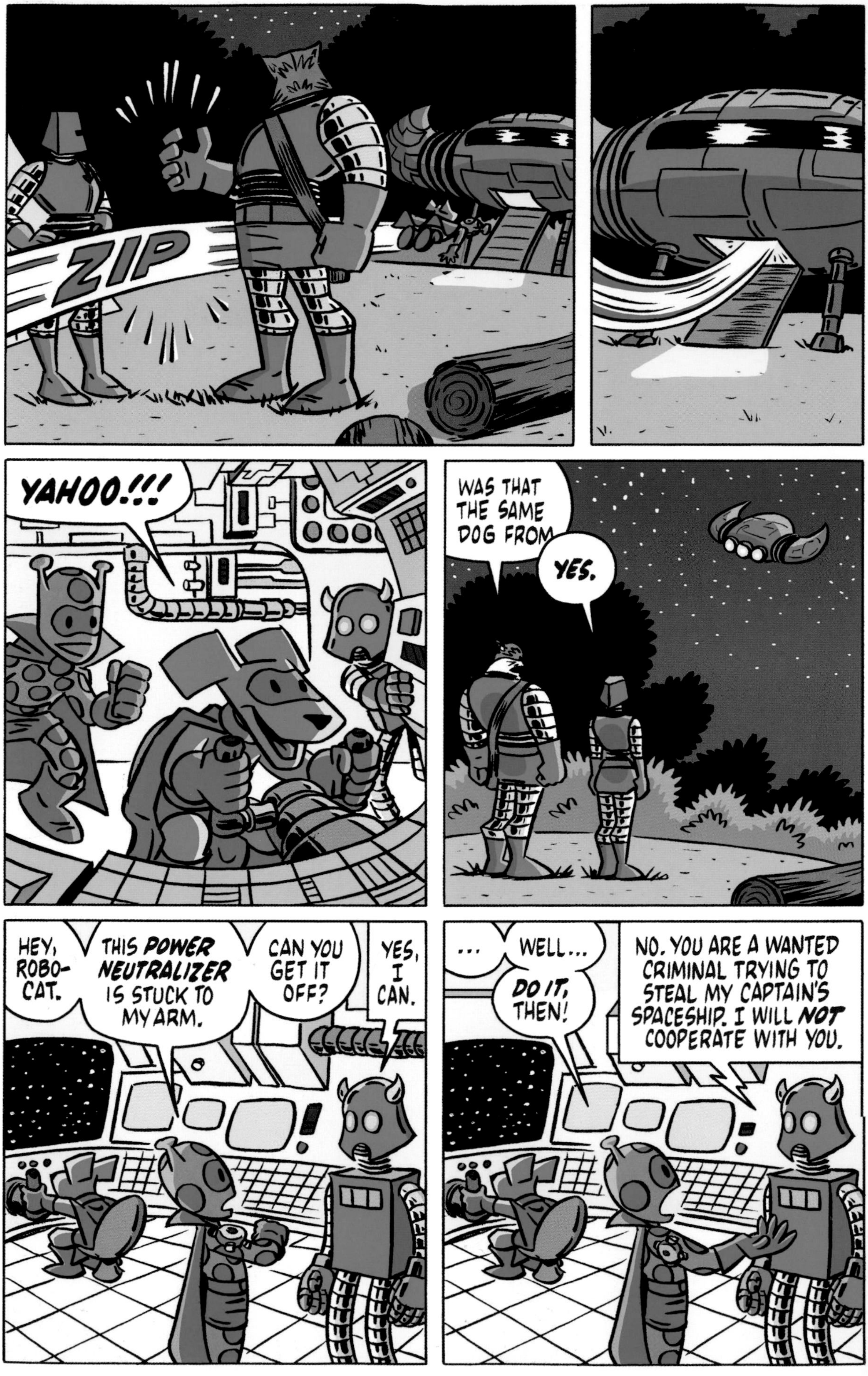
ZIP
YAHOO.!!!
WAS THAT THE SAME DOG FROM
YES.
HEY, ROBO-CAT.
THIS POWER NEUTRALIZER IS STUCK TO MY ARM.
CAN YOU GET IT OFF?
YES, I CAN.
...
WELL...
DO IT, THEN!
NO. YOU ARE A WANTED CRIMINAL TRYING TO STEAL MY CAPTAIN'S SPACESHIP. I WILL NOT COOPERATE WITH YOU.

DON'T WORRY, ENCOUNTER, YOU *KNOW* I'M A *TECH HOUND!*

THE NEUTRALIZER MUST BE CONNECTED TO THE SHIP'S MASTER CONTROLS!

I'LL FIGURE THIS OUT IN *NO TIME!*

CRASH!

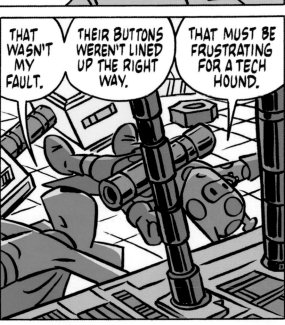

THAT WASN'T MY FAULT.

THEIR BUTTONS WEREN'T LINED UP THE RIGHT WAY.

THAT MUST BE FRUSTRATING FOR A TECH HOUND.

I BET ALL THE *OTHER* SPACESHIP BUTTONS YOU'VE SEEN WERE ALWAYS PROPERLY LINED UP.

LET'S NOT FIXATE ON BUTTONS RIGHT NOW. WE NEED TO GET THAT *NEUTRALIZER* OFF YOU.

PLEK

WE NEED TO GET THESE *NEUTRALIZERS* OFF US.

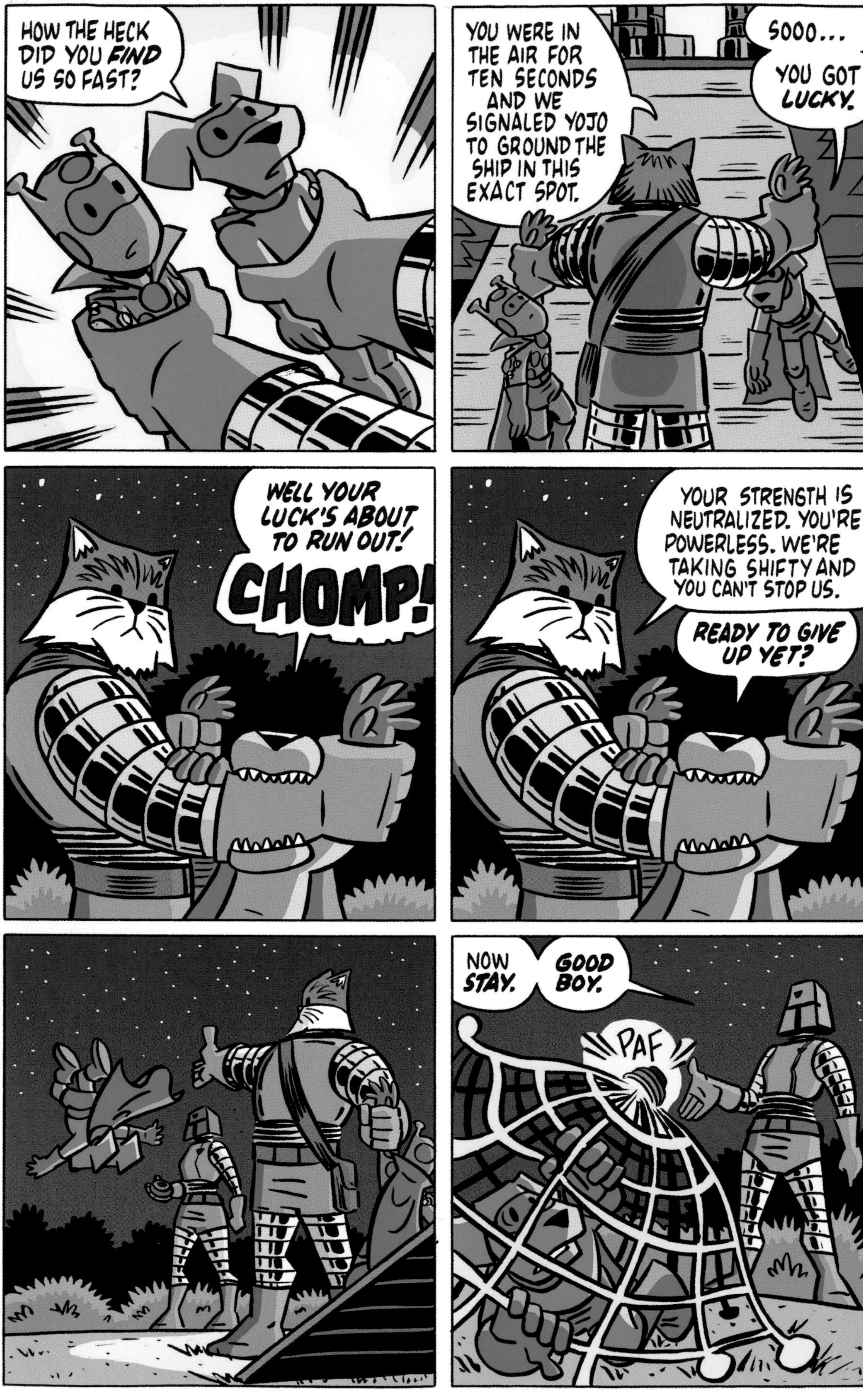
HOW THE HECK DID YOU FIND US SO FAST?
YOU WERE IN THE AIR FOR TEN SECONDS AND WE SIGNALED YOJO TO GROUND THE SHIP IN THIS EXACT SPOT.
SOOO...
YOU GOT LUCKY.
WELL YOUR LUCK'S ABOUT TO RUN OUT!
CHOMP!
YOUR STRENGTH IS NEUTRALIZED. YOU'RE POWERLESS. WE'RE TAKING SHIFTY AND YOU CAN'T STOP US.
READY TO GIVE UP YET?
NOW STAY.
GOOD BOY.
PAF

NO! YOU'RE NOT TAKING MY BEST FRIEND!

I'LL BITE YOUR UGLY SPACE CAT FACES OFF!

BARKO, THERE'S NO WAY OUT OF THIS ONE.

SURRENDER IS THE ONLY OPTION.

AT LEAST THIS WAY I MIGHT FINALLY GET SOME ANSWERS.

TELL KAYLA I SAID GOODBYE.

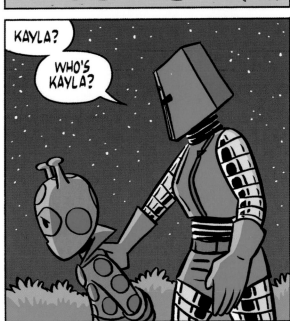

KAYLA?

WHO'S KAYLA?

SHE'S OUR SUPERHERO COACH. SHE WORKS AT THE COMIC SHOP AND KNOWS *EVERYTHING* ABOUT SUPERHEROES.

THE *WORST* PART OF BEING CAPTURED IS FEELING LIKE I'VE LET HER DOWN.

KAYLA FROM THE COMIC SHOP, EH?

HEH HEH HEH.

WHAT? *NO!* DON'T EVEN *THINK* ABOUT HURTING HER!

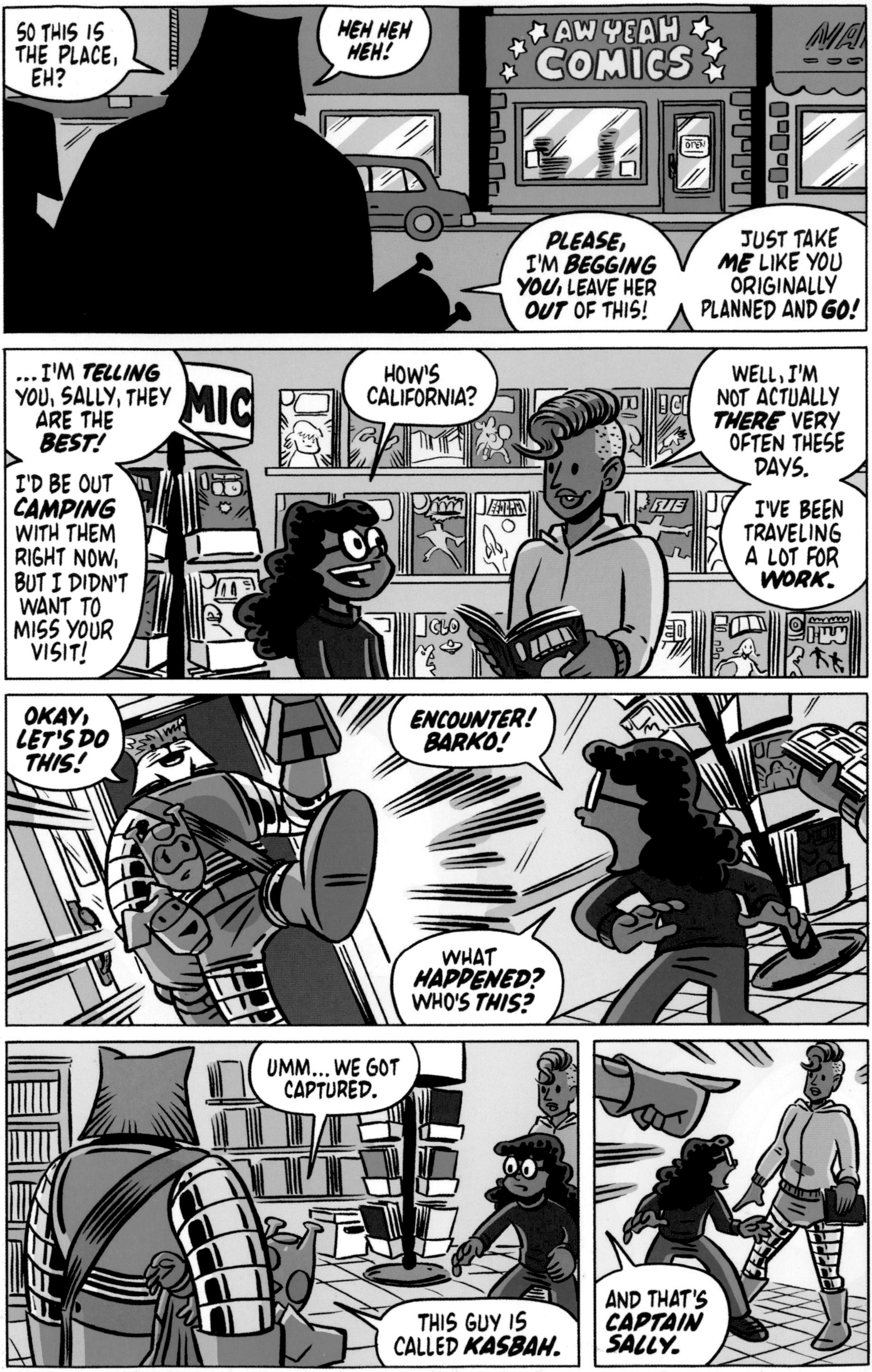
SO THIS IS THE PLACE, EH?
HEH HEH HEH!
AW YEAH COMICS
OPEN
PLEASE, I'M BEGGING YOU, LEAVE HER OUT OF THIS!
JUST TAKE ME LIKE YOU ORIGINALLY PLANNED AND GO!
...I'M TELLING YOU, SALLY, THEY ARE THE BEST!
I'D BE OUT CAMPING WITH THEM RIGHT NOW, BUT I DIDN'T WANT TO MISS YOUR VISIT!
HOW'S CALIFORNIA?
WELL, I'M NOT ACTUALLY THERE VERY OFTEN THESE DAYS.
I'VE BEEN TRAVELING A LOT FOR WORK.
OKAY, LET'S DO THIS!
ENCOUNTER! BARKO!
WHAT HAPPENED? WHO'S THIS?
UMM... WE GOT CAPTURED.
THIS GUY IS CALLED KASBAH.
AND THAT'S CAPTAIN SALLY.

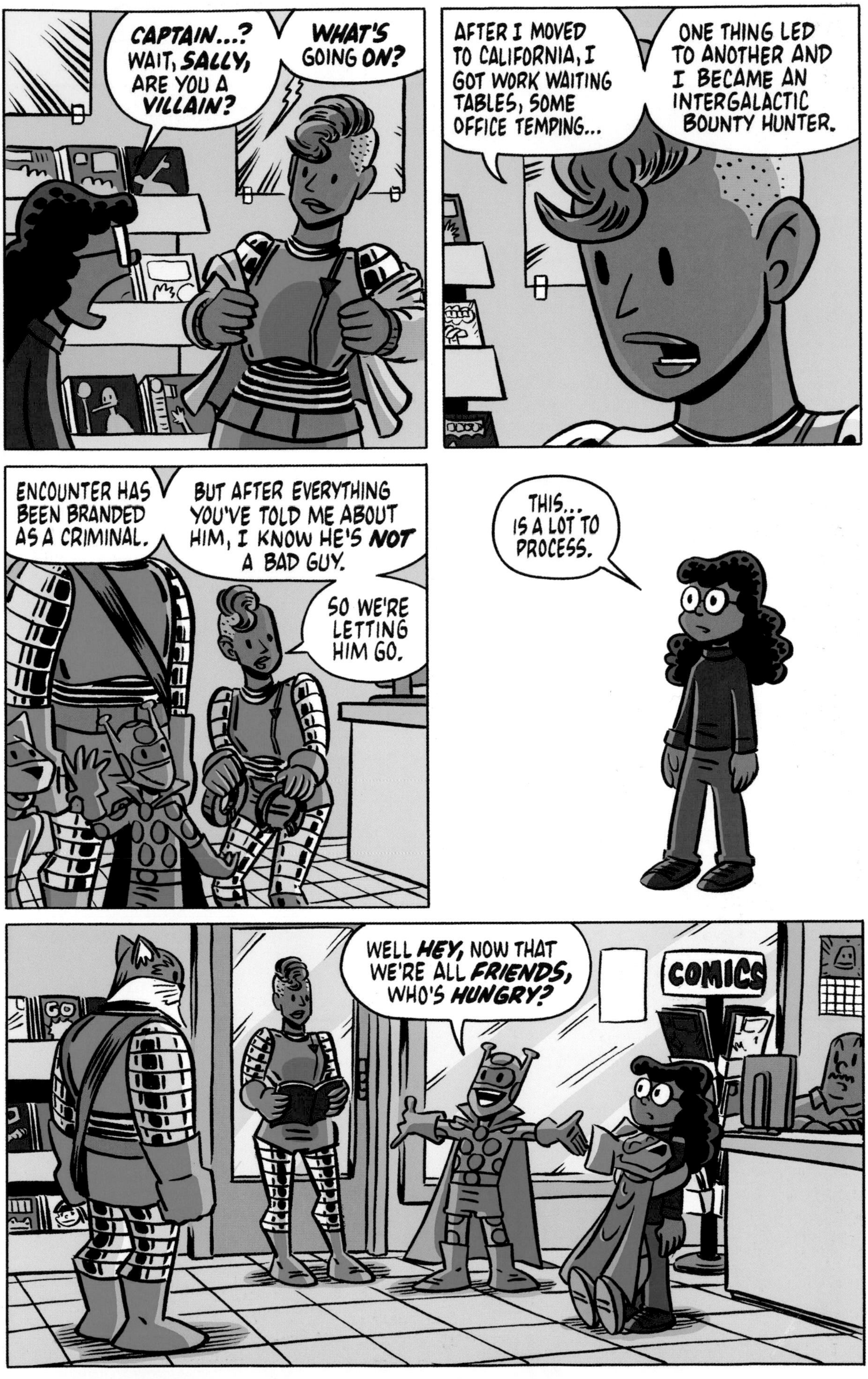
CAPTAIN...? WAIT, SALLY, ARE YOU A VILLAIN?
WHAT'S GOING ON?
AFTER I MOVED TO CALIFORNIA, I GOT WORK WAITING TABLES, SOME OFFICE TEMPING...
ONE THING LED TO ANOTHER AND I BECAME AN INTERGALACTIC BOUNTY HUNTER.
ENCOUNTER HAS BEEN BRANDED AS A CRIMINAL.
BUT AFTER EVERYTHING YOU'VE TOLD ME ABOUT HIM, I KNOW HE'S NOT A BAD GUY.
SO WE'RE LETTING HIM GO.
THIS... IS A LOT TO PROCESS.
WELL HEY, NOW THAT WE'RE ALL FRIENDS, WHO'S HUNGRY?
COMICS
GO

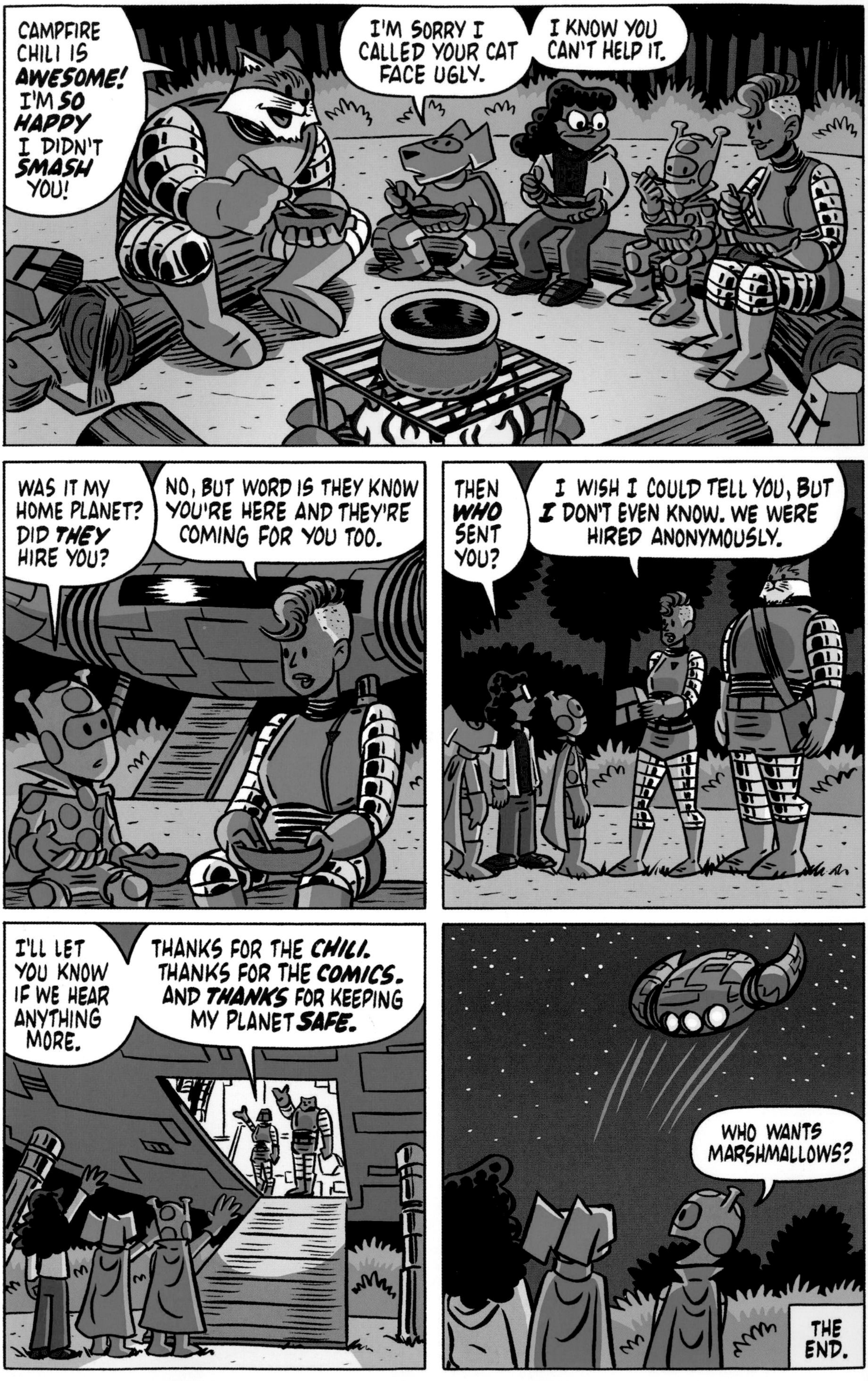
CAMPFIRE CHILI IS AWESOME! I'M SO HAPPY I DIDN'T SMASH YOU!
I'M SORRY I CALLED YOUR CAT FACE UGLY.
I KNOW YOU CAN'T HELP IT.
WAS IT MY HOME PLANET? DID THEY HIRE YOU?
NO, BUT WORD IS THEY KNOW YOU'RE HERE AND THEY'RE COMING FOR YOU TOO.
THEN WHO SENT YOU?
I WISH I COULD TELL YOU, BUT I DON'T EVEN KNOW. WE WERE HIRED ANONYMOUSLY.
I'LL LET YOU KNOW IF WE HEAR ANYTHING MORE.
THANKS FOR THE CHILI. THANKS FOR THE COMICS. AND THANKS FOR KEEPING MY PLANET SAFE.
WHO WANTS MARSHMALLOWS?
THE END.

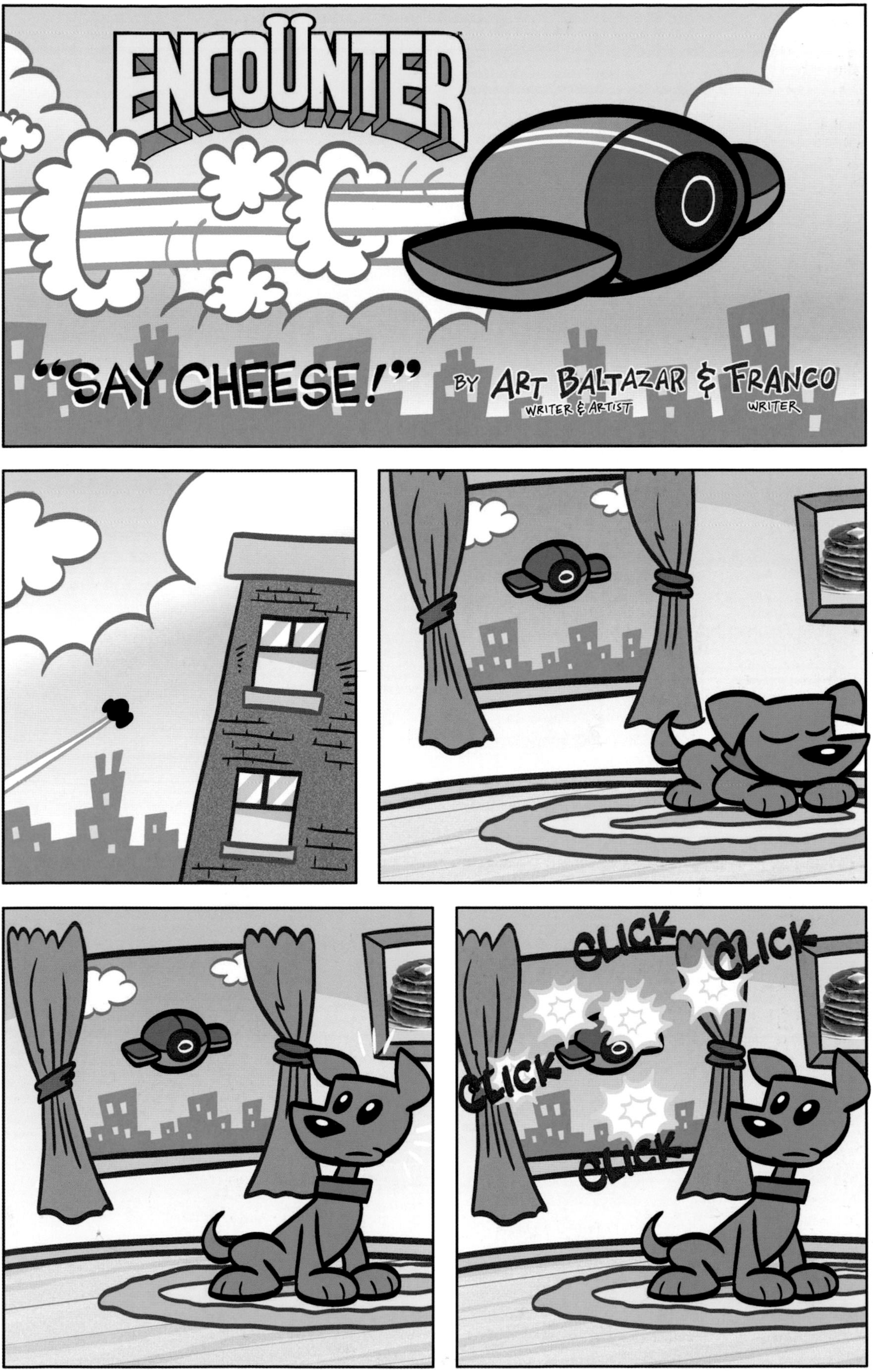

ENCOUNTER™
"SAY CHEESE!"
BY ART BALTAZAR WRITER & ARTIST & FRANCO WRITER
CLICK
CLICK
CLICK
CLICK

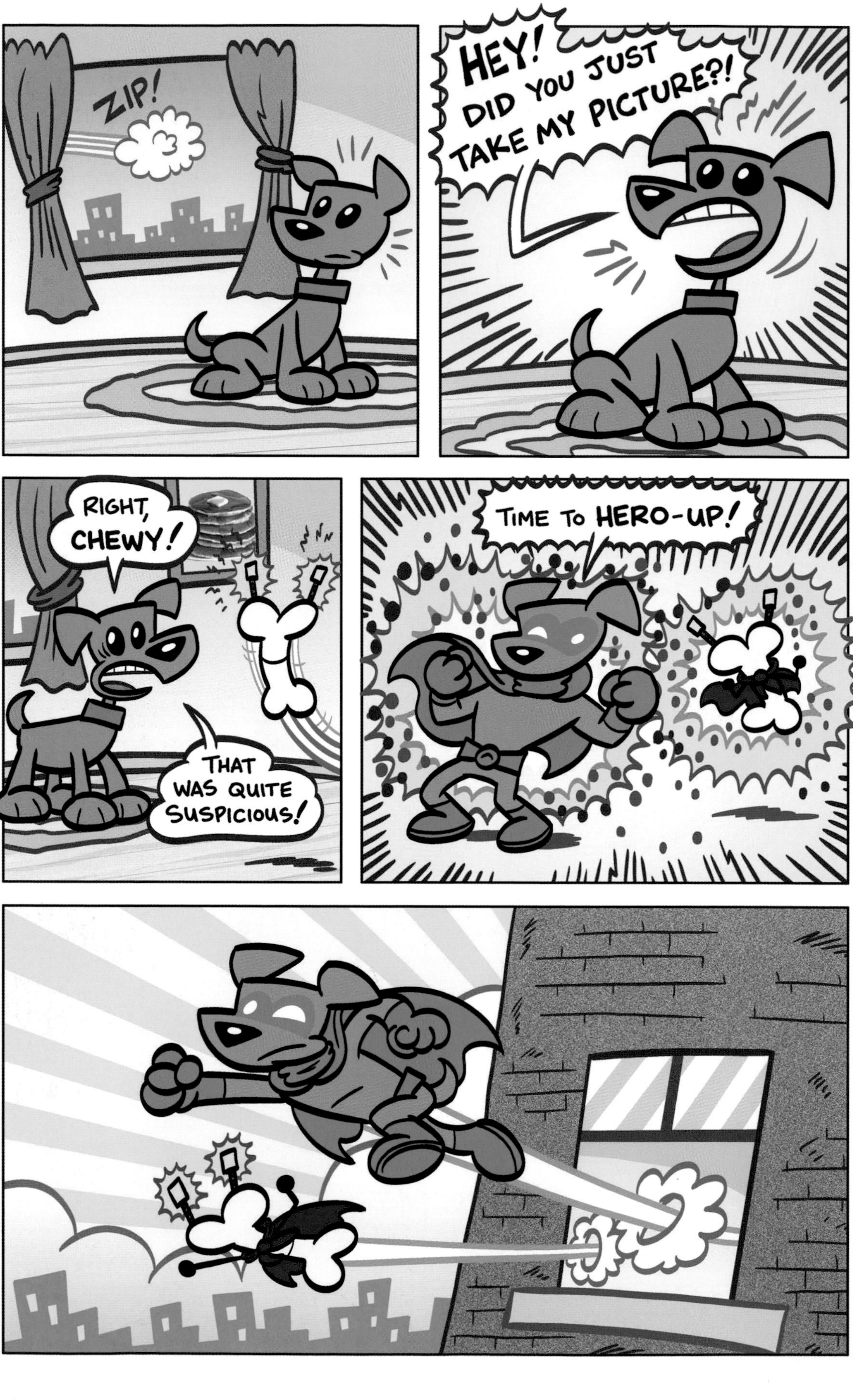
ZIP!
HEY! DID YOU JUST TAKE MY PICTURE?!
RIGHT, CHEWY!
THAT WAS QUITE SUSPICIOUS!
TIME TO HERO-UP!

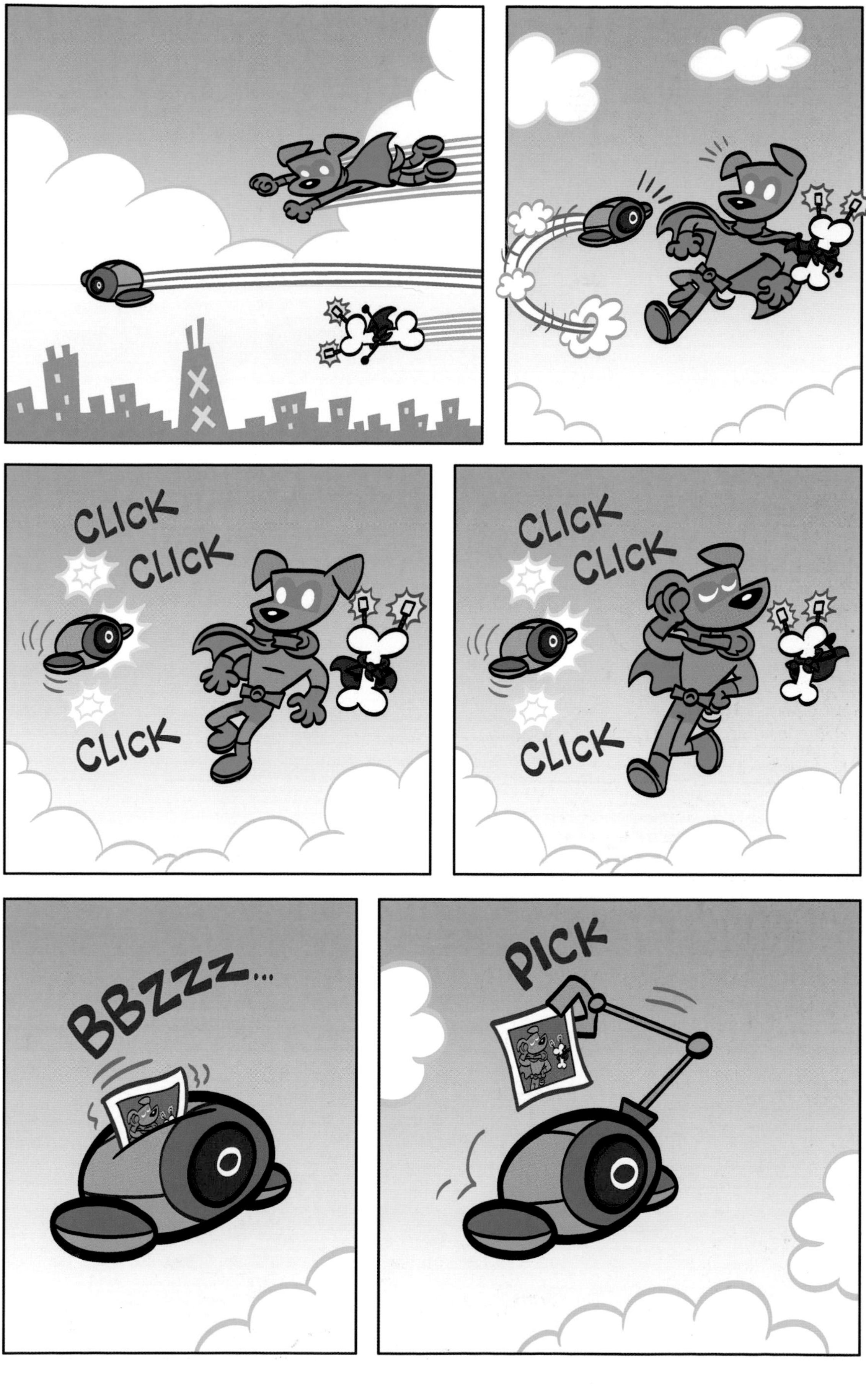
CLICK
CLICK
CLICK
CLICK
CLICK
CLICK
BBZZZ...
PICK

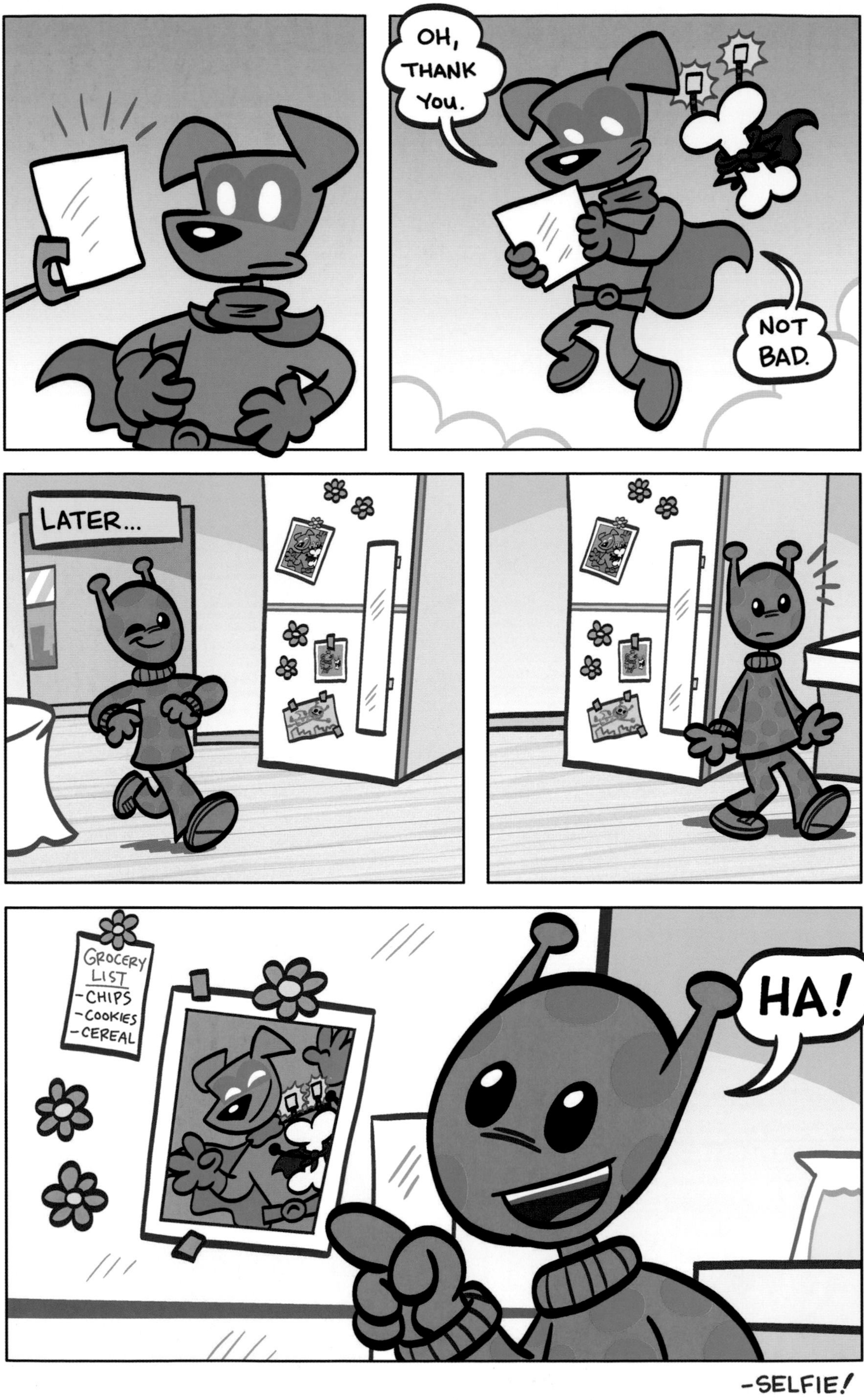
OH, THANK YOU.
NOT BAD.
LATER...
GROCERY LIST
-CHIPS
-COOKIES
-CEREAL
HA!

-SELFIE!

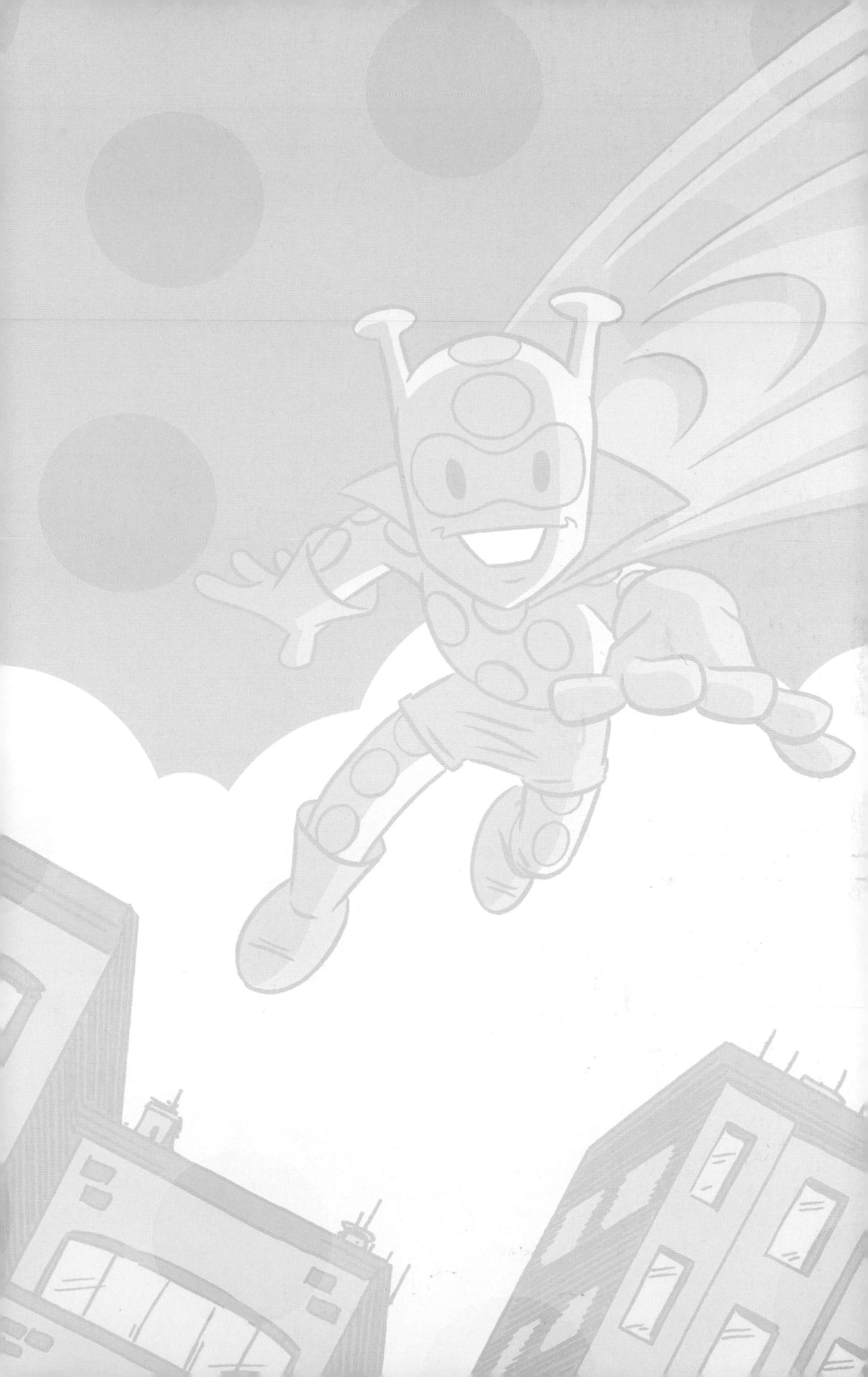

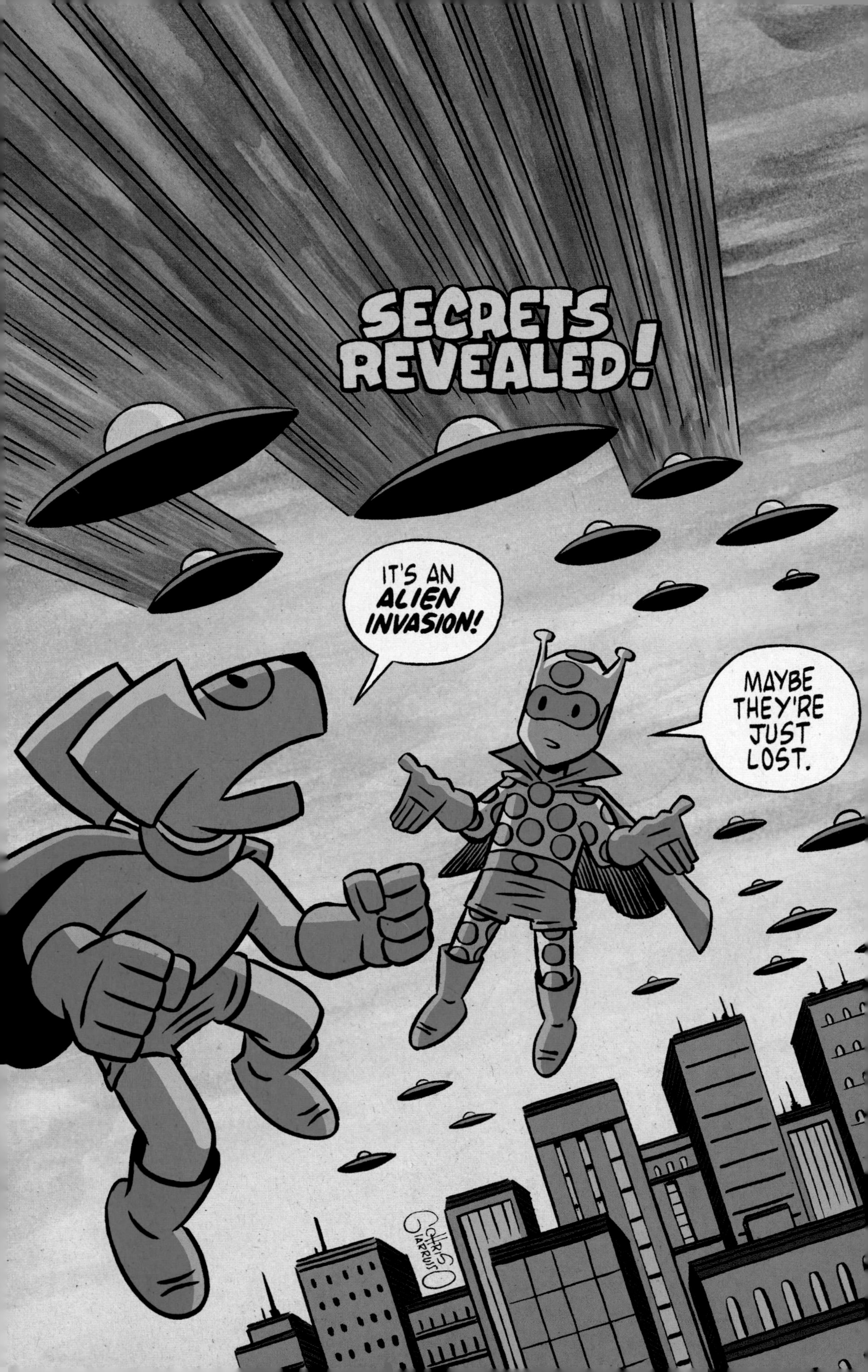
SECRETS REVEALED!
IT'S AN ALIEN INVASION!
MAYBE THEY'RE JUST LOST.
CHRIS GIARRUSSO

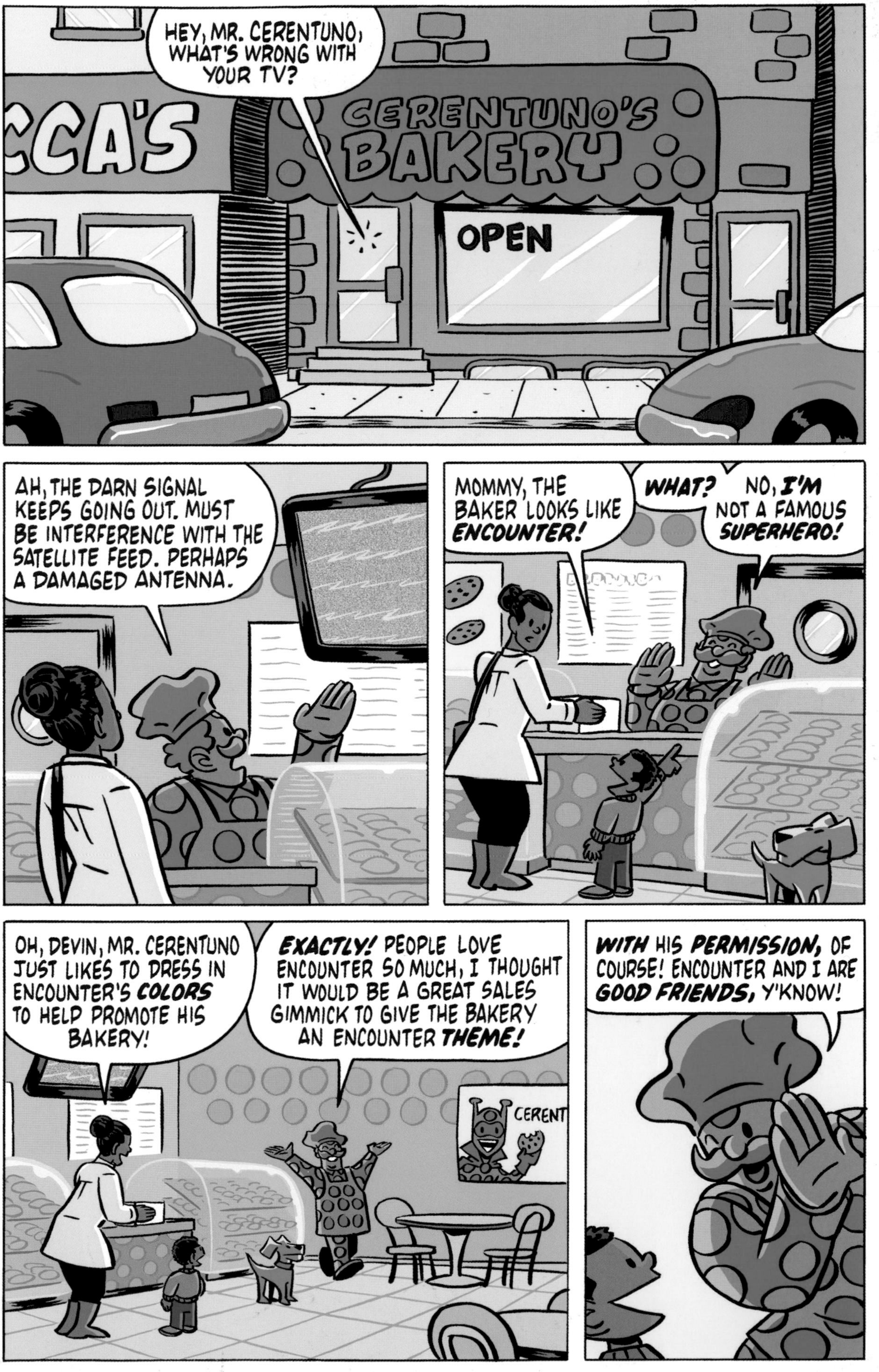
HEY, MR. CERENTUNO, WHAT'S WRONG WITH YOUR TV?
CCA'S
CERENTUNO'S BAKERY
OPEN
AH, THE DARN SIGNAL KEEPS GOING OUT. MUST BE INTERFERENCE WITH THE SATELLITE FEED. PERHAPS A DAMAGED ANTENNA.
MOMMY, THE BAKER LOOKS LIKE ENCOUNTER!
WHAT? NO, I'M NOT A FAMOUS SUPERHERO!
OH, DEVIN, MR. CERENTUNO JUST LIKES TO DRESS IN ENCOUNTER'S COLORS TO HELP PROMOTE HIS BAKERY!
EXACTLY! PEOPLE LOVE ENCOUNTER SO MUCH, I THOUGHT IT WOULD BE A GREAT SALES GIMMICK TO GIVE THE BAKERY AN ENCOUNTER THEME!
CERENT
WITH HIS PERMISSION, OF COURSE! ENCOUNTER AND I ARE GOOD FRIENDS, Y'KNOW!

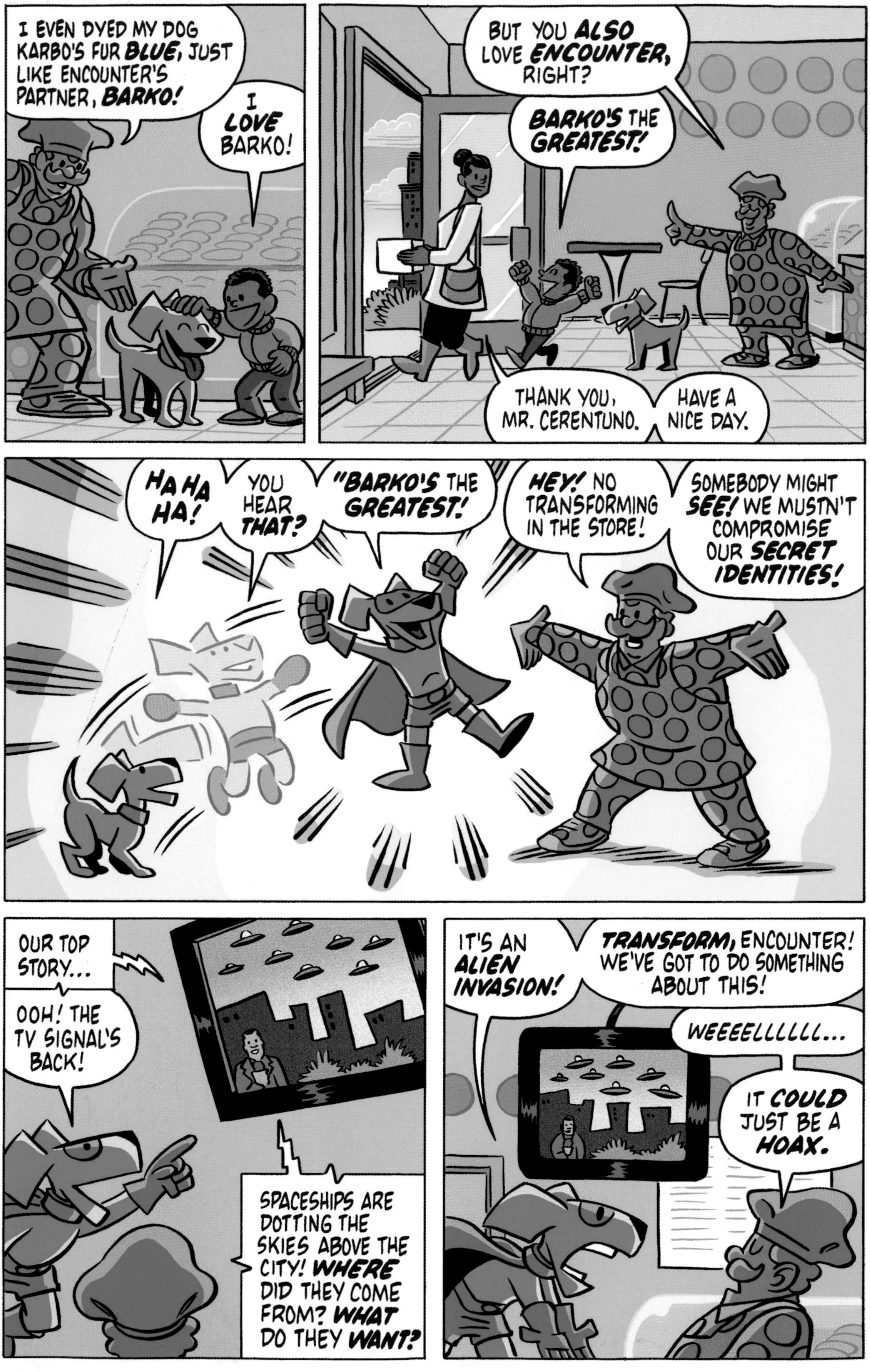
I EVEN DYED MY DOG KARBO'S FUR BLUE, JUST LIKE ENCOUNTER'S PARTNER, BARKO!
I LOVE BARKO!
BUT YOU ALSO LOVE ENCOUNTER, RIGHT?
BARKO'S THE GREATEST!
THANK YOU, MR. CERENTUNO.
HAVE A NICE DAY.
HA HA HA!
YOU HEAR THAT?
"BARKO'S THE GREATEST!
HEY! NO TRANSFORMING IN THE STORE!
SOMEBODY MIGHT SEE! WE MUSTN'T COMPROMISE OUR SECRET IDENTITIES!
OUR TOP STORY...
OOH! THE TV SIGNAL'S BACK!
SPACESHIPS ARE DOTTING THE SKIES ABOVE THE CITY! WHERE DID THEY COME FROM? WHAT DO THEY WANT?
IT'S AN ALIEN INVASION!
TRANSFORM, ENCOUNTER! WE'VE GOT TO DO SOMETHING ABOUT THIS!
WEEEELLLLLL...
IT COULD JUST BE A HOAX.

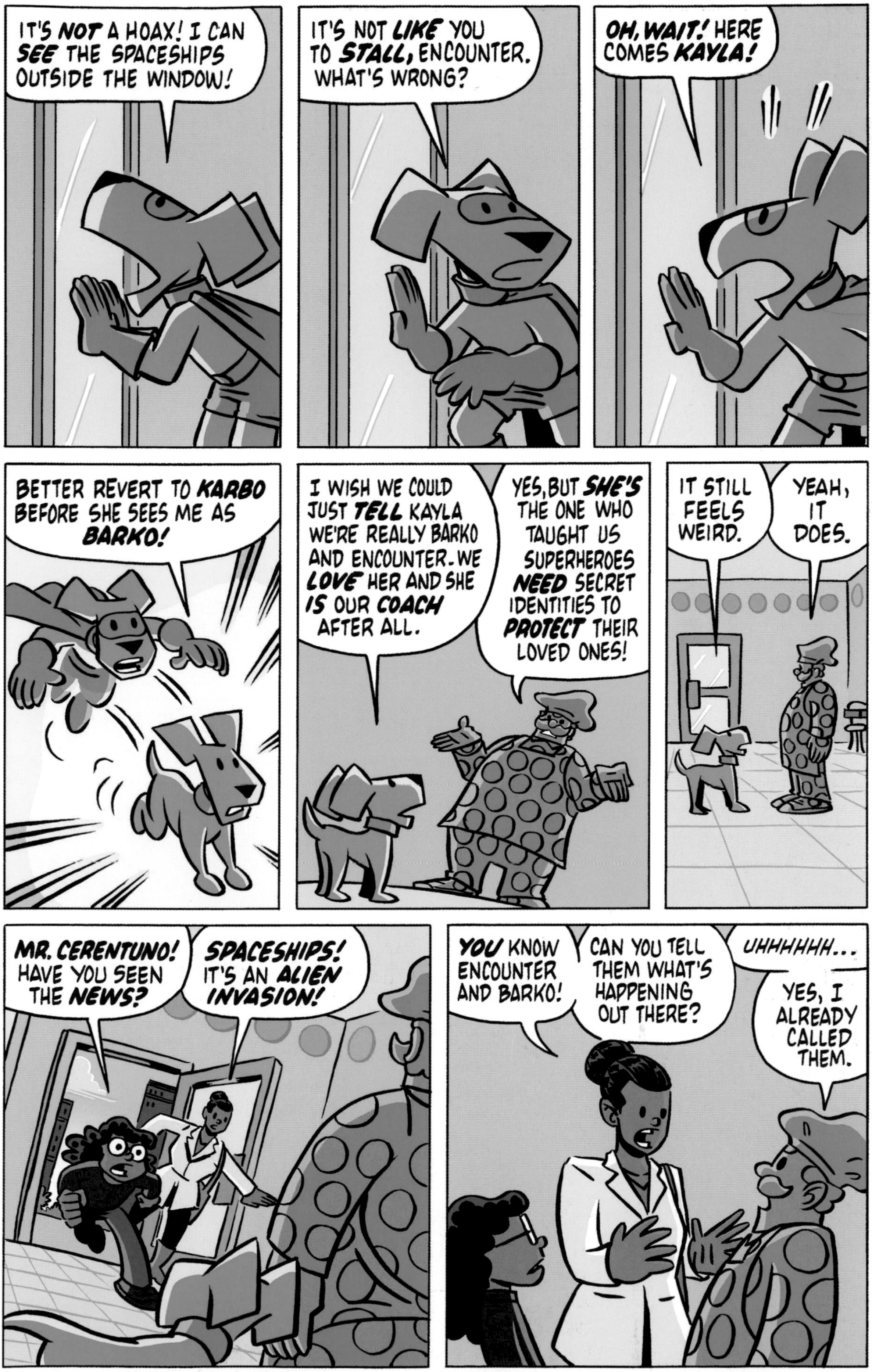
IT'S NOT A HOAX! I CAN SEE THE SPACESHIPS OUTSIDE THE WINDOW!
IT'S NOT LIKE YOU TO STALL, ENCOUNTER. WHAT'S WRONG?
OH, WAIT! HERE COMES KAYLA!
BETTER REVERT TO KARBO BEFORE SHE SEES ME AS BARKO!
I WISH WE COULD JUST TELL KAYLA WE'RE REALLY BARKO AND ENCOUNTER. WE LOVE HER AND SHE IS OUR COACH AFTER ALL.
YES, BUT SHE'S THE ONE WHO TAUGHT US SUPERHEROES NEED SECRET IDENTITIES TO PROTECT THEIR LOVED ONES!
IT STILL FEELS WEIRD.
YEAH, IT DOES.
MR. CERENTUNO! HAVE YOU SEEN THE NEWS?
SPACESHIPS! IT'S AN ALIEN INVASION!
YOU KNOW ENCOUNTER AND BARKO!
CAN YOU TELL THEM WHAT'S HAPPENING OUT THERE?
UHHHHHH...
YES, I ALREADY CALLED THEM.

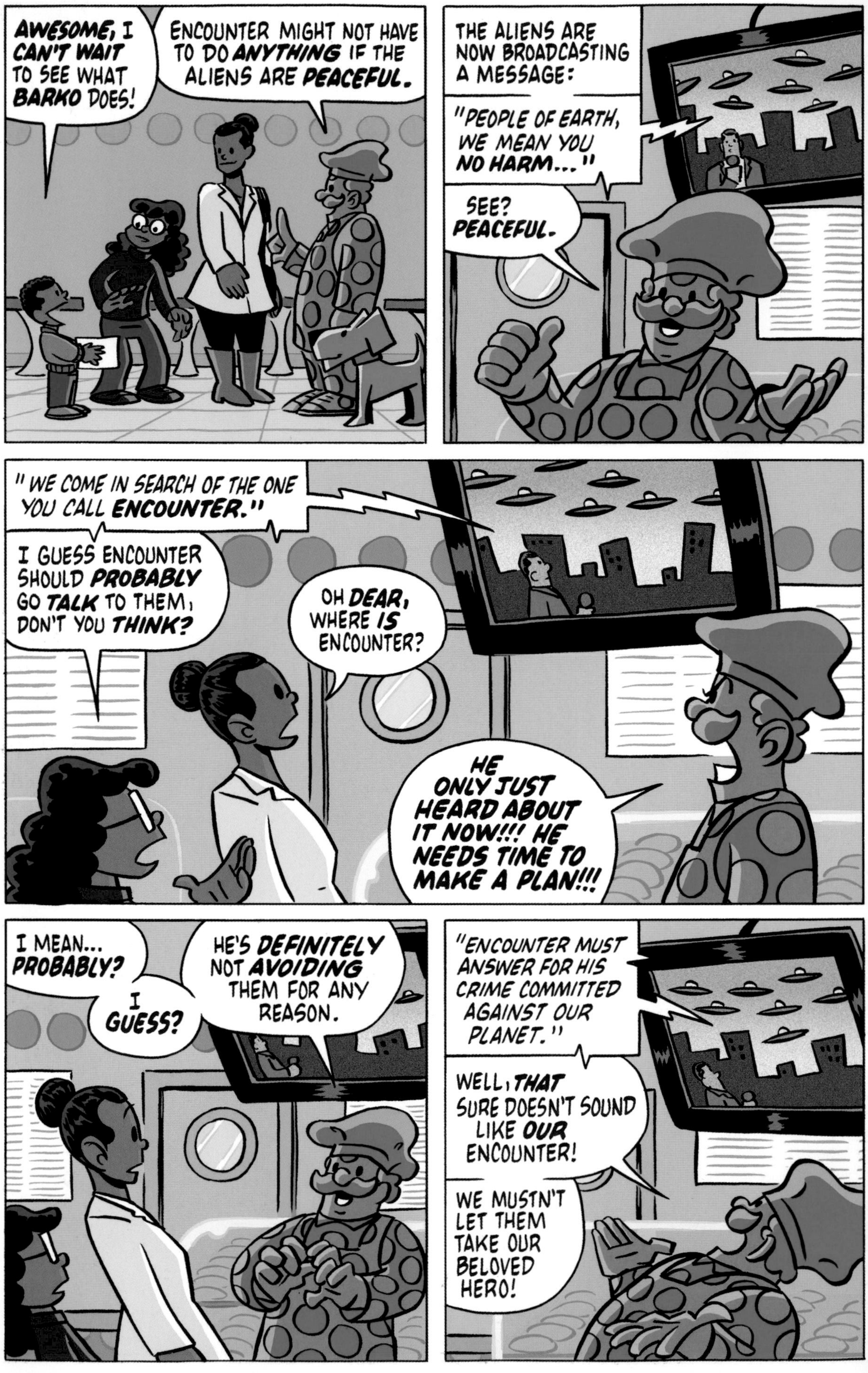
AWESOME, I CAN'T WAIT TO SEE WHAT BARKO DOES!
ENCOUNTER MIGHT NOT HAVE TO DO ANYTHING IF THE ALIENS ARE PEACEFUL.
THE ALIENS ARE NOW BROADCASTING A MESSAGE:
"PEOPLE OF EARTH, WE MEAN YOU NO HARM..."
SEE? PEACEFUL.
"WE COME IN SEARCH OF THE ONE YOU CALL ENCOUNTER."
I GUESS ENCOUNTER SHOULD PROBABLY GO TALK TO THEM, DON'T YOU THINK?
OH DEAR, WHERE IS ENCOUNTER?
HE ONLY JUST HEARD ABOUT IT NOW!!! HE NEEDS TIME TO MAKE A PLAN!!!
I MEAN... PROBABLY?
I GUESS?
HE'S DEFINITELY NOT AVOIDING THEM FOR ANY REASON.
"ENCOUNTER MUST ANSWER FOR HIS CRIME COMMITTED AGAINST OUR PLANET."
WELL, THAT SURE DOESN'T SOUND LIKE OUR ENCOUNTER!
WE MUSTN'T LET THEM TAKE OUR BELOVED HERO!

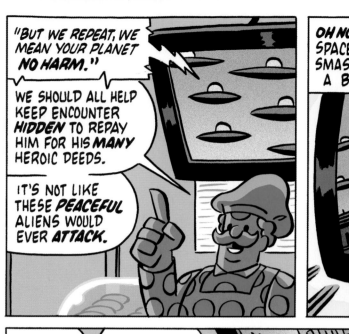

"BUT WE REPEAT, WE MEAN YOUR PLANET **NO HARM**."

WE SHOULD ALL HELP KEEP ENCOUNTER **HIDDEN** TO REPAY HIM FOR HIS **MANY** HEROIC DEEDS.

IT'S NOT LIKE THESE **PEACEFUL** ALIENS WOULD EVER **ATTACK**.

OH NO! ONE OF THE SPACESHIPS HAS JUST SMASHED INTO A BUILDING!

WELL, SO MUCH FOR "**NO HARM**"!

OH, I JUST REMEMBERED I HAVE TO... UM...

... GET A BATCH OF **DONUTS** FROM THE BACK HERE!

WE ARE UNDER ATTACK! POLICE URGE CITIZENS TO EVACUATE THE CITY!

LET'S GET **OUT** OF HERE, FOLKS!

I'LL HELP YOU GET TO SAFETY!

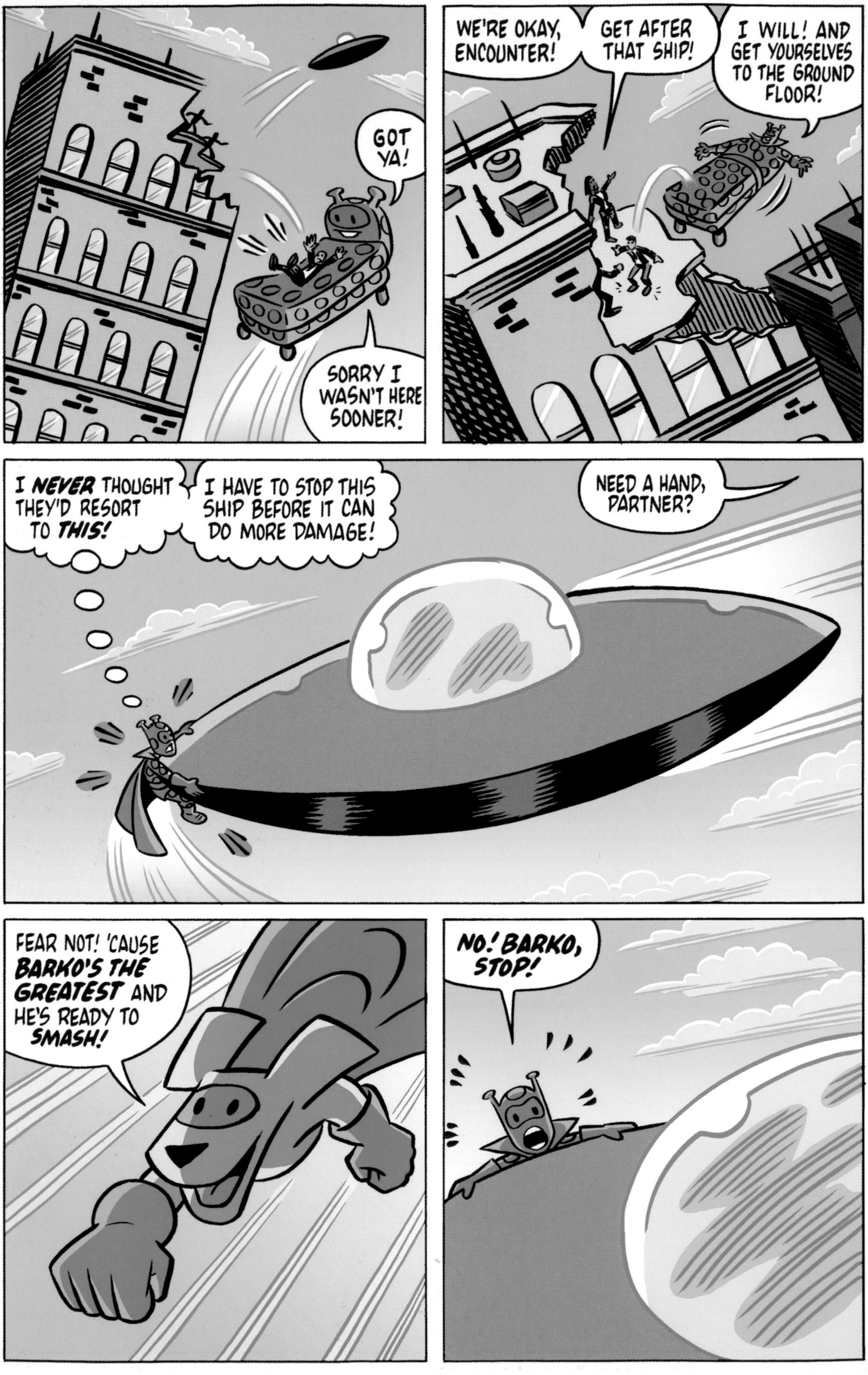
GOT YA!
SORRY I WASN'T HERE SOONER!
WE'RE OKAY, ENCOUNTER!
GET AFTER THAT SHIP!
I WILL! AND GET YOURSELVES TO THE GROUND FLOOR!
I NEVER THOUGHT THEY'D RESORT TO THIS!
I HAVE TO STOP THIS SHIP BEFORE IT CAN DO MORE DAMAGE!
NEED A HAND, PARTNER?
FEAR NOT! 'CAUSE BARKO'S THE GREATEST AND HE'S READY TO SMASH!
NO! BARKO, STOP!

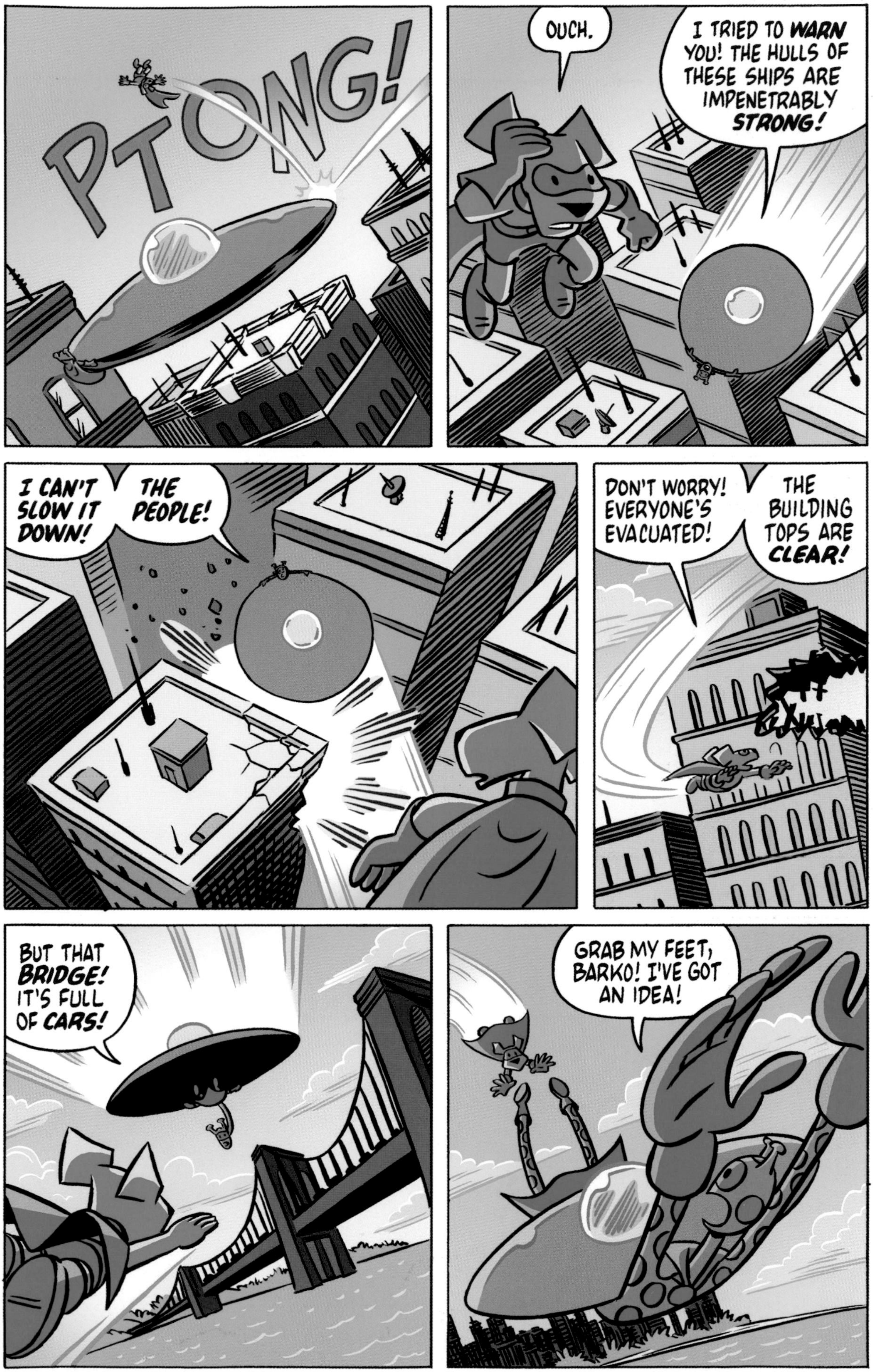
PTONG!
OUCH.
I TRIED TO WARN YOU! THE HULLS OF THESE SHIPS ARE IMPENETRABLY STRONG!
I CAN'T SLOW IT DOWN!
THE PEOPLE!
DON'T WORRY! EVERYONE'S EVACUATED!
THE BUILDING TOPS ARE CLEAR!
BUT THAT BRIDGE! IT'S FULL OF CARS!
GRAB MY FEET, BARKO! I'VE GOT AN IDEA!

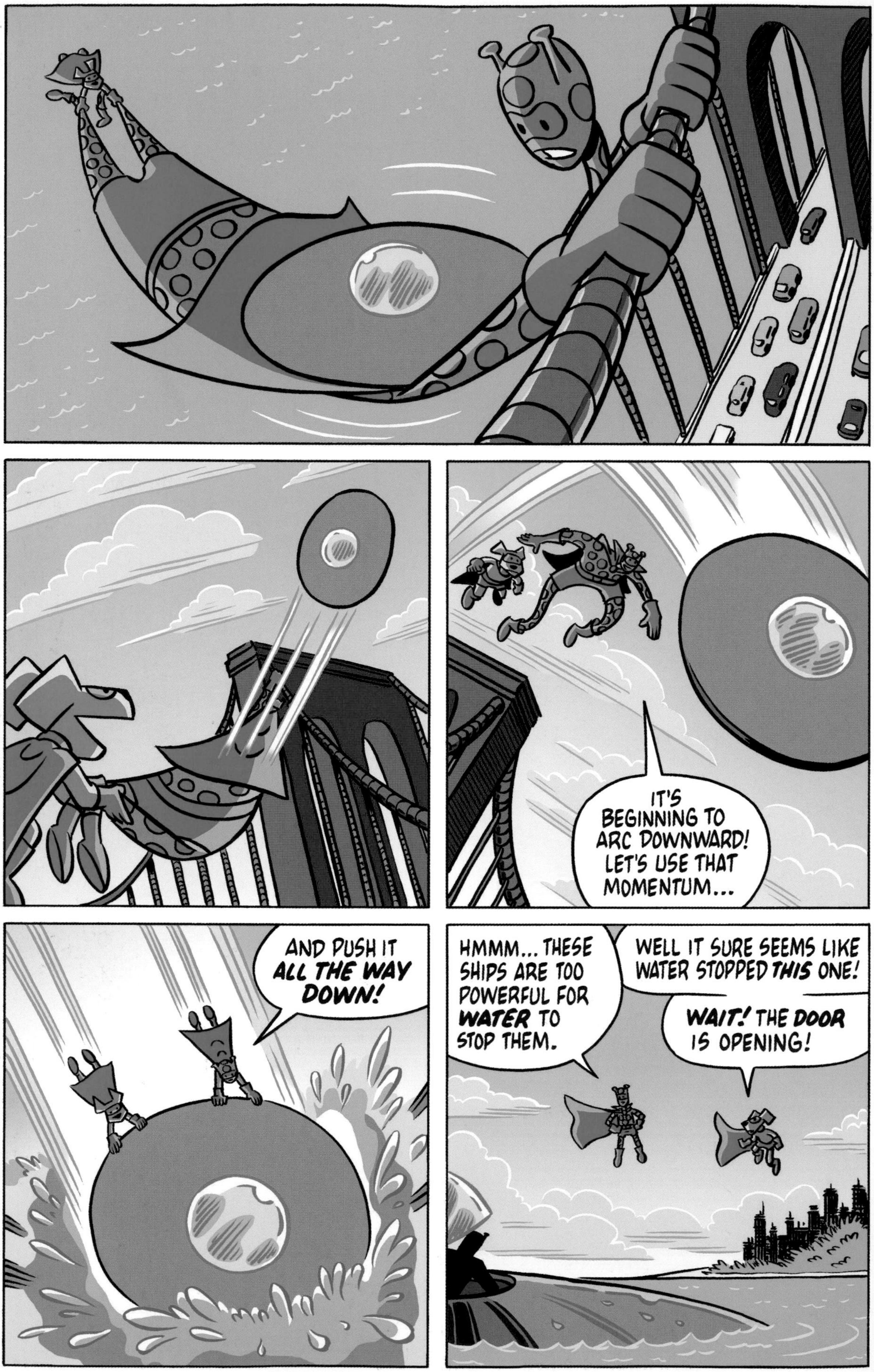
IT'S BEGINNING TO ARC DOWNWARD! LET'S USE THAT MOMENTUM...
AND PUSH IT ALL THE WAY DOWN!
HMMM... THESE SHIPS ARE TOO POWERFUL FOR WATER TO STOP THEM.
WELL IT SURE SEEMS LIKE WATER STOPPED THIS ONE!
WAIT! THE DOOR IS OPENING!

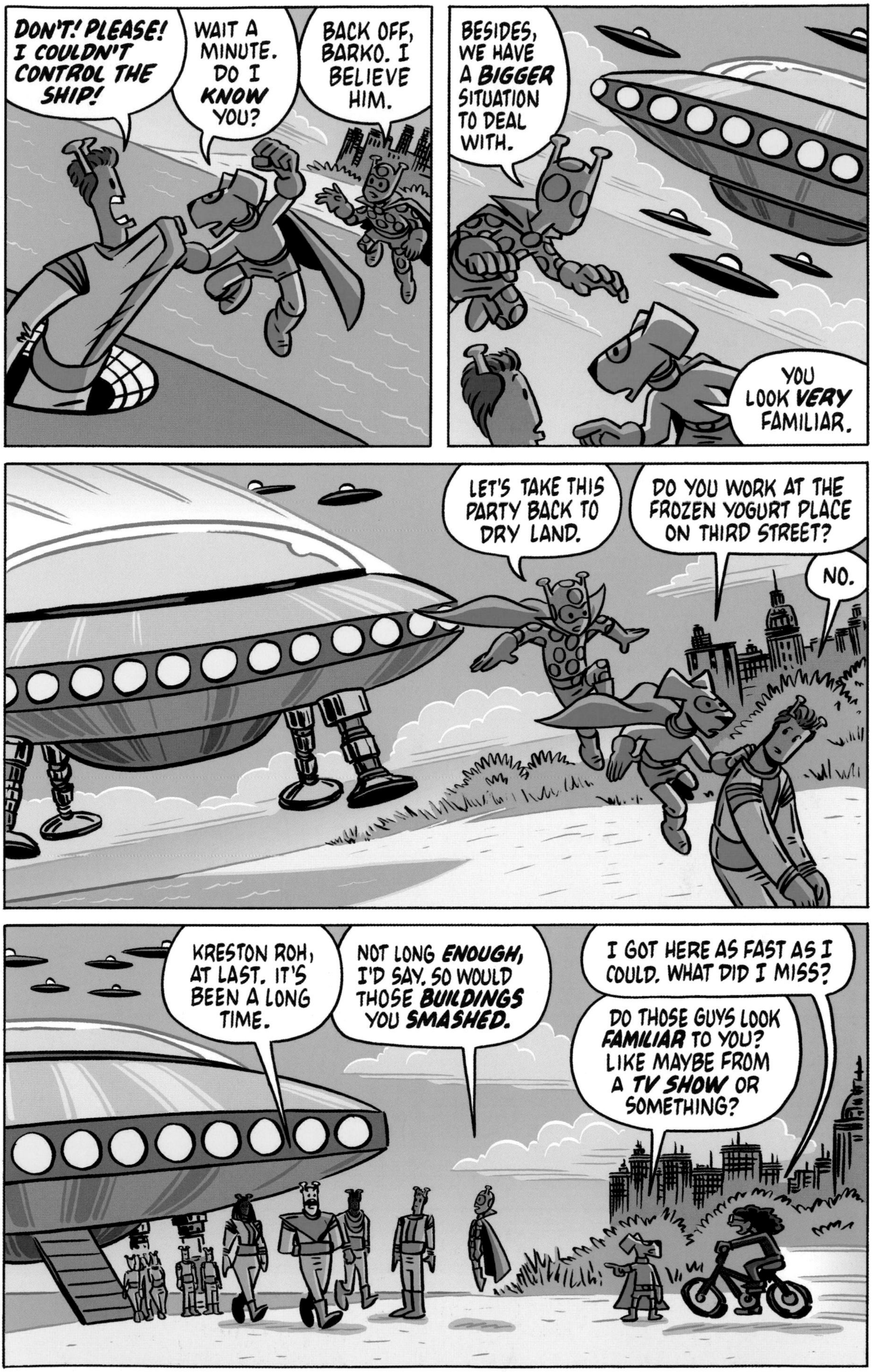
DON'T! PLEASE! I COULDN'T CONTROL THE SHIP!
WAIT A MINUTE. DO I KNOW YOU?
BACK OFF, BARKO. I BELIEVE HIM.
BESIDES, WE HAVE A BIGGER SITUATION TO DEAL WITH.
YOU LOOK VERY FAMILIAR.
LET'S TAKE THIS PARTY BACK TO DRY LAND.
DO YOU WORK AT THE FROZEN YOGURT PLACE ON THIRD STREET?
NO.
KRESTON ROH, AT LAST. IT'S BEEN A LONG TIME.
NOT LONG ENOUGH, I'D SAY. SO WOULD THOSE BUILDINGS YOU SMASHED.
I GOT HERE AS FAST AS I COULD. WHAT DID I MISS?
DO THOSE GUYS LOOK FAMILIAR TO YOU? LIKE MAYBE FROM A TV SHOW OR SOMETHING?

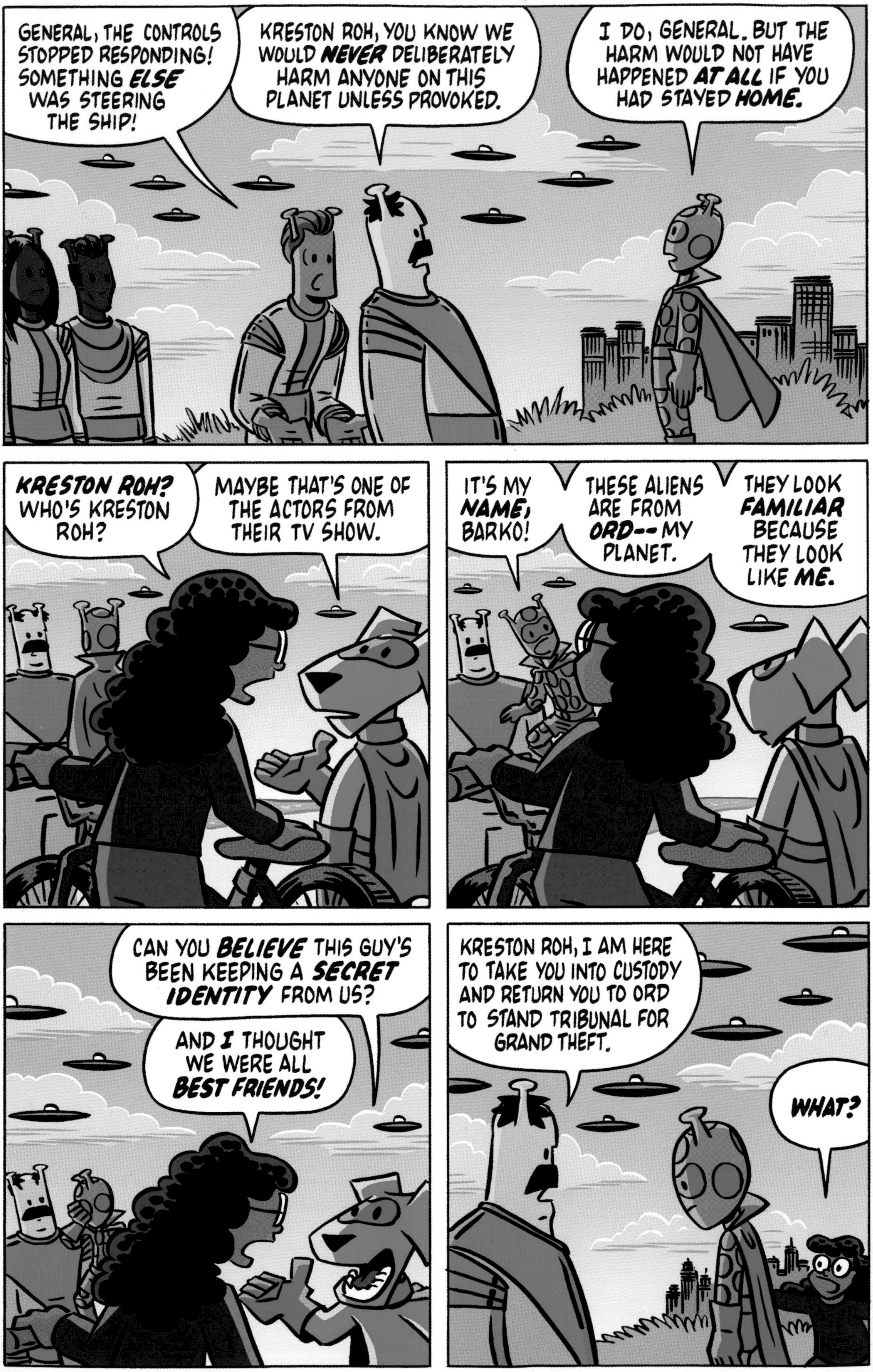
GENERAL, THE CONTROLS STOPPED RESPONDING! SOMETHING ELSE WAS STEERING THE SHIP!
KRESTON ROH, YOU KNOW WE WOULD NEVER DELIBERATELY HARM ANYONE ON THIS PLANET UNLESS PROVOKED.
I DO, GENERAL. BUT THE HARM WOULD NOT HAVE HAPPENED AT ALL IF YOU HAD STAYED HOME.
KRESTON ROH? WHO'S KRESTON ROH?
MAYBE THAT'S ONE OF THE ACTORS FROM THEIR TV SHOW.
IT'S MY NAME, BARKO!
THESE ALIENS ARE FROM ORD-- MY PLANET.
THEY LOOK FAMILIAR BECAUSE THEY LOOK LIKE ME.
CAN YOU BELIEVE THIS GUY'S BEEN KEEPING A SECRET IDENTITY FROM US?
AND I THOUGHT WE WERE ALL BEST FRIENDS!
KRESTON ROH, I AM HERE TO TAKE YOU INTO CUSTODY AND RETURN YOU TO ORD TO STAND TRIBUNAL FOR GRAND THEFT.
WHAT?

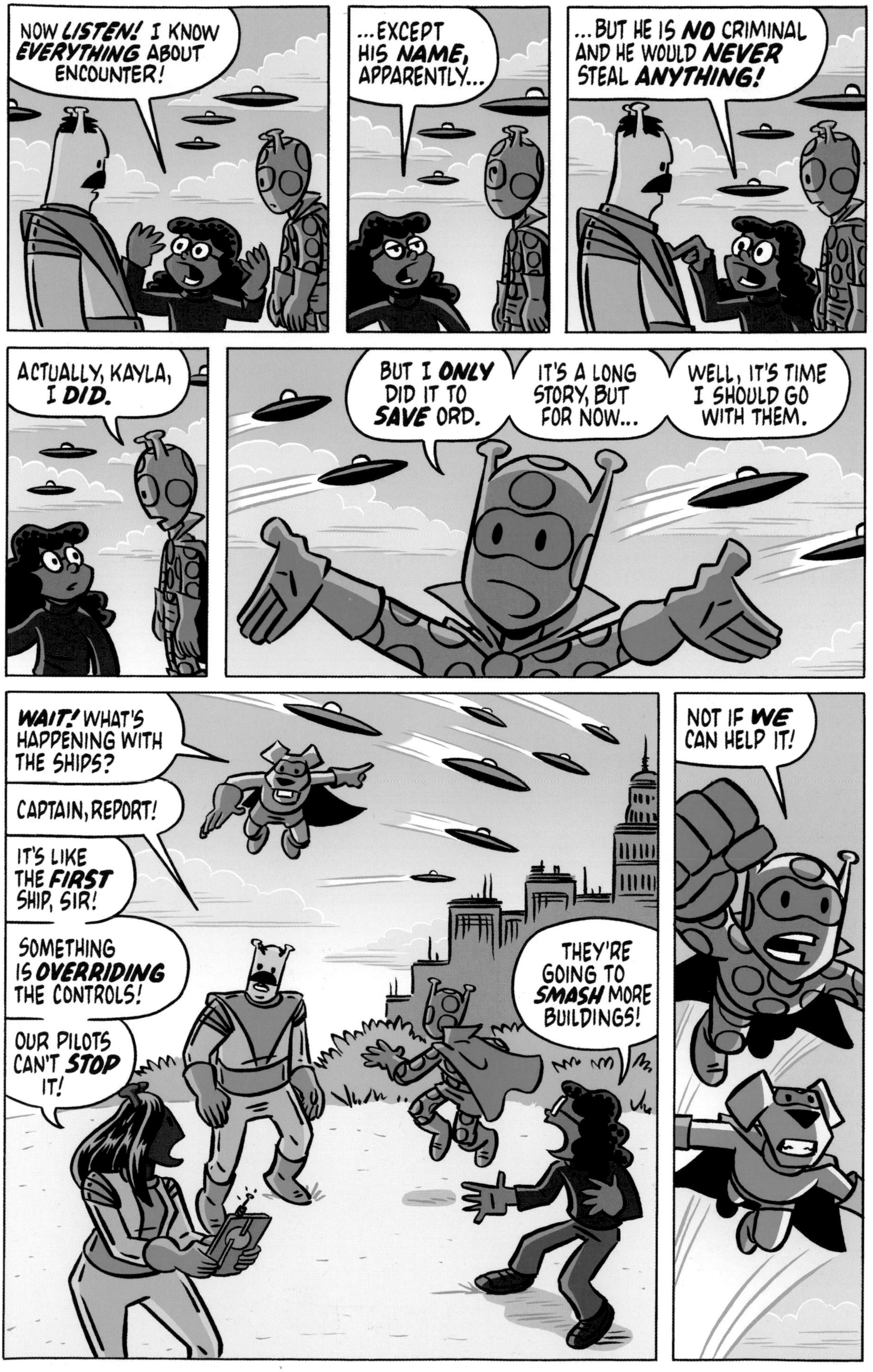
NOW LISTEN! I KNOW EVERYTHING ABOUT ENCOUNTER!
...EXCEPT HIS NAME, APPARENTLY...
...BUT HE IS NO CRIMINAL AND HE WOULD NEVER STEAL ANYTHING!
ACTUALLY, KAYLA, I DID.
BUT I ONLY DID IT TO SAVE ORD.
IT'S A LONG STORY, BUT FOR NOW...
WELL, IT'S TIME I SHOULD GO WITH THEM.
WAIT! WHAT'S HAPPENING WITH THE SHIPS?
CAPTAIN, REPORT!
IT'S LIKE THE FIRST SHIP, SIR!
SOMETHING IS OVERRIDING THE CONTROLS!
OUR PILOTS CAN'T STOP IT!
THEY'RE GOING TO SMASH MORE BUILDINGS!
NOT IF WE CAN HELP IT!

SO... HE FLIES OFF INTO DANGER WHEN OTHERS ARE IN TROUBLE.

SHOULDN'T *YOU* BE DOING THE *SAME?* THEY'RE *YOUR* SHIPS!

ONLY KRESTON ROH HAS SUPERPOWERS. THE *REST* OF US ORDANS DO *NOT.*

OH. I'D ALWAYS ASSUMED ENCOUNTER'S POWERS WERE A NATURAL PART OF HIS ALIEN HERITAGE.

SO HOW'D HE GET POWERS?

KRESTON WAS PART OF A SERIES OF *EXPERIMENTS* INVOLVING POWERFUL *ENERGY PODS.*

THEY GAVE HIM INCREDIBLE *POWERS,* BUT AT TERRIBLE *CONSEQUENCE!* KRESTON WAS LEFT WITH THOSE HORRIFYINGLY UGLY *SPOTS* ALL OVER HIS BODY!

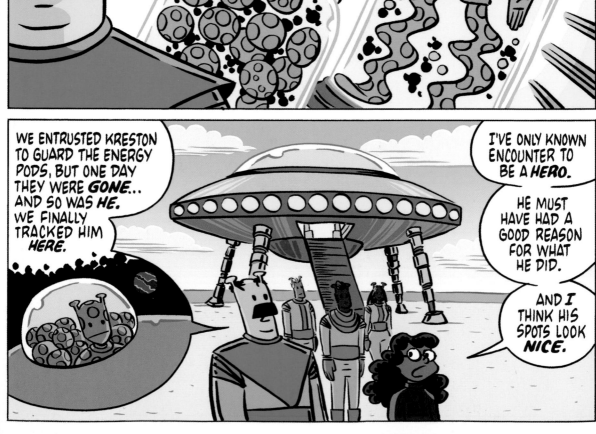

WE ENTRUSTED KRESTON TO GUARD THE ENERGY PODS, BUT ONE DAY THEY WERE *GONE...* AND SO WAS *HE.* WE FINALLY TRACKED HIM *HERE.*

I'VE ONLY KNOWN ENCOUNTER TO BE A *HERO.*

HE MUST HAVE HAD A GOOD REASON FOR WHAT HE DID.

AND *I* THINK HIS SPOTS LOOK *NICE.*

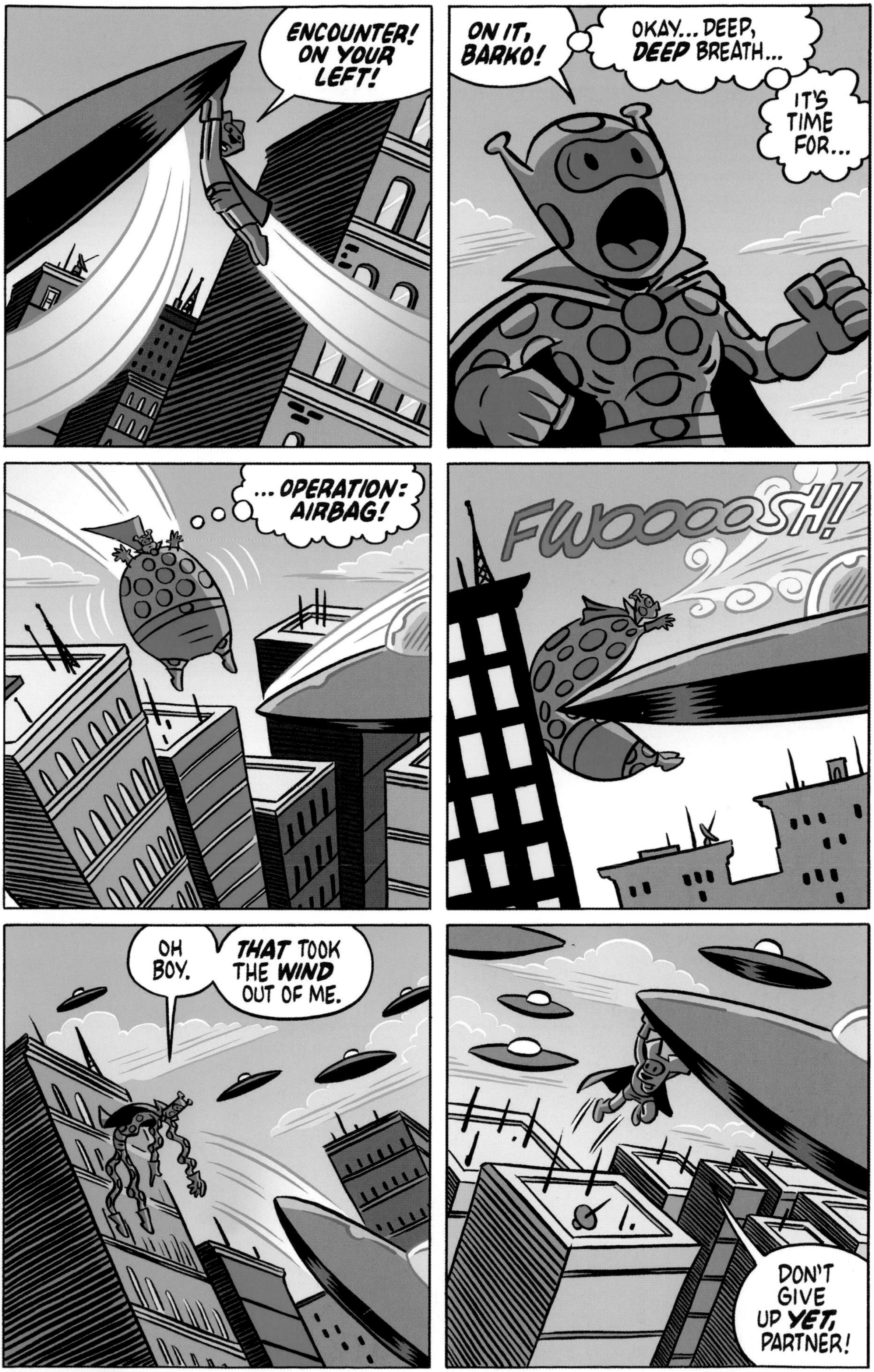
ENCOUNTER! ON YOUR LEFT!
ON IT, BARKO!
OKAY... DEEP, DEEP BREATH...
IT'S TIME FOR...
... OPERATION: AIRBAG!
FWOOOOOSH!
OH BOY.
THAT TOOK THE WIND OUT OF ME.
DON'T GIVE UP YET, PARTNER!

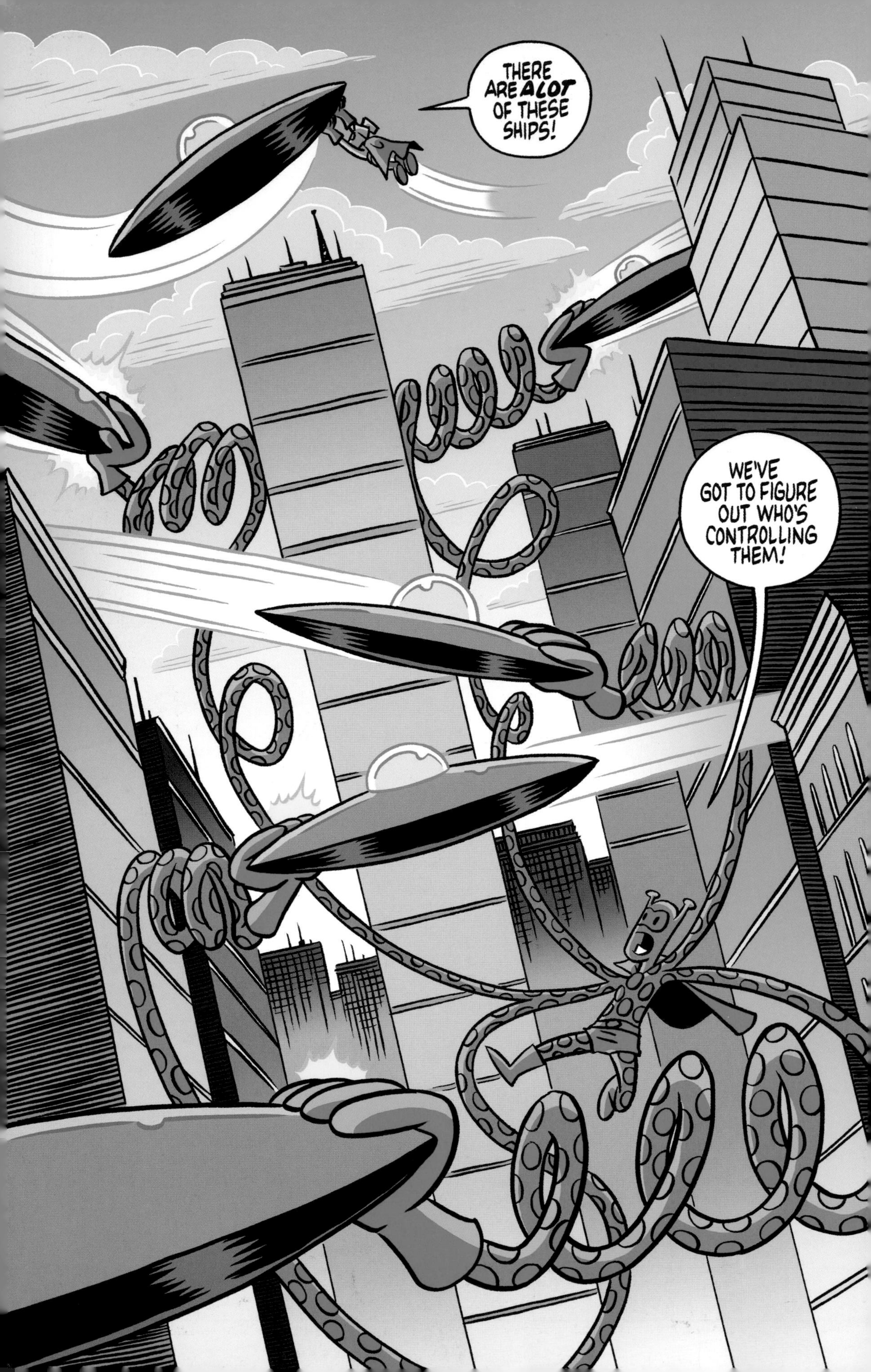
THERE ARE A LOT OF THESE SHIPS!
WE'VE GOT TO FIGURE OUT WHO'S CONTROLLING THEM!

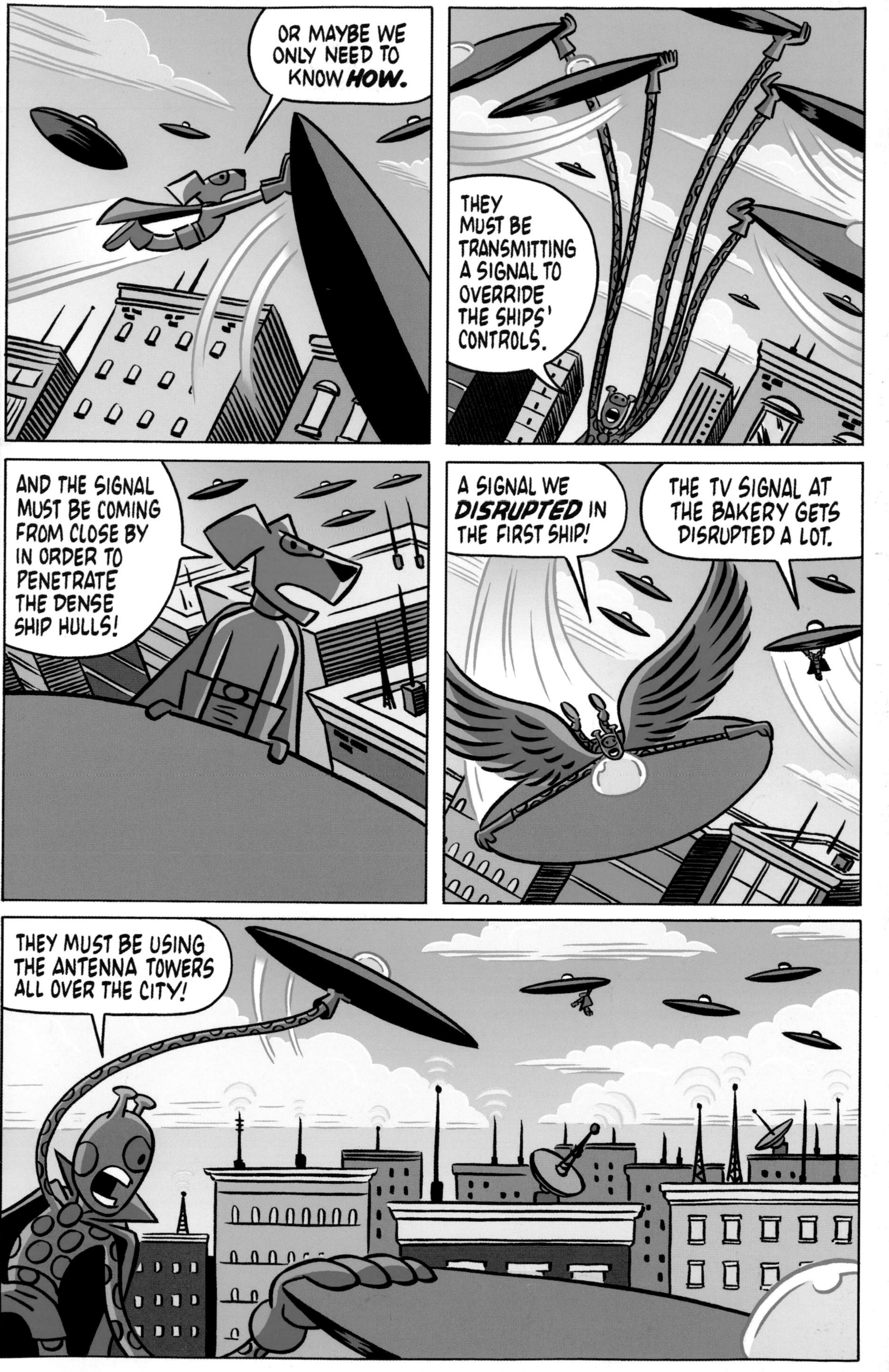
OR MAYBE WE ONLY NEED TO KNOW **HOW.**
THEY MUST BE TRANSMITTING A SIGNAL TO OVERRIDE THE SHIPS' CONTROLS.
AND THE SIGNAL MUST BE COMING FROM CLOSE BY IN ORDER TO PENETRATE THE DENSE SHIP HULLS!
A SIGNAL WE ***DISRUPTED*** IN THE FIRST SHIP!
THE TV SIGNAL AT THE BAKERY GETS DISRUPTED A LOT.
THEY MUST BE USING THE ANTENNA TOWERS ALL OVER THE CITY!

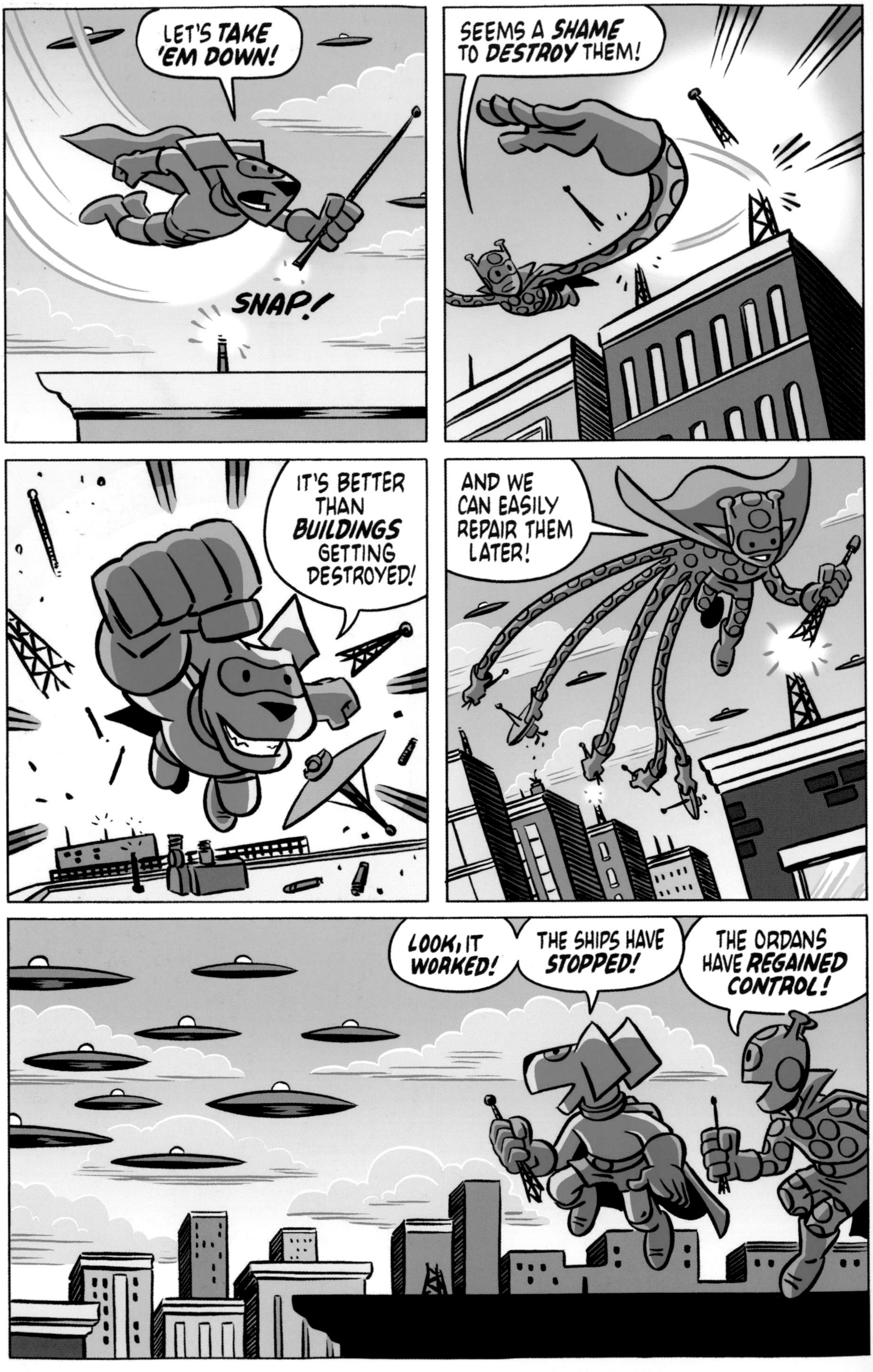
LET'S TAKE 'EM DOWN!
SNAP!
SEEMS A SHAME TO DESTROY THEM!
IT'S BETTER THAN BUILDINGS GETTING DESTROYED!
AND WE CAN EASILY REPAIR THEM LATER!
LOOK, IT WORKED!
THE SHIPS HAVE STOPPED!
THE ORDANS HAVE REGAINED CONTROL!

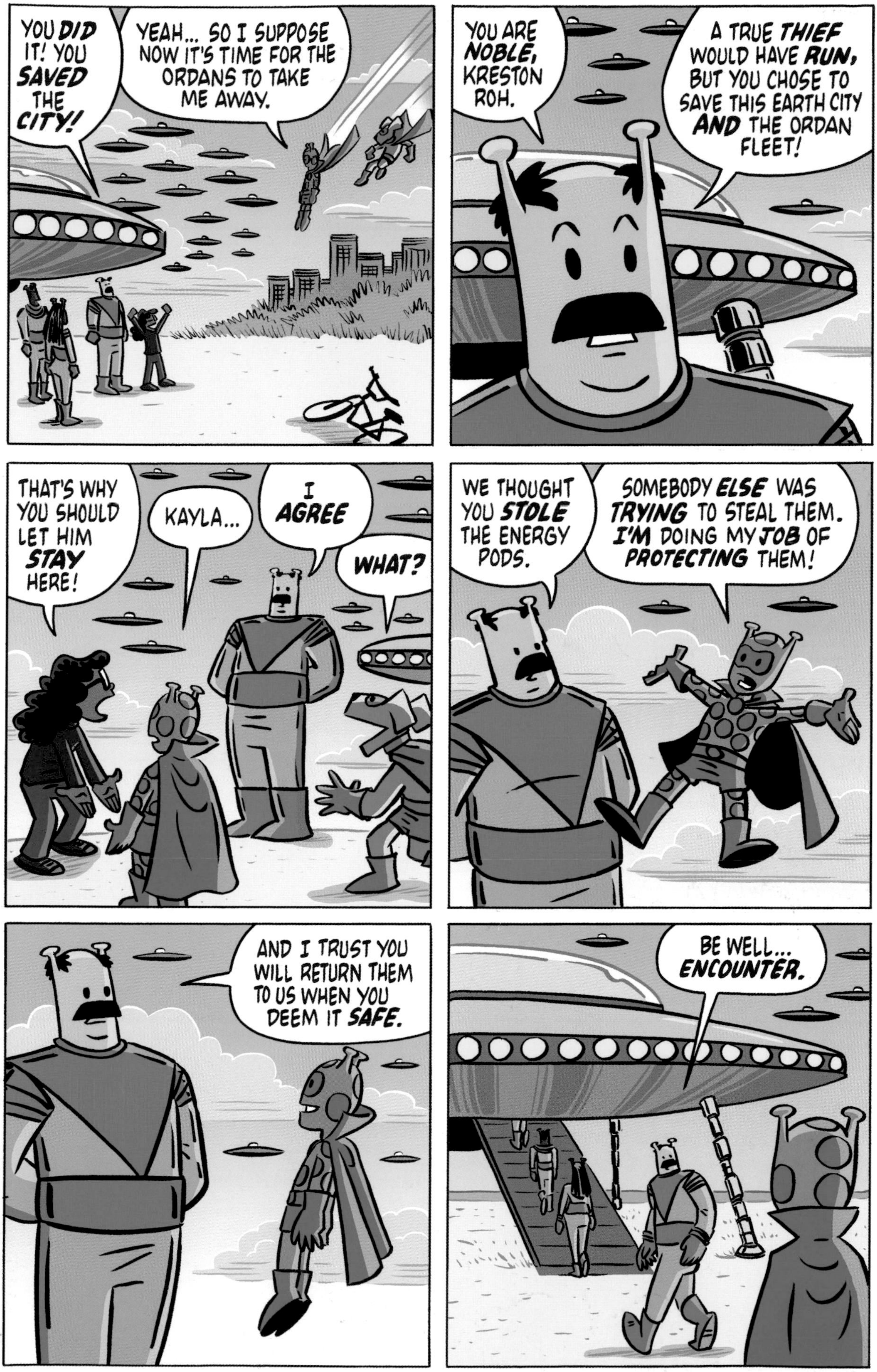
YOU DID IT! YOU SAVED THE CITY!
YEAH... SO I SUPPOSE NOW IT'S TIME FOR THE ORDANS TO TAKE ME AWAY.
YOU ARE NOBLE, KRESTON ROH.
A TRUE THIEF WOULD HAVE RUN, BUT YOU CHOSE TO SAVE THIS EARTH CITY AND THE ORDAN FLEET!
THAT'S WHY YOU SHOULD LET HIM STAY HERE!
KAYLA...
I AGREE
WHAT?
WE THOUGHT YOU STOLE THE ENERGY PODS.
SOMEBODY ELSE WAS TRYING TO STEAL THEM. I'M DOING MY JOB OF PROTECTING THEM!
AND I TRUST YOU WILL RETURN THEM TO US WHEN YOU DEEM IT SAFE.
BE WELL... ENCOUNTER.

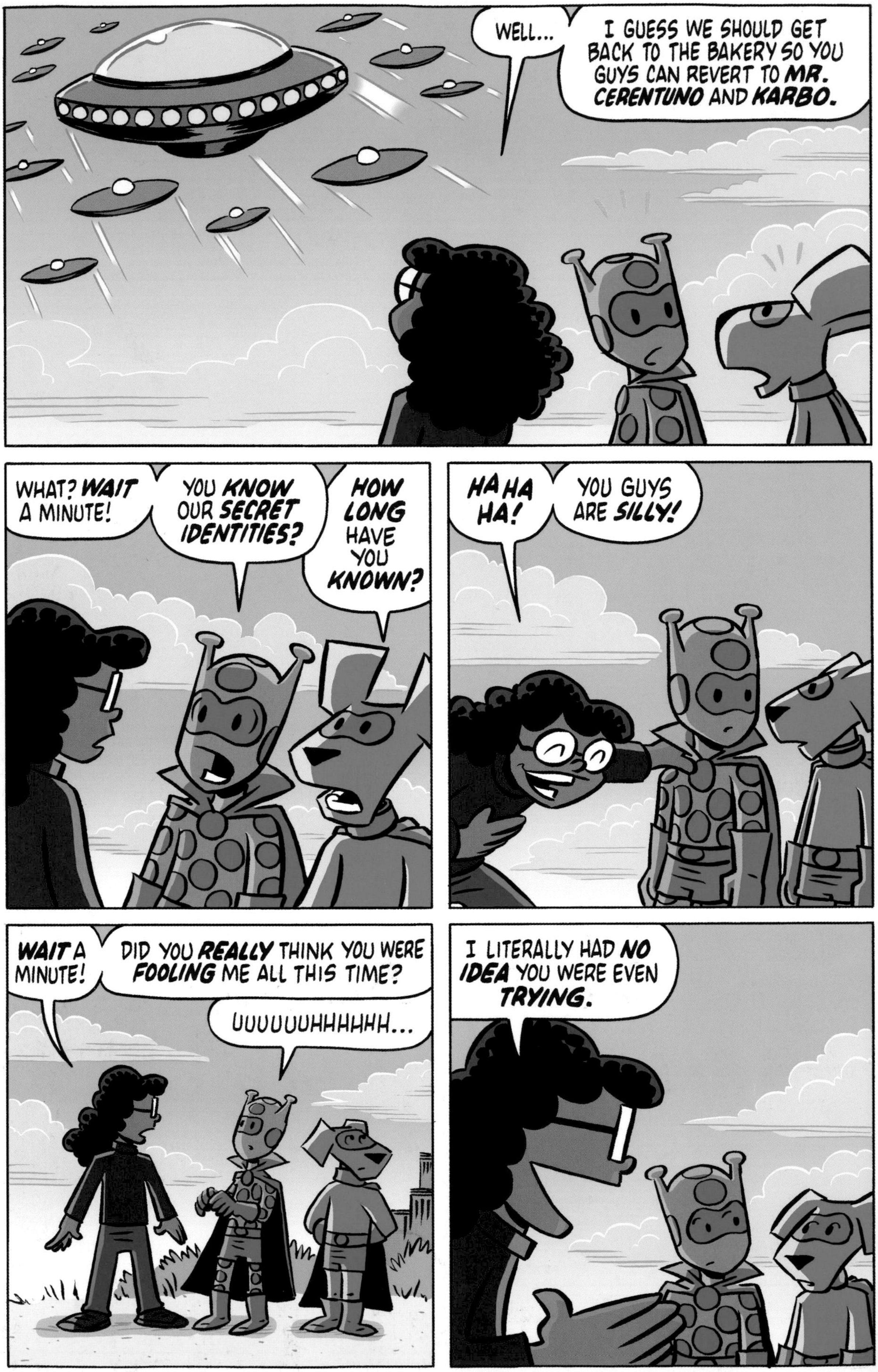
WELL...
I GUESS WE SHOULD GET BACK TO THE BAKERY SO YOU GUYS CAN REVERT TO MR. CERENTUNO AND KARBO.
WHAT? WAIT A MINUTE!
YOU KNOW OUR SECRET IDENTITIES?
HOW LONG HAVE YOU KNOWN?
HA HA HA!
YOU GUYS ARE SILLY!
WAIT A MINUTE!
DID YOU REALLY THINK YOU WERE FOOLING ME ALL THIS TIME?
UUUUUUHHHHHH...
I LITERALLY HAD NO IDEA YOU WERE EVEN TRYING.

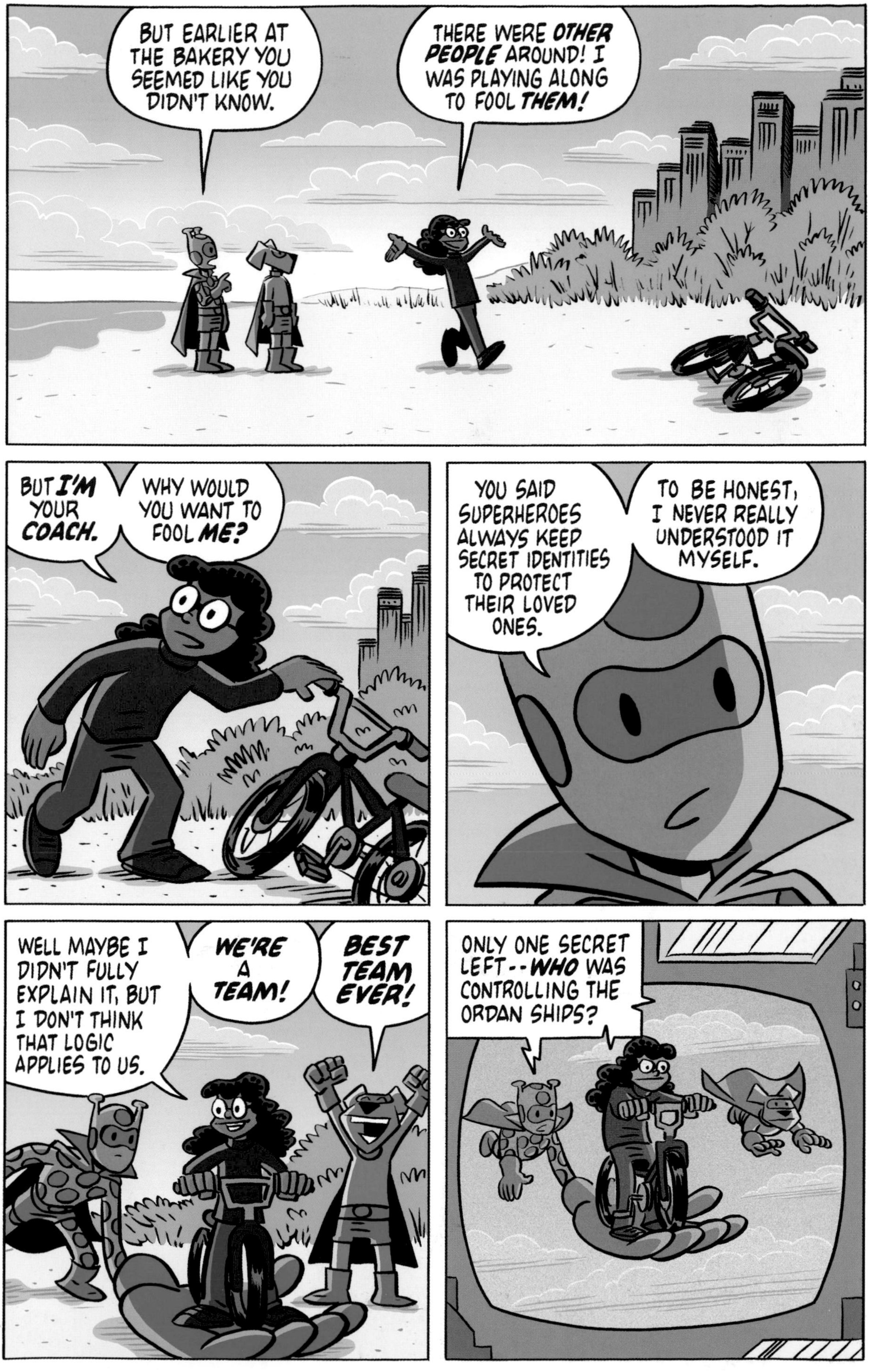
BUT EARLIER AT THE BAKERY YOU SEEMED LIKE YOU DIDN'T KNOW.
THERE WERE OTHER PEOPLE AROUND! I WAS PLAYING ALONG TO FOOL THEM!
BUT I'M YOUR COACH.
WHY WOULD YOU WANT TO FOOL ME?
YOU SAID SUPERHEROES ALWAYS KEEP SECRET IDENTITIES TO PROTECT THEIR LOVED ONES.
TO BE HONEST, I NEVER REALLY UNDERSTOOD IT MYSELF.
WELL MAYBE I DIDN'T FULLY EXPLAIN IT, BUT I DON'T THINK THAT LOGIC APPLIES TO US.
WE'RE A TEAM!
BEST TEAM EVER!
ONLY ONE SECRET LEFT--WHO WAS CONTROLLING THE ORDAN SHIPS?

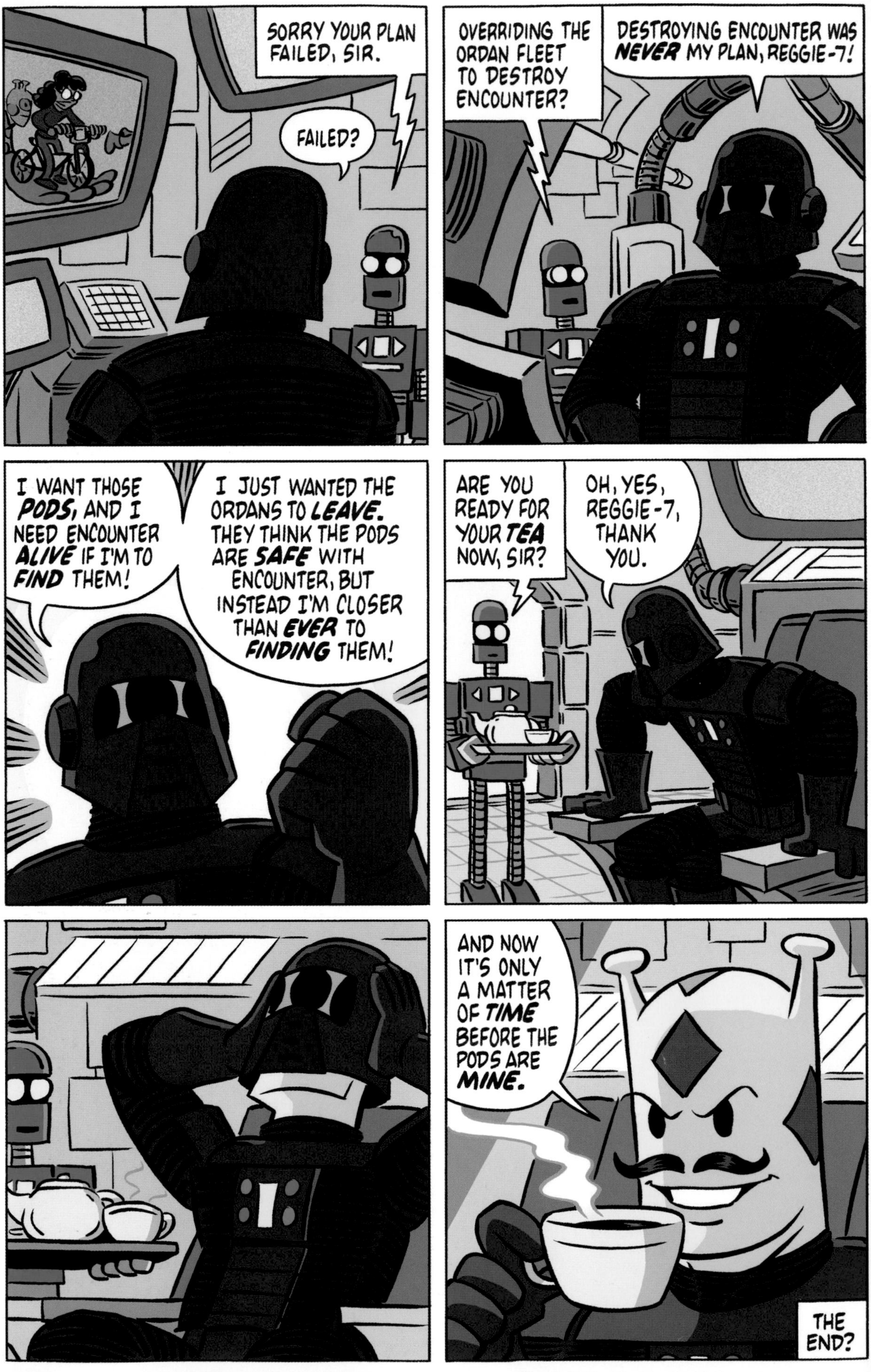
SORRY YOUR PLAN FAILED, SIR.
FAILED?
OVERRIDING THE ORDAN FLEET TO DESTROY ENCOUNTER?
DESTROYING ENCOUNTER WAS NEVER MY PLAN, REGGIE-7!
I WANT THOSE PODS, AND I NEED ENCOUNTER ALIVE IF I'M TO FIND THEM!
I JUST WANTED THE ORDANS TO LEAVE. THEY THINK THE PODS ARE SAFE WITH ENCOUNTER, BUT INSTEAD I'M CLOSER THAN EVER TO FINDING THEM!
ARE YOU READY FOR YOUR TEA NOW, SIR?
OH, YES, REGGIE-7, THANK YOU.
AND NOW IT'S ONLY A MATTER OF TIME BEFORE THE PODS ARE MINE.
THE END?

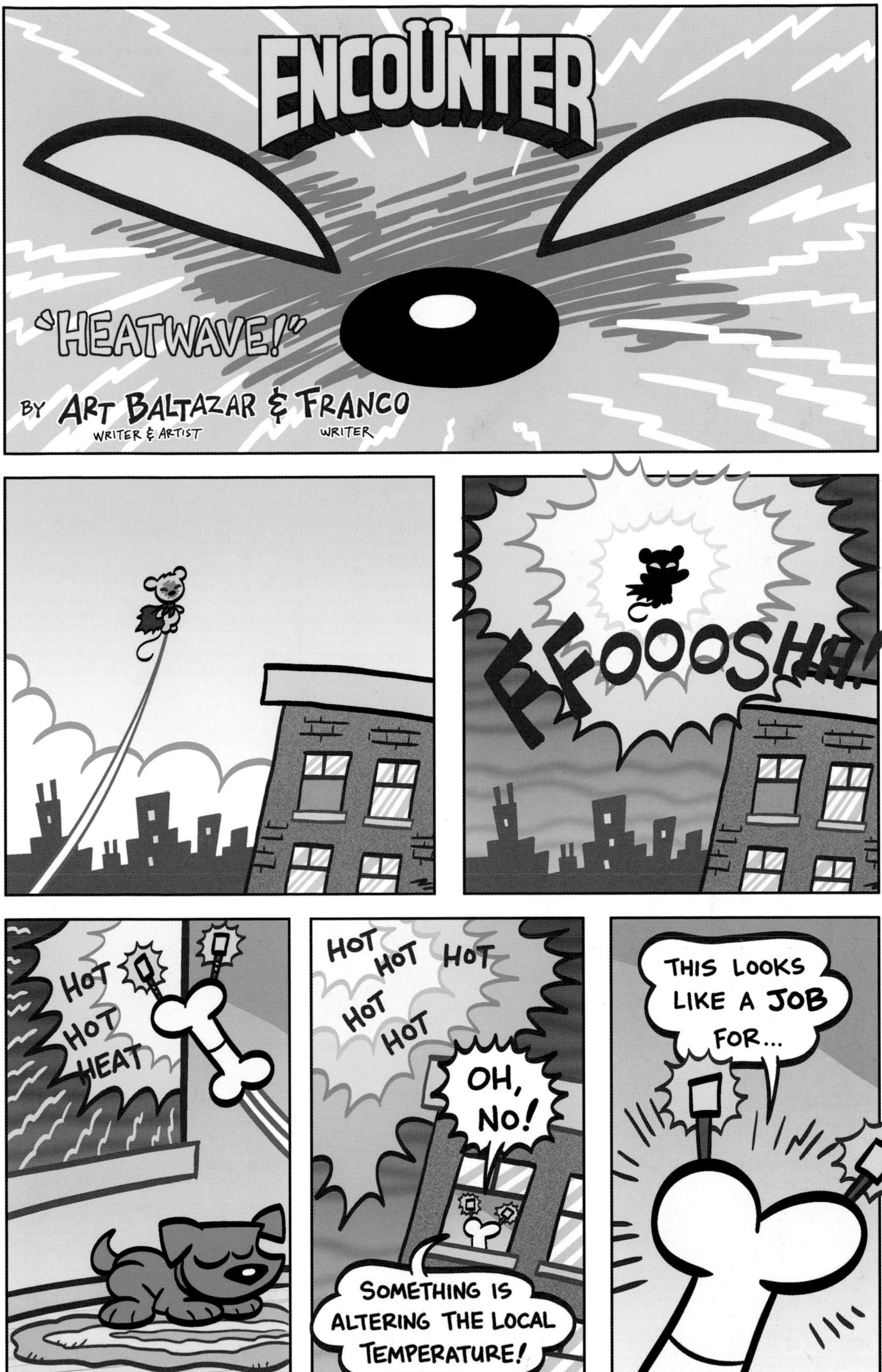
ENCOUNTER
"HEATWAVE!"
BY ART BALTAZAR & FRANCO
WRITER & ARTIST
WRITER
FFOOOSHH!
HOT
HOT
HEAT
HOT
HOT
HOT
HOT
HOT
OH, NO!
SOMETHING IS ALTERING THE LOCAL TEMPERATURE!
THIS LOOKS LIKE A JOB FOR...

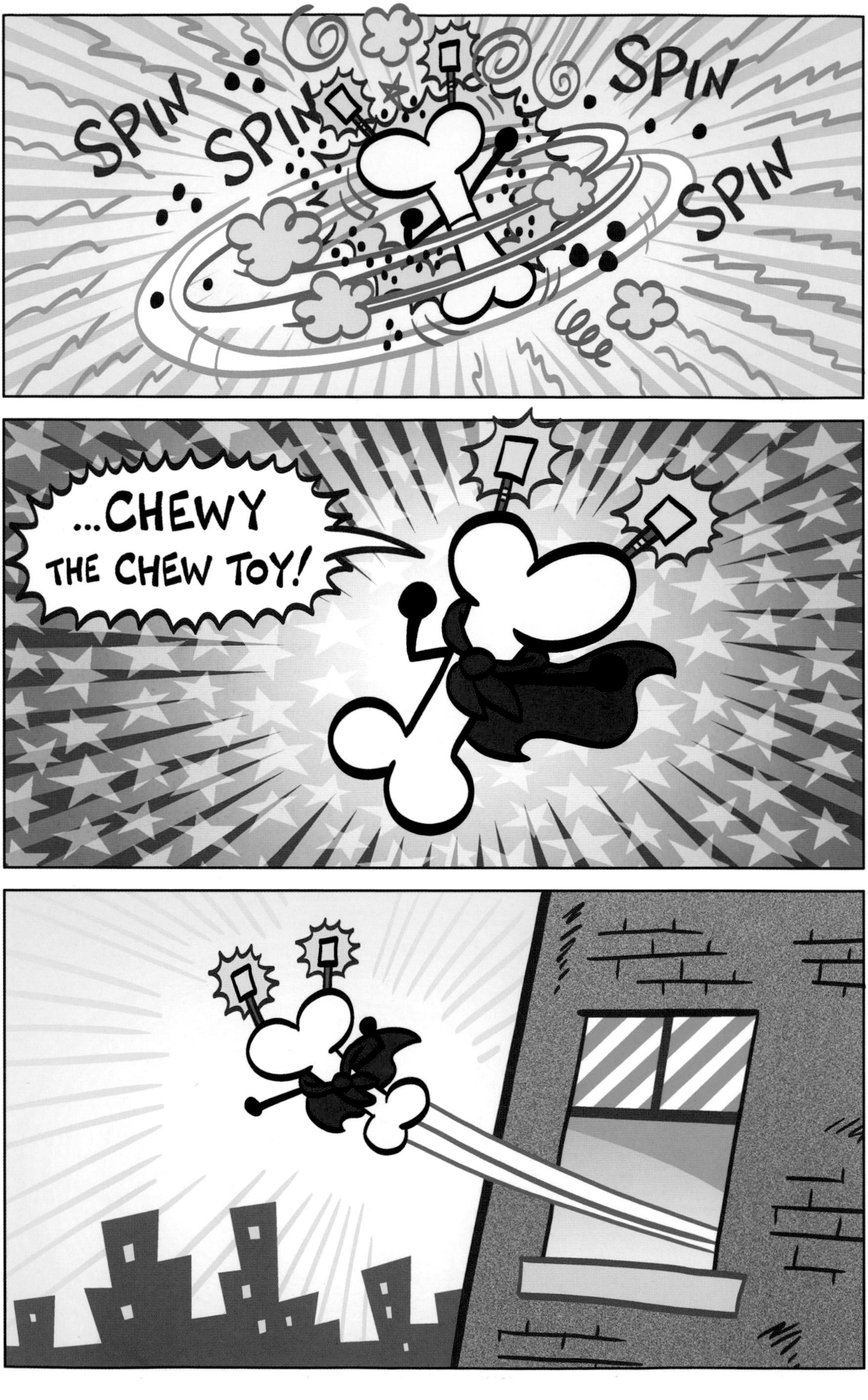
SPIN
SPIN
SPIN
SPIN
...CHEWY THE CHEW TOY!

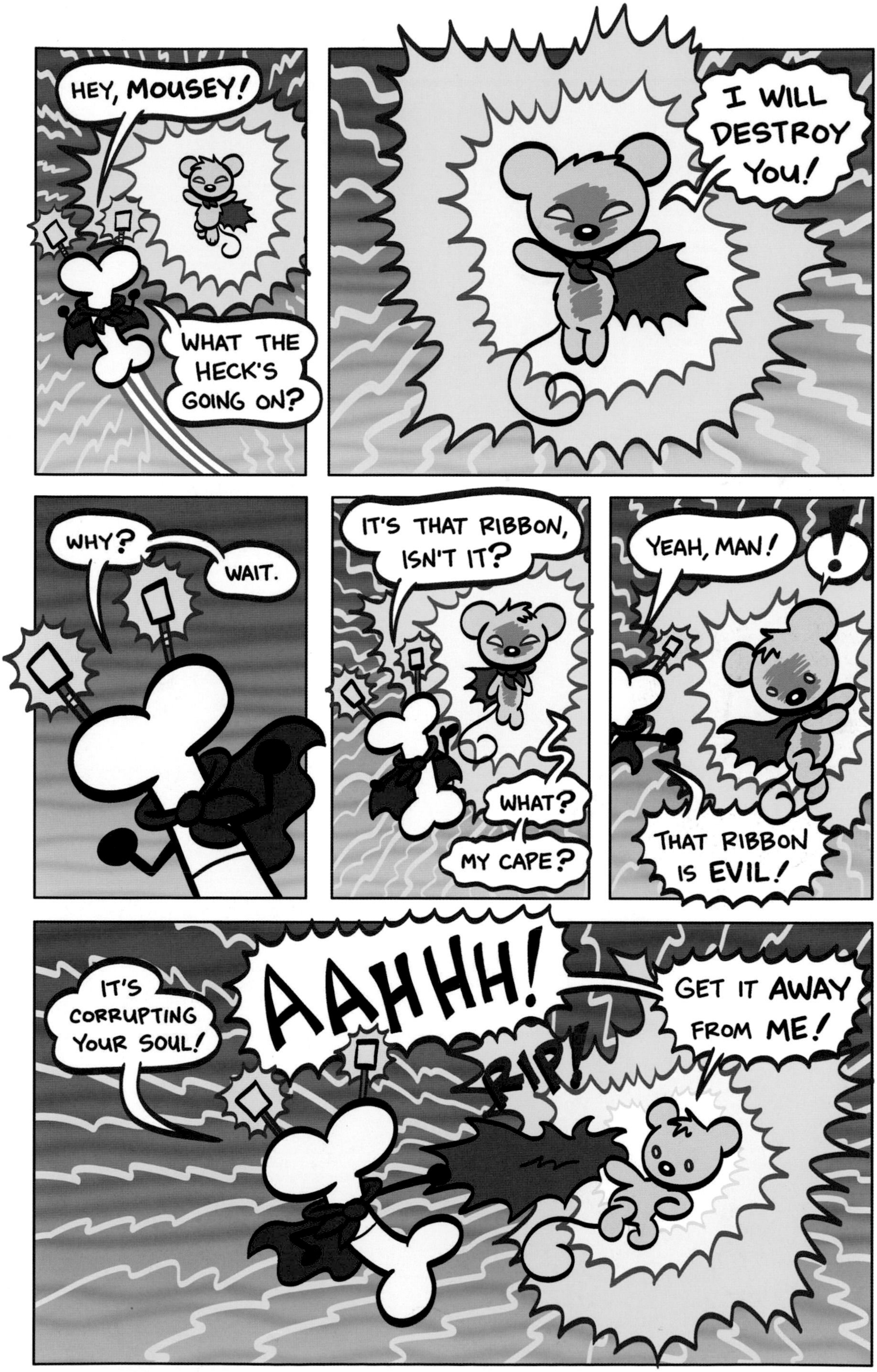
HEY, MOUSEY!
WHAT THE HECK'S GOING ON?
I WILL DESTROY YOU!
WHY?
WAIT.
IT'S THAT RIBBON, ISN'T IT?
WHAT?
MY CAPE?
YEAH, MAN!
!
THAT RIBBON IS EVIL!
IT'S CORRUPTING YOUR SOUL!
AAHHH!
GET IT AWAY FROM ME!
RIP!

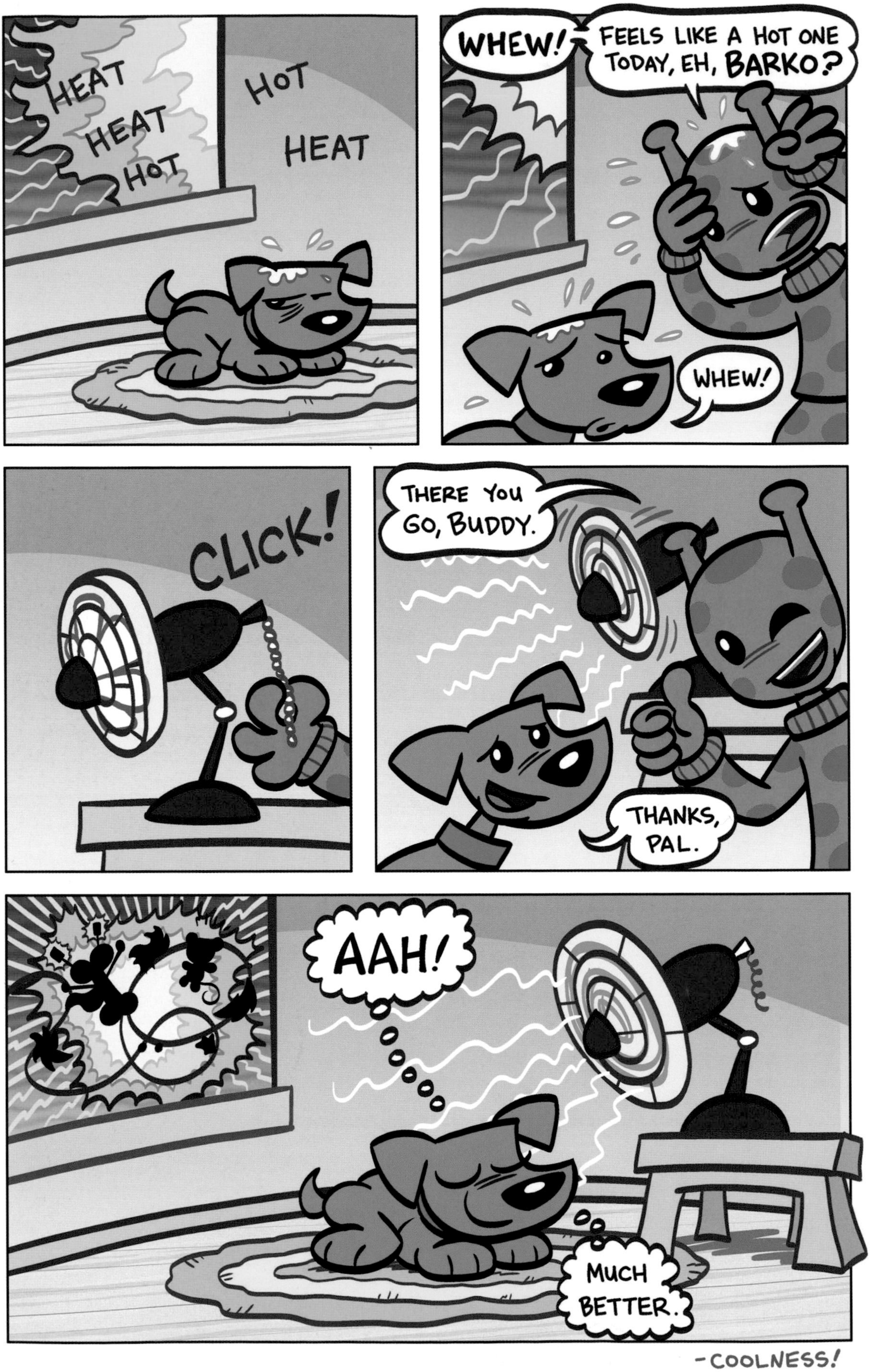
HEAT
HEAT
HOT
HOT
HEAT
WHEW!
FEELS LIKE A HOT ONE TODAY, EH, BARKO?
WHEW!
CLICK!
THERE YOU GO, BUDDY.
THANKS, PAL.
AAH!
MUCH BETTER.

-COOLNESS!

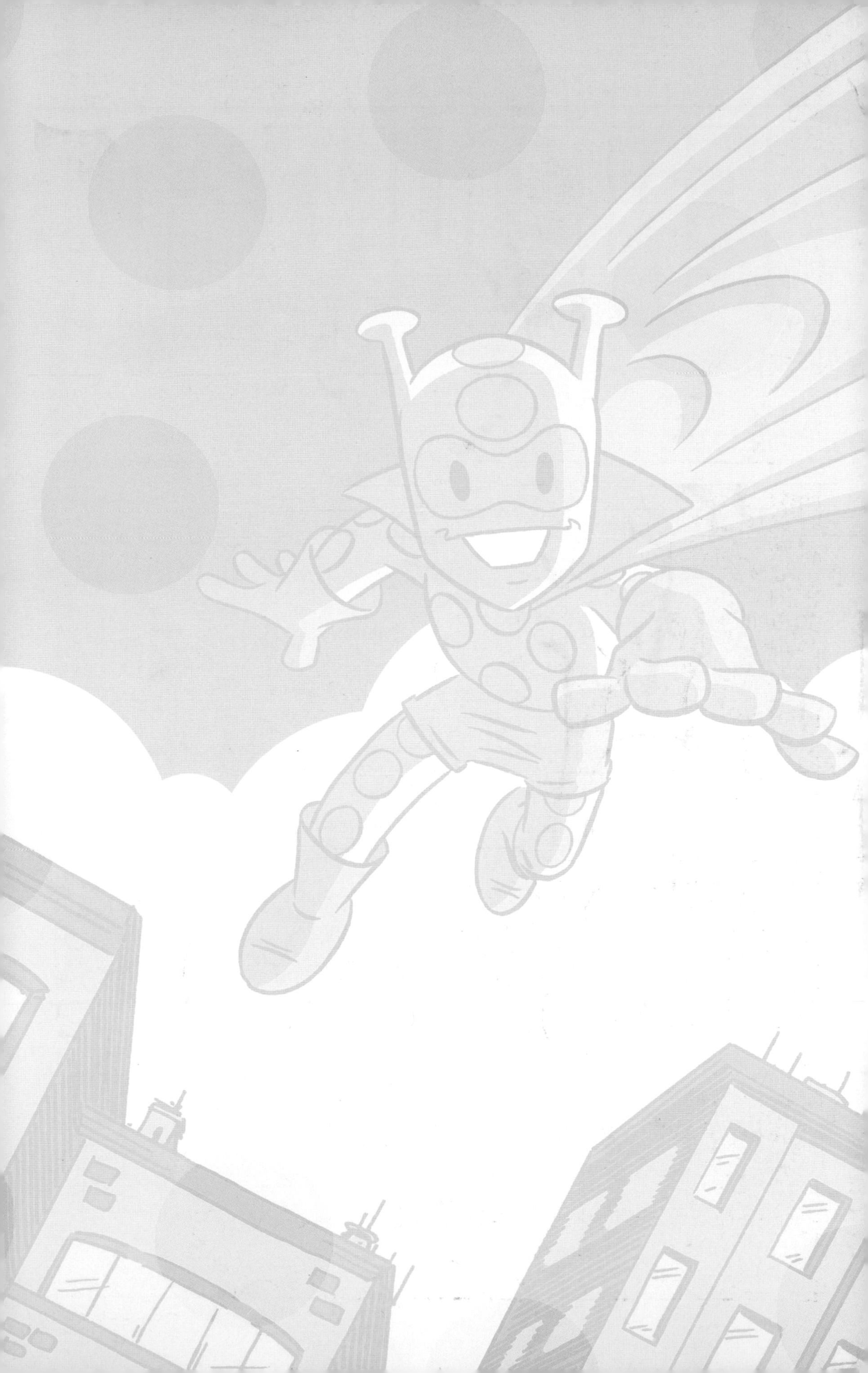

HOW TO DRAW ENCOUNTER

THIS IS SKETCHY ENCOUNTER
(A SKETCH VERSION OF OUR FAVORITE HERO)
THIS IS HOW HE LOOKS WHEN WE FIRST
USE A PENCIL TO FIGURE OUT HOW AND WHERE
HE WILL BE ON A PAGE

EVEN ENCOUNTER!

IF YOU CAN DRAW THESE SHAPES...

CIRCLE

SQUARE

TRIANGLE

...YOU CAN DRAW ANYTHING

ARRANGE THE SHAPES LIKE THIS

DRAW AROUND THE SHAPES TO MAKE THE SHAPE OF THE HEAD

USE BASIC SHAPES TO DRAW THE MASK AND MOUTH (YOU CAN USE A GIANT 'T' TO HELP PLACE THESE IN THE MIDDLE)

ERASE THE LINES YOU DON'T NEED

FRANCO

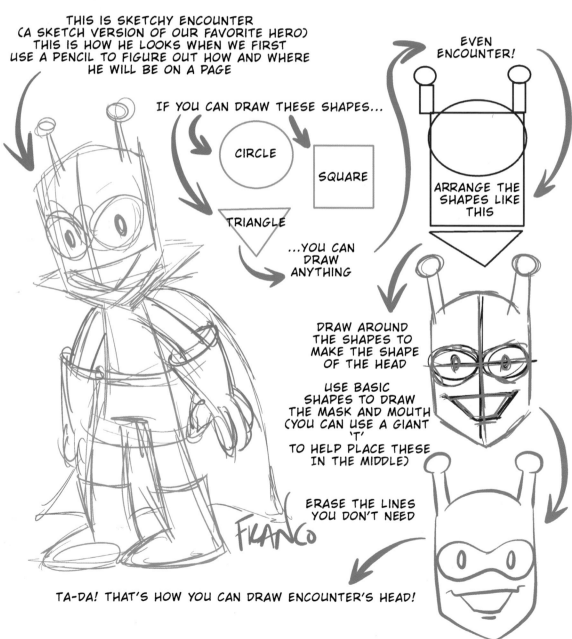

TA-DA! THAT'S HOW YOU CAN DRAW ENCOUNTER'S HEAD!

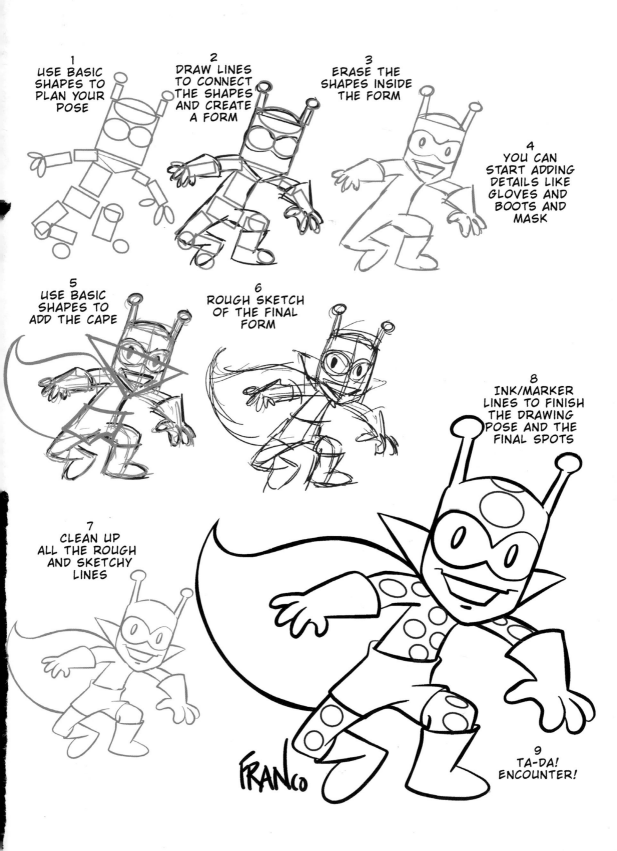

1
USE BASIC SHAPES TO PLAN YOUR POSE

2
DRAW LINES TO CONNECT THE SHAPES AND CREATE A FORM

3
ERASE THE SHAPES INSIDE THE FORM

4
YOU CAN START ADDING DETAILS LIKE GLOVES AND BOOTS AND MASK

5
USE BASIC SHAPES TO ADD THE CAPE

6
ROUGH SKETCH OF THE FINAL FORM

7
CLEAN UP ALL THE ROUGH AND SKETCHY LINES

8
INK/MARKER LINES TO FINISH THE DRAWING POSE AND THE FINAL SPOTS

9
TA-DA! ENCOUNTER!

FRANCo

Famous cartoonist **ART BALTAZAR** is the creative force behind the *New York Times* bestselling, Eisner Award-winning DC Comics's *Tiny Titans*, co-writer for *Billy Batson and the Magic of Shazam!, Young Justice, Green Lantern: The Animated Series*, and artist/co-writer for the awesome *Tiny Titans/Little Archie* crossover, *Superman Family Adventures*, and *Itty Bitty Hellboy!* Art is one of the founders of AW YEAH COMICS comic shop and the ongoing comic series!

FRANCO is from the great state of New York. He and his forehead have traveled the world and in between he writes and draws stuff and sometimes throws paint around on canvas. He is the creator, artist, and writer of *Patrick the Wolf Boy* and *AW YEAH COMICS!* He has also worked on titles for various comic companies, including the critically acclaimed *Superman Family Adventures, Young Justice, Billy Batson and the Magic of Shazam!, Green Lantern: The Animated Series, Itty Bitty Hellboy, Battlestar Galactica,* and the *New York Times* bestselling, multi-Eisner Award–winning series *Tiny Titans.*

CHRIS GIARRUSSO is the Harvey Award-nominated artist and writer best known for creating, writing, and drawing *G-Man,* a series of books about a young superhero who gains fantastic powers when he wears a magic cape, and *Mini Marvels*, the comic series featuring pint-sized versions of Marvel's most famous heroes! Chris's work has been published by Andrews McMeel, Scholastic, Marvel, Image, IDW, and several independent publishers.